The Hookmen

Timothy Hillmer

SCRIBNER PAPERBACK FICTION
Published by Simon & Schuster

SCRIBNER PAPERBACK FICTION
Simon & Schuster Inc.
Rockefeller Center
1230 Avenue of the Americas
New York, NY 10020

First Scribner Paperback Fiction edition 1996
Published by arrangement with University Press of Colorado

SCRIBNER PAPERBACK FICTION and design are trademarks of Simon & Schuster Inc.

Manufactured in the United States of America

1 3 5 7 9 10 8 6 4 2

Library of Congress Cataloging-in-Publication Data
Hillmer, Timothy, date.
The hookmen / Timothy Hillmer. —1st Scribner
Paperback Fiction ed.
p.   cm.
1. Young men—California—Kern River Valley—Fiction.
2. Man–woman relationships—California—Kern River
Valley—Fiction. 3. Fathers and sons—California—Kern River
Valley—Fiction. 4. Park rangers—California—Kern River
Valley—Fiction. 5. Kern River Valley (Calif.)—Navigation—
Fiction. I. Title,
[PS3558.I4532H66   1996]
813'.54—dc20   96-7262
CIP

ISBN 0-684-81386-6

"The Walking," © 1948 by Theodore Roethke, from *The Collected Poems of Theodore Roethke* by Theodore Roethke. Used by permission of Doubleday, a division of Bantam Doubleday Dell Publishing Group, Inc.

For Nancy, who has faith,
and for Rachel and Carly.

For my parents, Vernon and Catherine Hillmer.

And very much for Lloyd Kropp and Robert Meyer.

Acknowledgments

My thanks to the men and women at Whitewater Voyages and the Boulder Outdoor Center who shared the river with me; to the teachers and staff at the University of New Hampshire's Summer Institutes, especially Rebecca Rule, Tom Newkirk, Jane Hansen, and Lester Fisher, who provided encouragement and direction over the long haul; to the members of the Canyon Club, especially Juliet Wittman, for their careful reading of the early portions of this novel; to the Colorado Council on the Arts and the University of Colorado Kayden Advisory Committee for their recognition and financial support; and special thanks to my students and fellow teachers at Louisville Middle School and Platt Middle School.

This book could never have been completed without the help and support of Jane Carlson, Polly Greist, Bill Cross, my brother Michael, who shares the vision, and the late Kevin Munn, who was there to the end.

Acknowledgments

And all the waters
Of all the streams
Sang in my veins
That summer day.

— "The Waking"
Theodore Roethke

The Hookmen

CHAPTER ONE

It was the first week in June. Dark night. No stars, and clouds swirling in. When Cruz arrived, the other men were already fanning out methodically, as if walking to church. Lou the boss was there to fill him in. "A tourist thinks he saw a guy fall in the river. We found a jacket and camping gear and a Porsche parked near the springs. The water's hauling ass so you'll have to hustle to get him out before he gets into the gorge."

Cruz was the new man on the crew, barely nineteen, so he was given the job of handling the hooks. He went with old Crawdad, who showed him the best places to look, where the strong eddies carved out pockets in the shore and the current reversed upstream. Near Trout Bridge. Across from Hobo Campground. In the tangle of trees parallel to the abandoned mine. The hooks were heavy, clanking together in the silence. When Cruz reached the bank he saw the river, all foam and whirlpool, slamming into a jam-up of willows and scrub brush. "Good spot," he heard Crawdad say. "Good place to get hung up."

Crawdad's voice was raspy, like a creaking hinge being shut on a cage, and he dangled the hooks at his side as casually as a string of trout. Ten pounds of metal-pronged claw attached to thick gold-line rope. "Like throwing a lead shot underhanded on a string," he told him. "Ain't no picnic being a hookman. Dead bodies is heavy at the bottom. They'll fight you." He showed Cruz how to coil the line, then belay it out after throwing as the barbed talons dragged along the bottom in the tugging current.

"Never tie it to yourself," Crawdad said, "or you'll be as dead as the ones you're looking for. Drag you right under."

Cruz was sweating when he threw the first one. The hooks rose straight up and then bounced in the shallows. "Hell," Crawdad said. "Get it out in the meat of the water where it counts. Ain't much time. No mercy in that river." Cruz listened to him, balancing the hooks in one hand. He kept three loose coils of the heavy rope in the other, then began to rock back and forth, swinging the grappler like a pendulum gaining momentum. When he released, the hooks flew like a steel bouquet, soared in a wide arc and plummeted into the river, the rope hissing through his fingers. The current was strong, sucking the claws down into the violent flow and away from him in seconds.

"Work your way down like I showed you," Crawdad said. "Keep the line taut so's you can feel for something catching. I've pulled up a lotta junk before. Branches. Pieces of scrap iron. I even hooked a kitchen sink once. Thought I had a monster under there."

Cruz listened to him, dragging the steel across the bottom toward the jam-up. He used the black gloves with the extra padding sewn into the palms. They grew hot from the friction of hemp on leather.

"I know all the good fishing holes," Crawdad said. "I pulled up six in one summer." The old man laughed and Cruz saw a flash of black gums. "It's not pretty, kid. Spooky line of work."

Cruz needed the money. He had to pay rent and buy groceries and take care of Frank, his old man. They lived in a trailer in the alley behind the Shady Grove Saloon. Two bedrooms and a bath. Cruz kept the blinds drawn so the dust would stay out. Frank liked it that way. Dark.

It was the only work Cruz could find since getting laid off from a roofing job in Bakersfield. Kern River Search and Rescue was the official name. Lou told him that they got a lot of drifters who needed some quick money. Not many of them stayed on through the summer. They wore yellow hard hats and khaki shirts with the brown-and-green Forest Service logo emblazoned like a tattoo on the sleeves. Fires up in Sequoia. Cars going off the road from Los Angeles and into the canyon.

It was mostly river work on the Kern. A tourist tangled up in a snag island at midstream. A fisherman with his leg trapped in a rock crack. Hunting for a body after a drowning. They lost three or four each summer, usually during high water. Someone would get too close, slip, and they'd be gone in the froth of white. Two days later the body might wash through the Cataract Gorge. Sometimes it took months.

Cruz liked listening to the other workers talking while they rode together in the big trucks. Especially the stories Walker told. "Pulled a biker out from under the bumper of a Mercedes in my first week. Skull crushed and head split open like a coconut. I zipped him up in the plastic and let an EMT haul him away. I went behind the truck and threw up in the ditch. Get the hell out if you don't like it."

Walker was an odd one. He looked to be in his thirties and was a ten-year veteran with the Forest Service. Only Lou and Crawdad had been around longer. He didn't fit in with the others on the crew. Harrison and Sims and some of the rednecks cussed at him under their breath, calling him a "goddamn hippie" because he wore his hair in a braided ponytail that dangled halfway down his back. With his scraggly beard and long hair he seemed out of place, like he belonged in some hermit's shack out in the desert. He ignored the others most of the time and kept to himself. But when it came to the grunt work like digging firebreaks and clearing brush, Cruz had never seen a man work so hard with a shovel or machete. On the hottest days he did the work of two or three men while others rested in the shade. He never joined the others for a beer at the end of the week. He simply collected his paycheck and climbed into an old station wagon and drove away.

The work kept Cruz busy. Landslides over the road in the high country. Nothing serious. They'd started sandbagging in May for the big water they knew was coming. There had been a huge snowpack at Mount Whitney, and the river would swell in June, icy water rushing down from the Sierras in a torrent. Chico, a stocky Mexican from Stockton, made bets with the others on the first geek. *Geeks.* Cruz hated the word. That's what they called the dead ones. *Before the first of July,* Chico would say. *Put your money down. All proceeds to the Geek Funeral Parlor.*

Cruz never bet. It disgusted him. The other men called him "rookie" and "greenhorn," and it reminded him of the taunts he'd heard from the crew-cut jocks in high school about his long black hair and dark skin. *Look at the girl,* they'd yell from their lockers. *We're talking to you, taco.* Cruz had hung out with the gear-heads who drove Camaros and Mustangs and GTOs, all built for racing. He couldn't afford a car, but he liked to ride along when they'd race guys from Bakersfield down on the flats near Rio Bravo at the mouth of the canyon. He always rode shotgun for Danny Trujillo in his red Chevy, and sometimes helped him work on the engine, handing him wrenches and bolts as they listened to Springsteen. Since high school he hadn't seen much of the old crowd. Most of them took their fast cars and moved to L.A. or Bakersfield to work construction or in garages. Danny had wanted Cruz to go with him and get a place together. *I can't,* Cruz had told him, *at least not right now. My old man needs me around.* But there were plenty of times when Cruz thought about getting the hell out of Lake Isabella and taking Danny up on his offer.

The men on the crew kidded him about other things. His old man. Women mostly. They talked about the waitresses and the nurses they'd done it to on blankets by the river and in motels and on the seats of trucks. He ignored them and turned away. He knew the difference between a one-nighter and falling in love. There had been a girl in high school named Teresa. Her father was a migrant worker, and he'd met her during his senior year at a Friday night party down by the river.

Right away he'd liked her silence, the way she hung back and took everything in through eyes the color of almonds. There were evenings when they took their beers and walked down the highway so they could talk away from the others. She made it easy for him, always being the first to get the conversation started about music or friends or family, and she called him by his first name, Roy, instead of Cruz. She was Catholic and her mother made her go to church every Sunday and pin a scarf over her head in honor of the Blessed Virgin. *When I get on my own,* she said, *I'm gonna burn that damn scarf.*

She called him on the phone one night in April. *We're moving at the end of the week. My father has work in the north.* He could tell she'd been crying and he didn't know what to say except that he had to see her before she left. *Come to my house tomorrow,* she said. *My family's going to Bakersfield. I'll stay home sick.*

The next evening he walked to the twenty-four-hour truck stop and waited outside the rest room until he was sure it was empty. Then he went in and bought a rubber out of the machine that hung on the wall and slipped it into his pocket as if it were a coin. He stared at the faces of the women on the outside of the machine, how their heads were thrown back, their mouths open in an O of pleasure.

When he reached Teresa's trailer behind the city park, she was waiting for him at the door. She put her arms around his neck, her hair still wet from the shower, and he could taste the salt of tears on her cheeks when he kissed her. She led him into her parents' room. The bed was crude, unmade, next to a statue of the Virgin mounted on the wall. *I want Her to see us, Roy,* she said, pulling him onto the bed. They fumbled with each other's clothes, and he stumbled while kicking off his jeans and she started laughing at him. He touched her breasts, the nipples dark as chocolate. When they were both naked, she came up behind him and wrapped her arms around his neck and began to kiss him while he tried to unroll the rubber. But before he knew it, before he even had a chance to turn and push her back onto the bed and make love the way it was supposed to happen, the way he'd seen it in all the movies, he ejaculated, and his head filled with a rush of shame.

She was kind to him after he flushed the rubber down the toilet and came back to bed. *It's okay,* she whispered into his ear. *It doesn't matter. This is what matters.* Then she kissed him on the mouth, her tongue alive and sweet. And Cruz never forgot that kiss. When they said goodbye outside the trailer, she promised to write him. Within a few days her family moved north and she was gone. He never saw her again. She never wrote.

* * *

A rhythm began as they worked, Crawdad shining the light, Cruz throwing the hooks. He'd measure the distance, toss the grapplers, haul them in. A few snags, mostly wood or rock caught in the webbed talons. Water glistened on the black steel. He felt Crawdad's breath on his neck when he threw, the light flashing over his shoulder and tracing the arc of the hooks through the air. Crawdad was eager, watching for a sudden tension in the line. A trembling. A pulling down. It would be all the old man needed. Cruz smelled whiskey on his breath.

"It's probably some rich geek from L.A.," Crawdad said.

Cruz had never seen a geek before. The other workers joked with him about it now that he was working the hooks. Especially Chico. *Just wait,* he'd say to Cruz, *your turn's coming.*

He'd been waiting at home with Frank. They watched TV. The refrigerator was filled with Coke. It was all Frank could drink since he'd quit the hard stuff. Six times a month for two years Cruz had gone with him to A.A. in Bodfish. They listened to old pot-bellied men talk about being born again and wanting it bad enough to kill. It was all Frank had to hold on to. He never looked back. Couldn't.

Three years ago Cruz had come home one night and found an ambulance in the driveway, the interior of the house in shambles. Marta, his mother, and little Donna were in the yard holding one another and sobbing. *He was drunk as hell,* Marta said to him. *You know how mean he gets. He's like a crazy man.*

She sounded exhausted, her voice cracking. *I had no choice. He went after Donna with a cane pole and started whipping her. I couldn't take it anymore.*

Cruz went inside and found two white-shirted paramedics kneeling next to his father. Frank lay unconscious on the floor in the living room beside a splintered wooden table, blood oozing from an ear. Cruz's baseball bat, the Louisville Slugger with the Willie Davis autograph, was on the floor next to his father, and an empty bottle of tequila lay in the corner.

He spent the next two days at the hospital. His old man had a fractured skull, and by the time Marta called from a motel in Bakersfield, Cruz knew his parents were splitting. *It's over between us,* she said. *I'm taking Donna to live with my family in San Diego. You're welcome to come with us.*

Afterward he went back to Frank's hospital room. His father was asleep and Cruz stood next to the bed, staring down at his bandaged skull. He wanted to make all the pain stop, wanted somehow to make things safe again. It would be so easy. He could take one of the clean hospital pillows and press it over his old man's face and hold it there until he stopped struggling. It would be over in a few minutes and Marta and little Donna could come home. The harsh light from the single window hurt his eyes and he wanted to go somewhere quiet and think. He leaned close and watched Frank's chest rise and fall.

It hadn't always been this way between them. There had been good times. His old man used to take him out for barbecue over at Blackie's in Kernville and they'd laugh and talk amid a pile of greasy ribs, just the two of them, their faces painted with red sauce. Last summer they'd rebuilt the jeep engine and spent most of June hunting through junkyards for old parts. On Sunday mornings he and Frank would go fishing out at Lake Isabella and listen to a doubleheader as they cast out into the water, eating Spam sandwiches for lunch with vanilla wafers and apples. He loved standing next to his father, the water shining like a pool of light, not a ripple breaking their reflections. It was supposed to be like this between a man and his son, their histories intertwined in a knot that grew tighter with age.

Marta and Donna moved south. They never came back to Lake Isabella, not even for a visit. His sister sent postcards of beaches and golden surf at sunset. *Saw Burt Reynolds driving in La Jolla. Went swimming in the Pacific and found a rainbow shell at the bottom in the sand.* There were a couple times when Cruz had planned to take the bus down to see them. But it always fell through because Frank needed him for something or they didn't have the money.

Cruz stayed on with his old man. He knew Marta was angry with him for remaining, as if he'd purposely taken sides against her. She wrote him occasional letters and they'd talk on the phone every now and then. There were times when Cruz wasn't sure why he stayed. Once he and Frank argued bitterly and Cruz drove the jeep halfway to Los Angeles. He'd decided to get a place with Danny T. and start up a new life. But he turned around and drove home. Fear brought him back. There was no one else to watch out for his father, and he was afraid that if he left, his old man would die like some abandoned bum.

The divorce went quiet and smooth. No charges were pressed, and by Christmas all traces of Marta and Donna were gone. Frank sold the house and they moved into the trailer. He drank himself under every night for a year. One night Cruz came home and found him lying in a pool of vomit. Frank couldn't stop shaking. He talked of red devils in the wallpaper breathing fire, taking him to hell. He went into the hospital with a case of jaundice. His skin turned yellow as piss.

After he was out, Cruz got him into a dry-out program. He'd go and visit Frank in the damp, white-walled rooms. They'd sit in the lounge with the others, his old man chain-smoking Lucky Strikes and talking about going back to the real world, as he called it. *I know what it's like. I been out there. It's a bitch.* Cruz remembered all the ceiling fans and how they whirled overhead, clearing the air like the ghostly propellers of bomber planes. He'd go back to Lake Isabella and sleep for a few hours, then work the graveyard shift at the twenty-four-hour gas station.

He turned eighteen two days after Frank came back. Cruz bought him an aquarium as a welcome home gift. A big one with orange and turquoise and black tropical fish. Frank stayed on the wagon, but he wasn't ever the same. *It's simple mathematics,* the doctor told Cruz in his dry, uppity way; *alcohol destroys brain cells.* Frank would get lost walking to the grocery store or the post office, and Cruz would find him dazed and exhausted out by the highway, wandering along the roadside.

After a while he hardly ever ventured out of the house. He'd sit by the aquarium and smoke his cigarettes and talk to the fish. He named them after famous Dodger baseball players. Koufax. Drysdale. Wills. He'd forget the day of the week or the year, and sometimes Cruz would come home and find the table set for his mother and Donna too. One night they returned to the trailer after driving to Bodfish and Frank suddenly turned to Cruz and said, *Your mother's birthday is soon, isn't it? What should I get her?*

* * *

It was near dawn, the sky like slate, when the hooks caught. Cruz felt the change in the rope, heard Crawdad's breath quicken. "He's down there, kid," he said. "I know these things." The hooks came free and they tried again, this time throwing upstream and letting the claws drift down. Three attempts and nothing grabbed.

Cruz was scared. He wanted to get away from the river, to run and let Crawdad finish this. He wanted the hooks to break off or the rope to snap. But the old man was there, pressing. "He's stuck on something; work fast; he might get away." They continued, trying to relocate where in the riverbed the obstruction had been, the hooks sinking down each time into the oily dark and then pulling in, empty.

The line went taut on the ninth try. Cruz felt it slithering away from him and down. The weight was moving under there, shifting, the swift current trying to tear it loose. Crawdad helped him, their arms straining to bring it in. Breath puffed out in short gasps. Legs shook. Cruz wanted to cut it, let it go, but Crawdad pulled on, his eyes fixed on the line and the point of descent. They felt the rope jerk suddenly, the weight breaking free and inching downstream. Their feet slid in the mud toward the water. "Dammit, tie it off!" yelled Crawdad. "Wrap it around something!" Cruz let go briefly and secured the rope around a tree trunk. For ten minutes they heaved at the line, hauling it in against the force of the river. Forearms throbbed. Fingers cramped.

Then he saw it. A shoulder breaking the surface. A head, the scalp pink and wet in the light. A hand, limp and bent against the current. They pulled it into the shallows. Crawdad held the line. Cruz went in after the body.

Cold skin. Like fingertips on a freezer wall. The smell enveloped him. Not death. River scent. When he gripped the shoulder to ease it out of the shallows, he saw a torn red T-shirt. Jeans, heavy with water. He picked the body up in his arms and set it on the bank in the high grass.

Crawdad shone the light down. Cruz saw a slender woman. Young. Maybe early twenties. "Look at her skin," Crawdad said. "Hardly been touched. Only dead a few hours. It's like she's sleeping." Cruz saw long, flowing hair and closed eyes. Lips parted in mid-dream. The face was pure and milky, as if scrubbed by sand and water. Cruz thought of the chalky smooth face of a statue in a church. He put his hand on her cheek, in her hair, over her eyelids. Pure, like moist cotton. As if one touch could bring her back. One kiss.

"She's beautiful," Crawdad said. "Like a rose."

Cruz felt his eyes blur, his stomach twist. Then Crawdad's hand on his shoulder. "The first is the hardest, kid. Go easy. Let's wrap her up." But Cruz couldn't and stumbled away. So the old man covered her in the tarp. They drove back to the others, Cruz not saying a word.

* * *

It was early when he got home. He sat in the dark kitchen by the aquarium. The river smell was still with him. In his hair. On his clothes. He put his head down. Hardly any sound, save for the parched sobs from his own throat. He felt ashamed for crying, his cheeks and skin hot. A slice of light glowed under Frank's door. He heard the approaching shuffle of slippers. A hand on his bowed head. Frank was behind him now, the familiar irregular pattern of his breathing, a clearing of the throat.

"I know what it's like, Roy," he heard his father say. "I been there. It hurts but you get over it. Talk to me like we used to at the lake. Is she pretty? Is she as pretty as your mother?"

CHAPTER TWO

Mid-June brought the heat. It descended on the Kern like a veil of flame. Cruz put in twelve-hour days in the hundred-degree weather. The snowpack near Mount Whitney broke all records, and each day the river inched further above the high-water mark as the sun melted the mountain snow and fueled the torrent. The crew sandbagged along the bridges and near the riverside cabins and homes. Eighty-pound bags stacked six to eight feet high. "Ballbreakers," Crawdad called them. When that was done they started on the firebreaks up in Sequoia, tearing out sage and cactus with picks and shovels, always listening for the sharp buzz of a rattler's tail. The forest was parched and crisp, ready to burn. Crawdad was on their asses no matter what.

"Flood or fire, water or smoke," he'd sing out. "It's hot as Hades and you're working like ladies."

There were accidents. A drunken motorcyclist plunged his Harley one hundred feet off Lovers' Leap into the Kern. A three-year-old was swept out of the hands of a preacher while being baptized near Trout Bridge. Each time Cruz was called out with the hooks, he waited for the task to get easier, for the victims to somehow become faceless in his dreams. By the third body he knew he could never cleanse his memory of the dead. "All victims whose time has come," Crawdad liked to say. "All resting with the Kern."

Crawdad was always there, his silver hair hanging like tassels from under the stained hat. Cruz knew little about his history. No family anyone knew of. Only the river and forest for as long as anybody could remember. Cruz trusted the old man's knowledge of the land and liked the way he kept Chico and the others at a distance. Liked his vulture nose. The whiskey smell of his breath. The acrid, sweet scent of the little Dutch Masters cigars he smoked.

"Two packs a day for twenty years," he'd howl, "and lungs white as snow."

The daily grind took everything out of Cruz. He came home to the cramped trailer, his skin like scorched copper. Frank was usually asleep, the faraway sound of the Dodgers game on the radio. Cruz would shower, then rub lotion on his raw skin. The heat took away his appetite. He drank glasses of iced ginger ale to kill the bitter taste of sand and dust in his mouth.

At night he hauled an old air mattress on top of the trailer and slept under a gulf of stars. He imagined a cool breeze drifting inland from the Pacific to soothe him from the heat. In the distance he could see the twitching pink and green neon of the Kern Valley Motel. He listened to the sound of traffic out on the interstate. Sometimes he dreamt of the drowned girl.

In the dream she was always alive and staring up at him with eyes black as eels, her mouth so close he could feel her breath on his lips. Looking down he could see the hook thrust into her side and the blood seeping into the grass like syrup. He would awaken suddenly, cursing the dream. All he knew was her name. He had read it in the newspaper obituaries after they'd found the body. *Denise Kaufmann. Age Nineteen. Born in 1960. Parents deceased. No surviving family.*

On Saturday he drove to Bakersfield to buy a new window fan for the trailer. As he approached the city limits, he saw oil derricks and steel refinery towers looming out of the dry fields like scrap monuments. He had never liked Bakersfield. It was an ugly city, landscaped with cactus and white gravel and trash, and it always seemed to be twice as hot as it was in the mountains. The air didn't move here. It hung like a heavy curtain over the town, trapping all the factory smoke and car exhaust. While working on a roofing crew in south Bakersfield once, he'd gotten second-degree burns on his hands from the black shingles. The city was hell in the summer as sleek low-riders rumbled up and down the main streets.

He bought the fan at Sears, then walked around in the air-conditioned mall for a while. The place was packed with locals trying to escape the heat, so he decided to go to a matinee at the Cineplex movie theater. He loved sitting in the darkness as the cool air soaked into his skin and images exploded on the screen. After the movie, something called *Street Law* about a policeman in Los Angeles during a nuclear disaster, he went to a Mexican place, Señor Speedy's, for lunch. He'd eaten there before when he was working in the city. The yellow building was in the shape of a giant sombrero and decorated with garish red and green streamers. Piñatas swung from the ceiling like bloated calves, and the steam that rolled from the kitchen smelled of refried beans and tortillas and ground beef. At noon the place was usually packed with workers on their lunch hour. Cruz ordered the soft tacos and a bottle of Dos Equis. When the food arrived he devoured it and ordered another beer halfway through his meal.

In the restaurant he thought about driving to Los Angeles. He had some cash and he could be down there in three hours and spend the night with some high school friends. On Sunday they could go to Venice Beach and hang out at the boardwalk. Even though he had never been there before, he'd seen pictures on TV of women who rollerskated in swimsuits up and down the crowded boulevard, their outfits nothing more than pieces of bright string. He could see himself in one of the sidewalk cafes, sipping a tropical drink with one of these women, his hand relaxed and stroking her bare hip.

But there was no time for a vacation. Not right now, at least. A stack of unpaid bills waited for him back at the trailer, and he'd promised to drive Frank to the Baptist church in Kernville tomorrow morning. He would have to wait. Maybe by the end of August. Then he could visit L.A. and do it up right.

He started back in the late afternoon. The traffic was heavy near the malls and shopping areas, but once he was outside the city he made good time along the rolling hills near Rio Bravo. He played the radio loud and listened to Aerosmith on a Bakersfield station.

When he passed the Cataract Falls sign, he suddenly whipped the jeep off the main road and pulled into a small parking lot. There were no other cars around and he sat in the driver's seat listening to a sad, gravel-voiced love song on the radio, not really sure why he'd pulled off. Frank would be at home in the trailer chain-smoking Lucky Strikes, maybe doing a crossword puzzle. The evening promised nothing more than a frozen dinner and some bad TV.

He turned off the engine and swung down from the driver's seat. Cataract Falls was one of his favorite places. At one time it had been a rendezvous for his high school friends. He'd met Teresa here at a party. A dirt path at the end of the parking lot disappeared over the rim of the canyon and he followed it. The trail was steep and he had to dig in his heels to slow down, being careful to avoid the dense clusters of cactus on the hillside. Clouds of dust puffed up and coated his arms and T-shirt with a brown film.

After working his way down the trail, he curved to the left, and from there he could see his destination, a spectacular waterfall at least thirty feet high that plunged off a wide slab of rock. At the bottom was a circular pool surrounded by rock walls in the shape of an amphitheater. This was the last big drop in the Cataract Gorge. Below it the river calmed as it made its way south to the irrigation canals in Bakersfield. Cruz moved down the trail a few hundred feet and then stopped to sit on a rocky overlook. From his perch he could survey the Kern for a quarter mile in either direction. The rapids upstream were white and frothing and violent, but downstream of Cataract Falls the river was transformed into a serene channel that flowed toward the mouth of the canyon.

Twilight was his favorite time to be alone. He was glad he'd stopped. It gave him some time to relax, *chill the brain*, as Danny T. used to say, before heading back to Lake Isabella to deal with Frank. Cool air drifted up from the river bottom, and shadows darkened the thickly clustered chaparral, the coyote brush, manzanita, and chamise which choked the slopes leading down to the salt-and-pepper granite that lined the Kern.

He sat for more than an hour, listening to the roar of the waterfall below and thinking about his father. In the morning he'd take Frank to the Sunday service at church, and on the drive over it would be like all the other times, his old man preaching to him about religion and how he'd given up his life to Jesus since he'd quit drinking. It was a speech Cruz had heard before. *When you've been through the hell I've been through, you start believing in that guy upstairs,* he'd say. Frank always talked about a TV show he watched called *Road to Eternity*, the story of an angel who comes down to earth to save souls. *Makes me wanna cry,* he'd tell Cruz each week, his eyes red as grenadine swirling through tequila. *Jesus is my only guardian angel. Jesus saves the sinner.*

Cruz never went into the church with him. He'd buy a couple of donuts at a local bakery, then go back to sit outside in the parking lot and listen to the choir singing, all those sweet voices shouting to heaven for salvation. He hadn't been inside a church since Marta and Donna left. They used to go to Mass every Sunday, just the three of them, at Sacred Heart of Jesus over near Bodfish. Marta had been raised Catholic and he went along to please her, for the most part. He enjoyed seeing the change that came over his mother during the Mass, as if a great weight had been lifted from her shoulders. Marta had a beautiful voice and she'd gracefully sing each of the hymns, never missing a note. On the drive home she seemed younger and full of hope. She'd talk and laugh with her children about summer vacations and plans for the house. Cruz wondered if Marta and Donna still went to Mass in San Diego, and he pictured a church near the ocean, a white steeple and cross against a backdrop of blue waves.

After the Baptist service Cruz liked watching the young women as they came out the doorway in groups of three and four, their Sunday dresses ruffled in pastel swirls. He loved how they walked, the click of their high heels on concrete, and the way they smiled at one another in the sunlight.

Suddenly something upstream, a flash of color, caught his eye. At first he thought it was a boat that had gotten loose and was being flushed down empty, a yellow kayak with both ends pointed like needles, tumbling through the rapid above the falls. He scrambled down the trail but stopped when he saw the kayak right itself after being spit out upside down. Then Cruz saw the fluttering motion of a wooden paddle, and the red helmet and life jacket of a man who powered the kayak into an eddy against the far shore.

He's resting, thought Cruz. *But he's gonna have to paddle like hell to get over before the big drop.* The kayaker pivoted back into the main current. He was still upright as he sliced through a relentless train of waves, his tiny craft bobbing like a cork. Cruz stood on the shore transfixed by what he saw. He wanted to run down and help the man drag his boat out above the drop, but he froze in place, the sun a low, white glare in the sky. The kayaker made no attempt to pull over, instead heading straight for the falls.

There was no hesitation, no pulling back, as the kayak dropped off the lip of the waterfall and plummeted thirty feet, its lemon shell radiant against the white curtain of foam. Cruz saw the man raise his paddle into the air and lean back to brace himself for the bottom reversal. Then he was gone, sucked underwater and out of sight, only to reappear a second later in the shape of a yellow javelin being hurled from the depths. The kayak rolled upright, and the paddle flashed in an acceleration of quick strokes to move away from the drop.

From his place directly overhead Cruz saw the kayaker pause momentarily in the clear pool at the base of the falls and crane his neck upward as if looking at the heavens. It was then Cruz recognized the beard and the ponytail trailing out the back of the helmet. Walker let out a loud, yelping cry and whirled the double-bladed paddle in a helicopter motion with the grace of a baton twirler, then spun the kayak around and headed downstream. Cruz called after him, screaming as loud as he could so that Walker might know someone had witnessed his daredevil feat. But his voice was buried by the clamor of the falls, and he watched as Walker paddled away, unaware of his presence, the red helmet and life jacket fading from sight behind a veil of willows.

Cruz turned away from the river and scrambled up the loose scree and dirt of the hill, trying to avoid the sharp-edged leaves of the Spanish bayonet which grew along the trail. Within five minutes he reached the top and stood panting, out of breath from the climb. Then he got into his jeep and quickly started the engine and pulled back onto the main road to head south. If he hurried he might be able to catch Walker somewhere along the Kern at his takeout.

Cruz found the battered station wagon at a small picnic area next to the river, just downstream from the falls. He parked the jeep and got out, then saw Walker standing twenty-five feet away in the shallows, still wearing his life jacket, along with a pair of tattered denim cutoffs. He had the kayak turned upside down and was dumping water from the cockpit. A helmet and paddle had been tossed on the ground in front of the car.

"Hey!" Cruz yelled, walking down to the river. "I saw you upstream at the falls."

As he approached, Walker hoisted the boat to his shoulder and dropped it onshore with a hollow thump. "Cruz," he said, stepping out of the water. "What brings you down here?"

"I was just about to leave when I saw you coming through the rapid above Cataract. I thought you were crazy when you didn't pull out." Cruz bent down next to the kayak and ran his hand along the wet surface of the plastic.

"Yeah," Walker said, "I'm a kamikaze kayaker with a suicide wish." He unzipped his life jacket and tossed it toward the station wagon. His upper body was cocoa brown from the sun, and any signs of aging or a sagging belly were absent, as if dry leather had been stretched across his shoulders and chest and stomach to reveal only bone and muscle underneath.

"Won't be the first time somebody thought I was a little crazy," Walker said. "You were probably thinking I'd be the next poor bastard you'd have to drag out of the river." He smiled at Cruz, a crooked-toothed grin, then laughed and stared down at his ragged tennis shoes. "Crawdad would've gotten a kick from having to fish me out."

"I never even knew you kayaked."

"One of my little secrets," Walker said. "I grew up boating on the Kern. Every couple of weeks I try to run that drop just to keep my heart pumping."

"I was nervous just watching from the shore."

"You ever kayaked before, Cruz?"

"No."

"You should try it sometime. Nothing else even comes close."

"But the river's sky-high right now."

"I know what I'm getting into. I scout the rapids from the road before I run anything so I don't get ambushed. A lot of upstream shit gets washed down and the last thing I want is to get pinned under some cottonwood tree."

He picked up his paddle and the end of the kayak and began to drag it over to his car. Cruz grabbed the opposite end and helped carry it up to the wagon, where they hoisted it on top. The bottom of the boat was blemished with jagged scrapes and indentations, and Cruz imagined the sharp edge of a rock puncturing the thin surface.

"How'd you get your car down here?" Cruz asked.

"I've got a system," Walker said, grinning. "I stash my kayak and gear in the bushes upstream, then drive down to where I think I'll pull out. After I park the wagon, it's just a matter of hitching a ride back up the canyon. It usually works pretty well."

He lashed the boat down on the roof, then gathered up the rest of his gear and loaded it in the back. The inside of the station wagon was a jumbled mess of newspapers, grocery bags filled with glass bottles and cans, oily automobile parts, and a few large pipe wrenches scattered throughout.

"Are you on your way to the dump?" Cruz asked, peering in through a side window.

"No, I just like to keep the wagon looking a little messy."

"Why's that?"

"So no punk who wants a new toy for his car will suspect there's a five-hundred-dollar German stereo sitting inside this trashmobile." Walker leaned inside the car and within seconds the Grateful Dead blared out the windows. "Sweet music," Walker howled, "river music." He pulled out a plastic water jug, took a long swig, then offered some to Cruz.

"How's it going with the work crew?" Walker asked.

"It's not bad. Most of the guys are pretty friendly."

"Don't you ever get tired of listening to Chico talk about all the women he screws?"

"Sometimes," Cruz said. He took a drink from the jug, then passed it back to Walker.

"If he screws half as many women as he talks about, I think his pecker would've fallen off a long time ago."

"I don't mind Chico," Cruz said, laughing. "His stories help the day go a little faster."

"I especially liked the one about the twin female Jell-O wrestlers from Reno. That story even made Crawdad sit up and listen." Walker took another long pull from the jug, then capped it and slung it inside the wagon. "Jobs are hard to come by up here," Walker said. "It's not like Bakersfield where they're always tearing something down so they can build it back up again."

"I was lucky to get hired on when I did. I needed the money pretty bad," Cruz said.

"Hell, if you need money you oughta get out of here. The Kern Valley's no place to get rich. If I were you I'd head down to Los Angeles and get something in construction."

"I can't leave right now. My old man lives with me and I've got to help him out. I was roofing in Bakersfield until I got laid off."

"Roofing," Walker said, grimacing. "That's shit work. Hot as hell and hard on the back. At least with this job you get to sit in the shade now and then."

Walker went around to the driver's side and put on a black T-shirt. Cruz rested his hands on the hood of the car.

"How long have you worked on the crew?" Cruz asked.

"About ten years."

"And why haven't you gotten out?"

"Because I like living close to the Kern and working outside," Walker said. "No wife and family like some of the others, and no desire to make a lot of money either. I live in a trailer up in the foothills that's all paid off."

Walker sat on the hood and looked out over the river. It was getting dark and Cruz could see the dim headlights of cars moving up the canyon. They were both silent as they listened to the tape.

"So you're working a lot with the old man?" Walker said.

"Yeah."

"I heard you pulled that biker out. Sounded like a pain in the ass."

"A three-hundred pounder," said Cruz. "Took us four hours to get him in. He was snagged in a brush pile. A real pig."

"I know how it is," said Walker. "I put in my time with Crawdad on the hooks." He paused, then slid off the hood in a clean motion. "I'd watch that old guy if I were you. Don't trust him. He's crazy."

"How's that?" asked Cruz.

"He ain't together anymore," Walker said in an angry voice. He took a few steps toward the river. "He's cracked up. Lou nailed him for stealing off the bodies. Rings. Watches and bracelets. He said it was for his little collection. Garcia caught him red-handed with a victim's wallet once."

"I haven't worked with him very long," Cruz said. "He's a little strange, but he doesn't seem crazy. One thing's for sure, he knows the Kern like nobody else."

"True," said Walker, turning to face him, "but watch yourself. Don't let him get you into something you're not ready for. His life don't mean shit to him. All he's got to hang on to is a six-pack of beer."

Walker reached under the front bumper of the car and pulled out a set of keys. "I need to be leaving," he said. "I've got an hour's drive ahead of me."

"Thanks for the advice," Cruz said. He walked toward the jeep, but suddenly turned and asked, "What's it like? I mean, taking your boat over the falls?"

Walker stood next to the battered wagon and rested his hand on the kayak. He said nothing at first, just leaned against the car door and scratched his beard. "I was scared shitless the first time I went over. You come up on that big horizon line and right before you go off, you can see everything downriver, and it's like you're flying off the edge of the world."

He was silent for a moment, tugging at the rope that held the kayak on the roof. "When I was a kid in school we used to read these history books. They were about all the crazy explorers and how they were told the earth was flat and to sail off the edge meant you were gonna burn in hell and get eaten by dragons. Well, the way I see it, there aren't too many dragons left around anymore and it's up to me to find them." He took off his glasses and wiped them on his T-shirt. "Does that make any sense at all?" Walker asked.

"Yeah," Cruz said, "I think I know what you're saying."

"Good. I'd hate to sound like some moron tripping on acid."

Cruz shook his head. "No," he said, "not at all. It sounds cool."

Walker grinned. "I'm glad I can still say something that sounds cool. I used to be pretty good at that." He put his glasses back on and ran a hand through his long hair. "I'll see you on Monday," he said, then slipped into the wagon. "I'm sure Crawdad will have a nice surprise waiting for us. Maybe we can shovel out a truckload of rattlesnakes or something."

Cruz climbed into the jeep and watched as Walker pulled back onto the main road and drove away. He sat there for a moment in the darkness, thinking about all that Walker had said and trying to picture Crawdad stealing from the bodies. He took it all in. The slow murmur of the river as it turned to black in front of him. The quick flash of headlights as cars whipped by and vanished around a curve. Then he started the engine and drove slowly up the canyon to Lake Isabella, all the way back replaying in his mind the image of Walker flying off the edge of Cataract Falls and vanishing into the foam below.

* * *

The next morning Cruz found the bottle while looking for an old pair of steel-toed boots before work. It was hidden in a corner of the tin shed out back. A pint of Jack Daniels stuffed down inside a cardboard box and covered with yellowed newspaper. Cruz held the bottle in his hand and undid the cap, which was sticky to the touch. He turned it sideways and stared at the honey-colored fluid sliding back and forth. The pint reminded him of a toy he'd had as a child, a ship in a bottle which slid from side to side when tilted, always sinking at either end.

He wanted to smash it. He wanted to tear the trailer apart, searching for other bottles stashed away. *It's the heat,* thought Cruz. *Makes us all crazy.* He could envision his old man walking past the Shady Grove on his way to the post office. Stopping at the door and hearing the laughter from within. Feeling the tingle of cool air. Then a voice. *Hey Frank, you old lonesome stranger! C'mon in . . .* so he would.

It's from years ago, he wanted to hear Frank say. *Just one I forgot about. It's old as the hills. I been saved by Jesus and I'd die if one swig of that poison touched my lips.* He wanted to call Frank outside to the shed right then and pour the whiskey into the dirt in front of him. He wanted to watch his eyes as the bottle emptied.

But he couldn't, the shame like a stench that followed him, sour and unchanging. *You believe me son, don'tcha?* he could hear his father say. *I swear on the Good Book. Not a drop.*

Cruz drained the Jack Daniels into the dust, then placed the bottle back into the box where he'd found it. He went into the trailer to get ready for work, carrying the steel-toed boots at his side.

* * *

During the next few days the water level of the Kern rose even higher and Cruz saw the river transformed into a torrent of foam and power. There'd been no recent drownings, so Cruz hadn't worked the hooks. They rattled in the back of Crawdad's truck like skeleton bones. The Search and Rescue crew went on twenty-four-hour alert, eyeing the bridges and highway embankments as the raging waters tore at the shoreline. They posted DANGER signs in the parks and campgrounds and warned tourists to stay away from the Kern.

On Thursday evening he drove the jeep down to Hobo Campground. The riverside trailers had been abandoned and left to the mercy of the flooding. A ghost town, thought Cruz. A stray dog sniffed at an overturned garbage can and water lapped at the wheels of an abandoned truck. From the shore he could see giant willows that had collapsed into the river and floated downstream, their roots and foundations eaten away by the powerful current. A few trees had jammed up in a boulder garden and created an enormous strainer to sift the Kern like a gold dredge.

He sat near the river's edge and studied the water as it rushed by, glassy and green as jade. He liked the sound it made and the way it enveloped him and blocked out all other sounds. The coolness rose off the surface, cutting the heat like a razor. Again he thought of the drowned girl and wondered whether her death had been a suicide and if Crawdad had stolen something from her, a bracelet or ring or necklace, when Cruz's back was turned. He wondered if Crawdad ever inquired about the past lives of those he pulled from the river. He sat there until the Kern faded in the dusk and the water became a stream of gleaming oil rolling in front of him. His mind felt cleansed of sweat and work and dust.

As he sat onshore he thought about the hot springs at Miracle, a quarter mile downstream from the campground, and wondered if they'd been flooded as well. Cruz used to go there with friends to soak in the hot pools and drink beer, his muscles feeling like putty afterward. When it grew dark he decided to walk over to the springs. There was a back way, a crude path that cut through the trees bordering the river, and he followed it, stumbling in places where the trail vanished into tar-dark patches and his hands had to grope for a branch or boulder to balance himself with.

After ten minutes he found the main trail and walked easily down to the hot springs. During normal flows, the pools lay about ten feet from the Kern. But tonight, as Cruz came down the trail, steam rose up from where the river's main current mingled with the water of the springs.

The place was abandoned and Cruz quickly stripped off his clothes, then tested the closest pool with his foot. It was cooler than he'd expected, probably from the river's seeping in, but still plenty hot. He slipped in gradually, his feet and calves first, then his thighs, letting the initial sting of the heat subside. When he was all the way in, he rested his head on the cement rim. A fish splashed in the water, and he listened to the steady rumble of the Kern.

Suddenly a dark figure rose up from the edge of the river fifteen feet in front of him. It happened quickly, his breath catching, and the ghostly apparition so close that he was afraid to yell out. At first he could only distinguish a shadowy form moving toward him, but then he saw a faceless woman, her slim hips and breasts outlined against a backdrop of water and moon. In the few seconds it took for her to appear, Cruz somehow knew who it was, recognizing the curve of her neck and the long flowing hair. No need to see her face. He knew the smooth cheekbones and delicate forehead as well as his own profile. He didn't go toward her, didn't even move, afraid she might suddenly vanish.

She stepped into the far pool. Twice she bent down and dipped her hands into the steaming water and brought them to her face. Then, like a ritual, she began to rinse herself with the springwater, pouring handfuls over her arms and back and legs. She turned and he almost saw her face and he wanted to go to her.

She screamed suddenly, jumped back, then caught herself before falling. Her hands jerked up to cover her breasts and she scrambled out of the pool.

"Stay the hell away!" she screamed. He saw her bend over and fumble for something in her clothes, then jerk back around. She held a gun in her hand and was pointing it straight at him.

Startled, Cruz leaped out of the water and grabbed his shirt, trying to cover himself. She aimed the gun at his midsection, arms outstretched and locked in a shooter's pose. "I'll blow you away if you come one step closer!"

"I'm sorry," he said, backing away from her. "I didn't think anybody else was down here."

"What the hell — ?" she said. "You had to be sitting there the whole time watching me."

He quickly pulled on his jeans.

"I'm sorry," he said again. "I didn't mean to frighten you."

She groped for a towel off to the side and wrapped it around herself. She was shaking but continued to hold the gun on him.

"I mean it," she said. "I'll shoot."

"I believe you," he said, "but could you maybe hold the barrel down?"

She lowered the gun while Cruz slipped his shirt on.

"Why didn't you say something?" she said, exasperated. "Why'd you just sit there like that? You're lucky, you know. I could've shot you."

"I didn't know anyone else was down here. Honest. And when I saw you come out of the water, I thought you were somebody else. Somebody I saw once."

"Are you meeting someone down here?"

"No," Cruz said. "Look, I can go. I don't want to tangle with you."

She was still trembling, and he could see now that she was older, probably late twenties, and that her features were different from those of the drowned girl. Her face was thin, almost sunken in places, and her nose came to a soft point. Quickly moving to her left, she picked up a shirt and put it on, then tied the towel around her waist. Cruz grabbed his shoes and turned to leave, but she stopped him, saying, "Wait a minute." Her voice was calmer now. "I didn't mean to scare you like that. It's just a reflex, I guess."

"Some reflex," Cruz said. "Reflexes like that get people killed."

"I'm sorry," she said. "It's just not safe anymore for women. We have to look out for ourselves." She tucked a loose strand of wet hair behind an ear and looked away from him up the trail. The gun still dangled from one hand and she leaned down and tucked it inside a jacket.

"I guess I overreacted," she said. "It's a little spooky down here, though."

Cruz put his tennis shoes on. "I don't want to interrupt your evening," he said. "I can head back the same way I came." A long silence followed. From somewhere in the distance he heard the far-off roar of a motorcycle accelerating up the canyon. "But take a little local advice," Cruz said. "Coming here alone isn't a great idea. What if I were a maniac or something?"

"What if you were?" she said. "I can take care of myself."

"I'm sure you can. But my point is that you really shouldn't be down here alone after dark," he continued. "It's not safe. Some pretty weird people hang out around the river."

"And are you one of them?" she asked, crossing her arms and pulling her shirt closed. She looked up at him, her head tilted at a funny angle. "I could do without the lecture on what I should and shouldn't do." Her voice was suddenly defensive. "I'm pretty good when it comes to dealing with weird maniacs."

"I didn't mean it that way," he said.

"But that's how it sounded."

"I was just trying to help."

"Look," she said, "the last thing I need is somebody treating me as if I didn't have a brain in my head. I knew it was dark when I came down here. Maybe it wasn't such a great idea, but I can handle it."

"Can you handle that gun?" Cruz asked.

She pulled the pistol out from under the towel and smiled. "Trust me on that one," she said, holding it up. "If you'd come after me, you'd be a floater in one of those pools right now."

He stood there silently while she turned away to gather the rest of her things. She reached down and picked up a nylon windbreaker and put it on. Cruz ran a hand through his hair and watched as more steam billowed up from the pools. He kicked at a rock with his foot.

"Do you come here by yourself a lot?" he asked.

"Why do you want to know?"

"I was just curious."

"This is only the second time. I found out about the place last week." She zipped up the windbreaker and slipped on a pair of thongs. "I like to run in the evenings, especially up in the hills. I twisted my knee and a doctor in Kernville told me to come here and do hot and cold soaks in the river and the springs." She paused, then frowned at Cruz. "He forgot to tell me it was a hangout for maniacs."

Cruz laughed. "Do I look like some maniac?" he said. "I'm just trying to save you from being attacked by some damn biker gang."

Her face softened and she smiled. "Thanks," she said. "A noble gesture."

"I'm a pretty noble guy once you get to know me."

There was an awkward silence as they stood at opposite ends of the pools, and Cruz noticed that her features were delicate and pretty. She had the figure of a dancer and he wondered what she might look like in a skirt and blouse, twirling around a wooden floor.

"Can I at least walk you back to your car?"

"Another noble gesture," she said. "You can do that."

They set off in silence over a section of the trail where trees loomed close, blocking out any light from the moon. She walked a few feet away from him, carrying a pair of running shoes in her right hand.

"You're not from around here, are you?" Cruz asked.

"How could you tell?"

"Not many locals like to run up in the hills with this heat. By four o'clock, most of them are sitting in a bar with a cold beer."

She didn't respond at first. Then she said, "I'm from Los Angeles. I moved to Kernville a year ago to get out of the city."

"That must have been a switch," Cruz said. "Kernville's about fifty years behind L.A. in almost everything."

"Everything but peace and quiet. The air's clear up here and I can actually go running without sucking in a ton of car exhaust or having to worry about getting run over by some damn Mercedes."

"You're not one of those crazy marathon runners, are you?" Cruz asked.

"No, I couldn't do anything like that. I run because it helps me relax at the end of a day."

She walked next to him on the trail and he watched her from the side. He liked the way she carried herself. She had the stride of an athlete, and her dark hair hung wet and shining past her shoulders.

"I have some friends who live in L.A.," he said. "Buddies from high school. Most of them got jobs working in garages or down on the docks. They make some damn good money down there. Some of them said they make almost fifteen bucks an hour."

"Well, you'd need to make that to survive in Los Angeles. It's the rent that kills you." They walked on. At one point she stumbled on a root and Cruz turned to help, but she waved him off.

"Do you work in Lake Isabella?" Cruz said. *I ask too many questions,* he thought. *She probably thinks I really am some psycho.*

"Kernville," she said. "I cut hair at Laverne's House of Beauty and Style." She chuckled to herself. "I call it Laverne's House of B.S."

Cruz knew the place. He and the crew had driven past it on their way up into the high country. There was usually a pink Cadillac parked out front. Probably Laverne's.

"It's a job," she said. She walked next to him, barely a foot away. It was the closest she'd come all night. They were almost to the top of the trail, and Cruz could see the glow of highway lights in the distance.

"I'll be turning off here," he said. "I still have to hike over to where my jeep is."

She stopped, standing in the shadows a few feet away from him, her face barely visible. Cruz saw the physical resemblance again to the drowned girl, the slim figure and delicate shoulders.

"Thanks for walking me back," she said.

"No problem. I hope your knee feels better."

He expected her to turn and head up the trail, but instead she stood there, gently swinging the running shoes at her side.

"I'm curious," she said. "You mentioned earlier that at first you thought I was somebody you knew."

"Yeah."

"Who was it? An old girlfriend?"

"No," Cruz said. "Just someone I saw once. A pretty face I never forgot."

"And you never saw her again?"

"That's right."

"How sad." Then she smiled at him and said, "You never know. Maybe you'll run into her."

"Maybe so," Cruz said. He looked up the trail. "Watch your step as you head back. There's a lot of cactus near the highway."

"I'll be careful." She stood there, still swinging the tennis shoes. "I'm surprised. I nearly blew your head off and you're still friendly. A lot of guys would've called me a crazy bitch and gotten out of there."

"I'm just your friendly neighborhood weirdo," Cruz said.

"What's your name?" she asked.

"My real name's Roy, as in Roy Rogers. My old man was a cowboy fan. But I usually just go by Cruz."

"Well, Cruz, if you ever want a great haircut, stop by Laverne's and ask for Rita," she said.

"I don't get over to Kernville very often," he said.

"Doesn't look as if your hair gets cut much either."

Cruz smiled and looked down, running a hand through his thick, tangled hair. When he looked up she was gone.

He walked back down the main trail and then took the turnoff that led to Hobo and his jeep. He thought about Rita and the fact that he'd never talked much with an older woman before. In high school he'd been afraid the senior girls would laugh at him if he asked them out. He used to fantasize about what they might look like with their clothes off and standing in his shower waiting for him, like one of those letters in *Penthouse* magazine, the ones that always began with, *Even I was surprised when I came home one night and found Suzy, my hot little neighbor* . . .

But mostly he thought about the drowned girl and when he first saw the ghostly shape coming out of the water. There had been no fear or terror, which is what he might have expected. Instead, he felt as if it were part of some plan and that the girl had been waiting for him to find her. And when he'd reached out to bring her back, the Kern had suddenly ripped away the mask, revealing the truth as if it were some cheap magic trick.

CHAPTER THREE

On the morning the Kern reached its highest flow in twenty years, Lou called a meeting at headquarters before work. It was midweek and Cruz had been dreading another three days of chopping out cactus and mesquite in the high country. They gathered in the corrugated steel warehouse behind the main office, and Cruz spotted Crawdad standing off to the side, squinting out from under his baseball cap, while Walker sat on a rusty barrel in the back, wiping his face with a red bandanna.

"I need a couple of men for the river rescue team," Lou began. "Saunders and Martinez, my core crew, quit yesterday and moved up north to work in Fresno. I need volunteers to use a raft and oars in case we have to rescue stranded swimmers or search the shoreline for bodies. Got the word this morning that the river's not going down for a while, that there's enough snow up near Mount Whitney to keep it high until damn near August."

Lou paused. Cruz could tell he was nervous by the way he shifted his weight from one boot to the other and kept scratching at a red patch on his neck. Fidgety.

"With the big water here to stay," he continued, "we might as well gear up for some more accidents. There could be some overtime pay involved. Any volunteers?"

Cruz could hear Chico and the others mumbling to one another. Then there was a long silence, interrupted only by the roar of a gravel truck passing by outside. He looked toward the back and could see Walker with his head down, sitting quietly on the barrel. Cruz wondered why he didn't volunteer to help with his kayak. Lou cleared his throat and spoke again.

"How about it? I need some help here."

"Sounds pretty loco," Garcia said from the front.

"I ain't going near the Kern," Chico said. "It's a deathtrap."

A rumble of voices began and Lou stared at the men, his pudgy face ragged and sweating in the heat. He started to say something but stopped, only to turn and look away.

"I think the bottom line is this," Chico said. "None of us vets are gonna touch this job. No way in hell. We put in our time. Besides, that damn river's suicide right now."

"Why should I stick my ass on the line just because some drunk falls in?" Garcia said angrily. "Let 'em drown."

Then Cruz saw a hand go up from the side of the crowd. Crawdad's.

"I'll help out," he said. He stepped forward and eased through the crowd of men. "Back in the late fifties we had a flood like this and I went out on the river. Scared the hell out of me but I didn't have much choice. People's lives depended on it. But I'm getting too old for this. I need somebody to help out."

Cruz felt his skin tingle when he heard Crawdad, a layer of quiet settling over the group. He could feel the old man's eyes on him and he looked down at his dusty boots. He knew what the rest of them were thinking, that he was the rookie, the greenhorn. He didn't have a wife or kids, no real family except for his father. He looked up and saw Crawdad still glaring in his direction, waiting for Cruz to step forward and back him up. He thought of their time by the river and how the old man had taught him to use the hooks and the way he'd covered the drowned girl when Cruz couldn't stomach it.

He also thought about what Walker had said below Cataract Falls. *He ain't together anymore. Cracked up. Don't let him get you into something you're not ready for.* But maybe Walker had a grudge against Crawdad, something that went back to when they were on the hooks together. He felt his face redden, the skin on his cheeks heating up. He raised his hand.

"Okay, Cruz," Lou said. "You and Crawdad get the river gear. Training starts this morning and — "

Walker's voice cut him off in midsentence. "I'm not saying this because I want to take his place, but the Kern's no place for rookies." His voice was loud and resonated from the back of the warehouse. He wiped his face with the red bandanna, then continued. "Especially now. Cruz doesn't know what he's getting into and the rapids down there will eat him alive. Hell, nobody should be going near that river unless they know what they're in for. Like Chico said, it's a deathtrap."

Then Cruz saw Crawdad stride to the back of the warehouse. He spoke directly to Walker. "If you're so concerned about Cruz, then why don't you take his place?"

Walker didn't move off the barrel. The warehouse was silent now, and the men had turned their backs on Lou in order to see what was happening behind them.

"Hell, it'll be a reunion," said Crawdad. "You and me and the hooks. Just like old times." He spit out the sentences as if he had a bad taste in his mouth, then turned to grin at some of the men. "You can even bring your little kayak. We need all the help we can get."

"That's not the point."

"What is the point then?" Crawdad said angrily, his face turning red. "That you and everybody else here are too scared to help out?"

"Not scared," Walker said, sliding off the barrel. "Just smart. Some of us know better. We know that when the Kern gets sky-high, things start getting weird. The dragons come out and they're hungry." He grabbed a shovel that was leaning against the wall and started toward the warehouse door. Suddenly he turned and looked back at Crawdad.

"Why don't you ask Cruz what he thinks?" Walker said. "It's his decision."

Until that point Cruz had felt like an outsider, a spectator standing on the outskirts observing. But suddenly he saw the focus of the crowd shift as the men turned to face him.

"What do you say, Cruz?" said Crawdad. "You heard Walker say what he thinks. Now it's your turn."

The old man's gaze was unblinking, intense, and Cruz could see his red eyes waiting for an answer. He knew what Crawdad needed from him this time, just like he'd known when they'd gone to the river with the hooks. But he let the dark weight of the question hang in the air for a moment, let the silence fill the space between him and the others like a wall. He wasn't sure who to believe or trust, but he felt that he owed the old man something.

"You can back out," Crawdad said. "I'll find someone else. You decide."

Cruz could feel the old man pressing again, could hear his words haunting him. *Ain't much time. No mercy in that river.*

"Somebody has to go out on the Kern," Cruz said. "It might as well be us."

Then Crawdad turned toward Lou. "He'll know the river when I'm done working with him. He'll know the river or we'll both drown like rats in the willows, and I don't plan on dying soon. Didn't he take on the hooks when nobody else wanted them? Didn't he?"

"You can kiss his ass goodbye," said Walker, turning away from them as he stepped out of the warehouse.

Cruz heard a buzzing of voices around him as the men grabbed tools and axes and began heading out to the trucks. He turned and saw Crawdad approaching. "Don't listen to Walker," the old man told him. "He's a first-class bullshit artist. C'mon. Stay close and I'll make a boatman out of you."

*   *   *

"Geek patrol" was what Crawdad called it in the beginning. Cruz felt spooked that morning as they drove down to some slow sections of the Kern where the river opened up out of the willows. When they reached the put-in, Crawdad dragged the old boat from the back, a sixteen-foot black military raft, and stretched it out in the sand.

"It looks ancient," Cruz said.

"Hell," Crawdad said, chuckling, "it's old all right, but it's hauled too many bodies out of the river to go under now. It's a river hearse. Look at this."

He showed him the grey, rectangular patches checkering the seams and tubes. Cruz ran his hands along the rough surface, feeling the irregularities as if they were zippered scars against his fingertips.

"You sew up a raft just like a man," Crawdad said. "There's needle and thread under all these rubber Band-aids."

Then the old man took a bucket of river water and washed the boat down until the black exterior was shining like sealskin. They took turns inflating the six chambers with a metal cylinder pump, going at it until Cruz could feel his forearms and back throb.

They unloaded the ten-foot oars, each one sleek and heavy as a wooden beam in Cruz's arms, and set them next to the raft. There were other things in the back of the truck. Rusty ammo cans, supposedly watertight, but smelling sour and dank when the metal lids were popped off. A metal rowing frame with a slanted wooden seat attached. Frayed coils of rope wound tight as a hangman's noose. Two thick plastic body bags for drowning victims. "Corpse condoms," the old man called them. All of the gear carried the scent of mildew and decay, like items unearthed from a long storage underground. The musty odor filled Cruz's nostrils with an awareness of the tools and their trade. To carry the dead from water to an earthen grave.

Crawdad taught him the knots, the sheet bend and bowline and trucker's hitch. At first the rope was awkward in Cruz's fingers, like stiff wire in the hands of a child, but the old man stood beside him and guided his hands through the invisible patterns. They used red webbing to lash the steel frame into the center of the raft, cinching it down taut to the metal D-rings. They slid the boat into the river and tied it off to a tree, then watched it bob and sway in the green current. Crawdad slid two of the oars into the U-shaped metal oarlocks jutting skyward from either side of the frame, then lashed the third to the side of the raft.

He showed Cruz the orange life jackets, which were bulky and ballooned out in front. "Mae Wests" was what the old man called them. "I knew a flat-chested girl named Doris that could've used one of these," he said. He made sure the front straps were cinched tight so Cruz would pop up quickly if he ever got tossed into the river.

"How'd you learn all this?" Cruz asked him at one point. "There's so much to know."

"Taught myself," said Crawdad.

"That sounds a little dangerous."

"It was. Twenty years ago there wasn't a soul who knew anything about rafting. I talked my boss, this old guy named Sam, into letting me buy some gear so I could learn. The first time I went out I didn't even wear a life jacket. Flipped the boat in the first rapid and nearly drowned."

"And you got the raft back?" Cruz asked.

Crawdad smiled and slipped into the shallows. "Damn right I did," he said. "I jumped back in the Kern and swam after it. I wasn't gonna let Sam pin a big bill on me."

He suddenly stopped and pointed down at the water. "Now here's something you'll like." Cruz stepped into the icy river and walked over to Crawdad. They saw a cluster of tiny water striders hovering near the green surface, their spidery legs barely visible.

"Jesus bugs," Crawdad said. "Look how they dance on top of the water. Light as a feather and quick. That's what we're gonna have to do, with the river being so high. Dance or drown."

"But the boat's heavy with all that gear," Cruz said. "I've never seen a barge dance."

"Don't worry. Once you've learned to row, she's a black bullet in the water."

He made Cruz begin that morning at the oars, sitting in the wooden slant-board rowing seat. Crawdad perched in the stern, directly behind the rower. "Be careful how you slide or you'll get splinters up your butt," the old man told him. He called it a crash course in river sense, in learning to row by rowing. "Sometimes you got to be a fortune teller. That's what it takes. Seeing the unseen," he said.

The oars were bulky and awkward in Cruz's hands and he struggled, catching the wooden tips on rocks or thick roots buried in the shallows. Even the calm sections were deceptive. The swirling undercurrent twisted the oar blades flat beneath the surface and they plunged down, ripping Cruz forward as he clutched the handles and was nearly jolted from the boat. He flailed impatiently at the river and hoped the oars would bite into the water for a powerful stroke. He felt overwhelmed and frustrated that first morning, as if the Kern were conspiring to trick him at every turn.

Crawdad showed him how to feather the oars so the blades would dip back into the water and slice through the emerald current like fins. He taught him the basics: the pivot, the double-oar turn, the portogee.

"Use your legs more!" he'd shout. "Drive up with your legs. That's where your power is." Sometimes the old man was like a barking demon, always positioned directly behind Cruz in the stern of the raft. "Pull with the left oar," he'd say. "Too hard, dammit! Correct with the right. Keep the angle. Now point your bow at the shore and pull away. Don't lose it. Pull!"

For a week they worked the slow stretches, ferrying back and forth across the current, practicing angle pivots and catching the calm pockets of water behind boulders. Cruz would go home at night with nickel-sized blisters on his palms. He bought leather gloves and cut the fingers off to protect his hands when he rowed. The old life jacket chafed his skin raw under the armpits, and his lower back was inflamed after the first day. But he learned to relax at the oars and listen to Crawdad. "You're picking it up fast. A real natural. Now let the river do the work for you. Go with it."

Throughout the days of training, Cruz grew accustomed to the icy tingle of water on his ankles in the morning, the itch of poison oak breaking out on his skin in small patches. The river world slowly became more than just a place of the dead. The days of working the hooks and sandbagging and digging firebreaks up in Sequoia seemed long ago, replaced with a sense of timelessness, of watching a wave curl back endlessly, repeating the cycle of water and its motion. Each morning revealed blue sky and a gold wafer of sun slanting down from the canyon rim as they rigged the boat. When he felt the river streaming beneath the raft and taking over, he sensed an electricity within himself, as if he were gliding across stormy waters in a magic vessel.

But each day when Cruz returned home after work he felt distant and somehow insulated from the world his father lived in. He saw the river beckoning with adventure while Frank stayed firmly planted in a life where it was enough just to hang on from Sunday to Sunday. There were nights when Cruz felt exhilarated after a new training run through a challenging section of the Kern, only to listen to his old man babble on about the heat and how the Dodgers lost the doubleheader in Pittsburgh and whether or not Cruz's mother and Donna would ever come from San Diego for a visit.

He wasn't sure if his father was drinking again. He didn't search the house after finding the bottle, nor did he return to check the box in the tin shed. He only knew that Frank spent most of his days sitting on the porch facing the alley, dressed in denim cutoffs, pink thongs from K-Mart, and a straw cowboy hat. His huge potbelly hung over the rim of his shorts, and a scar from an operation ran across his shirtless skin like a jagged crease. He would yell and shake his Bible at motorcyclists who roared up and down the alley, leaving dust and cinders in the wake of their Harleys.

One night Cruz came home and found him asleep on the tattered sofa, the cloth cover soaked with urine. Cruz walked him to the bathroom to shower, then washed his soiled pants and underwear. He quietly helped his father to bed and turned out the light. Afterward, as Cruz listened to Frank's fluttered breath, he realized that he'd never once asked him if he had been drinking. The lies weren't necessary anymore.

The questions had been shut away and avoided long ago. Cruz remembered a Christmas Eve when he'd been eleven and Frank had gotten drunk and had begun to fight with Marta. Donna started to cry and Cruz took her outside into the cold, away from the house. They walked around the block, her tiny hand inside his, and softly hummed Christmas carols until the shouting stopped. Then they entered the house and put their coats away. He could tell Marta had been crying, but she wiped away the tears and sat them down at the kitchen table. She poured eggnog into the tiny red and white Christmas glasses they liked so much and slid a tray of cookies out of the warm oven. They opened presents afterward. Cruz got a pair of plastic walkie-talkies and an Etch-A-Sketch. His father was silent throughout, staring at them from his chair near the Christmas tree. His gaze was glassy-eyed, unblinking, as if Cruz were transparent as tissue paper to be burned and thrown away. It was as if his father stared right through his heart and mind and soul into the shadowed hallway beyond.

*   *   *

During the second week of training they moved downstream to where the river narrowed, a section Crawdad called the Jungle. Willows arched out over the river, their roots stabbing up through the surface, the water boiling as it slithered in and out of the tangled foliage along the shore. The rapids had been christened by Crawdad with names like Strangler, the Cauldron, and Executioner. They all contained short bursts of frothing waves within tight channels. "The trees are the killers," he heard Crawdad say one morning at put-in. "Get pinned underwater by a willow and the water'll hold you there forever."

The undercurrents and twisted passages of the Jungle were a frightening maze of traps for Cruz. He grew afraid each time he felt a sudden burst of speed as they blindly accelerated around a bend; each time the dark water tugged the raft toward a partially submerged mass of vines and branches.

One morning, in a rare calm stretch between rapids, Crawdad surprised him. Cruz was gripping the oars, waiting intently for the next command, when suddenly the old man asked, "You got a girlfriend?" Before Cruz even had a chance to respond, Crawdad said, "You need a girlfriend. Somebody to take your mind off the river. And don't think she has to be a looker. Just make sure she's got good hands. That's the sign of a beautiful woman. Her hands tell it all. All the decent women I've known have always had good strong hands." Then, as if this brief exchange had never occurred, they rounded a bend and Crawdad's voice jumped him from behind, yelling, "Pull away, dammit! Stay to the right!"

Crawdad showed little mercy, continually pushing and correcting his every stroke. When they stopped for lunch, Cruz ate little, his mouth tasting sour as he remembered the hot days of breaking trails in rattlesnake country. Late one day they went farther downstream and approached a new rapid, Nightmare Corner, and Crawdad refused to describe it beforehand as he had with the others. "You're on your own," he said. "I ain't always gonna be sitting back here like your guardian angel. Read it and run it."

Cruz looked downstream and saw a series of cresting waves surging into a tangled stand of low-hanging willows on the right. He pointed the stern left and began to pull away from the trees. The first powerful wave crashed into the boat, spinning it backward and out of control. Cruz strained at the oars, trying to pivot the boat back around as they descended into the rapid, when suddenly he heard Crawdad scream, "Get down!" Too late, he felt something solid and heavy explode like a hammer into his head and he was swept into the river.

Dazed, he saw water swirling around him, endless and deep. *I'm drowning,* he thought in a panic. *This river is my grave.* Then he felt iron hands on the collar of his life jacket as he was pulled from the depths and thrown onto the floor of the raft. Choking, he spit out water and panted for air. He looked up and saw a grinning Crawdad at the oars, rowing the boat away from the willows.

"You okay?" Crawdad asked. "That was one helluva branch that decked you."

He didn't answer immediately. There was a burning sensation in his nostrils from the water. His head pounded, and he felt a walnut-sized swelling on the back of his neck. "I think so," he finally said.

"You're lucky," Crawdad said. "The river gods were smiling on you today. Those willows aren't usually so merciful."

Still dizzy, Cruz got up from the raft's floor and sat on the front thwart. "Hell," Crawdad cackled, "just remember: there are two kinds of boatmen. Those that have screwed up, and those that are gonna. And now you're an official screwup!"

Cruz rubbed his head and said, "What an honor." Suddenly Crawdad pivoted the bow around and a huge wave slapped over the tube, dousing Cruz with water. They both began to laugh, softly at first, then louder. Cruz could feel the adrenalin seeping away, easing into the air as Crawdad guided the raft through a series of rollercoaster waves.

"This is crazy," Cruz said, laughing.

"Maybe so," said Crawdad, "but I'd rather be doing this than chopping out cactus and digging firebreaks." The old man slid off the rowing seat and motioned at him. "Get back in the seat and finish up."

So Cruz clambered over the thwart and Crawdad moved back to the stern. As he began to maneuver the boat downstream, Cruz said, "Thanks for grabbing me."

"You're welcome," he said. "I'll expect the same from you if I ever go for a swim."

"It's a deal," Cruz said, pulling back on the oars to avoid a black rock. Suddenly he felt a hand on his shoulder.

"You did good back there," said Crawdad. "You didn't quit."

Then the hand was gone and Cruz pointed the bow downstream. He waited for Crawdad's voice, a shout of caution or direction. Nothing came. So he pushed forward on the oars, moving the boat toward the steady rumble of the next rapid looming around the bend.

* * *

On the last Saturday in June the old jeep broke down and Cruz had to hitchhike to the auto parts store in Kernville for a new fan belt. It was late morning by the time he got there. He waited fifteen minutes while the guy at the desk rummaged around in the storeroom. The entire back wall behind the counter and cash register was covered with advertising calendars that showed big-breasted women in tight bikinis holding the latest in shock absorbers or mufflers.

He had time to kill before heading back home. Unlike the dust and gravel of Lake Isabella, Kernville had green lawns and wide shade trees, as well as a beautiful park bordering the river. Cruz thought about buying some lunch and eating it down by the Kern, or going over to the new air-conditioned Safeway to escape the heat and read some magazines. But as the salesman appeared from the back with the fan belt, Cruz ran a hand through his long hair and realized that what he really wanted was to stop off at Laverne's for the haircut Rita had promised him.

The pink Cadillac was parked in front of the shop when he arrived. Laverne's House of Beauty and Style was located across the street from one of Kernville's fanciest motels, the Hi-Ho Lodge, and the parking lot of the beauty parlor was packed. He walked through the front door with the fan belt tucked under his arm and was immediately assaulted by the strong aroma of perm solution and creme rinse. It tickled his nostrils and he almost sneezed in the face of Laverne herself, a big woman with thick glasses and a beehive hairdo which sat like a small mountain on top of her head. She wore a pink name tag that was pinned to her tight green shirt.

"You looking for someone, honey?" she said to Cruz.

"I'm here for a haircut."

"Well, we usually don't cut men's hair. There's a good barber just down the street."

"I'm looking for Rita," Cruz said. "She told me to stop by and she'd cut my hair."

"Oh, I see." The woman paused and a sour look came over her face. She glanced at the back of the shop. "This is a busy time, being Saturday and all. And Rita is one of our most popular stylists." She pursed her lips together. "Let me see if she can squeeze you in."

Cruz looked toward the back as Laverne wriggled her way through a corridor of older women sitting under pink plastic drying domes. There was a hum to the place, and Cruz noticed that a number of the women were staring at him.

He finally saw Rita hovering over a customer. She looked different, her dark hair pulled up and exposing a pale, thin neck. She wore a denim skirt and a white cotton blouse, and he watched as Laverne spoke to her. Rita leaned over and said something to the woman she was attending to, then made her way toward the front, stopping along the way to talk with another woman under a dryer. Rita looked older, more professional. As she approached, he noticed a pale scar that ran across the right side of her chin.

"It's you," she said. "The maniac from the hot springs."

He nodded. "That's me, the noble maniac."

She laughed, then said, "I didn't think I'd see you again after the way I treated you. I guess you decided to come back for some more."

"Is this a bad time?" he asked. "You seem pretty busy."

"Saturdays are always like this. If you can wait five minutes while I finish with Mrs. McCalister, I can fit you in."

"You're sure?"

She smiled. "I'm sure. Besides," she reached out and ran a hand through his hair, "I haven't seen this much hair in six months. It'll be a challenge."

He sat down in a pink vinyl chair and looked at the magazines and papers. *National Enquirer, The Star, Better Homes and Gardens.* When he was a kid he used to go to the barber shop with his father just so he could read the men's magazines like *True Adventure* and *Argosy.* He was halfway through the *Enquirer* article "Kansas Housewife Impregnated With Alien Sperm" when he looked up and saw Rita standing in front of him.

"That looks like fascinating reading," she said.

He slid it back on the magazine rack and stood up. "I feel a little out of place," he said in a low voice. He could see Laverne glaring at him from her post at the main counter and cash register.

"Don't worry about Laverne," Rita whispered. "You're probably giving her a thrill just walking in here." Rita took his arm and started back. "We don't get a lot of male customers. Most go to Curly's up the street."

"I kinda figured that out," he said.

Cruz followed her down the center aisle until they reached Rita's station. He sat down and she draped a pink plastic apron over him.

"Is everything pink around here?" he asked.

"It's Laverne's favorite color. She sells Mary Kay cosmetics on the side. That's how she got that big Cadillac parked out front."

She turned Cruz around so that he faced the mirror, then ran her fingers through his hair.

"Geez," she said, "I've known some guys who would've killed for all this hair. One thing's for sure, you'll never go bald."

She spun the chair back around, popped a lever at the bottom with her foot, and tilted the whole thing so that Cruz's head rested in a low sink. Turning on a faucet, she ran warm water over his hair, then added some shampoo and began to wash it. She was careful not to tug or pull at any of the tangled places as she worked the soap into his scalp.

"You should take better care of your hair," she said. "Use a little conditioner once in a while."

"Maybe so," Cruz said. "I've never given it much thought."

After rinsing off the soap, she tilted the chair back up, combed his hair straight down so that it hung in his eyes, and began to snip off black strands with a long pair of scissors. She worked fast and talked with him about his job and growing up in Lake Isabella.

"How'd you end up in Kernville?" Cruz asked her at one point.

"I just wanted to get out of Los Angeles and go someplace different."

"I'd say you found it."

"Yeah," she said, "Laverne's is different all right. But I've always loved the mountains. My dad used to bring me to Kernville when I was a kid. He liked to fly-fish and we would go on these weekend trips up in the Sierras. I guess I've always wanted to come back here."

As they talked, there were moments when her hip would press against his shoulder, or she would rest her hand on his neck as she studied him in the mirror. At first he wanted to deny any pleasure he felt when she touched him, but as her fingers moved through his hair, he felt a secret intimacy with her. But it was unrealistic to think that an attractive woman like Rita didn't have a boyfriend, somebody she was already involved with. After all, Kernville was a small town. A beautiful woman didn't go unnoticed.

He studied her hands in the mirror as she worked. Her fingers were unusually long and slender. The high desert air tended to crack and dry out skin, and his own hands were blistered and peeling from the oars. Yet hers were smooth, unblemished.

"How's that?" she said. He glanced up into the mirror and saw that the ragged edges had been neatly trimmed and the bulk thinned out. "It's a big improvement," he said, smiling. "My head looks smaller."

She laughed and began to blow-dry the hair off his neck and shoulders. "Seriously," he said. "It looks great. I'll recommend you to all my friends at work who still have any hair left."

When he was cleaned up and standing next to her, he reached for his wallet. "How much do I owe you?" he asked.

"Five for the cut and one for the shampoo," she said.

He pulled a ten from his wallet and handed it to her.

"C'mon, I'll walk you out," she said. "I've got a break coming anyway."

The shop was buzzing with hair dryers and chatter. He followed her to the front, then past the pink chairs, where a few older women sat browsing through magazines as they waited. Rita stopped at the main counter to talk with Laverne, who looked at Cruz and smiled.

"Rita turned you into a new man, honey," Laverne said. "Now you're almost as handsome as my boy Wiley. He's a big singer in Las Vegas." She pointed at some photographs hanging on the wall behind her of a tan guy in a tuxedo with a pencil-thin mustache and slicked-back hair. "I'm so proud of him," she said. "He's gonna be the next Elvis." Then she handed Cruz a pink plastic comb. "Take this as a little gift, compliments of Laverne's."

"Thanks," Cruz said, sticking the comb in his pocket. Rita winked at him and grinned. As they stepped outside, she whispered, "Wiley's just a lounge lizard in Vegas. He came to visit Laverne last year and tried to pick me up. He ended up over at the Hi-Ho with fat Wanda. She came back the next day acting like she'd seen God."

The heat was sweltering out on the porch, so they stayed in the shade. Rita took a pack of cigarettes out of her pocket and slipped one into her mouth, then lit up. She rested her foot on the bumper of Laverne's Cadillac.

"It's hot," she said. "All I've got in my apartment is a window fan. Sometimes I want to just sleep here at the shop."

"It's not as bad down by the river," he said. "In the evening there's a layer of coolness coming off the water. Natural air-conditioning."

"Sounds nice."

Cruz leaned against the wall of the shop. He said nothing, even though what he wanted to say was *Let's do something Friday night* or *I'd like to see you again.* But the words sounded all wrong, as if he'd been planning to say them for the last hour. Besides, she'd probably heard this a million times before from men like Wiley and others.

"Are you surprised I smoke?" she asked suddenly.

"Not really," he said.

"Some people are, especially when they find out I run." She exhaled, the smoke streaming from her nostrils. "It's a bad habit I haven't been able to kick. But I plan to quit someday." She stared down at the porch. "One thing at a time."

"Were you surprised when I showed up today?" he asked.

"Yeah. Like I said, I didn't think I'd see you again after the way I acted toward you, all paranoid and bitchy. I mean why would a cute guy want to hassle with some woman who just treated him like a convict."

Cute. The word stayed with him for a moment. He'd never thought of himself as being cute or handsome. And no one had ever said it to his face, not even in high school. Not even Teresa.

She looked at him and laughed, the cigarette in her hand. "Seriously," she said. "What you said when we were at the hot springs, about being down there alone after dark. You were right."

"We all make mistakes."

"Some more than others." She took her foot off the bumper and walked to the end of the porch, the denim skirt swinging around her legs. "It just makes me mad."

"Why's that?" Cruz asked.

"Because there are places a woman can't go after dark. Sometimes I like to think I can do anything I want, that there aren't any rules. Then I get myself in trouble and I feel stupid all over again."

"What kind of trouble?"

She flicked the cigarette out into the parking lot and looked over at him. Her face softened and she raised a hand to her face, covering the scar on her chin.

"I'll tell you about it sometime," she said.

"I'd like that."

She walked over to where he leaned against the wall. Her blouse was low cut, a thin slit leading down to her breasts.

"I need to get back inside," she said. "I don't want Laverne to have a stroke or anything."

"Can I call you later in the week?" Cruz asked.

"If you want to. My last name's Clark," she said. "I'm in the phone book and I like to dance."

"I'm not much of a dancer," Cruz said.

"Don't worry," she said. "Some things you learn just by doing."

Then she went back inside the shop. Cruz stood on the porch for a minute longer, staring at Laverne's pink Cadillac and wondering what he might look like cruising through Lake Isabella in that car with Rita sitting next to him. Then he shook the notion off and walked back to the main business district of Kernville so he could find a pay telephone with a directory and write down Rita's number. By the time he headed back to Lake Isabella on the Reservoir Road, it was late afternoon and the sky had darkened to a plum color in the west. He stood by the roadside, keeping an eye on approaching vehicles as well as the distant storm, silently repeating the phone number again and again in his head and committing it to memory.

CHAPTER FOUR

A storm front moved in on Monday of the first week in July. The early morning was overcast, the sky darkening with deep shades of purple. Lou called Cruz at 4 a.m., startling him from sleep.

"I just heard," Lou said. "Crawdad called. Says he was coming up the canyon from Bakersfield last night when a Mexican family flagged him down near Hobo. They said their son was missing." Lou paused and Cruz could hear a crackling on the line. "Go ahead and meet Crawdad at Manning's Bridge. Take the raft and search the willows. There's a chance the kid might be pinned and still alive. And watch yourself down there, Cruz. The Kern's still running high."

They were on the river by dawn, rescue gear and ropes lashed tight into the boat. They wore faded yellow raincoats that smelled damp and musty under their life jackets. They brought the hooks, storing them in a thick canvas bag and tying it to the rowing frame. Cruz felt a chill when he touched them, the prongs rust-tipped, like blood dried and baked from the sun.

He rowed the Jungle section again, working hard at the oars until he felt sweat inching down his ribs. He saw the river now as a narrow ribbon of landmarks. The buffalo-shaped rock perched on a cliff marked the entrance to Executioner Rapid. The hermit's abandoned cabin near Trout Bridge. The powerhouse at Borel. Thunder rumbled from the south and he glimpsed jagged veins of lightning.

Crawdad sat behind him and said little as he studied the shore and the strainers and looked for pinned bodies. Cruz focused on the river. They worked their way down methodically, moving from one side to the other like a zigzagging water strider, Crawdad's crooked finger pointing the way. There were moments when Cruz imagined he was alone and rowing in solitude. Then he would hear a rasp behind him, a voice of warning.

"Be ready, Cruz. There's a family waiting to know if their kin is drowned or alive. Sweating it out. This ain't no time for relaxing."

It was drizzling when they reached the towering granite wall near takeout; the wall was streaked with mineral deposits, each strand a tributary of color. The rain felt cold and stung Cruz's cheeks. He began to ease the boat over to shore when Crawdad stopped him.

"Not here. We're going farther down today, where the river's tighter. More places to get hung up. Just row. Leave the fishing to me."

Cruz hesitated, letting the oars drift free in the water.

"I've never seen this section before," he said.

"That don't matter," said Crawdad. "I can talk you down it."

"Shouldn't we get some backup from shore?"

"There's no time for that. Something's telling me the kid's down there. I know it."

Cruz could feel a drumming inside his chest. *Watch yourself,* Walker had said. He longed for Crawdad to spot the body before they went farther into the canyon. He hadn't even seen this lower section from the road high above. Shielded by an overhanging shelf of granite, it had always been a place of shadows for Cruz, a dark slit in the landscape where the river narrowed.

In the first mile the tangled foliage of willows and scrub brush gave way to vertical sheets of granite and basalt slanting down to the lip of the river. No sign of a body. Then the rapids began. "Ass kickers," Crawdad called them. Cruz had never seen water so huge. White-tipped waves poured over the bow, filling the boat as Crawdad scooped out muddy water with a plastic bucket. Cruz could feel the pulse of the current quicken beneath the raft, as if the stream tumbled down a staircase of time-hewn steps.

They were descending now, going deeper. No roads or takeout beaches visible. Rain fell in shimmering torrents, turning the walls into slabs of ebony. Water spilled from the cliffs above, cascading down and pumping the river with speed. Cruz felt the raft dive into the trough of a wave, then rise up and break through as if at sea in a storm. He thought of what Walker had said about going off Cataract Falls. *Where dragons wait* was the warning echoing in his mind as he approached each rapid, trusting only Crawdad's words as to what lay below. *The dragons are hungry.*

They reached Gravedigger Falls early in the afternoon. Still no sign of a body. Crawdad made him pull the boat over to scout. Walker's warning loomed clear in Cruz's mind. He was uncertain of everything now, even Crawdad's story about the Mexican family and the body. *Don't trust him,* Walker had said. *He's crazy.* But maybe Walker had been lying in order to discredit the old man.

They tied off in the trees and hiked down along a slippery ledge. Cruz saw a V-shaped tongue of glassy water sliding into the rapid like an arrow, then descending into a towering wave at the bottom. One hundred yards downstream the river vanished between two black monoliths of granite.

"This here's just the little brother," yelled Crawdad above the roar, pointing at the wave. "Down below is Gravedigger Falls, the big daddy deathtrap. No way are we going into that. I seen a kayaker try to run it once. His boat came out in pieces. We never did find the body."

Crawdad was silent for a moment, almost reverent as he stared at the horizon line downstream. "We'll pull over just above it on the right and portage. There's a footpath we can carry the boat around on. Only one way to run Gravedigger Falls. Onshore."

His directions for the rapid in front of them were straightforward. "This little one's called Tombstone. Don't let it fool you. There's no way to portage around it, so you have to break through the waves coming from the right, then keep pulling to slip by the big curler at the bottom. Maybe I'm getting too old for this, but stay clear of that bottom wave on the left. It's a boat-eater. Hit it dead on and we'll flip."

As they hiked back to the boat Cruz felt his mouth suddenly go dry as sand. He had no spit. He paused, letting Crawdad get ahead of him so he could stop and piss, all the while hearing the deafening clamor of the rapid. Doubt clouded his mind. Simple thoughts of self-preservation, of not wanting to drown. *His life don't mean shit to him,* Walker had said.

He went back to the raft where Crawdad waited.

"I ran into Walker a while ago," Cruz said as he stared down at his damp tennis shoes.

"So what?"

Cruz paused. A part of him wanted to hold back and not talk about any of his suspicions. Keep it to himself like he'd always done before. But he looked out at Tombstone and knew this was different. He had to know some truth before he set foot in the raft again.

Cruz kicked at a rock and said, "He told me not to trust you, that you were crazy."

"And what do you think?" Crawdad answered.

"Isn't this crazy?" Cruz said, pointing at the river. "I mean, look at this rapid. And look at what's waiting downstream."

"It's crazy if you don't think you can do it." He fixed Cruz with a questioning stare. "What's the matter, boy? Are you doubting old Crawdad now when you most need him? Are you blowing off everything I've taught you?"

"No."

"What else did Walker tell you?"

"Nothing else," Cruz said angrily, "but why haven't we found the body?"

"Because there is a body and there ain't," said Crawdad. "There is if you believe me and all we've been through together and why we're here. There ain't a body if you believe Walker. Which is it?"

Cruz stood at the water's edge and closed his eyes, smelling the dank scent of rotting wood, feeling his breath escape in shallow, uneven gasps. He longed for sunlight and warmth. He thought of Rita and how beautiful she'd looked that day on Laverne's porch, how he'd wanted to run his hand through her dark hair. He imagined being with her at the top of the canyon and peering down into the abyss where he now stood.

"Untie the boat when I'm ready," was all Cruz said as he stepped into the raft.

They launched from the trees after Crawdad had bailed the boat dry. The current was sleek, accelerating, and Cruz hung close to the shore, the raft's stern pointing right. Twenty feet above the drop, he began to sweep hard on the oars, gathering momentum to break through the first lateral waves of the tongue. Suddenly he felt the raft glance off something, perhaps a root or a finger of rock jutting up from the shallows. In a flash, the boat rebounded out into the center, then careened sideways into the maw of the rapid. He felt dizzy, a sickening emptiness in his stomach as his oars flailed madly at water.

"Straighten it!" Crawdad shouted, and he did, a last-second pivot swinging the bow around before they rocketed into the bottom wave. Cruz saw the black raft peel upward like a dagger pointing at the sky, straight and true, only to be buried by a colliding wall of darkness.

Flipped, he thought, stunned as he tumbled helplessly, head over heels, out the back of the boat. Like being in a washing machine filled with black ink, he felt the water pummeling him. He grabbed for a line, the raft, Crawdad's hand. Only churning water. In his nose. Throat. He felt himself spun upside down. He saw the fading surface light, the air bubbles exploding around him. He was dragged under as the current sucked at his life jacket, pounded him in the depths, then hurled him up again. He clawed for air. *No mercy,* thought Cruz as he was flung down into a white chamber of foam.

Then he felt a surge, a downward thrust, and his body was flushed away, released. He broke the surface directionless, choking, the air like ice in his throat. The waves broke over him and he began to swim toward what he thought was the right shore, his hands knifing through the water as the bulky rain gear and life jacket dragged in the current. He kicked through another wave, then lunged ahead, groping for a rock, a tree limb. He felt a stone outcropping and muscled his way up, crawling onto his stomach until he was out of the river, safe onshore, hacking water from his flooded lungs.

Crawdad? He turned and saw the black raft upside down and hurtling away from him downstream. He could see the old man clinging to the perimeter line on the side, tugging at it as he tried to pull the boat to shore. *Crawdad held on.* He watched the raft hovering near the entrance to Gravedigger Falls. "Swim!" he screamed. Then he saw Crawdad, his faded life jacket still visible as he hung frozen on the horizon line for an instant, then vanished into the foam spitting up from below. Gone. Off the edge of the world.

He perched on the rock, staring at the void where Crawdad and the raft had been only seconds earlier. He expected to hear a scream, a shout of fear or pain. Nothing. Only the roar. In shock, he got to his feet and began to stumble along the shoreline. A feeling of helplessness overwhelmed him. He was aware that Crawdad could be trapped downstream and that he couldn't reach him. Cruz saw the haunting image of the boat disappearing over the ledge, Crawdad beside it. He gasped for breath. A swarm of insects buzzed relentlessly around his head.

He scrambled over car-sized boulders, his tennis shoes heavy with water. He slipped on the wet stone, fell down, then rose to climb again. He struggled up a granite slab to its crow's-nest pinnacle. What he saw was breathtaking. A white maelstrom. At the top of the waterfall the river narrowed into a tight channel, then spilled thirty feet down into a cauldron of thrashing waves and reversals. In the center of it all loomed a towering fang of rock with geysers of spray exploding off the sides. It was as if some demonic force beneath the streambed had erupted into a tempest.

He couldn't survive this, Cruz thought. *Nobody could.* He scanned the rapid for signs of the boat or Crawdad. At first there was nothing, only raging water. Then he saw a single oar, unbroken, jutting up from the river like a miraculous golden staff, shaking violently. Looking closer, Cruz saw it had been driven down into a rock crack and imbedded there, like a chisel into marble. He searched for a flash of orange or yellow, any sign to reveal that Crawdad might be trapped somewhere within the rapid. Then he hurried downstream to look below Gravedigger Falls.

It was slow going in the rain and storm. The shoreline seemed impenetrable, with layer upon layer of brambles and hanging vines. Within fifteen minutes, Cruz was trembling uncontrollably. He stopped near the water's edge to calm himself. Blood dripped from a gash in his forehead. He sat on a low rock and took deep breaths, then exhaled forcefully. Adrenaline shot through his arms and legs. There was no time to think of fear or death. Only calm.

He searched throughout the late afternoon and evening. All thoughts of time vanished from his mind. When it was near dusk and he could feel the darkness lowering itself over the canyon, he forced himself to mechanically sweep the shallows for any sign of the raft or Crawdad. Thick branches and thorny plants tore at his exposed face and hands. At one point he seemed numb to the pain, hardly aware that a cluster of cactus needles had penetrated the rain gear and pierced his leg. But then he became ensnared in a mass of vines and he thrashed like an animal, lashing out until he broke free and ran blindly through the undergrowth.

He needed help. He couldn't continue the search alone in the darkness. He watched the sky for signs of a clearing in the storm, an opening to stars or moon. And when he saw the first glint of constellations, his hope soared. He could now see he was out of the main canyon and that the steepness of the surrounding walls had lessened. He knew the highway was somewhere above him. He stripped off his life jacket and rain gear, the plastic pants torn and flapping loosely at the knees, and began to climb.

The rock and scree beneath him were unstable, as if he were ascending an endless dune aimed at the heavens. He climbed cautiously, testing each hand- and foothold before trusting his weight to it. Imbedded rocks and scrub brush aided his footing as he crisscrossed the face of the canyon wall to avoid cliffs or overhangs. He would set his vision on some shadowy object in the distance, then scramble up until he reached it. Rest. Climb again.

Fear pushed him higher. He knew that if Crawdad had somehow survived and was on the river shoreline below, he would be badly injured and in need of medical treatment. He remembered when the old man had yanked him from the water like some guardian angel hovering overhead, and how later he'd said to Cruz, *I'll expect the same from you if I ever go for a swim.* He would find Crawdad somehow. He would get to him and carry his body to shore so the Kern could not claim it.

He knew there was no going down. His chest heaved like a bellows, each breath searing him. If he were to stumble or collapse he would surely plummet to his death. Occasionally he saw headlights above him, shooting out over the canyon rim like lasers, then vanishing. *This is the way it is,* thought Cruz, *this holding on.* He could remember hopping a slow train on a dare when he was twelve, and the terror he felt as he dangled from the boxcar, his feet only inches from the sparking wheels. He wondered if Crawdad was clinging to a willow somewhere below, his legs broken. Cruz felt connected to the old man, as if some invisible line ran from his body to Crawdad's. Each step toward the road lifted his spirit. Each breath. Each second of holding on.

When he reached the highway, he clambered over the guardrail and saw he was on a long straightaway. He looked for road signs but saw none, so he sat by the road's edge, his ragged breathing beginning to slow. He could taste blood on his lips and noticed that his knees had been scraped raw. He waited for headlights to pierce the night.

He was sitting in a daze when he heard the far-off hum of a car. Limping out onto the road until the glare of high beams illuminated his tattered figure, he raised his weak arms to signal, then saw the vehicle slow and pull off. He could hear the voices of strangers approaching, and he lifted a hand to shield his eyes from the light.

"This guy's a mess," he heard someone say. Rough hands eased him down into a sitting position against the guardrail. He sat with one of the men for what seemed like hours.

Later he saw a truck grind to a halt, then heard the slamming of doors. "Use the radio and get an ambulance," a familiar voice called out. He could see Lou approaching.

"Cruz, are you okay?" Lou asked, kneeling beside him. "We've been looking everywhere."

"We flipped and I got thrown out," Cruz answered, gripping Lou's arm. "Crawdad's still down there. He stayed with the boat and went over Gravedigger Falls. I couldn't get to him."

"Take it easy," said Lou. "We'll find him. You're in no shape to go searching for his body."

"But maybe he's not dead. He could've made it through."

"Maybe so. If anybody could survive a swim over Gravedigger Falls, it'd be Crawdad. Now we gotta get you to the hospital."

Cruz closed his eyes. Minutes passed. He felt as if he were floating in a cloud of mist, his body supported only by air. He smelled the pungent odor of antiseptic from the first-aid kit. He heard the rip of paper as rolls of sterile gauze were torn open, and in the distance, the shrill sound of a siren approaching.

When he opened his eyes he saw Walker standing in front of him. He was staring down as if gazing at some wounded animal found by the roadside. Lou was over by the truck, a crowd of men huddled around him as he talked with headquarters on the radio.

"He almost killed you," Walker said. "I tried to warn you. He has no respect for the power of the Kern. None. Never did. And that's what killed him."

"Why aren't you out looking for him?" Cruz asked. "He might still be alive down there. He could be dying."

"Because I respect the river," said Walker. "I've got more sense than to go out searching for a dead man in the middle of the night when the Kern's in flood."

Cruz felt nothing at first, no pain, no anger, not even exhaustion. He noticed a rip in the left knee of Walker's jeans. A stranger smoked a cigarette nearby, its red tip gleaming like a firefly in the darkness. Then a wave of heat, perilous and unchanging, rolled through him. He wanted to kill Walker, crush his skull like pulp on the asphalt. He wanted to scream and hear his own voice shatter the stillness. He wanted to hit him with his fists in the ribs, shoulder, face, until teeth cut into his knuckles.

Lou came and led him to the ambulance, helped him inside where he could sit on a stretcher. He felt pain everywhere, deep and sudden, as if he'd been stung by a scorpion hidden in the dust. Before the ambulance doors closed he looked up and saw Walker standing there again, staring at him in silence.

"These things happen," Walker said. "Sometimes people die in this line of work."

Then the doors slammed shut and the dark interior closed around him.

* * *

The next morning Cruz awoke in a small room in the Kern Valley Hospital. Daylight seeped in from a window to his left, giving the pale walls a reddish adobe color. His eyes ached with a relentless pounding somewhere in the back of his head, and he listened to the steady drone of an air conditioner. He was hot with fever and when he moved he felt thick gauze bandages raking across his open wounds.

He remembered things about the accident. The black raft rising over him in the rapid called Tombstone. The storm pressing down as he searched for Crawdad. Then later, the emergency room lights glaring like bright suns, and the ripping of cloth as his pant leg was torn away at the seam.

He was waiting for Crawdad to come striding in, his stained baseball cap cocked at a funny angle. *Another close call,* he might say, *but the river gods were there when I needed 'em.* Crawdad might have a cast on his wrist, or a bandage on his forehead. However, Cruz saw nothing, heard only the occasional slap-slap of hospital slippers in the hallway.

Vivid dreams had laced his sleep and he had awakened unsure of his surroundings. In one dream his mother and sister knelt at his bedside holding candles. They were dressed in black and in the faint light he could see tears of blood streaking their pale cheeks. When he rose from the bed to comfort them, they receded into the shadows. In another, a beautiful nurse stepped into his room, her white skirt glowing like a luminous orchid. As she took his temperature, he felt a cool glass thermometer slip under his tongue. Her dress was tight and Cruz could see the outline of her figure as she placed her hand on his forehead. Then she slipped out of her dress as if shedding a skin and lay down beside him, her soft hands on his forehead and chest. *Angel of mercy,* he thought.

Lou had come by earlier that morning while Cruz had been asleep. He left word with the doctor that he'd contacted Cruz's father and had told him that his son was doing okay and recovering in the hospital. Cruz didn't expect any calls or visits from Frank. When he'd been sick as a child, it had always been Marta who cared for him. Frank had never been the one to bring him a cold glass of 7-Up or to step in and see how Cruz was feeling. Instead, his father would stand outside the doorway and peer in as if afraid he might catch the virus. Cruz had learned long ago that any outward signs of emotion or sympathy were things that Frank kept locked away in quarantine. Yet he still wanted his father to enter the room and place a hand on his forehead to see if there was any sign of fever. He still wanted Frank to pour the Pepto Bismol into a trembling spoon.

Later in the evening, the door to his room opened and Walker stepped in.

"How you doing?" Walker said, pulling up a chair beside the bed. His face was drawn and tired and he hung his head low. "You look a helluva lot better than the last time I saw you."

"I didn't expect to see you here," Cruz said.

"Well, after our last chat out on the highway I felt I owed you a visit. I figured it was best if I came and told you."

"Told me what?"

"We found Crawdad last night." He paused, lifted his head and looked at the window. "He was a few miles downstream from Gravedigger Falls. I was in charge of one of the search crews."

Cruz said nothing. Exhaustion washed through him in a dizzy rush, and he felt as if he were underwater again above the falls, his hands groping for the raft. The anger toward Walker resurfaced and he longed for the strength to climb from the bed and knock him to the floor.

Cruz snapped back at him in a sarcastic voice. "I thought you said you had more sense than to go out looking for a dead man in the middle of the night."

"Crawdad's alive," Walker said. He grew silent for a moment, staring down at the carpet. "We found him tangled up in a bunch of willow roots. I thought he was dead for sure. I had my hands on him and was trying to drag him out when I saw his eyes roll open, big as quarters. I nearly dropped him back in the river. He was delirious, rattling on about seeing visions of the dead. All this crazy shit. Then he looked right at me and said, 'The hooks are gonna have to wait.' He was hurt pretty bad. His leg was busted up and there was blood coming out of one ear. But the old guy hung on. He finally shut up when we got him on the stretcher. His eyes were wide open, watching me. Like he was afraid I might try to throw him back so the river could finish the job."

Walker paused to stand up and walk over to the window. The sun flashed through and illuminated patches of grey stubble on his face as he squinted into the light.

"We hauled him up a fire trail on the south side of the river. I thought for sure he'd go unconscious on us. But he stayed awake all the way back to the Emergency Room, yelling at anybody who laid a hand on him. And when we got to the ER, he told the doctor to put a cast on the leg and release him so he could get home. The doctor tried to convince Crawdad to at least spend the night, but the old buzzard threw a fit and started tearing the IVs out. Finally the doctor gave in. They patched him up and Lou drove him back to his cabin over in Kernville. That's where he is now."

"Did he say anything about the accident?"

"Not really. But he did ask for you, Cruz. It was one of the few things he said without acting crazy. I told him that you'd made it to shore above the falls and that you'd climbed up the north canyon wall. Then he pulled me aside and told me to give you a message. 'You tell Cruz that I want to see him. Tell him he owes me and to come up to the cabin. I'll be waiting.' Then he was gone."

Walker turned away from the window and stared back at the hospital bed. His eyes looked sleepy and he tugged at his beard. Cruz felt the old anger softening and knew that Walker could've easily sent someone else to deliver the message but had chosen to come himself. He noticed an admiring tone in Walker's voice when he talked about Crawdad now. A tone that was almost respectful.

"We've been looking for the Mexican kid and dragging the river in all the usual places," Walker said, "but there's still no sign of him. We did find the kid's family at Hobo, like Crawdad said. By the time we got there, the mother was pretty hysterical, screaming in Spanish that the river was 'El Diablo' and all that shit. We put the family up at a motel."

"Did they check Trout Bridge?" Cruz asked.

"Yeah," Walker said. "I know the places to look. I was a hookman once, remember?" He walked across the room toward the door. "I better be going. I need to head home and get some sleep."

"Thanks for stopping by to tell me the news," Cruz said.

"When are you getting outta here?" he asked.

"The doctor said I can go home tomorrow."

Walker opened the door halfway and stood there as if to leave.

"Do you still think he's crazy?" Cruz asked.

"I don't trust him, if that's what you're getting at," Walker said. "It's damn spooky that he's alive. I couldn't sleep last night. I just lay awake and kept seeing those eyes of his popping open after we pulled him out. I don't know if he's crazy or just lucky." He paused, "I guess you're the one who's gonna find that out."

Then Walker was gone, leaving Cruz alone in the cool hospital room.

* * *

He was released the next day at noon. Lou had called earlier and offered him a ride back to Lake Isabella and he'd gratefully accepted. Before he left, a young intern with pale, fleshy hands changed the heavy bandages on his arms, replacing them with lighter gauze. He gave Cruz some aspirin to keep the fever down.

Lou met him at the main entrance. Cruz noticed the heat as soon as he stepped out of the air-conditioned hospital, feeling a dry itch under the bandages. They drove back on the Reservoir Road in one of the pale green Forest Service trucks, the ones Chico said were the perfect shade of piss. Cruz hadn't realized it was the Fourth of July until Lou started talking about fireworks and all the hazards they created for the work crews.

"The forest is dry as dust right now," Lou said. "Always is around this time. Drop a match up there and you might as well toss on a bucket of gasoline. Poof!" Drops of sweat rolled down Lou's cheeks. Cruz knew his boss perspired when he got worked up over something, sometimes going through two or three shirts in a day. *The only way to cool Lou off,* Walker would say, *is to send him up to Alaska to rub noses with the damn Eskimos.*

"It's the biker gangs," Lou was saying, his cheeks red as tomatoes. "They think it's a circus to shoot their Roman candles across the river. I'd like to shoot one up some biker's ass and see how funny he thought that was."

Lou was still ranting when he dropped Cruz off at the trailer. He was talking about stacking all of the gangs' black Harleys in a huge pile and tossing on a hand grenade. "They want fireworks? Hell, I'll give 'em a show." Then he roared off in the piss green truck.

The air was stale and hot when Cruz stepped into the trailer. He went into the kitchen and found the plastic trash can overflowing with stained paper towels, chicken bones, and soup cans. The sink was crammed with greasy dishes, and a rank smell emanated from a gallon of warm milk on the counter.

When he walked into the living room he saw an empty bottle of tequila sitting like a centerpiece on the low table, and it stopped him in his tracks. For a moment he imagined little Donna's face after the whipping, her skin bruised and swollen. Frank hadn't even bothered to hide the bottle in the shed this time. Suddenly the air in the trailer seemed thin and hard to breathe. Cruz felt a hot, feverish wave rising through his chest and he slumped into a chair, his head spinning.

He didn't move the bottle from the table. Still dizzy, he got up and walked into Frank's bedroom at the back of the trailer. The place smelled of sweat and alcohol. Wrinkled clothes were heaped in the corner, and the mattress sheets were rumpled and stained. No sign of Frank.

He went back into the living room and picked up the empty bottle, stopping to examine the gold label for a moment and noticing that the ingredients were written in both Spanish and English. Then he hurled it at the far wall, whipping it the same way his father had taught him to throw a baseball. It shattered against a mirror, sending a web of cracks up through the glass panel. *Traitor. Homewrecker.* He thought of all the times he'd driven to Bakersfield to visit Frank while he was drying out. *It'll be different now,* he'd told Cruz, *we'll get things back to normal.* He wanted to take a sledgehammer and trash the room. He wanted to scream *Go to hell!* in his father's face.

Cruz went into the kitchen and made some tuna sandwiches, then washed it all down with three glasses of ice water. The food calmed him and helped soothe his anger. He knew that he needed to find Frank before it got dark, so he grabbed the keys to the jeep and drove over to the main drag of Lake Isabella. He checked all the bars and asked if anyone had seen his old man. No one had. The Safeway store was crowded with tourists buying beer and ice for the weekend, but none of the clerks had spotted Frank. In the dusty light of late afternoon he headed out toward the reservoir.

The picnic area on the east side of the lake was crowded with tourists and campers when Cruz arrived. RVs were pulled up next to the water like beached whales. Powerboats roared by just offshore, while kids on four-wheeled cycles raced up and down the sand. Bikers clad in leather and denim lounged on their Harleys, drinking beer. After parking the jeep, Cruz began searching through the crowds asking if anyone had noticed an old man wearing cutoffs and a blue Dodger baseball cap. He found a biker mama, her skin decorated with ruby-red tattoos, who claimed to have seen a man fitting Frank's description. "I thought the old guy was drunk," she told Cruz. "I seen him heading off that way," she said, pointing toward the rocky bank along the north end of the reservoir.

Cruz searched the shoreline for nearly an hour. His ribs ached when he breathed, and his mind seemed cloudy as he imagined Frank losing his balance and stumbling into the water. He knew that his father couldn't swim and that just beyond the jagged rim of the lake was a steep, fifteen-foot drop-off. In the distance behind him lanterns were glowing outside the doors of pale Winnebagos. The water on the lake was black and still.

Suddenly there was a far-off whistle of a rocket cutting toward the sky. Cruz saw the first barrage of fireworks out over the lake, a web of red and gold streamers. In the faint glow from the explosion, he saw a hunched over figure sitting among the rocks.

He quickened his stride, jumping from boulder to boulder until he came up alongside his father. There was another burst of fireworks and it startled Frank. He turned and glared at Cruz as if his son were a stranger. He'd been crying and his lips trembled.

"Where the hell have you been?" Frank said. "I've been looking for hours. Why aren't you ever around when I need you?"

"What are you looking for?" Cruz asked.

"Little Donna. She got lost in the crowd and wandered off. We've got to find her. She could be drowning this very moment." He staggered to his feet. "I've just been resting for a second. Gotta keep looking."

Cruz moved in front of him to block his path. He put his hands on Frank's shoulders.

"Sit down and rest some more," Cruz said.

"I don't need to sit down. There's no time to waste."

Frank struggled with him for a moment. Then Cruz was able to ease him down onto a flat rock. His father was sweating and his breath heaved out in uneven gasps. More fireworks lit up the blackness. Each time a new barrage illuminated the sky, Frank jumped as if shocked, his face staring up at the heavens in fear.

"Donna's in San Diego," Cruz said. "She's with Marta."

Frank looked up at the fireworks and was silent for a moment.

"I always hated goddamn San Diego," he said. "A guy could get killed on the freeway down there."

His eyes were lost. He would close them momentarily, then jerk them wide open when the sky ignited with tracers of fluorescent green. His right hand was shaking. He licked his lips repeatedly, searching for moisture.

"Is Donna safe in San Diego?" he asked.

Cruz paused before answering. He looked out over the black reservoir, thinking of the tequila bottle and how easily he'd smashed it in the trailer. He knew what he wanted to say to his father. *Donna's as good as dead to you.* But when he finally spoke, it was in a soft voice, as if he were talking to a child.

"Yes," Cruz said, "she's doing fine. She wrote and told me about going to the beach nearly every day to swim. She hunts for these beautiful Pacific shells." He paused and stared up at the fireworks, searching for the right words, then continued. "She calls them her 'water rainbows' and keeps them on a table in her room. At night when she sleeps, she can hear the shell music, and it's like the ocean's singing to her through the walls."

"Is she careful when she swims?" Frank blurted out. "Does she watch for the riptide?"

"Yeah, she's careful. She swims in the shallows and never goes alone."

"I miss little Donna," Frank said. "I'd go crazy if anything ever happened to her. Do you remember what she used to call the fireworks?"

"No."

"She called them the 'fire rain' because they used to scare her so bad. The first time she saw them, she thought the sky was blowing up. She said, 'Save me, Daddy, save me from the fire rain — ' and then she'd hug my neck for dear life. 'There's nothing to be afraid of, sweetie,' I'd tell her, 'not when your old man's here.'"

Frank paused. He looked down at the rocks, then wiped beads of sweat from his forehead. Cruz listened to his father's labored breathing and smelled the tequila.

"I was wrong. There was plenty to be afraid of," said Frank.

They sat there quietly until the fireworks were over. Then Cruz helped Frank up and they walked back along the shoreline until they reached the parking area. He drove slowly back to Lake Isabella and stopped twice so that his old man could stumble out of the jeep and vomit into the ditch.

* * *

In the morning while Frank was in the shower Cruz found a bottle of whiskey under his father's mattress. He poured it down the sink and then pitched it into the trash can. He put coffee on and began to fix eggs and toast in the kitchen.

When Frank walked in and saw breakfast on the stove he said nothing at first. He took a few shuffling steps into the kitchen, his lips pressed together in a scowl, and stopped near the table. The air smelled of burnt toast, just the way Frank liked his bread.

"How's your arm?" Frank asked. "Looks pretty nasty."

"I'll survive."

"I'm glad you're all right. It scared the hell out of me when your boss called and told me what happened."

"It was pretty crazy."

"How's the other guy?"

"He broke his leg, but at least he's alive."

"Thank God," Frank said.

Cruz put the eggs and toast on plates and set them down on the table.

"Let's eat," Cruz said. "I don't want this million-dollar breakfast to get cold."

"You didn't have to do this," said Frank. "I can fix my own breakfast. You should be the one sleeping in after all you've been through."

"I'm not the one that's hungover," Cruz said as he stared down at his plate. "I found the bottle under your bed and dumped it."

Frank walked to the window and stared outside. He turned to look at Cruz for a moment as if to say something, but then shook it off.

"What is it?" Cruz asked.

"That bottle don't mean nothing. I just had a bad time of it yesterday. The heat and all got to me."

A long silence followed. Cruz took a bite of toast and listened to the garbage truck roar by in the alley. Already he could feel the day heating up as the sun flooded the kitchen.

"A drink now and then don't mean shit," Frank said. "I can quit anytime."

"I don't think so," Cruz said. "I've been thinking about what we need to do. After breakfast I'm gonna drive you down to the shelter in Bakersfield so you can dry out. I packed some things for you last night."

Frank stared over at the kitchen table, at the food on his plate. He seemed numb to what Cruz had said. Emotionless. Like it was just another morning and nothing had happened yesterday or the day before that. He brought his hand up to his face and rubbed his eyes, then suddenly slammed his fist against the wall, leaving a V-shaped dent in the flimsy wood panel.

"Since when did you start making decisions for me?" Frank said. "Let me tell you something." He shook his fist at Cruz, his face red and straining. *Heart attack,* Cruz thought, a rush of panic and dread sweeping through him. *He could drop dead on the kitchen floor.* "I want to tell you something — " He was struggling with the words. He slammed his fist into the wall again. Cruz remained seated, still holding the fork in his right hand. "You know why this is happening, don't you?" he said angrily. "Because you ain't been around enough to ask me what the hell I've been doing. Well, I'll tell you. I've been sitting in this tin shit house watching the carpet squirm while you've been off on that damn river."

"Somebody has to work around here," Cruz said.

"You're damn right somebody has to work. I busted my ass for twenty years so you'd have a decent place to live. Now it's your turn. You owe me that much, boy."

Frank was breathing hard. His right hand trembled, and sweat formed a ring under each arm.

"I used to work the big construction jobs. The bosses would call me when they needed a crane operator who could swing a fifty-ton boom over the workers' heads and not even think about messing up. I helped build every bridge on the Kern."

Cruz had heard these stories before. *Hell, if it weren't for me, half the damn bridges would've fallen in the river by now.* But Frank wasn't bragging this time. It was like listening to one of those embarrassing street preachers down in Bakersfield as they tried to witness to a crowd. All passion and no poise. Not caring that there might be somebody in the crowd laughing.

"I was important back then," Frank said. "I knew engines like nobody else. Half the time I never even had to pop the hood to tell you what the problem was. All I had to do was listen. But now," he gestured with his arm at the window, pointing at the engine pieces scattered in the yard, "I can't even put a busted-up Chevy back together."

Silence enveloped the room, as if they were speaking from within a bubble and sealed off from the outside. He waited until he was sure Frank was done talking.

"I never told you this," Cruz said, "but when I was in grade school and I used to take the bus, I'd tell kids about you. When they'd be bragging about their dads and how this one had been a soldier or a truck driver, I'd wait until we were going over one of the big bridges that crossed the river and I'd say, 'My old man built this,' and they'd all look at it and stop their bragging 'cause they knew they couldn't top me."

Cruz stood up from the table and carried his plate to the counter. He ran some water in the sink, added soap, then set the dish in to soak. With his back to Frank, he said, "I might've stayed around the trailer more if you'd asked me."

"A father's not supposed to have to ask," said Frank. "I guess I expected you to know."

"Well, I didn't know," Cruz said. "There've been lots of times when I wondered why I stayed around here at all. I could've gotten the hell out and gone to San Diego. But I stayed because you were here and I thought you needed me." Cruz turned around. His father hadn't moved, still standing next to the window and the dented wall. "But I can't get on with my life when I'm always watching out for you. I want a life of my own and I won't get dragged down with you again. You're sick and I can't help you get better."

He turned back to the sink and the dishes. The skin on his face was burning and he knew Frank was staring at him. He waited for the anger that might follow. A chair thrown across the room. His right hand made a fist in the soapy water.

"Okay," Frank said. His voice softened. "If it'll help any, I'll get out of here and go back to the shelter. I'll do it for you." Then Cruz heard the sliding of a chair as his old man sat down to eat his breakfast.

* * *

They took the canyon road that bordered the river. It paralleled a section of the Kern which the locals had nicknamed the Cataracts. The two-lane pavement was narrow and tight, with few guardrails on the sharp curves. As Cruz drove he kept his eye on Frank, who looked sourly at the landscape. The Kern was still running high. There were several places where the entire river simply vanished off a granite shelf and dropped eighty feet into a pool below. The rapids were long and steep, each one tumbling over slick grey domes and jagged fins of pale rock. Cruz tried to envision taking a raft through some of the swift channels and he felt his breath quicken.

"Keep your eyes on the damn road!" Frank yelled at one point. "What if you had a blowout? We'd be goners for sure."

Cruz didn't argue. He kept both hands on the wheel and stole glances at the river with every opportunity.

At the bottom the canyon opened up into a wide valley of rolling hills. There was a sign posted near the Kern that listed the number of people who had drowned since 1930. Each time there was a drowning, the total was painted over and replaced with a higher figure. The Forest Service crew called it "the geek count."

After driving another thirty minutes they reached Bakersfield. St. Vincent's Recovery Shelter was near downtown, next to an abandoned block of shops and offices that had been vacant for as long as Cruz could remember. It was run by an old Catholic priest named Father Sam, an ex-alcoholic himself, who had started the center years ago. The men who stayed there paid what they could afford, but otherwise it was kept alive through charity donations. As Cruz pulled into the parking lot next to the plain brick building, he heard the hiss of the jeep tires as they rolled over the hot black asphalt. GET BAKED IN BAKERSFIELD! read the back bumper of an old Plymouth he parked behind.

He helped Frank get his things out of the jeep, then walked with him to the main entrance. His father hesitated and leaned back against the fender of a red truck. He seemed out of breath, the sweat running down his temples onto his pale blue shirt.

"It's the heat," Frank gasped.

"You'll feel better once you're inside," Cruz said.

Frank nodded, resting his hands on his knees. Cruz thought for a moment that his father might get sick in the parking lot.

"It's harder this time," he said, slowly straightening up. "When I left this place I swore I'd never come back." Frank's voice grew suddenly angry. "I don't think I can stand to listen to that sonovabitch Father Sam and his breakfast sermons. Who knows? Maybe he's dead by now."

Cruz laughed. "You're probably his favorite guest."

"Maybe so." Frank took in a big breath of air and then released it, his ruddy cheeks puffing out as he blew. "I think I need to go in by myself."

Cruz nodded. "That's fine. Do what you have to."

He could feel the heat seeping up into his boots from the black parking surface. A car raced by, its radio blasting out a song in Spanish.

"I need to tell you something," said Frank. "I didn't mean what I said this morning about you not being around."

"I know," Cruz said.

"You should just tell me to go to hell once in a while. It'd do us both some good." He hesitated, looked toward the shelter, then back at Cruz. "I never have understood why you didn't just take off on your own."

"Maybe I thought you'd come around."

"Well, don't expect any miracles. I've never been much good at changing my ways."

"I know," Cruz said. "Give me a call when you're ready to come back."

They didn't embrace or shake hands. Frank picked up his battered suitcase and shuffled toward the main entrance. He suddenly turned and yelled over his shoulder, "Sometime when you got a day off, go down and look at them bridges. Your old man used to run a pretty mean crane."

"I'll do that," Cruz said. Then he stood in the parking lot and watched as his father vanished through the double doors, the hems of his baggy pants dragging on the ground.

CHAPTER FIVE

When Cruz awoke Saturday morning he was famished, his stomach empty and weak. He went to the Safeway and bought bread and eggs and orange juice, then came home and fixed breakfast. After eating, he showered and changed the bandages on his forearms, then called Rita. Her phone rang three times before she picked it up.

"It's Cruz. I would've called sooner but — "

"That's okay," she said, cutting in. "I figured you were either busy or an incredibly bad dancer and I'd scared you off."

"I couldn't have called if I'd wanted to." He paused, his voice dropping. "There was an accident on the river. A friend of mine was almost killed."

A long silence. "I'm sorry to hear that," she said. "Are you all right?"

He laughed nervously, trying to find the right words. "It's been a helluva week. I spent some time in the hospital because I got dumped in the river and banged up pretty good. But I'm still in one piece."

"Is your friend gonna be okay?" she asked.

"He's resting at home with a broken leg."

Cruz could picture her face, the receiver only inches from the scar on her chin.

"Maybe it's time to look into a safer line of work," she said.

"I could always wash dishes at the Dam Corner Cafe. But I still might catch a disease from their biker biscuits and gravy."

She laughed. "Seriously. I'm glad you called." Her voice was different over the phone. Softer.

"And why's that?" he said.

"There's a place I want to show you. I think you'd appreciate it. My father and I used to go there when I was a kid. We can hike up to it when you feel ready."

"I'm free tomorrow," he said.

"Then meet me in Kernville at two o'clock. I live in an apartment building called Whitney Court about three blocks south of Laverne's."

"I'll be there with my jeep." He paused, not wanting to hang up. There was something he wanted to say, but he was unsure of the words. Finally, "When I was on the river and things got scary, I thought about you."

"Terrifying," she said. "You were probably afraid I'd shoot you the next time we got together."

"That's not what I meant." He waited for her, the silence awkward over the phone. "I was afraid I might not see you again," he said.

"I know," Rita said. "You're sweet. It's been a long time since anyone said something like that to me."

"I'm surprised."

"Why?"

He paused again, wanting to be clear. "I thought guys would be lining up to sweet-talk you."

"Some have. But they didn't mean what they said."

"I mean it."

"I know you do."

Then she hung up. He put the phone down and closed his eyes, resting his head on a bandaged forearm. *What'll we talk about tomorrow?* he thought. He imagined her smooth, beautiful hands moving through his hair again, stroking his temples. The trailer was quiet and he wanted to drift off. Vivid scenes of him and Rita as they embraced, kissed, slipped each other's clothes off, interrupted his weak attempts at sleep. *Soap opera fantasies.* He tried pushing them out of his head, but they poured in like dark water. Her hands peeling down his underwear. Her tongue finding his mouth. The dry smell of clean sheets as she pushed him back onto the bed.

* * *

Rita was waiting for him the next day when he pulled up in front of the brick apartment building. She wore denim cutoffs and a yellow T-shirt and sat on the center stairs with a small nylon backpack. She jogged toward the jeep but stopped when she saw his bandaged arms resting on the steering wheel.

"That looks serious," she said, climbing into the passenger side.

"It's just scratched up. I need to keep the bandages on because it got infected." He put in the clutch and accelerated out of the lot.

"This is a classic," she said, looking at the interior of the jeep. "A real beauty."

"My father put it together a long time ago. He used to be pretty good with engines. He ordered it out of some army catalogue and they shipped him the whole damn thing, unassembled."

The wind blew through her hair and she pulled a red bandanna from the pack and tied it around her forehead.

"What do you drive?" he asked.

"I've got an old Fiat that bleeds oil all over the road. I should probably get rid of it, but it's the only car I've ever owned. We're kind of attached."

"A sportscar, huh?"

"I like to drive fast."

Rita gave Cruz directions, telling him to stay on the main road and go north. They drove ten miles into the mountains until the pavement narrowed into a thin two lanes, then turned left onto a dirt road that wound through thick clusters of cottonwood and willow. The road was more of a jeep trail than anything, crisscrossed by deep ruts and trenches that caused him to swerve back and forth to avoid bottoming out. He liked the seclusion, the way the skinny road threaded its way back into the woods.

"How'd your father ever find this place?"

"It was one of his favorite spots to camp and fish for trout," she said. "An old friend who used to live up here showed it to him."

A half mile back the road came to a dead end in a stand of trees. He parked and turned the engine off. "We'll walk from here," she said, stepping out of the jeep and slinging the backpack over her shoulders. There was a dusty path off to the left and they followed it into the dense forest. After zig-zagging a quarter mile down a slope and a series of switchbacks, they emerged from the woods into an open meadow.

Suddenly Rita stopped. She stood quietly next to him and said, "Listen." At first he didn't hear anything peculiar, just the sound of the wind and birds. A locust croaked its sad song. After a few seconds he glanced over at Rita with a puzzled look. "You've got to listen closely," she said. Again they were silent and this time Cruz heard the faint murmur, steady and rhythmic, of water.

They hurried across the meadow for a few hundred yards, and by then there was little doubt that the rushing, sweeping sound coming from beyond the trees was the Kern, nearly hidden by a steep bank that bordered the woods. Cruz peered over the edge and saw the river unfold before him in a foaming channel of green. There were calm pockets near shore, but the current grew swift at the center, perhaps the beginning of a rapid, then vanished down-stream around a bend.

"Isn't this fantastic," she said, "the way it sneaks up on you? The first time my father brought me here, he made me stand in that meadow and listen until I heard it. I've never forgotten that feeling. It was magic."

"It's beautiful," he said. "Not like the lower Kern, with the tourists and trash all over the place. This is different."

"And there's more. Follow me."

They stayed close to the river and moved upstream along a different trail. They'd gone a half mile when Cruz noticed an odor in the air, an overpowering stench of rotting fish and excrement. At first he thought it might be coming from the nearby river, but then he saw the source of the smell off in the distance, the frail bundles of twigs and scrap wood clustered high in the trees, all carefully balanced amid a network of branches. Heron nests.

As they walked on he saw the curved silhouette of a heron on a limb, its sharp beak pointing skyward. The nests were everywhere, at least fifty of them perched in the heights, and soon Cruz began to see through the camouflage of leaves to where the birds stood like sentries. Their spindly legs were invisible from a distance and they seemed to float on air. The bases of the trees and the forest floor itself were plastered white from the droppings as if a thin blanket of snow had fallen overnight. There were feathers lying scattered on the ground, dark blue and grey with an occasional silver edge, and Rita bent down, picked up a grey one, and tucked it under her bandanna.

He stared upward, mystified. The herons were outlined against the heavens, their shapes foreign and prehistoric. The silence was unnerving and he anticipated a sudden attack, an explosion of wings as they descended upon him in a flurry of talons. *Intruder,* he thought.

"My father brought me here when I was eight years old," she said, "and I looked up into those trees and thought I'd gone back in time. I used to beg him to bring me back on weekends so we could camp nearby and I could watch them."

She walked ahead of him, her hands on her hips, and turned a slow circle, all the while staring upward at the herons. "I used to study them when they fished down by the river, strutting around like kings or queens, and sometimes I'd bring colored pencils and paper and try to draw them. My dad made up stories about the heron kingdom, giving each bird a name like Silverwing, Troutkiller, and Brother Blue. We talked about doing a children's book together. He would write it and I'd do the illustrations. Once I even had a dream that the herons flew down to Los Angeles to visit me and were in my backyard when I woke up in the morning."

They made their way deeper into the glade, studying the nests, which towered at least sixty feet off the ground. A jumble of sounds floated down toward Cruz and he listened to the squawks and croaks as if hearing a new language for the first time. Young herons teetered on the edges of their nests, then hurled themselves a few feet into the air, only to land precariously on a nearby limb. They repeated the effort, each time violently flapping their wings as they jumped from branch to branch. Cruz admired their courage, the way they leaped over the edge into space. The larger adults stood nearby on lordly perches and watched the young as they attempted to fly.

Sunlight filtered down through the branches, and the herons cast twisted shadows on the forest floor. The strong scent was overwhelming, intoxicating. He stared overhead at a mad carousel of swooping, winged figures and remembered a childhood visit with his family to the zoo in San Diego. At one point he wandered away from his parents and into a large dome-shaped building where the air was moist and humid, like a jungle. He thought of Tarzan movies he'd seen at matinees, and he anticipated that an ivory-tusked elephant would burst from the tropical ferns and attack him. There had been brightly colored birds looping through the air like crazed bomber pilots splattered with paint, and he grew dizzy spinning about in circles, trying to watch their mad flight patterns. He'd collected feathers wherever he could, and the further he moved into the heart of the aviary, the more he loved the rich smell of the place and the musical clicks and chirps. When Frank found him, Cruz was scolded and spanked for getting lost, but he held back the tears as he secretly clutched a palmful of exotic feathers. Later, he would take these priceless mementos and wrap them in tissue paper and hide them in his suitcase.

As Cruz walked past a nearby tree there was a sudden rustling sound directly above him. He glanced up. A small pointed head darted over the lip of the nest and released a shower of grey matter. He tried to duck, but the brunt of it struck him on the nose and chin.

"Bastard!" he yelled.

It was foul stuff, somewhere between fish guts and bird droppings. Disgusted, he stumbled away, trying to wipe the substance from his face. He could hear Rita laughing behind him.

"That's something I forgot to tell you about," she said. "You have to be careful around here."

Cruz stripped off his shirt and used it to wipe away the sticky liquid.

"It's their way of telling you to stay away from the nests," Rita said. "Some people put up signs and fences. Herons just vomit on you when you get too close."

"Now I know why this place stinks," Cruz said, holding his shirt at a distance.

"I'm sorry I laughed, but the look on your face was perfect."

Cruz smiled and said, "A little bird barf on the face is probably great for the complexion."

They cut through the trees down to the river and Cruz washed his face off in the icy water, then rinsed his shirt clean. When he was done they walked on, Cruz trailing a few yards behind Rita. The green veil of the woods enveloped them in coolness. The wind blew and more feathers glided down. They stopped in the large clearing and stood silently, watching the graceful motion of the herons above them. Cruz felt as if he were in a lush and private landscape, a world apart from Lake Isabella.

"This is great," Cruz said. "All of it."

"I try to come here at least once a week."

"Do you still draw the birds?"

"Sometimes," she said, looking down at the forest floor. "I guess you could say I try to draw them, but it never turns out very well. Most of them end up in the trash."

Her face seemed suddenly tense, the skin tight around her mouth and eyes. She looked away. "There was a time when I thought I could be an artist," she said. "I took all the classes in high school and even tried a drawing course at a junior college. But things never worked out. I guess I didn't have a good enough eye or something."

"Well, if you ever save any of your drawings, I'd love to see them."

Rita didn't respond. Cruz dug the toe of his boot into the soft ground and unearthed a small pocket of ants.

"Is this the part where we tell our life stories?" she asked.

"I don't know," Cruz said. "Is it?"

She continued to look at him in silence, taking her hands out of her pockets and crossing her arms. Cruz felt uncomfortable, the quiet beginning to rattle him.

"Listen," she finally said. "I brought you here because I thought you'd appreciate this place. But you need to know something." Her bottom lip quivered. "There are just some things I don't like to talk about."

"Like your drawing?"

"That's one of them. There are others. I came to the mountains for a lot of reasons and one of them was to get out of Los Angeles."

He took a step toward her. "It's okay," he said. "I'm not pushy."

She looked up at him and a strand of hair fell from behind the bandanna in front of her eyes. She smiled, dropping her hands to her sides. They stood silently in the clearing, a few feet apart, and then he reached out and put his hands on her shoulders and drew her to him. At first she hesitated, pulling away.

"A hug?" he said, looking at her.

She took an awkward step forward and he slid his arms around her. He could feel the warmth of her shirt on his bare skin. She was trembling. They stood in the clearing for some time. Finally Cruz said, "I'm glad you brought me here."

They separated and Rita took a step backward, her hand sliding up to adjust the bandanna around her forehead. Suddenly an object flashed through the trees. "Look," she said, and he turned to see a heron soaring upward, its wings long and extended like black kites attached to its sides, the neck arching out ahead, the beak keen as a compass needle. Gangly legs dangled beneath the airborne frame. It looked bold to Cruz as it flew toward the river. As he tracked its flight, he looked at Rita and felt a sudden trust with her. She'd brought him to see her treasure, a realm of herons protected by a cathedral of willow and cottonwood. They watched until the bird vanished in a sudden plunge toward the river, and then they headed back along the trail through the lengthening shadows of the heronry.

* * *

He slept late again the next day, staying in bed until midmorning, when the sun broke through the window blinds and cast hot gold bands on the dirty sheet he'd slept under. Turning on the radio, he was surprised to hear an old song from a jazz station, probably out of Los Angeles, that played music from the thirties and forties. He knew that Frank borrowed the radio from his room sometimes and took it into the kitchen. Cruz usually hated this kind of music, but the song was different somehow, slow and romantic, the words almost painful. It made Cruz think of smoky bars and a black female singer in a sequined dress standing in a spotlight while couples swayed in the shadows around her. He thought about dancing with Rita in a dark bar after midnight, his hand stroking her back as she laid her head on his shoulder.

Then he tried to picture his father listening to this song, tried to imagine him sitting at the shelter in Bakersfield. It would be early for him, before he'd even smoked his first cigarette. Maybe the song would take his mind off wanting a drink, then trigger something, a memory of Marta or an old girlfriend.

He might suddenly be a different man, the handsome one with a flat stomach who could hang a six-ton girder above a steel trestle and then lower it smack on target. His mind would clear with the music, and silky images would come forward, glossy and tinted with perfume.

Marta sitting in a convertible after they'd first started dating as he tried to impress her with the car, even though it was borrowed from a friend. *Your father was a slick one,* Marta had told Cruz once. *He'd bring roses and wine, even a box of candy for my mom. Then he'd take me dancing at some roadhouse bar. I was only seventeen and didn't know a thing, so I followed his lead. A real smoothie.*

He turned the radio off and got out of bed, feeling stronger and rested from the long sleep. The wounds on his arms no longer ached beneath the bandages. He thought about calling his father, then threw out the idea. He could call him tomorrow. Today was a different story. Today he needed to visit a man who had returned from the dead.

Ever since Walker had come to the hospital to tell him of Crawdad's miraculous survival, he'd been putting the visit off, feeling uneasy, afraid of what he might discover. In his own mind he felt that he'd done everything possible to locate and rescue Crawdad the night of the accident. But he'd been remembering Nightmare Corner and the way the old man had fished him out of the river. When Lou had driven him back from the hospital, Cruz had asked for directions on how to get to Crawdad's cabin. *Are you sure you wanna go up there so soon?* Lou had blurted out. *The old buzzard could be pissed off at you, thinking you left him down in that canyon to die. For all I know he could be waiting for you with a shotgun.* Had he done the right thing in climbing out when he did? Should he have swum across the river to search on the other side?

He went in the bathroom and stripped down to shower, but stopped when he saw himself shirtless in the mirror. For the first time he noticed a change, something different. His shoulders and biceps were muscular, reminding him of the athletes he used to see at the high school who lifted weights. Cruz had never played any sports, although he would've liked to have tried football or wrestling. He was always too busy hustling jobs and working on cars with his friends. But as he looked in the mirror this morning, he wondered what Rita saw when she looked at him. *A cute guy,* she'd said when they stood on the porch outside Laverne's.

After breakfast, Cruz got the keys to the jeep and filled it up with gas over at the Sportsman's Station, then drove north to Kernville. He went straight through the city and headed upriver about a mile until he turned left onto a gravel road that cut through a stand of pine trees. Within minutes he emerged from the woods into a clearing and saw the cabin, a low structure of dark wood with windows across the front. It was what he'd expected, something rustic and weather-beaten, a loner's hideaway. The slanted roof was shingled, and a stone chimney poked up from within. He parked the jeep next to Crawdad's old red truck, then got out and walked toward the cabin.

As he approached the building he noticed something odd. Things had been left unfinished. It looked as if Crawdad had started to stain the cabin's wood exterior to a dark tone, but then stopped, leaving a black ring around the bottom portion. An old truck was jacked up in the side yard, the right front tire off. A white stone wall was partially completed on the side of the cabin, and Cruz saw piles of the stones at various places in the yard. There were tools scattered in the dirt. A rusty metal shovel. A garden hose. A hammer.

Once on the porch, he stepped around a wire-enmeshed crate which was leaning against the wall. A rattling hum suddenly erupted from within the cage and Cruz snapped back. Peering down, he saw a rattlesnake coiled upon a gathering of straw, its diamond head arched and twitching, hissing at the chicken wire which separated them. A faded piece of paper was nailed to the top of the crate with the word *Jasper* scrawled onto it.

There were two gigantic rattlesnake skins nailed to the front door, their fangs protruding like hypodermic needles. Cruz knocked firmly, then waited for the sound of movement from within the cabin. No response. The doorknob turned easily in his hand and he paused on the threshold.

"Anybody here?" he called. "Crawdad?"

It was all one large room, dimly lit by the windows to his left. Daylight spilled from the doorway onto a braided rug, and Cruz saw a large wooden table covered with maps, a sink and cabinet, a bookshelf, a metal bed and mattress. The scent of Dutch Masters cigars filled the air. In the silence he heard the brittle crunch of dirt under his feet as he moved into the room. A part of him was scared, wanting to turn and run to the jeep so he could drive like hell back to Kernville. But he moved to his right and saw Crawdad slumped in a rocker, his foot propped up on a small wooden table. Cruz could see the whiteness of the cast encircling his leg.

"Crawdad?" Cruz said. The old man stirred in the chair, slowly looking up until he stared directly at Cruz with red, tired eyes. *Saturday morning eyes* was what Cruz used to say when his father would come to the breakfast table hungover. A bottle of Jack Daniels rested next to Crawdad's leg, along with two shot glasses and an old cigar box. A hunting knife with a white pearl handle was stuck in the top of the table.

"I've been waiting," Crawdad said in a weak, slurred voice. "Guess you got the message from Walker."

"Yeah," Cruz said.

"At least Walker finally did something right."

"He told me where to find you. I'm just glad to see you all in one piece."

"Hardly," Crawdad said. He slapped his hand against the white cast. "My leg's screwed up, but I'll get by."

"I would've come sooner," Cruz said, "but I was in the hospital for a few days."

"No need to rush," Crawdad said, his voice quavering. "Time don't matter to me. Time don't mean nothing up here." Flies had settled on his face and he slapped them away. He slowly hoisted his leg off the table and straightened up in the rocker, then reached over and grabbed the bottle of whiskey, wincing as he stretched for the glasses. "I was just glad to hear you made it. Let's have us a drink to survival." He raised the bottle and poured. "I couldn't wait to get out of that hospital. Too afraid that one of them doctors might cut something important off, if you know what I mean." He winked at Cruz and grinned.

Cruz stepped farther into the room and pulled up a rickety folding chair while Crawdad filled the shot glasses to the brim and passed one over. He sipped the whiskey and felt it burn in the back of his throat. The old man stared at the ceiling, head tilted upward.

A long silence followed and Cruz swore Crawdad was drifting off to sleep. He looked exhausted. His weathered features had a hard edge, and wrinkles cut into his forehead and cheekbones like deep slits. Crawdad sat hunched over, his back slightly crooked, his hair as thin and wispy as cobwebs. He grimaced before sipping the whiskey, and Cruz saw a brown stain on his teeth.

"You look tired," Cruz said, breaking the quiet.

"A bit. I haven't been sleeping too well since the accident." Crawdad squinted at him, then finished the shot of whiskey. "Tell me your story," he finally said, "about what happened at Gravedigger. All I want is a little piece of the facts. You can do that, can't you?"

"Where do I start?"

The old man laughed, a shrill cackle that startled Cruz. "It's easy," he said. "Tell me what you saw that day."

Cruz took another drink from the glass. He could feel the stuffy heat in the room, the dead air. The smell of alcohol and dust and smoke filled his nostrils. Sweat trickled down his chest and arms under the T-shirt. He was trying to think fast, stay a step ahead of the old man.

"I was scared as we waited above Tombstone," Cruz began. He waited, saw the old man nod his head in agreement, then continued. "I didn't want to run it. We still hadn't found the boy and the sky was black from the storm and the river was running fast. I wanted to portage but the shore seemed too rocky and steep. I was afraid to say anything."

Crawdad nodded again, a fresh glass of whiskey trembling in his hand. Cruz stared at the old man, not sure where this was going.

"So we ran it," Cruz said. "Only I bumped into something at the top and it turned the boat sideways and we went into the big wave all wrong. Things happened so fast when the raft flipped. Suddenly I was swimming for shore and I saw you being washed over Gravedigger Falls. That was the last I saw of you."

Crawdad slapped at the flies on his face, swatting them into the air. "I bet Walker figured I was some crazy old dog out to drown myself," he said.

Cruz set the glass down on the table. He thought Crawdad was playing some game, trying to get a rise out of him.

"I don't think you're crazy," Cruz said. "I told Walker that when he came to see me in the hospital."

"Walker thinks I'm nuts."

"But he doesn't know you like I do."

"Maybe so," Crawdad said. "Maybe he don't."

They sat there for a while after that, not talking or even looking at one another. Crawdad filled the glasses again and they drank. A stillness hovered in the room, and Cruz felt nauseous from the whiskey.

Suddenly Crawdad said, "Bet you thought I was hookmeat when you saw me go over Gravedigger Falls."

"I thought you had a chance. I searched the shoreline until it got dark, then figured the odds of finding you were slim without getting some help."

Cruz felt a dampness under his arms from where he'd been sweating.

Crawdad went to pour him another drink, but he covered the glass with his hand. A hurt look came over Crawdad's face. "You gonna come all this way and not drink with your old friend?"

"Okay," Cruz said, pulling his hand away, "you convinced me."

"That's more like it," he said, pouring the whiskey. "Did I tell you how Gravedigger Falls got its name?" His words were slurred and came out slowly.

"No, you never did."

"Years ago there was a mining camp down there. A local found this gold vein when he was in the canyon screwing around. He got his friends, and they hauled down all their gear and set up camp next to the falls."

Suddenly Crawdad was seized with a violent fit of coughing. His entire body shuddered as if he'd been kicked in the stomach. Cruz leaned forward in his chair and said, "Are you all right?" The old man waved him off, waited until the coughing passed, then swigged down the glass of whiskey.

"My story," he said, "there's more to it. After a year of digging, they got hit with the spotted fever. Most of them died quick. The one bastard who survived didn't know what to do with the bodies 'cause there was no place to bury 'em, and it was too hard to haul them out of the canyon. So he chucked them over the falls and let the river do the rest."

"Not a bad way to get rid of your dead," Cruz said.

"Amen," Crawdad said, pausing to pour himself more whiskey and then lean back in the rocker. "I was thinking about the miners when I went over the edge. All their skeletons caught in the rocks, waiting for me to join them. All them river bones." He ran a hand through his gnarled hair. "But there's another story I have to tell," he said, continuing. "That's why I gave Walker the message for you. I figured you were the only one who wouldn't think I was some crazy fool." A shadow came over the old man's face, a look of helplessness that Cruz had never seen before. A pleading in his eyes.

"When I went over the drop, it all happened like lightning. No time to think. I remember trying to get my feet downstream so I'd hit the rocks with my legs, but then everything exploded and the river was ripping at me, yanking me under and trying to drown me. I felt the leg snap when I hit the boulders, and then I smacked my head and everything went black. All I remember is waking up and floating in the water at the bottom of the falls. My head hurt and there was blood coming out of my nose."

"I ran downstream to look for you," Cruz said. "I couldn't see anything except one of the oars stuck in the rocks. Couldn't even find the raft."

"The life jacket's what saved me," Crawdad said. "I got swept downstream with the current, but the river slowed after a quarter mile. I grabbed hold of a root onshore, but couldn't climb out 'cause the bank was too steep. My leg was hurting like a sonovabitch and it was getting dark and I was afraid to let go 'cause I couldn't see if there was a rapid around the bend."

He finished the whiskey and then leaned forward, resting an elbow on his knee. He looked straight at Cruz with an unblinking, almost glassy stare, the same kind of look he'd used with Walker when they squared off in the warehouse.

"Then something crazy happened," he continued. "When I couldn't hang on anymore and my arms and legs were going numb and I was getting the shakes, I started seeing things. Things that most folks never want to see. The faces of the drowned."

Cruz said nothing. He thought of the girl he'd carried from the river. Her cold skin. Her eyes black as eels in his dream.

"There were men and women. A few children. I could see their faces clear as day right next to me in the water. And their faces weren't dead and scary like what you'd expect. They were clean and smooth and fresh. Shiny. And they told me things."

"Like what?" Cruz said.

"Stories," he said. "About these."

He opened the cigar box and emptied the contents around the knife. Bracelets and rings and gold chains spilled onto the table. One by one Crawdad held up the pieces of jewelry and told Cruz the stories. A sapphire ring bought in Los Angeles on the eve of World War II with the winnings from a stud poker hand. A turquoise necklace given as a gift on a tenth wedding anniversary and purchased from an old Indian named Charlie Eagle Plume. A St. Christopher's medal passed down from generation to generation on the day of First Communion. A copper bracelet with the words *Jesus Was a Fisherman* emblazoned on the side and given to a minister on his forty-seventh birthday.

"How do you know these things?" Cruz asked.

"They told me," Crawdad said. "Only it don't stop there. Ever since they pulled me out of the river, I still see their faces. That's why I can't sleep. They keep coming back to me at night like a damn movie in my head I can't turn off."

Cruz leaned forward, elbows resting on his knees, and stared down at the wood grain in the floor, unsure what to say to the old man. He wanted to tell Crawdad that he believed him, even though he wasn't sure he did. It was as if a stranger sat in the rocking chair across from him.

"I'm not going batty," Crawdad said. "How else could I know unless I heard it from their own voices?"

"You've been through a lot. You need to rest."

"I survived," he said, his face straining. "That's what counts, right, being a survivor?"

"Sure, that's the important part. You're alive and you'll be back to work in no time."

"Back to work," Crawdad said, scowling. "No way."

"What do you mean?" Cruz said, leaning forward in the chair.

"I'm quitting. I ain't going back."

Crawdad grabbed a wooden crutch from the floor and stood up, then hobbled over to the kitchen table. Cruz didn't move.

"Have you said anything to Lou?" Cruz asked.

"No. You're the only one I've told."

He began to shuffle back and forth across the cabin, talking to Cruz.

"I got money saved. I got my pension. It ain't much but I can get by."

"I don't blame you for retiring," Cruz said. "You've been at it a long time."

"Too damn long. Almost thirty years." He walked over to the kitchen sink and stood there with his back to Cruz, head down, as if looking for a cup or plate in the basin. Then he spoke, his voice weak and hollow. "The first time I dragged a geek out with the hooks I could hardly stand the smell and got sick right there on the bank. So I quit looking at their faces, and pretty soon they were nothing but meat on the end of a hook. It got to the point where I even liked fishing 'em out. But that's all changed. I don't look at things the way I used to. I see those faces at night and it spooks me. Like they've come back from the dead." He turned away from the sink and faced Cruz, the look on his face haunted and sorrowful. "And there's one that's worse than all the others. A woman. A real beauty in her twenties. Her hair's black as midnight and her face is just under the surface. When her lover kicked her out, she jumped off a bridge into the Kern and drowned. Only she's lost her gold ring and she can't find it. Now she knows I have it."

Crawdad turned and walked to the kitchen table, then stood there staring down at the maps. "I'm glad you came up here. Not too many others would listen to this. They wouldn't know what the hell I was talking about 'cause they don't know the hooks like you and me." Suddenly he began to cough and a harsh, rattling sound erupted from his throat, almost doubling him over. He straightened and shook out one of the little cigars from a pack in his shirt pocket, then lit up. It seemed to calm him and he looked at Cruz, saying, "But I didn't ask you up here just to tell you I was quitting. I need your help with something."

"I'll help if I can," Cruz said.

"Find the raft. I don't care if it's ripped to shreds. Find it and bring it back to me."

"Then what?" Cruz asked, rising from the chair and going over to the table. The faded topographic maps were spread across the large surface at odd angles, a blend of contour lines and creases and pale green swirls. Crawdad lined them up until all the edges were connected, and then Cruz noticed a crooked red line, cherry-colored and as wide as a trickle of ink, running from the upper right-hand corner of one map and streaking down across the others to the bottom left.

"It's the upper section of the Kern," Crawdad said. "I've had these maps for years, ever since I went up there for the Forest Service in the late fifties to scout out some new trails." His finger traced the line, starting at the top and then curving down in a crooked descent. "It starts near Mount Whitney and then cuts through the Sierras until it reaches Kernville. Not many people have ever seen this part of the river. Maybe a couple of backcountry rangers or mule packers or hunters. It's damn near untouched. I want to go back there in a raft and I need your help."

"What about your leg? You can't do any rafting with a broken leg."

"The cast comes off in six weeks. We'd have to wait that long anyway for the river level to come down. In 1958 I hiked along certain parts of the run, and the water has to be just right to sneak through some of the rapids. But it'll be worth it, Cruz. Twenty-five miles of virgin water."

Cruz hesitated, moving the palm of his hand over the surface of the map. He could sense Crawdad pressuring him and he wanted to stall a little. Take some time to think it through. "The north and south forks meet here?" he asked, pointing at the corner. Crawdad nodded, tapping the place with his finger.

"How would we get the gear in?" Cruz asked.

"I know an outfitter in the high country with mules. His name's Half Pint and he can get us anywhere we want."

Cruz walked away from the table and stood next to the kitchen window. Through the trees he could see the river below and how the water reflected silver when the sun struck it full-on. His head was buzzing from the whiskey and he needed to clear his mind before making any decisions.

"I'm not sure I'm ready for something like this," he said. "I'm still feeling a little shaky."

"I know," Crawdad said. He slid a folding chair up to the table and sat down. "But it would mean a lot to me. There's something I need to do up there." He placed his palms on the maps and drew his hands across them as if probing for some invisible texture or contour. "Anyway," he said with a grin, "before you know it some jackass from the Army Corps of Engineers will come in and throw up a dam and flood the whole canyon and it'll be gone." He leaned back in the chair and exhaled a cloud of cigar smoke. "I figure it's my last chance to get up there. Who knows? A year from now I could be sitting in some damn wheelchair out on a pink houseboat in the middle of Lake

Isabella. I can't leave the Kern like this. I need to finish something, and I need your help to do it."

"What is it you need to finish?" Cruz asked.

"I'll tell you soon enough," Crawdad said.

Cruz turned away from the window and said, "What if we run into a rapid like Gravedigger Falls again? What do we do then?"

"Unload the raft and carry it onshore. We can take some heavy-duty rope just in case we have to line the boat around."

Cruz shook his head. "I'm still not sure. It sounds risky."

"Of course it's risky. Everything is." Crawdad slapped the map with his hand. "You don't get laid unless you ask the girl to dance. And sometimes you get slapped. That's just how it works."

Cruz got up, then walked in front of the table. "I'll have to think about it. I've got some things I need to take care of first."

"Like talk to Walker?" Crawdad asked.

Cruz stared down at the old man. "No," he said firmly. "That's not on the list."

"Well, don't think too long or the water'll be gone up there."

"I'll let you know," Cruz said. "I need to be going now. I've got to get back to town."

"Don't let me keep you," Crawdad said weakly from the other side of the table.

"Is there anything I can get for you?" Cruz asked. "Do you need any groceries or supplies?"

"Just find the raft."

Cruz made his way to the door, his back to Crawdad. Suddenly he heard the old man's voice say, "The girl you hooked out of the river that first time. Do you remember her?"

Cruz turned to face him. "Yeah," he said. "What about her?"

Crawdad came forward and held out his hand. There were two pearl earrings that gleamed against the cracked skin of his palm like silver tears. "She wore pearls," the old man said. "Her parents gave them to her when she graduated from high school. Expensive ones, the real thing. She got to pick them out and liked to keep 'em in a velvet-lined box in her dresser." He extended his hand toward Cruz. "Take them."

So Cruz did, slipping them into his pocket. Then he closed the door without saying thanks or looking back at the old man who stood in the window and watched him go.

CHAPTER SIX

Cruz called Frank the next morning from the trailer. He was planning to go in at nine to see Lou about starting back to work, but he wanted to talk with his old man before leaving. In the kitchen, holding the receiver to his ear, he felt the day heating up as sweat beads trickled down his neck like warm dew.

The man who answered the phone had a gruff, scratchy voice. Cruz guessed it was Father Sam.

"Can I speak to Frank Cruz?" he said.

"Is this Frankie's boy?" the voice said.

"Yeah."

"I remember you from the last time your old man was in. You were a good kid. You never forgot your father. A lot of men here don't get visitors because people have given up on 'em."

"That's too bad," Cruz said. He knew Father Sam was a talker and might keep him on the phone for a while, so he said, "I need to speak to my father if he's up and around. Could you get him for me?"

"Sure," said Father Sam. "Just saw him at breakfast. You should be proud of your old man. Frankie's doing better after a rough coupla days. But I think the good Lord's got plans for him."

"Right."

"Will you be coming to see us this week? Your old man could use a visitor."

"Maybe," Cruz said. "I might do that."

"Let me get him for you."

As he waited, Cruz heard sounds in the background. A television was playing, and sporadic laughter filled the receiver with sound. The last time he'd visited Frank in the shelter, he'd watched his father and some of the other men gather every morning to watch *Jeopardy* on TV. They'd each take one of the question categories to see how they competed against the people on the show. One morning Cruz sat with them and played the game. He remembered a man who stood against the wall of the recreation area and watched, but never played. They called him Professor because he used to be some kind of a teacher at the college in Bakersfield before he started drinking. He would hold a metal frying pan and a spoon, and every time somebody missed a question he would hit the pan with a resounding gong, then blurt out *dumbshit*.

The others ignored him most of the time, treated him as if he were invisible. Sometimes the Professor would blurt out the answers to difficult questions and the others would yell and tell him to get the hell out. *That guy had brains, though,* Frank used to tell Cruz. *He had all the answers. But too many brains ain't a healthy condition for nobody.*

Suddenly he heard his father's voice at the other end. "Roy?" Frank said.

"How you doing?" Cruz asked. "I would've called sooner, but I've been busy with some things."

"I'm hanging in there. This place hasn't changed a bit. Just the faces." His father sounded winded, his breath rapid on the phone.

"I talked with Father Sam for a moment," Cruz said.

"Same old bastard," Frank said. "How that guy got to be a priest I'll never know."

"He told me things were rough at first."

"Hell, it's like that for anybody who's on the wagon. I still get the shakes at night, but I'm getting through it. I'm talking to the other guys here and getting to know 'em."

"Do you need anything?" Cruz asked. "Can I bring you some things from home or the store?"

"Not right now," Frank said. "I've got most of what I need." There was a pause and Cruz could still hear his labored breath. "I read the Bible every day. I'm still trying to look for something there, but not like I used to. This time I'm staying more to myself. Working from the inside out, if you know what I mean."

"I think so," Cruz said, even though he didn't. "I was thinking I might come down to visit you over the weekend. Maybe on Saturday."

A long silence followed at the other end. Cruz heard the TV again in the background, only this time a man was saying something angry and a woman was screaming. "Not yet," Frank said. "It's too soon. I need time to get through it myself."

"Okay," Cruz said.

"Don't worry about me," his old man said. "There are men here I can talk with. They're in my shoes and they know what I'm saying. We all know what we have to do and what will happen if we don't."

"Do you remember that guy you called Professor?" Cruz asked suddenly. "I'll never forget him. He used to watch *Jeopardy* and beat on that old frying pan. What a nut."

"I remember him," Frank said. "Father Sam still talks about him. Sort of a lesson about what can go wrong when you think you've got it beat on the outside."

"What do you mean?" Cruz asked.

"The Professor went back to teaching and had himself a real good job at the college. Then something snapped. Father Sam said he used to see him sitting out in the St. Vincent's parking lot on weekends. It was like he wanted to come in, but couldn't. About a year ago he got up in front of one of his classes, took out a gun and blew his brains all over the chalkboard. I guess it was in all the Bakersfield papers. Can you imagine what the kids thought after that? You don't get that kind of lesson every day."

"I know what you mean," Cruz said.

"The Professor was always too damn smart. That was his problem."

They were quiet for a moment. Finally Frank said, "What about you? Have you gone back to work yet?"

"No," Cruz said. "I'm going in to see Lou this morning, and maybe start back on Wednesday. I don't know what they'll have me doing. Whatever it is, I'm sure I'll be busting ass."

"That's the name of the game."

Cruz sensed a hesitation, a holding back, in his own voice. There was more that he wanted to say to Frank, more about being scared. He was afraid that Lou would assign him back on the river, and he knew that fear was something Frank could've been an expert in.

"Is the old guy doing all right?" Frank asked. "That friend of yours who broke his leg. Catfish or whatever his name is?"

"Crawdad? Yeah. I drove over to Kernville to see him the other day. He's doing okay, but he's gonna retire from the Forest Service. I think the accident was kind of the last straw for him."

"Sounds like a good thing to do. Get away, I mean. Go someplace and do something different."

"You could do the same," Cruz said.

"I'm too damn old to be going off and starting all over again. I just want to get through this and take it slow. But maybe it's something you should think about."

Are you scared? Cruz wanted to ask him. *Are you afraid of going back and starting over again? Are you afraid of dying?* He didn't ask these questions. Instead, they talked about other things: the Dodgers, local news, taking care of the jeep. *Fill in the gaps,* Cruz thought. When it was time to end the conversation, Cruz told him he'd call again over the weekend.

"That would be fine," Frank said.

"I'll try to call in the morning."

"The morning's a good time. My head's clearer then. Sharp as a tack. Talk to you then, Roy."

* * *

The Forest Service warehouse seemed quiet and nearly empty when Cruz arrived to see Lou. There were a few workers, men he didn't recognize, who were unloading sandbags from a flatbed truck. Otherwise the place was abandoned, and as Cruz walked past the big metal doors he thought of all the times when the place was teeming with trucks and motion. But the men were gone now, probably out working on a firebreak or building a trail in the foothills.

The door to Lou's office was open and he stepped inside. The walls were covered with slick centerfolds and pinups and spreads of nude women from magazines like *Hustler* and *Gallery* and *Fox* that Lou kept on his desk. Cruz had seen these magazines behind the counter at some of the gas stations, and it made him uneasy walking into that office and being surrounded by all these women spreading their legs, heads kicked back in pleasure as they stared at a camera. *Wall to wall pussy,* was what Chico said. The place always startled him, and for the first time Cruz realized that maybe this was intentional, just what Lou wanted, kind of like throwing a curveball at your head when you stepped into the batter's box.

Lou was behind his desk and he looked up from some papers. "Cruz," he said. "I'm glad to see you're still breathing. I was wondering when you'd show up." He got up and shook Cruz's hand. His face was red and flushed and he continued talking. "How are those arms of yours doing? About ready for a little work?"

"I took the bandages off yesterday. Still a little tender, though."

Cruz sat down in a chair across from the desk. He motioned with his hand at the pictures. "Still got your girlfriends around, huh?"

Lou chuckled. "Yeah. I like to keep a little company during the day. Having all these pretty gals to stare at keeps me awake. My little collection."

Cruz glanced down at his arms for a moment, running a hand gently across the scrapes and cuts. Without looking up he said, "I could use some work."

"Good," Lou said. "I've been counting on that. I've kept a place open for you."

"But not on the river," Cruz said. "At least not at first."

Lou leaned back in his chair, unwrapped a piece of gum and popped it into his mouth. "The river's gone down," he said. "It's nowhere near as high as when you and Crawdad went out. More manageable."

"Maybe so."

"A little spooked?" Lou asked.

"You could say that."

"Nothing to be ashamed of," Lou said, his lips grinning as he smacked the gum. "But we need to have an understanding. I spent a lot of time having you trained on that river. A lot of money. Hell, I can get ten guys off the street to shovel out ditches. But you've got a skill I need."

"I know that," Cruz said. He felt the heat Lou was putting on him, knew what was coming, so he tried to think fast and look at the possibilities. He needed cash. Money for the trailer and jeep and groceries, along with Frank's expenses.

"Then understand this, too," Lou said. "Jobs are scarce. A lot of hungry men come through here every day looking for work and I have to say, 'Adios, amigo.' They got families to feed and are willing to do damn near anything. So don't come back too slow. I need to be able to count on you when it comes to the river. It don't look too good when a rescue needs to be done and there's nobody around to do the rescuing."

Lou got up from his chair and came around in front of the desk. He tucked his shirt in over a huge belly, straightened up and sat on the corner of the table. Cruz felt a slow anger building and he tried to temper it. *You go out in that raft, fatso,* he wanted to say. *You'll be floating belly-up with the fish.*

"I don't mean to be a hard-liner," Lou continued. "I'm just telling you the way it is. A lot of people started asking questions after you and Crawdad had your little accident. I don't need that kind of a headache. I like things smooth and easy around here. Dependable. Understand?"

"I think so," Cruz said.

"Good. I'm glad we talked."

"But there's something I need to know," said Cruz. "When Walker and the others found Crawdad, did they see any signs of the raft?"

Lou smiled. "I'm one step ahead of you." He motioned for Cruz to follow. They went through the warehouse, past the men unloading sandbags, and then outside to a small shed. Lou opened the padlock, swung the door open, and almost immediately Cruz could smell it. The musty, damp scent of the river.

The raft was crudely rolled, burrito-style, around one of the oars. The steel rowing frame leaned against a wall of the shed, and a variety of other things that had been tied to the frame were spread along the dirt floor. A black watertight bag containing the pump and first-aid kit. Tattered straps dangled from the frame, the only remains of where the current had stripped some of the gear clean off. Cruz saw the canvas bag containing the hooks in the far corner.

"The raft was about a half mile downstream from where Crawdad washed up. It got snagged in a huge pileup of brush and willows. I'm not sure if it's salvageable, though. It got ripped up pretty good, and there's a big gash in the floor."

Cruz stared at the raft and gear for a moment, then entered the shed. He ran his hands over the coarse black rubber and pulled the hooks from the bag.

"Thank Chico and Garcia and some of the others for this," said Lou. "They had to bust ass to get all the stuff back up that fire trail. I think old Chico might've given himself a hernia, he worked so hard." Lou laughed, tugged at his crotch with his hand. "He'll be out of commission for a bit."

Lou helped him and they hauled the raft out into the sunlight. It was covered with dirt and sand, and as they unrolled it, Cruz could already see the damage. The floor had been slashed wide open, maybe a seven-foot tear. The line running around the outside of the boat had been ripped away. There were long, jagged scratches in the sides, and one of the valves had popped out, allowing water to flood into the tube.

"Good luck," Lou said, staring down at the raft, shaking his head. "It's one helluva cleanup job."

"I promised Crawdad that I'd bring it to him no matter what kind of condition it was in. He said he had the materials to repair it."

Cruz pulled his jeep over to the shed. He rolled the raft up and wedged it into the back. "I'll pick the rest of the stuff up later."

"Do what you have to do," Lou said. "You're the expert when it comes to this stuff. I don't know shit about rafting." Lou took out a can of chewing tobacco and shoved a huge pinch into his mouth. "I'm trying to quit smoking," he said, grinning, and for a moment Cruz thought the boss's lower lip might explode.

"If it's all right with you, I'll start back tomorrow," Cruz said.

"Sounds fair enough. I'll try to get you on Walker's crew."

"I'd appreciate it."

As Cruz drove away he thought about Lou's words. *You're the expert.* It surprised him. It had always seemed that everyone else had something they were good at, such as working on cars, playing sports, or building things. He'd always been good when it came to helping them out, but he'd never seen himself as an expert on anything. Until now.

*   *   *

When Crawdad saw the raft he didn't say much. Cruz unrolled it on a large canvas tarp in the side yard next to the cabin. The old man wasn't using the crutch anymore, instead putting his weight on the cast itself and hobbling around. He glanced at the boat momentarily, then vanished inside the cabin. It was almost as if he expected the worst and didn't need to see the actual damage.

A few minutes later he returned with a large metal ammo can in one hand, filled with an assortment of glass jars, paintbrushes, sandpaper, and shiny rolls of black patching material. In the other hand he carried a twelve-pack of beer. "The main ingredient," Crawdad said, swinging the beer onto the ground. "Part of my private reserve. Keeps you patient when you'd like to take a chainsaw to the old boat."

Cruz waited as Crawdad tossed him one, then he popped it open and took a long swig. The can was icy in his palm and for a moment he rested it against his face to feel the cold surface.

Crawdad took a long drink from his beer, then gestured at the raft.

"This reminds me of something," he said.

"What?" Cruz asked.

"I read a story once about this beauty queen. I think it was in one of them papers you see at the grocery store while you're waiting in line."

Cruz nodded, drank some more of his beer.

"She was in this car accident," Crawdad said, "and her face got all bashed in and cut up. She lost an eye and part of her nose. They had these before and after pictures of her in the paper, and she was ugly as sin. They had to do plastic surgery. Only thing is, when they were done with her, she didn't look anything like she used to. She was a different person. 'I want to look better than before,' she told them jackass doctors. And she took 'em to court and got her money's worth. The next year she won another damn beauty pageant. Can you believe that? Fooled all them judges. I'd like to find that gal and marry her."

Crawdad laughed, drank some more beer, then moved toward the boat. "Maybe we should take some pictures of the raft," he said. "Kinda like what they did with that beauty queen. You know, before and after shots. So people will know what kind of a job we did here." He went into the house for a few minutes and came back with a dusty old camera. He circled the raft and started taking pictures. He looked like some old tourist, Cruz thought, the way he limped around, camera pointed down at the deflated raft. There was a funny liveliness to him, like some character out of a cartoon.

"I'd marry her on the spot," Crawdad said, camera clicking. "I would indeed."

They dragged the boat over to the shade of a nearby tree. It was late morning and the sun cast down a relentless white heat, giving the yard a pale, bleached color. "We need the coolness for patching," Crawdad said. "If the rubber and glue get too hot, the surfaces won't bond." Cruz sat on the ammo can watching Crawdad and waiting for directions. Every now and then the old man bent down and poked at a deflated thwart or one of the tubes. Cruz saw him feeling the situation out, seeing what he was up against.

They turned the boat over and began with the floor rip. River water sloshed around inside one of the tubes and began to drain onto the tarp as Crawdad emptied out the ammo can. There were tubes of Bostik adhesive and toluene cleaner, thick rolls of duct tape, a heavy pair of scissors, coarse sandpaper, a handful of thin, wispy paintbrushes, a spool of thick thread and a needle, an old pair of channel locks, and a small wooden roller. He showed Cruz how to trim off the tattered edges around the rip, then outlined the rectangular area of the patch with a heavy-duty marking pen. They poured toluene onto some rags and cleaned off the sand and dust from the surface and roughed it up with a piece of sandpaper.

"You ever get sewn up?" Crawdad asked while he took the heavy thread and tied it onto the steel needle. Cruz shook his head no and said, "It's amazing that the meat in somebody's arm or leg or stomach can grow back together the way it does." The old man pierced the rubber around the torn area with the needle, then used the channel locks to yank it through. With each puncture, he began to smoothly weave the thread back and forth in a zigzag pattern.

He let Cruz do some of the sewing. "Keep the spacing even," Crawdad said. "If you get big gaps between the holes, it won't cinch up tight." The needle was awkward in Cruz's hands as he tried to punch the blunt tip through the leathery rubber. He stayed with it, making sure to pull the thread taut after each hole was made. When the sewing was finished along the length of the tear, they worked their way down one more time and tightened it up as one pair of hands yanked the rubber edges of the gash together while the other pulled in any slack.

He liked watching the old man. Crawdad stopped now and then for a beer, completely in tune with the job at hand. There was a peace to the way he worked, his eyes rarely straying from the raft in front of them. With a flourish, he unfurled one of the long rolls of black material and cut out the patch, then roughed up one side with the sandpaper. When they were ready to apply the Bostik adhesive to both the sewed area and the patch, Crawdad showed Cruz how to brush on the glue in a thin coat so the thick, milky substance spread out over the dark surface. "It's sticky but it ain't sweet," the old man said, laughing.

They let the glue dry a little on both the rubber patch and the torn seam. Then, with Crawdad slowly sticking down the patch, Cruz followed with the roller and pressed out any ripples or air bubbles.

"What about that girlfriend?" Crawdad said at one point.

"She's not my girlfriend," Cruz said. "She works in Kernville at a beauty shop. I see her now and then. I might stop by her place today on my way back through town."

"A beautician," Crawdad said, whistling. "I bet she'll give you a blow-dry you'll never forget."

Cruz blushed. "It's nothing like that."

Crawdad stood up and admired his patch work, whistled again. "Hell, you're young. You'll figure it out. Just keep me posted on all the juicy details." After finishing the big rip, they started on the little holes and abrasions. Crawdad had an amazing eye for spotting the smallest puncture or scrape in the material and he wasn't lazy about pointing it out. As they worked on the bow, Crawdad said, "I've been thinking about our trip to the upper Kern and I've got another favor."

"Name it," Cruz said.

"I want you to ask Walker to go with us."

Cruz looked up from his patch job, surprised. "Why Walker?" he said. "I thought you two didn't get along. Why him?"

"It's something personal. Something that happened a long time ago between us and never got settled. He might listen to you if you're the one doing the asking."

Cruz paused before answering, taking everything in.

"I'll try," he said, "but I won't guarantee he'll go."

"I can't ask for anything more," Crawdad said. "Just make sure to tell him." The old man stopped suddenly, his voice faltering in midsentence as if he'd forgotten the words. Then a sly smile came over his face and he spoke in a tone Cruz hardly recognized.

"You tell Walker that being scared won't cut it this time around. Chickenshit don't float on the upper Kern."

"I'll tell him," Cruz said.

* * *

In the late afternoon Cruz drove back into Kernville, leaving Crawdad sitting in a folding chair next to the boat, surrounded by a clutter of empty beer cans. He stopped along the way and bought a six-pack of cheap beer at Gus's Liquor Store, then went by Laverne's. He waited in the parking lot and watched a few older women come out, then saw Rita step onto the porch with her purse and a paper sack. She'd unfastened the clip that usually held her hair in place and now it flowed down her back, loose and dark against her brown shoulders. She wore jeans and a black tank top and sandals, and when she saw Cruz sitting in the jeep, she came over and leaned her arm on the roll bar.

"We don't let your kind hang out around here," she said. "No maniacs allowed."

"I just look tough," Cruz said. "I'm actually here to pick up Laverne for a hot date."

"You're too late. She's already left with Curly from down the street. I think they're scheming to control the hair market in Kernville."

Cruz held up the beer. "How about a little siesta down by the river?"

"I could definitely use one of those," she said, smiling as she climbed in. "It's been a helluva day."

They drove to Kern Park, which bordered the river, and found a place in the shade. Rita took her sandals off and walked barefoot to the water's edge. Cruz followed with the beer. The Schlitz was cold and he opened two, giving one to Rita and setting his own on the bank. Then he gathered rocks and formed a little pool next to the shore and set the rest of the beer in the river to chill.

"Sometimes I hate that shop," Rita said. "Pampering all those old women with 1950s hairdos." She started laughing, then paused to sip her beer. "One night I had a dream that this bitchy old lady, Mrs. Olive, fell asleep in my chair at the shop and I gave her a crewcut. I swear that some of these women don't know a thing except cooking and kids and their fat husbands."

It struck Cruz then, as they sat on the bank and laughed and drank their beers, that his mother had never once gone to the beauty parlor. She usually trimmed her own hair and kept it short because of the heat. Sometimes Cruz and Donna sat on the counter and watched as she took the long-handled scissors and snipped off strands of hair that fell into the sink. *Gotta get all those grey ones. I don't want your father thinking he's married to some old woman.* He wondered what Marta's hair might look like now and whether or not she'd let it grow out.

Rita finished her beer and opened another. She dangled her feet in the water and lay back on the grass.

"Laverne can be a real pain sometimes," she said.

"How's that?" asked Cruz.

"She docked me an hour's pay this morning for not keeping my area clean. Sometimes I think the woman's a cleaning witch, the way she scoots around with her broom."

"Sounds like a long day."

"It was. I just get sick of being on my feet and smelling shampoo and conditioner." She stopped and looked out over the river and grew quiet. A breeze caught her hair for a moment and partially obscured her face. Cruz lay back next to her so that their shoulders were touching.

"I'm gonna start back to work tomorrow," Cruz said. "I talked with my boss this morning." He opened another beer and set the empty on the grass. "I'm gonna have to get used to Chico's dirty jokes all over again."

"Sometimes I think I'd like working outside," Rita said. "I hate being cooped up in that shop all day."

"I need the money. My old man never did pay off that trailer."

They didn't talk for a while, just sat and watched the Kern as it rolled by in front of them.

"I went up to Crawdad's today," Cruz said at one point. "I got the raft back and he showed me how to patch it."

"How's his leg?" she asked.

"He gets around okay. I think the cast stays on for another five weeks or so."

"I'd like to meet him sometime. Maybe you could drive me up to his cabin."

"I'm not sure you'd like him. He's a tough old bastard. He can get pretty crude when he's been drinking."

She lowered her eyes and glared. "I happen to adore tough old bastards," she said. Cruz grinned at her and she reached over and gave him a shove. "I hate overprotective men," she snapped playfully. "You should know that about me."

"I learn something new about you every time. It's part of my strategy."

"What strategy?"

"So you'll go out with me."

"Not a chance. You don't have a prayer. I only date millionaires and motorcycle hoods. The cream of society."

"What about Laverne's boy, Wiley? Where does he fit in?"

"No lounge lizards either. Too slick and scaly. I break out in a rash when they touch me."

Cruz rested his elbow on the grass. "What about me?" he said. "Where do I fit in?"

"You're in the cute maniac category," said Rita. "You've got possibilities."

"For what?" Cruz asked.

She looked at him with a crooked grin. "All the things that excite a typical girl from L.A. Deviant sexual behavior. Bizarre dining habits. The usual."

"I'm not like that at all," Cruz said in mock seriousness. "I'm a traditional guy. I'll buy you a pizza and take you dancing."

"Just don't be predictable," she said. "I hate predictability."

"Is Friday night too predictable?" Cruz asked.

"Friday night is fine," she said smiling. "By the way, does it always take you this long to ask somebody out?"

"I'm a little rusty. Does it show?"

"I'm not sure." She moved toward him until she was only inches away, then kissed him on the mouth. It was a slow, lingering kiss that silenced everything around him, as if the river and wind and the sound of cars from the road all stopped to lean in and listen. Then she moved back, leaving a warmth still on his lips, the scent of lilac in her hair. He wanted to go to her. It was like she'd opened a door and he wanted to step through it. But he held back, waiting.

"That was nice," she said. "I like kissing younger men. It still matters to them."

"What do you mean?" Cruz asked.

"You're still untouched by all the crap. I could tell by the way you looked around up at the heronry. A kiss still matters to you."

"It does," Cruz said. "It means a lot." He wanted to say more to her, tell her he was scared about going back to work on the river, afraid of drowning and being pulled out with the hooks. But he held back again. *Not yet,* he thought. *Enough for now.*

"I once dated a girl for seven weeks and never kissed her once," Cruz said. "I was in the ninth grade. Every time we'd get to her door I'd say goodnight and walk away."

"How come?" Rita asked.

"I liked her too much," he said. "I was afraid I'd ruin it."

She laughed. "You're funny, Cruz. You remind me of somebody. An old boyfriend. He was sweet, too."

"What happened?"

"Bad timing. There was a problem and he couldn't handle it, so he left for a while. Things were different when he came back."

She sat up and looked at him for a long time without saying anything. It was awkward and Cruz gazed out over the river. She was studying him as if searching for something odd and peculiar in his features. A dark mole on his neck, perhaps, or a tiny birthmark tucked under his chin.

"What about Friday night?" he said. "What time can I pick you up?"

"I get off from work around five. Give me some time to get ready."

"I'll be there at six-thirty. We could get something to eat or go to a movie."

"Take me dancing," was all she said.

"Like I said before, I'm not much of a dancer, but I'll try."

She pulled him up with her hands until they were standing, then started to sway. "It's easy," Rita said. He could feel her bare feet on his shoes, hardly any weight at all. "Slow dances are what I like best." She pressed against him, her breasts soft against his own chest, and stood that way for a long time. He didn't kiss her, just moved with her across the grassy carpet. A car drove by and honked, but neither of them turned. At one point she whispered, "I'm scared," into his ear and Cruz nodded. "But I like being scared," she said.

Suddenly she pulled away from him and started running across the park, waving for him to follow. He ran after her and saw that she was headed toward the road, where a concrete bridge spanned the river and led to the other side of town. She reached the bridge first and leaped up onto the narrow cement railing, where she began to walk it carefully, arms outstretched like a tightrope performer. Cars whipped by a few feet from where she stood. She walked confidently out to the center of the bridge, at least thirty feet above the river, then turned to look back at Cruz. He didn't say anything, expecting her to hop down at any minute. Another car raced by and swerved upon seeing Rita perched on the railing.

"Do you like me?" she asked.

"Of course," Cruz said. "Now get the hell down before you fall off and break your neck."

"Would you walk through fire for me?" she asked. "Would you do something dangerous?"

Cruz began to approach her, but she waved him off.

"I used to be a gymnast," she said. "This is child's play. I could do this in my sleep." Suddenly she bent down and placed her hands on the railing, then sprang up into a handstand. She quickly flipped into a graceful cartwheel and landed on the railing feet first again.

Cruz knew she wanted him to come after her. Make a big deal out of it. He stood at the end of the bridge about ten feet from her and watched a truck blitz past, the backdraft nearly knocking her into the river. She swayed momentarily as the trucker honked and shouted a curse out the window.

She regained her balance, then said, "C'mon Cruz, Get up here and walk with the devil. I dare you."

Cruz smiled at her, waited for a car to pass, then went out to the center of the bridge where she stood on the railing.

"No guts," she said, looking down at him. "All I want is a little nerve."

In one quick motion, Cruz hopped up onto the concrete railing and grabbed her hand. "You want a little nerve?" he asked. "Is that it?" Then he leaped off the bridge, pulling her along with him. She screamed as they plummeted toward the river, then hit the water in a tangle of arms and legs. The current was slow, gently swirling about them, and Cruz grabbed Rita's arm and tugged her over to shore. Hair hung in her face like a wet curtain. When they reached the shallows and stood up, Rita swatted at him with her fist, landing a few solid blows on his arms and shoulders.

"Shit!" she said. "Look at me."

Cruz smiled. "Was that what you wanted?" he asked. "A little nerve?"

Rita sat down on shore, brushing the hair out of her eyes. "You didn't have to do that," she said. "I would've gotten down. I was just kidding."

"I never kid," Cruz said, sitting down next to her. "That's something you should know about me."

"What else should I know?" Rita asked, looking at him.

"Nothing really." Then he reached over and kissed her, his hand moving boldly through her wet hair. He began to pull away, but she drew him back, her lips moist, her skin and hair smelling of the river. He thought of the drowned girl he'd wanted to awaken with a kiss, but pushed the image from his mind as he pulled Rita close to him. He felt her breath on his throat and wondered why she'd left Los Angeles in the first place. Maybe there had been a boyfriend who slapped her around, or some involvement in drugs, or perhaps she'd been raped. *Then I get myself in trouble* was all she'd said to him. *I'll tell you about it sometime.* Whatever it was, he could wait.

* * *

Later that night Cruz hauled the air mattress onto the roof of the trailer. The sky was clear and black and the stars seemed close. When he shut his eyes he still felt Rita's lips on his and remembered the confident way he'd kissed her. He was sleepy and drifted off. Rita's face suddenly merged with the women in Lou's office, their eyes closed, mouths open, lips curled back and parted as if in pain.

He tried to separate Rita's image from the other women. When she'd stood close he'd seen freckles on her shoulders and he longed to press his mouth to each one and watch as they blossomed into tiny flowers. He'd held back, trying to be gentle and not push things. Move at her pace. Yet there was a part of him that needed her in the same way he'd needed Teresa. But only when the time was right. Only when he knew Rita wanted him in return.

But when would he get his chance? The fact that he was a virgin nagged at him, probably the result of being around the men on the crew, especially Chico. When it came to sex, he felt cheated and unprepared, as if all the other men he knew had somehow been given information or lessons that he'd missed out on. Frank and Marta had never even tried to talk with him about his body or about sex, so he'd educated himself through the only means available. Conversations with other guys around town and at school. The slick magazines that he found on the shelves at Gas 'N Go, the ones with names like *Stag* and *Hustler* and *Stud*.

Once in Bakersfield he'd gone into a porno shop called The Pink Pussycat. He was red-faced and ashamed as he stared at the contents. What overwhelmed him was not the sheer lust that he'd expected, but an immense sympathy for the women who were exposed on the glossy pages. He wondered if the women had fathers and mothers and husbands and how they had come to this, their mouths open, heads tilted back, eyes shut, as if they too were afraid to look into the camera's lens.

For years he'd masturbated in the privacy of the trailer's bathroom, often late at night when Frank slept. His fantasies were sometimes with girls that he knew from school, but often with strange women he'd seen on the street or the faces of beautiful celebrities. The sexual encounters took place in trailers, on a train, in the school locker room, at a plush apartment in L.A., or some other location. And when he was finished, he would always feel the same rush of shame, the knowledge that if he were a real man he wouldn't need to resort to such a disgraceful act. Each time he vowed to find a lover so he could end the lonely ceremonies of relief that allowed him to finally sleep at night.

* * *

Walker stood in the warehouse the next morning when Cruz showed up for work. He wore a sleeveless orange T-shirt, already damp with sweat.

"Welcome back," Walker said. "You picked a hot day to start again. It was 110 yesterday. Ramirez damn near passed out on me."

They shook hands and Walker grunted when he saw the scratches and reddish scabs just visible under the dark hair on Cruz's forearms.

"Hamburger," Walker said. "Looks like you stuck your arm in the garbage disposal for a chew."

"Now that things are starting to heal up, I actually feel like working."

"We've got plenty of that. With the high water going down, there's a shit-load of sandbags to haul out. Are you up to it?"

"I think so," Cruz said.

"It's good to have you on the crew again," Walker said, placing a hand on Cruz's shoulder. "Some of these guys could use a kick in the ass when it comes to working hard. I need all the help I can get."

Cruz nodded and they walked out to the truck, where the other men were waiting. Some of them greeted him with a handshake or a slap on the back. There were new faces, men with tired eyes that Cruz had never met who merely smiled. *Probably fresh over the border,* he thought, and doubted if they spoke any English.

As they rode in the back of the flatbed down to the river, Cruz noticed something else. Occasionally he saw one of the veterans staring in his direction, and when he caught his eye the man would only smile and nod or give him a thumbs-up. They seemed friendlier, almost respectful. Throughout the morning as they heaved the sandbags into the truck, they were quiet around him, as if unsure what to talk about. None of the usual sarcasm and teasing.

During a water break, Ramirez pulled him aside and said, "I heard about you and Crawdad on the river. Looking for a body and then almost drowning. Tell me about it, man. What was it like?" His voice was pleading, hungry for a few scraps of morbid information to pass on to the others.

"Have some respect," was all Cruz said. Then he walked away and left Ramirez standing with a soggy paper cup in his hand.

The rest of the day he shoveled rock and swung a pickax. The sun was merciless, but he wore a baseball cap with a soaked bandanna underneath to keep his scalp cool. Unlike Crawdad, Walker worked side by side with him, his biceps glistening with sweat as he set a tempo and asked Cruz to follow. Cruz lost himself in the work, sometimes thinking only of the dust swirling up from the trail and how it looked like thick, golden smoke in the afternoon heat.

At the end of the day when they'd arrived back at the warehouse, Cruz pulled his jeep over to the shed where the remaining river gear had been stored. He filled the jeep's interior with ammo boxes and dry bags and a few of the extra life jackets, then lashed the metal rowing frame onto the roll bar.

He drove up to Kernville to see Crawdad and deliver the gear as well as work on the raft. When he arrived, he hardly recognized the boat. Old patches had been ripped away and new ones put in their place. D-rings on the sides had been reglued. The rusty metal valves were pulled out and shiny new ones screwed in. Crawdad had replaced the old bow, stern, and perimeter lines with thick nylon rope that blazed like a white snake against the black hypalon rubber.

Crawdad never asked about Walker. It was as if he knew that Cruz would talk to him when the time was right. As the evening cooled, the old man fixed thick steaks over a fire, cooking them with sliced potatoes and onions in a huge blackened skillet. Afterward, they hooked up an overhead lamp that dangled above the boat and bathed it in intense white light. They worked until long after midnight, a steady flow of beer and glue and toluene cleaner fueling the activity, and when Cruz finally said goodnight to the old man, Crawdad waved his hand at the boat, which gleamed under the spotlight. "Back from the dead," he said. "More lives than a damn cat."

* * *

On Friday morning Lou put them on garbage detail. There'd been a biker wedding the weekend before and they'd trashed the campground down near Caulkins Flats. Beer cans were strewn everywhere and broken glass shone like cut diamonds on the granite surface of the rock. The place was a mess, as if an army had been through and trashed every inch of the property, leaving the landscape scarred.

The work was easy. Walker passed out heavy plastic trash bags and they spread out in a line, working their way toward the river, picking up everything in sight. Sometimes Cruz felt the shade of a tree spread over him and he slowed his pace, not wanting to step back into the hot blaze of sun. The place smelled of beer and urine and cigarette butts.

They stopped for lunch at noon and walked down to the river. There were eight of them and they found a cool, grassy place next to a calm pool protected from the main current by a finger of rock. Some of the men stripped down and waded in. Some soaked their feet. Walker did neither, sitting shirtless on a rock and chewing on an apple. He hardly ever ate anything and Cruz wondered how he could make it through a day with just fruit and a jug of water.

Cruz sat next to him. "Do you ever go dancing?" he asked Walker.

He took a bite out of his apple and said, "Occasionally. Dancing and getting drunk make a nice combination. Why are you asking?"

"I've got a date Friday night and she wants to go dancing."

Walker's eyebrows arched up and he whistled. "Damn, Cruz. A date. I was beginning to think you were some kind of monk in training." He grinned at him. "Is this a special lady?" he asked.

"Yeah," Cruz said.

"Take her to Don's Crossroads. They've got the best dance bands around on the weekend."

"Sounds good."

"But if you take her to Don's, I hope she won't mind the bikers. It's their hangout and the crowd gets a little rough sometimes. I've had my share of runins with the Harleyheads. They don't like anyone asking their biker mamas to dance. Sometimes I do it just to piss 'em off."

"I'll remember," Cruz said. "Thanks."

They stood in silence for a while and ate their lunches. Chico had just come out of the water and was drying off with his T-shirt. Some new guy whom Cruz didn't know was talking about his brother who was in prison.

"It ain't right," the new guy was saying. "My little brother wasn't fucked up before. He was a church boy in high school, man, and a great running back. Fast as shit. Had a full ride to San Diego State and all set until he got drafted. He comes back from 'Nam all fucked up in the head, his knees blown away, drinking every night till he blacks out. Then he tries to rob this Jack in the Box in the drive-thru and shoots off the clown's head. The judge calls him a damn menace and now he's doing time. No way out. He's gone for five years at least."

Chico was listening while the guy told the story. Cruz knew what was coming. Chico was shifty, liked to jerk people around when there wasn't anything to do. He carried a knife in his boot, a switchblade. He'd shown it to Cruz once. *I'm gonna cut off some biker balls with this,* he'd said, grinning.

"Quit your crying, Paco," Chico said. "Your brother got what he deserved. It ain't Vietnam that fucked him. It was his own head. Pretty damn stupid to try and rob a Jack in the Box."

"It was the war," Paco said. "Fried his brain, I'm telling you."

"Shit," Chico said. "A lot of vets got it made. Damn GI bill and extra benefits. I know this guy who got shot in the leg over there. He comes back with a little limp and now he don't have to work the rest of his life. He sits at home with his old lady or hangs out at the bar. I get sick of his shit. Hell, I'll let somebody shoot me in the leg if it means I don't have to work no more."

"You don't know nothing," Paco said.

"Fuck you," Chico said. "Fuck you and your brother."

"Fuck the both of you," said Walker. He sat next to a granite boulder, still chewing his apple. "Neither of you knows what you're talking about."

"This ain't your business, Walker," Chico said. "This is me and Paco talking now."

"I was in Vietnam for two years," Walker said, "and I don't need this. You guys don't know anything."

"What'd you do over there?" Chico asked, his voice probing. "Clean out latrines?"

Walker didn't move from where he sat. He knew the others were listening, waiting to hear him.

"I was the point man in our platoon. That means the first one up the trail on night patrol. You ain't seen dark till you been in the jungle." He looked at Chico and nodded. "It's enough to fry anybody's brain."

Chico was leaning forward now, his eyes on Walker.

"Did you shoot anybody?" Chico asked.

"Yeah," Walker said. "I killed my share. We used to play poker with what we took off the bodies afterward. Ears. Tongues. Fingers. We ran out of chips so we got creative. Somebody threw a gook dick on the table once. That was a royal flush."

Chico didn't say anything. He stood with the others, shaking his head and looking at Walker.

"Is that what you wanted to hear, Chico?" Walker said. "Do you believe it now?"

Chico backed off, leaned against a rock.

"Good," Walker said. "'Cause it's all horseshit. I made it all up. It was worse than that. Poker was what we did for kicks. The real party started in the jungle when the lights went out. Night hunts. Those were my favorite. Seeing what can't be seen. Psycho psychics."

Cruz watched Walker closely, the way he leaned toward Chico when he talked, and it scared him to see this side of the man. It was like he was daring him to yank out that switchblade. There was hate in his voice, real menace. Evil stuff that Chico couldn't even touch. Then Walker backed down, eased out of it. It was as if he knew there was no need to take it any further.

"Enough of this," Walker said. "Let's get back to work. We still got a lot to do. Those bikers throw a mean wedding." The rest of the men picked up their clothes and lunches and headed back to the truck as Chico lagged a few steps behind, his head down, his fists clenched. Cruz stayed close to Walker and when they got back to the truck, Walker turned and grinned at him. "Mind games," he said. "Everybody plays them." He thrust a new trash bag at Cruz. "But some people play 'em better than others." Then they headed down to the camp area.

CHAPTER SEVEN

On Friday night when he picked Rita up at her apartment, she was sitting out on the front steps waiting for him. Cruz had gotten off work late, and there had only been time to grab a shower, fill the jeep with gas and then drive over. Rita wore new jeans, a pair of expensive black cowboy boots, and a dark halter top tied off at the neck. Her hair was down, combed out and shiny, and for a moment Cruz hardly recognized her from the beauty shop. She looked like a model on the cover of some magazine in the grocery stores. Lean and athletic. He knew what Chico and the others might say if they saw him with Rita. *Fuck her lights out. Heavy humping, hombre.*

Cruz was mad at himself when he saw her. If he'd planned better he would've taken the time during the last few days to buy a new shirt or a pair of pants. Instead he wore an old western shirt with long sleeves to hide the bandages and some faded jeans that were the only clean ones in his closet.

"You look nice tonight," he said as she climbed in.

"Thanks," she said. "Not bad for just getting home fifteen minutes ago."

"Good day?" he asked.

"Not bad. Better than others, I guess."

She took out a cigarette and tapped the filter on the pack, then stared ahead as they drove out of the parking lot and onto the main road.

"Maybe it's time for a change," Cruz said.

"Maybe so. I could always get a job at the funeral home giving styles and clips. At least they wouldn't complain. A mortician beautician. Catchy."

She smiled at him and slipped the cigarette into her mouth.

"You bring out my morbid sense of humor," she said. "Why is that?"

"It must be my line of work. You're hooked on me."

She rolled her eyes. "Very sick."

"I knew you'd like it."

He took her to the Gold Pan in North Kernville for pizza and made sure they got a seat on the back deck overlooking the Kern. The place was crowded and a softball team was eating in the main dining area. Now and then raucous laughter rolled out onto the deck, overwhelming the sound of the river below.

"Those guys have some pipes," Cruz said.

"My theory," Rita said, "is that softball teams should be exterminated. If they can't play baseball, get rid of them."

"You're a baseball fan?"

"I lived and died for the Dodgers when I was growing up."

"Me too," Cruz said. "I listened to all their games on the radio."

"We used to take a bus to Dodger Stadium for all their doubleheaders. My dad and I would sit in the cheap seats and scream our lungs out."

"Favorite player?" Cruz asked.

"Maury Wills," she said. "Fastest feet in the west. Size 9. I knew everything about him."

"Mine was Willie Davis. I swear he had a magic bat."

When the waitress came he ordered thick slices of pizza and a pitcher of beer. Rita interrupted him and said, "No beer for me tonight." Cruz changed the order to some iced teas, and as the waitress walked away, he said, "Any reason for not drinking?"

"Not really," she said. "Any reason for not asking me before you order?"

She lit another cigarette and looked across the table at him, waiting.

"No," he said, flushing red. "I take it you like to order for yourself."

"When it comes to liquor, you bet," she said. "And by the way, I love it when you blush." She flicked some ash off the side of the deck and took a long pull from the cigarette. "Sometimes alcohol and I don't mix. I need to see things real level and clear when I've got a lot on my mind."

"And what's on your mind," he said, "besides a future in the funeral home business and the Dodgers?"

"Tonight." She smiled. "It's been a long time since I've been out on a date, and it's not because I haven't been asked."

"Then why'd you go out with me?"

She set the cigarette in the foil ashtray and leaned back in her chair. "You seemed safe," she said. "But there was something else. I liked listening to you talk about your father and your job. You never condemn anyone, even though they might hurt you or put you down. That's rare. You give people a chance."

They sat quietly for a while, looking down at the river. Cruz didn't know what to say to her in return, but felt an overwhelming sadness slipping over him. Everything about this moment was hopeful. Their talking and the things she said as they tried to get to know each other. Yet he knew it could all end in a flash. It wouldn't take much. A careless sentence or two. The wrong tone of voice. A misunderstanding. Time worked that way. Everything was temporary and could eventually fade. Love. Friendship. All to dust.

The waitress brought the iced teas and pizza and they ate. She talked about her sister who lived back east with her mother and how they used to get together at Christmas and exchange expensive gifts. They talked about their parents, each marriage ending in divorce, and Cruz told her about Frank and little Donna and the letters she wrote from San Diego.

"I act like she's still a baby or something," he said. "Donna's twelve and probably a foot taller by now." He took a sip of his iced tea. "I need to find some time to go visit her. I don't want her to forget she's got a big brother."

"I know what you mean," Rita said. "My sister sends pictures occasionally, but we haven't talked on the phone in over three years. I don't think my mother approves. I was always Daddy's girl, the bad influence."

"I have a hard time believing that," Cruz said.

"Things change," she said. "What about your father? When's he coming back?"

"I don't know. Drying out takes a while."

After they ate, she smoked another cigarette and grew quiet. She seemed tense and he didn't push a conversation. The softball team had left and the deck was clearing. "The water's nice," she said at one point, "soothing." He simply nodded in agreement, wondering what others might think when they saw the two of them together on the back deck. Lovers? Friends? Were they breaking up after a long relationship?

"Are you still up for dancing?" she asked.

"I wasn't sure if you were," he said. "You seem tired."

"Just distracted." She smiled. "Believe it or not, dancing sounds wonderful."

"Don't expect anything fancy."

"It's all in your attitude. If you act like you know what you're doing, then nobody'll know the difference."

"Attitude dancing," he said.

"You got it."

He followed Walker's advice and drove to Don's Crossroads, a biker bar over near Lake Isabella. He'd only been inside once, but had driven by and seen the big Harleys parked outside in a row, their chrome gleaming and polished.

When they arrived, the place was packed with cars and trucks and cycles all crammed into the front lot, so they parked in the alley. Music blared from the side doors. As they walked in, a hot wave of sweat and beer and smoke swept over them. Bikers had taken over the far side of the place, a wall of black leather, chains, and bare flesh. Metal glistened on their fingers or wrists or around their wide necks. Some of the biker women were tattooed, their arms covered with pale markings and symbols. Many of them kept their hair long and braided like a piece of rope that dangled down their backs. Even in the heat, the men wore leather jackets emblazoned on the back with gold and red and yellow logos.

The band was set up on a stage to the left, a cluster of guys wearing cowboy hats who called themselves The Rural Route Rebels. An enormous Confederate flag hung overhead. The dance floor was in the center of the bar and couples were moving together in a steady rhythm.

Cruz felt off balance from the commotion and familiar smells of the place. In many ways, the scene was all too familiar. As a child he'd often been sent by his mother to find Frank and bring him home from the bars. The odors of cigarettes and stale beer, the way the sticky floor made his tennis shoes squeak, the loud voices and sudden jolts of laughter, all of it threw him off guard with a shock of recognition. Most of these places were the same. A wooden bar, some tables and a stage, a few pinball machines set against the walls. But when he was a kid he felt funny walking in, as if he were intruding on some private club where he was not a member.

The bars where Frank hung out were like bad dreams, and it was awkward when Cruz found his old man perched on a stool, his hand on the knee of some strange woman. Cruz never told anyone about the women he saw his father with. He never said anything to Marta. It was like an unspoken code, a secret that men refused to talk about. One evening he'd been out looking for Frank and he passed the Kern Valley Motel and saw him coming out of a room with a blonde he recognized from the bars. He'd watched them get into her car, a beat-up Cadillac, and drive off. Later he'd wanted to use the secret against Frank, use it wickedly somehow to hurt him. But he never did. Kept it inside. *You never condemn anyone,* was what Rita had said.

They found a couple of chairs at a table near the door and Cruz ordered a beer and a Coke. The music was imitation Charlie Daniels and Marshall Tucker, driven by wailing guitar riffs and a thumping bass and interspersed with hoots and screams from the dancers themselves. They sat for a few songs and listened, checking out the crowd and watching the spinning motion on the dance floor. At one point Rita leaned over and said in a loud voice, "Nervous about getting out there?"

"A little," he said. "They're moving pretty fast."

"We can wait for a slower number."

"Sounds good."

"Just remember," she said, "it's all a primitive mating ritual anyway."

Cruz laughed. "Remember that when I stomp on your toes."

A few minutes later she pulled him up from the chair and they made their way through the crowd. It was a slower tune and they stayed on the outer fringe of the large dancing area. Rita tried to teach him a few basic steps, holding both of his hands and tracing out a simple pattern that he could follow and repeat. It was awkward glancing out at the other men, who seemed to swing and twirl their partners with flair and ease, and he felt as if all eyes in the place were trained on him.

"Listen for the bass," Rita said, and they began, her hips swaying as she took the lead and guided him through it. They seemed off balance, bumping shoulders or getting steps crossed as their feet collided, but she was patient with him, laughing after each mistake. He began to pick up the beat while still holding Rita's hands. She swung in next to him so they were hip to hip, slid his hand across her back, and began to alternate a two-step slide to the left, then the right, ending with a final kick. It seemed to go perfectly with the song and Cruz noticed there were other couples on the floor doing the same.

"Where'd you learn how to do this?" Cruz said.

"From my urban cowgirl days," she said. "It's like cutting hair. Once you've done it enough, you never forget."

"I feel like an urban klutz."

"You're doing fine. Just remember to kick."

They stayed with it for another song and Cruz began to relax, his feet in time with the music and his arm nestled around Rita's waist. He loved being close to her, and the sweet, clean scent of her hair and skin made his head swim. When the song ended they made their way through the crowd and back to the table.

As he sat down, Cruz glanced over and saw Walker at the bar, a bottle of whiskey perched in front of him. His head rolled from side to side with the music. "Hold up a minute," he said to Rita. "I see a friend." Walker was about twenty feet away and Cruz shouted his name and waved. He looked up and saw them, then hoisted his shot glass in a salute. Cruz yelled, "C'mon over and join us."

Wobbling a little, he got up from the stool and grabbed the bottle. Almost instantly he collided with three bikers who'd been coming up from behind. One of them held a pitcher of beer and it flew into the air, spilling its contents on the three husky men. They started shoving Walker, surrounding him with their barking faces and pinning him to the bar. Then, in a blur of black leather and chain, they grabbed him by the hair and throat as if he were a stick puppet and quickly ushered him out a side exit as a wall of bikers parted to let them through. The band continued playing without missing a beat and a wave of dancers started up again.

Cruz looked quickly at Rita. "Something's going down outside," he said. "Stay here." He made his way to a nearby door and dashed out of the brightly lit hall into the darkness. Streetlights illuminated the parking lot and he ran around the side of the building to the alley. Turning the corner, he saw them near the metal fence that bordered the back.

They had Walker up against a truck, two of them holding him there while the other flailed at his face and ribs. The truck vibrated from the blows and Cruz could see Walker's face, already smeared with blood, and he could hear the sounds coming from him as they struck again and again. He froze in a panic, looked around for some kind of a weapon, anything he might use to attack with. Then he ran blindly at the pack, flung himself on the back of the nearest assailant, and tried to jerk the biker away with a wrenching headlock. The man was enormous and Cruz could feel the raw stubble of beard against his forearm as he tried to pull him down. An elbow knifed into his side, followed by an explosion against his face and he went down, his cheek raked by cinders in the alley.

He heard running, the slide of feet grinding to a halt. An object hit the ground. Someone twisted his arm, then quickly dropped it. He looked up and saw Rita standing twenty yards away, her purse in the dirt at her feet. At first Cruz thought it was odd that she stood there by herself, a blank look on her face, staring at them. *Get help,* he thought. *Call someone.* Then Cruz saw the gun. The same black revolver she'd pulled at the hot springs. It looked large in her hands, like some big toy, but she dangled it loosely at her side. Cruz thought of old westerns and gunfighters he'd seen on TV, the way innocent bystanders would scatter when John Wayne walked out for a showdown. Only there was no place to run to and Rita was definitely not John Wayne. "Back away," she said firmly.

The first shot came from her hip and it shattered a window of the truck, glass raining down on him. Cruz tried to get up, felt a stab of pain in his ribs and gasped for breath. A heavy boot came down on his back.

"Who the hell are you? Policewoman?" a deep voice said from behind him. Music filtered out of the bar, only he could barely make out the sounds over the ringing in his ears.

"I'll use it," Rita said. "Don't think I won't. Now get away from them."

One of the men, red hair tied back with a bandanna, whirled and charged her like a bull, a flash of steel in his hand. Rita swung the gun upward, supporting it with her free hand, the barrel straight and true. Her arm kicked when she fired and the man was slammed back, a chunk of flesh from his thigh landing in the cinders as he sprawled on the ground. "Bitch!" one of them yelled. "Crazy bitch!"

"You figure it out," she said. "It's all self-defense."

The boot lifted from Cruz's back and he got to his knees, then saw Walker in a heap next to the truck. He scrambled over to help him up. Walker was bleeding from the mouth and forehead. The men had been wearing rings, and his face was peppered with crescent-moon cuts. His breath wheezed out and he held one hand against his ribs. "Get him in the jeep," Rita said.

He supported Walker on his shoulder and dragged him over, then fumbled momentarily with the door before swinging it open. When Walker was in the backseat, he started the engine and swung the jeep around so they faced away from the men. Out the window he saw Rita pick up her purse, then walk toward the vehicle, still holding the gun on the men, who were moving with her, inching closer. "I don't want to be followed," she said.

"You're gonna die!" one of them yelled. "We'll catch you!"

"I seriously doubt it," Rita said.

She fired two quick shots over their heads and Cruz saw the men buckle and dive into the cinders. Then she was in the jeep, shouting for him to drive, and he floored it, accelerating down the alley and onto a side street. He was sweating, the tension breaking on his forehead like a fever. She sat next to him, looking back at the alley, the gun still in her hand.

Cruz drove north at a breakneck pace down more alleys and back roads, the town whirling by in shadows and streetlights. He glanced in the rearview mirror for any sign of followers. Rita climbed in the back with Walker and began to wipe the blood away with a rag. His breathing was heavy and deep like a wounded animal.

"No hospital," Walker mumbled at one point. "No insurance."

A bloodied hand came forward and rested on Cruz's shoulder. It was Rita. "Drive to my place," she said calmly. She'd left the gun on the seat and Cruz looked over and saw it.

"You saved us," he said. "But I can't believe you shot that guy."

"What was I supposed to do," she said from the back. "Ask them to please stop kicking the shit out of you or I was gonna plug them? They deserved it."

"I still can't believe you shot him."

Rita climbed into the front seat and cradled the gun in her lap. Cruz turned onto the Reservoir Road and floored the gas pedal. "Kind of like Bonnie and Clyde," she said. Her tone was flat, emotionless. "Except I'm the only shooter. I'm the one who could've blown their brains out."

"Where'd you learn how to shoot like that?"

"In L.A.," she said. "I took lessons from an old guy who had a firing range in his basement." She took the gun and pushed it into her purse. "I like to shoot."

"That's pretty obvious." Cruz touched the right side of his face and realized it was swollen and puffy.

She grew quiet, looked out the window at the wide expanse of water to the east, then reached over and rested her hand on Cruz's shoulder. "They needed a lesson," she said. "I bet it's been a while since a woman told them what to do."

When they reached her apartment, he parked in the front while she ran to open the door. Then they eased Walker out of the jeep and helped him up the stairs. He was coughing violently but seemed more coherent and aware of what was happening. When she flipped on the lights, her place seemed empty, almost barren, as if decoration was too much effort. A couch, a coffee table with some paperbacks and magazines, a wooden rocker. They put Walker on the couch with a white sheet under him, then Rita went into the bathroom and came back with towels and some first-aid supplies.

A wound had opened over Walker's eye and the blood oozed down his cheek. She started there, holding a damp towel over the cut until the bleeding stopped. Then she cleaned the wounds with hydrogen peroxide. Cruz helped with the bandaging and the compresses. He got ice from the fridge and put it in a plastic bag for Walker to press against his swollen ribs.

Cruz watched Rita as she cared for him. The cool anger he'd seen in the alley behind Don's and on the drive back had been replaced with a look of absolute tenderness. She touched Walker as if he were a sleepy child, gently guiding his hands away as he reached for his face. There was blood clotted in his beard and she washed it out. Cruz thought of the luminous nurse who'd come to him in a dream when he was burning with fever after the river accident. *Angel of mercy,* he said to himself again, staring at Rita and the dark sweep of her hair as it rolled down her back.

"He's gonna be hurting in the morning," she said. "Beer and whiskey are only temporary painkillers."

"He'll never forget this hangover," Cruz said.

Walker stirred, tried to prop himself up on an elbow. His eyes were red and flashed around the room, disoriented. Then he sank back onto the couch.

"You're at my apartment," she said to him. "I'm Rita."

He looked up at her, then at Cruz. Suddenly he smiled. "St. Rita," he said. "St. Rita of the Crossroads." Then he closed his eyes and slept.

Rita turned out the light while Cruz carried the towels and first-aid materials into the bathroom. In the mirror he saw the bruise on his own face, a plum-sized swelling around the right eye. He'd been lucky to only get an elbow in the side and not a steel-toed motorcycle boot that could snap ribs like plastic. His stomach ached and he sat on the toilet and put his head down. "We'll have to keep an eye on him tonight," Rita said from the hall. "Make sure he's okay."

She came in and saw Cruz and knelt down beside him. "I forgot about you, didn't I?" she said. She ran her fingers across his face, then got some ice and wrapped it in a washcloth and gave it to him. They sat in the bathroom for a while as Cruz pressed the icepack against the swelling.

"What time is it?" he said.

She looked at her watch. "After one."

"Are all your dates this exciting?" he asked.

"Hardly."

"It happened so fast. It seems like only a few minutes ago that we were dancing together."

He looked up and saw four perfectly arranged photographs, all framed, hanging on the wall opposite the mirror. They were small black-and-white close-ups of various objects: a piece of driftwood, a sea shell, rusted bars of metal, and the cracked hull of a rowboat.

"Did you take these?" he asked.

"I used to have a 35-millimeter that I played around with. I took them when I was walking on the beach after a storm."

"They look like something you'd see in a museum."

"I wouldn't exactly call them art, but they remind me of the ocean."

The ice stung but he kept it over the bruise, then glanced over and saw the bloodstains on her halter top and jeans. She looked as if she'd been through a war.

"What about the police?" he said. "What will you tell them?"

"Simple self-defense," she said. "But I doubt if they'll come around. I don't think those bikers will admit that some woman shot them up. In any case, the gun has a license. I'm covered."

They got up and moved out into the narrow hall. In the dim light from the bathroom they could see Walker on the couch and listened to his uneven breathing. Cruz stood behind her and placed his hands on her shoulders, then drew her toward him.

"Will he be all right?" he asked, kissing the back of her head.

"I hope so," she said. "I'll check on him later tonight."

She led him down the hall and into a room on the left, then flipped on a light. What he saw made him step back and hesitate before entering. The walls and ceiling were covered with targets from a shooting range. Some were the circular red-and-white bulls-eyes. Others had the upper torso of a man. All were riddled with bullet holes and taped to the plaster like flags on display. One end of the room contained a large table covered with art supplies and paper and books. An easel stood next to it with a drawing tablet propped on the backing.

"You must do a lot of shooting," Cruz said.

"I like to stay in practice." She smiled and walked over to the easel. "You never know when you're gonna need it, right?"

"Right."

He went to the table and saw a number of drawings scattered across the top. On each was the swirling figure of a heron, its wings outstretched and flowing across the surface of the page. Most of the work was in pencil, but a few carried familiar hues of blue and silver and grey that Cruz remembered from the rookery. Each drawing was different yet lifelike, as if the birds might suddenly leap from the paper. Rita had captured the elegant beak and flowing neck, the plume of feathers that arched from the head, even the rippled edges of the wings.

"It's my studio," she said. "I come here to sketch before work and again in the evening."

"These are beautiful," Cruz said, holding up one of the drawings. "It's exactly the way I remember them. I didn't know you were this good. Why didn't you say something the other day?"

"What was I supposed to say? That I'm some great artist who cuts hair for a living?" Her voice had a sarcastic lilt to it and she turned away, took out a cigarette, then walked toward the only window in the room.

"That's not what I meant," he said. "You acted as if you couldn't draw worth a damn."

"That's how it feels sometimes." A hard edge had come into her voice. *Still tough,* Cruz thought. Rita turned to look at him, and for the first time all evening she seemed older and more tired. She began to smoke and sat on the floor, using a glass jar as an ashtray. "Please," she said, patting the carpet next to her. After sitting down, he took her hand and said, "Maybe we both need some sleep."

"I am definitely tired," she said. "But there are some things we need to get straight. Some facts."

"Like what?"

"That I enjoyed tonight."

"What do you mean?"

She cut him off. "I enjoyed shooting that man. It's a fact and it's something I've wanted for a long time. And that night at the hot springs, when we first met? If you'd touched me, I'd have blown your head off."

Cruz leaned away from her, rested against the back wall.

"But you were just defending yourself tonight," he said. "You said it yourself. You saved me and Walker."

"But it's what I wanted. When I saw those men and what they were doing and the way they acted, I wasn't scared. I felt relief. I'd been waiting for that moment." She stopped and motioned at all the targets. "It's what I'd been practicing for. A little revenge."

"But you didn't know those men before we went into that bar."

"No," she said. "But I was raped in L.A. by someone like them." She said it coldly, the words emotionless and detached, then stared down at the carpet.

He waited for her to continue. When she didn't, he said, "I'm sorry. I figured something had happened. But I didn't know how bad."

"I hide it pretty well," she said. "I'm good at that. It's become a kind of art for me. I bet I could hide at Laverne's for another twenty years." Her eyes were red and moist. "You should feel honored," she said, awkwardly smiling. "Other than my father and some police officers, you're the first man I've ever told. And I'm not really sure why I'm telling you, other than I trust you and feel you won't treat me like damaged goods."

"I'm glad you told me," Cruz said. "It means a lot."

"Every morning before I go to work I sit here and look outside — " she waved the cigarette at the window — "and wonder if he knows where I am and how to find me so he can come back and finish the job."

"They didn't catch him?" Cruz asked.

"Not that I know of. There was a series of rapes in Marina del Rey, and suddenly they stopped. The police figured he got scared and took off. I was his last victim."

She paused, looked at the window again, then wrapped her arms around herself as if cold. "It happened in May. I remember the harbor was filled with sailboats in the evening, and how pretty all the red and gold and orange spinnakers looked. I came home late one night after being at a party. I was pretty wasted and fumbled with the key at my door and that's when he jumped me. He was smart because he waited for me to get the door open a crack, and then he got his hand over my mouth." She began to rub her wrists, shaking her head back and forth.

"You don't have to tell me any more," he said.

"But I want to," she said. "You need to know this about me." She paused to press her hands against the carpet. "He was a real pro. He wore a stocking over his head and had a roll of duct tape around each wrist. You could tell he'd done it before, the way he cut the tape with a knife and wrapped it around my mouth and wrists. At one point he sliced open my chin with the blade, then rubbed some of the blood onto the carpet. *So you know I'll use it,* he said to me. Then he dragged me into the kitchen. He wore this sweet cologne, Old Spice, the kind you give your father for Christmas when you're a kid. Every now and then he'd whisper into my ear, *Do you like my scent?* I had a four-room apartment and he raped me in every room. Each time he finished he'd take out a can of red spray paint and use it to trace around the outline of my body, like what you see on TV when there's been a murder. Then he'd kick me in the stomach with his boot and whisper, *This is it, bitch. This is where they'll find your body.*"

Cruz didn't move. Couldn't. He made no effort to comfort or touch her. He listened, his mouth and throat dry. Rita told the story without flinching, her voice cool and detached as if remembering a dream.

"I've never forgotten his voice," she said. "It's been over two years and I can still remember what he sounded like. More of a hiss than anything. If I heard that voice on the street or on the radio, I'd know it immediately. I can't get away from the words he whispered. Words like *cunt* and *whore*. Hate words."

She stopped and looked at him, her eyes taking in the targets on the walls. "That's why I had the gun tonight. That's why I always have the gun. I take it with me everywhere, just in case I ever need it. Some women take tampons and aspirin in their purses. I take my gun."

Cruz sat a foot away and he could see the scar on her chin, a pink slash against her smooth skin.

"Will you hold me again?" she said. "Will you hold me like you did at the rookery?"

He nodded, then leaned close and drew her into his arms. He shut his eyes, tried to focus on her pain, and this time felt no pulling back or hesitation in their embrace. "I won't hurt you," he whispered. "I could never hurt you."

When she finally eased away from him and turned out the light and led him down the hall to her room, he seemed to move through a dream where minutes and hours no longer mattered. He felt welcome here, as if he were a child on some museum tour and he need only pay attention to her signs and gestures in order to understand who she was and why she was doing this. It was her gift.

All the fantasies from the previous nights, all the daydreams, seemed cheap and artificial. He had his own voices to contend with, the voices of Chico and the rest of the men talking about what they had done to women and what women really wanted. But right now, in this moment with Rita, he knew the others were wrong. No come-ons or games or sly one-liners. This was enough.

They sat on the bed in the dark, the only illumination coming from the streetlight outside. "I have something for you," he said. "I'd planned to give it to you earlier." He reached into his pocket and withdrew a white envelope, then took her hand and carefully placed the two pearl earrings into her palm. They glistened in the faint light.

"You didn't have to do this," she said. "They look expensive."

"But do you like them?"

She held them up as if cradling two delicate insects in the palm of her hand. "Of course. They're beautiful." She placed them on the dresser next to the bed. "Moon pearls," she said. Then they lay back and he felt her head on his shoulder and he wanted to make love to her. But his own voice told him it would be wrong, a mistake, that this holding was all she needed right now. An embrace. A trusting to hold her through the night until morning.

* * *

When Cruz awoke, Rita was already in the other room, looking after Walker and changing his bandages. Cruz's face and stomach throbbed and he took some aspirin, then showered. When he emerged from the bathroom, Walker was sitting up on the couch, his face puffy and bruised. The smell of coffee and toast came from the kitchen.

"How you doing?" Cruz said as he sat down in the rocker across from him.

"Hungover and hammered," Walker said. "Like someone took a stapler to my face." He winced, flexed his shoulder, then leaned back onto a pillow. Rita brought over some toast and fruit on a tray and set it between them.

"It's all I had in the fridge," she said. "Coffee'll be ready in a moment."

"Rita," Walker said, "you amaze me. First, you shoot one of the guys that's beating the hell out of me. Then you bandage me up and cook me breakfast. Can I marry you now?"

Rita laughed. "Sorry, I'm already interested in a younger man."

"Ouch," Walker said, clutching at his chest. "A heartbreaker and a ball-buster all rolled into one."

Walker hardly ate anything, and after breakfast, Cruz offered to drive him home. "My wagon's still parked across the street from Don's," Walker said.

"I'll take care of it later," Cruz said. "I'll get one of the crew to help me shuttle it out to your place on Monday."

"Much appreciated." Walker rose slowly from the couch and took a few steps, testing his legs. He grimaced at one point and put a hand out to lean against the wall. "Everything's still a little tender," he said. "All I need is a month in Palm Springs and I'll be good as new."

Rita and Cruz helped him down the stairs and into the jeep. Before they left, Walker reached out through the window and took her hand. "I don't say thanks too often," he said, "but I appreciate what you did. It took guts to stand up to those bikers."

"You owe me one," she said.

"What Rita wants, she gets. You just name it."

"I'll remember that."

Walker looked at her, then turned to Cruz, who was behind the wheel. He laughed and said, "It's funny. Here I am, the old veteran. Shouldn't she be the one who owes me all the favors?"

Rita smiled. "Not necessarily." Then she leaned down and gave Walker a kiss on the cheek.

* * *

Junky was the word that came to mind when Cruz saw Walker's place. He lived over behind Bodfish off a gravel road that climbed steadily up the hillside for miles. "Five acres," Walker told him. "I bought it when I got back from Vietnam, hoping the property value would increase. Now I'm stuck and the price hasn't gone up a cent." It looked more like a compound than a home, and Cruz braked when he came to the web of barbed wire that encircled the perimeter. He climbed out and swung open a rusty metal gate, then drove the jeep through.

A long trailer lay at the center of the property, surrounded on all sides by a sea of chrome. Car bumpers littered the dirt yard in every direction. Some were stacked in piles and shining from the intense sun. But close to the trailer like a cluster of sentries stood an assortment of oddly shaped statues. As they drove into the yard Cruz saw that the sculptures were nearly seven feet tall and made of chrome that had been welded together. Some resembled bodies that were embracing and struggling, arms and legs wrapped together with torsos intertwined.

Cruz stared at the statues.

"Strange stuff, huh?" said Walker.

"I've never seen anything like it," Cruz said.

Walker chuckled. "It's a hobby. I think it adds a little magic to the place."

They climbed out of the jeep. Cruz tried to help Walker but he waved him off. "It's okay," he said, "I can handle it."

A scruffy dog with salt-and-pepper fur came up and sniffed at Cruz's shoe, then scurried under the trailer.

"That's Toby," Walker said. "I got him at the pound in Bakersfield. He's not good for much except killing a rattler now and then, but we've been together a long time. He's a good little amigo."

There were no trees or grass in the yard, only sand and dirt and a few large rocks. *Lunar landscaping,* Cruz thought. An assortment of battered red and yellow kayaks leaned against the trailer. The land was up high and the view east was an eye-catcher. Cruz could see the full panorama of the valley, with its scarves of green that branched out from the river and the dusty brown floor of the desert dominating almost everything.

Cruz walked over to one of the sculptures and ran his hand along the hot surface of the chrome. "How do you make them?" he said as Walker shuffled up from behind.

"I love to weld and I put them together piece by piece. I pick up the chrome at junkyards and from wrecks we get called out on. It's just a matter of eyeballing it as you go. I weigh each piece before welding it on and make sure the thing's not gonna go lopsided on me and dump over." Cruz could see his reflection in the chrome. Walker laughed. "I'm inspired by auto accidents. This one's titled *Reflections of Roadkill* because I got most of the metal off a '67 T-bird that hit a deer up in the high country. That one over there," he said, pointing at a statue to the side of the trailer, "I call it *Hog Heaven*. All the chrome came from smashed Harleys that I picked up down in the canyon."

"I like it," Cruz said. "It's like something out of a science fiction movie."

"Right. Picasso goes to Pluto." Cruz circled the statue, then Walker said, "The sun's getting to me and I'm feeling a little dizzy. C'mon inside." Cruz followed him into the trailer. The interior was dim and shadowy until Walker popped open some blinds. The carpet was worn away in places, and there were kayak paddles and helmets scattered across it. Bright, kaleidoscopic pictures hung on the cheap wood paneling. *Sixties art,* is what Cruz thought of. Swirling watercolors that looked to him like paint being flushed down a toilet. Some pinup calendars of naked women lounging in hammocks and on motorcycles were also on the walls.

Walker eased himself down onto the couch. "Grab a seat," he said.

"I can't stay long," Cruz said, sitting down. "I've got some things to take care of back in Isabella."

"No problem. Take off when you need to."

There was a coffee table in front of Cruz with a framed picture of Walker and a woman. His hair and beard were shorter, and he had his arm around her. They were smiling and in the background Cruz could see the river. She was blond and pretty, shorter than he was, and seemed to be in her early thirties.

"Your girlfriend?" Cruz asked, pointing at the picture.

"Ex-girlfriend," Walker said. "We broke up last winter after living together for a while."

"That's too bad," he said.

"Probably for the best. She was an emergency room nurse over at the hospital. She wanted to get married and move to L.A. I wasn't interested."

"What was her name?"

"Nancy," Walker said. "She left town right before Christmas and went south. I got a letter in the spring saying she was working at some ritzy hospital in Orange County. She's happy. It's what she wanted and I'm glad for her. Things don't always work out."

"I guess," Cruz said.

A long silence followed. Walker lifted his right leg and set it gently on the coffee table.

"I saw Crawdad the other day," Cruz said. "I took the raft over to him and we patched it up. It's good as new." Walker nodded and smiled.

"Those old military rafts are tough as hell," Walker said.

"Crawdad said he's gonna retire from the Forest Service," Cruz continued. "He told me the accident took something out of him."

"It's about time he got some sense."

Cruz leaned forward in the chair. "He wanted me to ask you something." He hesitated, then laughed nervously. "He said you'd probably tell him to go to hell but I should ask anyway." Walker was silent. Cruz heard the dog bark, then the wind pushing against the trailer. "Crawdad wants to do a river trip on the upper Kern. He says he wants to run it before he settles down. I'm thinking about going." Outside the dog continued to bark in shrill bursts. "He wanted me to ask you to come with us."

Walker smiled. "You don't learn too fast, do you?" he said.

Cruz looked away, stared through the screen door at the dust kicking up outside. "I'm just asking," he said.

"He almost got you killed once, didn't he? Wasn't that enough?"

"It was an accident," Cruz said. "Boats flip sometimes."

Walker shook his head and scowled. "I tried to warn you about him. He can't be trusted."

"What happened between you two anyway?" Cruz asked. "Crawdad told me that something happened a long time ago and never got settled."

Walker glared at him, swung his leg down hard off the table, then grabbed at his side and cursed. He ignored the question, saying, "The upper Kern is big-time water. I've kayaked sections of it before, and if you fuck up, there aren't any roads or ambulances or rescue squads to haul you out. You're on your own. There's rapids up there that'll curl your hair."

"That's why we need your kayak," Cruz said. "In case something goes wrong."

"If something goes wrong, that little kayak won't do shit. I might be able to pull one of you out, but not both. And you can forget about the raft." Walker coughed, glanced away from him with a sour look on his face.

"At least think about it," Cruz said. He paused, got up from the chair and went to the door. Walker didn't move, his head resting on the back of the couch. "He's not crazy," Cruz said, continuing. "He's changed since the accident. If you talked with him now, you'd see."

"Why do you trust him?" Walker asked.

Cruz stood in the doorway and looked out at the yard. "I'm not sure I do completely. I've had my moments of doubt, believe me." He turned and faced Walker. "But I owe him for teaching me about the river. He's pushed me to do things I never thought I could do. And for the first time in my life I'm good at something."

"Is it that simple?"

"No," Cruz said. "Nothing's ever that simple."

Walker got up from the couch and walked to the door. Cruz started to leave. "I'll call you," Cruz said, pushing open the screen and stepping outside. Then he felt Walker's hand on his arm. The grip was strong, viselike, and he turned to face him.

"There's something else. Crawdad's gonna bring it up sometime, but I want you to hear it from me first."

"What?" Cruz asked.

"There was a time when Crawdad and I were tight," Walker said, his voice flat and emotionless. "But that was a long time ago when we worked the hooks."

Cruz waited, then said, "You mentioned that when I met you."

"I know," Walker said, sitting down on the outside steps. "Then something happened. A woman died. This was over ten years ago."

"Who was she?" Cruz asked.

"Her name was Rose. She worked behind the bar at the Shady Grove. Crawdad and I used to hang out there after work."

"She died — ?"

"She drowned in the Kern," Walker said, interrupting him. "She fell off the Johnsondale Bridge one night. Crawdad pulled her out with the hooks the next day." Cruz let the screen door swing shut, then sat down next to Walker.

"How well did you know her?" Cruz asked.

"We'd been seeing each other for a while, but things hadn't worked out, so I broke it off." Walker coughed, a pained expression on his face. "Rose and Crawdad were real close. He used to get drunk and call her his long-lost daughter. Shit like that. And when she died, he took it hard. Said it wasn't an accident at all, but a suicide. The old guy blamed me and said I'd driven her to it when I broke things off."

"And that's when it all started between you and Crawdad?" Cruz asked.

"He refused to work with me after that," Walker said. "The whole thing with Rose made him crazy. A few months later I joined up in the army and got the hell out of town. Then Vietnam came along."

Cruz closed his eyes and pictured the old man dragging the woman from the river. *She's beautiful,* Crawdad had said to him when they'd stood over the drowned girl in the spring. *Like a rose,* he'd said. Or had it been *like Rose?*

He got up from the steps and walked out into the yard. The sun was intense and he shaded his eyes as he looked back at Walker.

"Thanks for telling me," he said.

"No problem," Walker said. "I wanted you to hear my side before Crawdad talked to you." He got up and opened the trailer door, preparing to go back in.

"Tell me something," Cruz said, stopping Walker on the porch. "Did you love her?"

Walker smiled. "Yeah," he said, his lips curved in an odd grin. "I remember Rose. She was my first."

"So why'd you break things off?"

He laughed. "It sounds stupid, but she loved me too much. The whole thing scared the hell out of me." His hand rested against the doorway and he stared down at his boots, pausing for a long while. Finally he glanced up at Cruz and said, "Thanks for the ride and all your help, especially last night. You didn't have to come after me and take on those bikers."

Cruz smiled and said, "You would've done the same."

"You're right," Walker said. "Absolutely."

He closed the inside door and left Cruz alone in the yard. Cruz stood there for a while, studying the chrome sculptures that sparkled in the late morning sun like huge silver pawns. Then he got into his jeep and drove back to town.

CHAPTER EIGHT

He called Rita early on Sunday and they arranged to go to the rookery in the afternoon. The rest of the morning was a blur as he pushed out any thoughts of Walker and Crawdad or the bikers Rita had shot at. *What if they got a good look at the jeep?* he thought. *What if they saw the license plate?* He tried to keep busy. He washed the jeep, then walked over to Safeway to buy a little food for lunch. He bought soft rolls, some meats and cheeses, a few apples. At the liquor store he found small bottles of wine that would fit neatly into a cooler. *She'll like that,* he thought. *Elegant.*

Back at the trailer he slipped on a Hawaiian shirt that Frank had bought for his birthday last year. He'd almost forgotten it was in his closet, folded neatly on the back shelf. The fabric had a swirling pattern of bright red parrots and green palm trees. It was bolder than anything he usually wore, and he tried to save it for special occasions. When he looked in the mirror it made him appear different, like a rich college boy on his way to the beach to meet friends and surf. *No more Señor Drab.* His life could be different now. With Rita, he felt confident that anything was possible and all he had to do was take charge. The shirt glowed with possibilities.

* * *

She whistled from the steps when he picked her up at the apartment.

"Nice shirt," she said. "Are you making a fashion statement?"

"I'm just trying to improve my image," he said.

"I like it. You look dashing."

She swung into the jeep, then pressed her feet up against the glove compartment. Cruz turned on the radio and they listened to a Bakersfield rock station as they drove along the river. At one point he asked, "Has anyone contacted you from the police?"

"Not a soul," Rita said. "I'll stay put in Kernville and away from Lake Isabella for a while. Keep a low profile and let some time pass."

"That sounds like a plan."

Cruz didn't say anything more. It was probably best not to push the conversation, give her a little room. If she wanted to talk about it, she would. Sunlight and a dry wind filled the air as they drove. She rested her hand on the back of his neck and talked about going to San Francisco to visit a friend who lived near Golden Gate Park. Cruz listened, the images of restaurants and museums and glass skyscrapers dazzling and clear in his mind.

"The weather stays so cool in the city," she said. "Nights are heavenly."

By the time they parked and hiked down to the clearing, the sun overhead was blazing. They found some shade and spread out a blanket, then made sandwiches and sipped the wine. Cruz lay back and rested his head on the small pack they'd brought the food in. He stared up at the trees and marveled at how straight they grew, like ancient towers of the forest, their reddish bark in contrast with the clusters of green pine branches. Closing his eyes he listened for the whirling rush of the river and picked it up within seconds. There was a certain comfort and reliability in that sound. He knew he could come back to this place anytime and still hear the Kern in the distance, steady and constant in its motion.

At one point he looked over at Rita, took a long sip from his bottle and said, "Do you see yourself as being brave?"

"Not really," she said.

"I think you are. What you did the other night took bravery."

"I'm not sure I'd call it that," she said. "I didn't really have a choice. I knew what I had to do."

"It still took guts."

She set her sandwich down and looked in the direction of the river.

"Running from L.A. wasn't brave. I was terrified and needed to escape and that's exactly what the rapist wanted. That's what he gets off on, knowing he left a scar."

"How does it feel now?" Cruz asked. "Do you still want to take off?"

"Sometimes," she said. "But that's the easy way out and I know it. I'm not going to run from him anymore."

Cruz reached over and took her hand and she turned to look at him.

"I guess we've both been through a lot," she said. "It's time we got some breaks, don't you think?"

"Definitely," he said.

She put her sandwich down and leaned over and kissed him. He could taste the sweet wine on her lips, and while they kissed he brought his hand up and touched her face. Everything around them was still, as if the world had taken a long breath and was waiting to exhale. He tried to memorize the smallest details in her features. The dark tendrils of her eyelashes. The gentle flare of her nose and its soft tip. The smooth curve of cheek and neck. The scent of skin lotion and pine and earth all swimming together in his head. Her body slid over him, weight pressing down, until leg and hip and breast seemed fused with his own, of one mold, as if they were made of clay and she'd left her imprint upon him.

No need to rush. She took the lead, unbuttoning her shirt so he could slide his hands along the back and trace the curve of her spine. She slid his shirt off, then kissed neck and shoulder and chest, her tongue moving in a swirl over his stomach, her hands sliding down his legs. He remembered what Crawdad had said about a woman's hands, and he thought it was beautiful the way she touched him, fingers stroking his skin like a brush.

He was flushed and warm, the heat moving through his head. He thought of Chico talking about *pussylicking* and *buttfucking* and suddenly grew terrified, unsure of what he wanted and afraid that he might hurt Rita. His arms stiffened and he looked up at her and she smiled. A bead of sweat trickled down his forehead and she wiped it off.

"Are you frightened?" he whispered.

She looked at him, her face only inches away. "A little," she said. "But I trust you. I know you won't hurt me." She reached out and ran a warm hand over his cheek.

Cruz felt her confidence, the way she looked at him and held his gaze with her clear eyes. There was still fear, a wanting to hold back and play it safe and think about all that could go wrong between them. But in her words and the way she looked at him, he felt cleansed of Chico's crude talk and of being afraid, and he knew that he loved her and that she wanted him.

"We could go down to the river," she said. "It's cooler there. We could go for a swim."

He nodded and they got up and walked in the direction of the Kern. At one point he stopped and they kissed for what seemed like minutes. She smiled at him and said, "Do you know how long you've been smiling? At least five minutes nonstop."

He laughed. "It feels that way. My face is starting to hurt."

They reached the riverbank and found a place to swim. It was an eddy pool, maybe four to five feet deep, where the water cut around a rock and then recirculated back upstream to form a calm pocket. The main current slipped around the edges of the pool in a slow glide. They took off the rest of their clothing. He'd only undressed one other woman before and had nearly forgotten what it was like to slide off the shorts and underwear, revealing a beautiful diamond of dark hair between her legs. They stood naked by the pool, shyly dipping their feet into the water. His arm was around her waist and she stared down at the river, watching some Jesus bugs skim across the surface.

Then he sensed an abrupt change in her breathing, a sudden hitch that caught him off guard. She pulled away and stood off to the side with her back to him. The awareness that they were not alone startled him, hit him like a knife sliding under his skin. Rape was in the air. He tried to go inside her head, imagine what she might be thinking. He felt desperate to understand what was happening right now in her mind. Could she still feel the stranger's breath on her neck? Had he tried to kiss her through the mesh of the stocking?

He draped a shirt over her shoulders. She was shaking and he put his arm around her.

"I thought I was ready for this," she said.

"It's okay," he said. "We can take our time."

She looked up at him. "I love being with you. It's been a long time since I felt this way. And it's not that I don't want to be here."

"I know," Cruz said.

They stood in the sun, leaning against a smooth granite boulder and she rested her head on his shoulder. Cruz watched shadows lengthen over the river, saw a white ripple of foam turn grey. Time passed. He wasn't sure how long they stood there. A few minutes, maybe a half hour. There were many times he started to say something but then stopped. He was willing to wait.

"It's hard to put into words," she finally said. "There's this part of me that was never raped, that he never touched. It's all I've got left. It's the part of me that draws and comes to watch the herons and wants to make love. But before I can show you that, I've got to be absolutely sure you won't steal it." She looked downstream for a moment. "I have nothing left after that. Nothing."

There was a change in the light and a gold streak of sun flashed across her hair and cheek and Cruz wished he could've taken a picture right then. He wanted to show her the beauty in that face.

"It's amazing," he said. "When I first met you down at the hot springs and we talked later at Laverne's, I thought you were one of the toughest women I'd ever met."

"Why were you interested?" Rita asked.

"Because there was a side of you I couldn't see and I wanted to. It's the side I see now."

She bit her lower lip and ran a hand through her hair. "The tough part was easy," she said. "I never used to be that way. I was this sweet kid who didn't have a clue that a man could push you into an apartment, rape you senseless, and then get away with it." Her eyes jumped as she spoke, flashing anger. "But I learned about violence. I learned that if I was going to survive, I'd have to do something with all the anger. Otherwise I'd drown in it and never set foot outside my door again. So I bought a gun and learned how to use it. I took self-defense classes and started weight lifting and running. I was in training for the next time somebody tried to attack me."

Her fists were clenched and she tapped them against the firm surface of the rock. "But the hardest thing," she said, her voice cracking, "the hardest thing of all is dealing with the lie in my head. When he sodomized me, it reached a point where the pain was too much. I had to go someplace in my mind, somewhere it didn't hurt. So I thought of the rookery and the herons and being there with my father. It was like I left the room to go somewhere else for a while until the pain was gone. It was a lie, but it saved me."

She stopped, her lower lip trembling, and started to cry. She tugged the shirt down over her breasts. "Only later it was like I didn't want to admit I'd been raped, like it hadn't happened to me. It happened to the woman in that apartment with the tape on her mouth and wrists. The woman I abandoned and left behind." She paused and looked over at him. "But she came back the other night in that alley. She pulled the trigger."

Cruz touched her shoulder. "I don't know how to love you," he said. "I only know that I do. But sometimes I feel like you don't want me around, that you'd rather be left alone."

"You're doing fine," she said. "You ask questions and listen. You brought me here. That's what I need more than anything."

She slipped the shirt off, then reached up and placed a finger on his lips, quieting him as they stepped into the water. His hands stroked her back, the inside of her thighs. She cupped water in her hands and poured it over his head. At first he was embarrassed by his hardness, how it poked at her and came between them. But then she slid her hand down across his chest and stomach and gripped him there, easing him back onto the mossy bank, her fingers tightening, and he closed his eyes as she moved her other hand through his hair. She stroked him, her hand sliding in a steady rhythm, and he heard the river and her breath next to his ear. It was like being underwater and feeling the slow lung burn, then suddenly breaking the surface to pull in the air, his breathing rapid-fire and quick. Muscles tightened and he felt a great pressure building inside his chest and shoulders and legs, an electricity that grew intense and hot and swept over him. Then a release, a tight knot suddenly popping free, and he was spurting into her hand as she stayed with him, brought him out of it with a rush, the sky spinning overhead.

He washed off in the river, then stopped to watch her lying on the bank. After a few seconds he began to laugh. "We're zebras," he said, pointing at their tan lines.

She got up from the bank and came to him while he stood in the pool. He noticed the firmness of her legs and thighs. Sunlight dappled the water and he felt the heat of the air merging with the river's chill. A heron flew overhead and they watched its flight upstream until it vanished around the far bend.

"I want to make love with you," she said. "I really do. But I can't right now. I still need time."

He hesitated, then kissed her shoulder. "It's all right," he said. "I can wait." He picked up her clothes and brought them to her. They dressed, then gathered the rest of their belongings and headed up the trail. All the way back to the jeep, Cruz felt as if he were glowing from the inside, a warmth that radiated out from his body. He wondered if Rita could see it and notice a change in the color of his skin or the temperature of his palms. He tried to remember everything about that moment. The way the small birds soared above the branch tops. How the path was littered with feathers, and the wind carried the dry, burnt smell of summer. He took it all in as if memory were something to be inhaled, absorbed, and never lost.

They returned to her apartment. Cruz hesitated in the doorway, but Rita took his hand and led him into the room. She kept the windows open, shades pulled up so that light streamed in and made the rooms sunny and bright. They undressed each other and left their clothes neatly folded by the bedroom door, then went to her bed and threw back the sheets so nothing covered them. They lay down together, the taste and smell of her staying with him.

While she slept, her head nestled against his shoulder, he lay awake and listened to the sound of her breathing, the rise and fall against his chest. He thought of an empty trailer in Lake Isabella, an empty bed, and at that moment he seemed unable to remember anything about the rooms or the furniture or the people that had once lived there.

* * *

Cruz went to work on Monday. Rita got up early with him, fixed some juice and eggs and toast, and they ate quietly at the kitchen table. When they said goodbye on the porch outside her door, she playfully reached for his belt and pulled him close.

"I feel like I'm in some dream," she said. "A lot happened yesterday."

"Yeah," he said, grinning. "What would Laverne say?"

She laughed. "Don't worry. I won't tell a soul at the shop about any of this. I don't want any *scandal.*"

"Thank God," he said. "I wouldn't want Laverne calling me on the phone and begging for a date."

She kicked him with her bare foot and he winced.

"I guess we could call in sick," she said.

"I'd like to, but I need to work. Money calls."

She sighed. "The voice of responsibility calls. You're no fun." Then she reached up and put her arms around his shoulders. "Take care today," she said. "Be careful." They embraced and he felt her hands slide around his neck.

"I'll call you tonight," he said.

"I know you will," she said, smiling.

* * *

Walker was absent from work that day. *Probably too damn hungover,* Lou said. Cruz remained silent, waiting to see if anyone had heard about the shooting Friday night. There were no comments from the other men as they climbed into the truck and headed out. They spent the rest of the day on some landscaping work over near the park headquarters in Kernville. *Cake job,* as Chico liked to say. But as Cruz planted bushes and dug postholes, he thought of Rita and all that had taken place the day before. It seemed as if, for the first time in his life, something was happening that was real and natural, and the way he'd always pictured falling in love with a woman.

He took a nap when he got home from work and fell asleep on the couch without even taking a shower. He wanted to feel rested when he talked with Rita on the phone later. But when he awoke, it was dark outside and someone was hammering on the trailer door. He cursed, realized that he'd overslept, then went to answer it.

It was Lou. His truck was still running in the driveway, its headlights beaming onto the tattered paint of the trailer. He seemed out of breath, huffing a little as if he'd been running.

"We've got a situation," he said. "Some car jumped the guardrail doing about sixty down in the canyon. It landed in a nasty place smack in the middle of a rapid. The car's wedged against a rock."

"When did it happen?" Cruz asked.

"I just got the call and I'm headed down there now. We could use your help."

Cruz ducked back into the trailer and grabbed his boots, a sweatshirt, and a pair of work gloves. As he slid into Lou's truck, he felt it lurch, cinders grinding under the tires. They drove most of the way in silence while Lou chain-smoked a couple of cigarettes down to the nubs.

"We might need you to go out on a line to the car," he said to Cruz. "Walker didn't answer my call, and the others can hardly do a goddamn pull-up."

Cruz hesitated. *Take care today,* Rita had said to him this morning. "I can do that," he said. He knew the traverse procedure and had practiced it with Walker and Crawdad and some of the other men earlier in the spring on a calm section of the lower Kern. They'd anchored a rope to the bumper of a truck on one side of the river, then to a big tree on the far shore. After setting up a pulley system and yanking the line firm, like a tightrope, they'd taken turns going out, hand over hand, connected to the rope with carabiners. It had only been a quickie practice run, a one-day shot, just like some of the other training they'd received. *In one ear and out the other,* Walker had whispered to him then, pointing at Chico and the others as they horsed around, dangling limply from the rope. *This don't mean shit to them.*

Cruz could tell Lou was edgy by the way he handled the truck, accelerating as he sped around the sharp bends in the road. At one point, as they came across a narrow bridge, he swerved into the other lane and narrowly avoided an oncoming car. "Guess I better slow down," he said. "Otherwise we'll be the ones who need rescuing."

When they arrived at the accident scene Cruz saw a county sheriff's truck and some of the highway patrol cars, their roof lights twirling with red and blue flashers. There were a few vehicles that belonged to men on the crew who had been on call for night work. He saw Ramirez and Smitty and Brozier down by the river hauling in a rope. Roadblocks and flares had been set out and the traffic was already starting to back up in the canyon in a procession of headlights. The trucks and police cars were turned so their high beams and spotlights illuminated the river. Cruz felt his stomach twist and tighten when he saw the whitewater.

It was a staircase rapid, steep and violent and choked with boulders. *Not a good place,* Cruz thought. *Nasty.* Foam spit into the air in the harsh light, and he saw the car, bathed in a white glow and pushed sideways against an enormous slab of rock. The front part of the vehicle jutted into the air like a small, sinking boat, while frothy current slammed into the upstream side, kicking up spray. The lights flashed off the partially submerged back windshield, and Cruz saw that it was cracked but unbroken. A deputy from the Sheriff's Department was training a floodlight on the car, playing it back and forth on the windows. "I know I saw it," he said as they approached. "Something moved inside there, dammit."

They'd already made a crossing upstream and had a heavy rope spanning the river. It hung taut directly above the trapped vehicle. He and Lou hurried over to a cluster of men huddled by a patrol car. A radio squawked with static and voices from the interior. The deputy who had held the floodlight was describing what he'd seen to the others. "It's worth checking out," a policeman said, "but we don't have much time."

"What'll it be?" Ramirez said to Lou.

Lou had a troubled look on his face and he turned to Cruz.

"Can you do this for me?" he said to him. "If Walker were here — "

Cruz hesitated, looked around at the circle of men, at Ramirez and the others, their sagging bellies hanging like sacks over their belts. "I'll go out," he finally said.

"Just do some checking," Lou said. "Don't try to be a hero. If we need some hotshot diver to go in, we can always call Bakersfield."

Cruz nodded, then went over to Lou's truck and readied himself in the glare of the headlights. He buckled on a battered orange safety helmet and tugged the chin strap tight, then clipped on a life jacket. The rest of the gear was simple and light. A climbing harness made of nylon webbing with metal carabiners attached that slipped around his waist and thighs like a diaper. A small walkie-talkie that fastened to the life jacket. A utility belt with a hammer and flashlight and knife. Cruz checked the blade and found it razor sharp. His mouth felt parched, and he thought of Rita sitting in her apartment, waiting for his call.

When he'd pulled his gloves on and was ready, they walked down to the rope and signaled the others on the far side. "I can hear you with the walkie-talkie while you're out there," Lou said. "We should be able to tell from the shore if anything's moving inside, or if the car's shifting."

"Okay," Cruz said. "Keep the line tight. I don't want to go swimming here."

"You bet," Lou said, gripping his arm.

Cruz said nothing, his breath short and quick now. He reached up, clipped the carabiners onto the main rope, and tried to push the roaring sound of the rapid from his mind. *Spiderman,* he thought. *Just like Spiderman.*

Suddenly a car braked to a halt on the pull-off above them. It was Walker's wagon, the kayak lashed to the top. He stumbled out, jerking around in a helter-skelter manner, the bandages still on his head and face. Then he saw Cruz and the others down by the river and came running. He was out of breath, sweating, when he approached.

"Where the hell you been?" Lou said. "Some damn dogfight?"

Walker ignored him, looked at Cruz, then out at the car in the river.

"This is no good," he said. "If anybody's still alive inside there, it's a miracle." He winced and rubbed a hand across his battered cheek.

"You shouldn't be here," Cruz said.

Walker smiled. "What's the deal? You trying to earn a little overtime working nights?"

"I can handle this."

Walker coughed, held a hand to his ribs. "I'm in no mood to argue. You're in a helluva lot better shape than I am right now." He reached out and gently tugged at one of the carabiners. "I'll be downstream in my boat. I'm not too banged up to run safety. If anything goes wrong or if you come off that line, I'll fish you out."

Cruz looked at him and swallowed, then reached out and grabbed hold of the rope. The line's tension vibrated through his hands as he pulled himself upward, letting the carabiners and harness support the weight momentarily. He swung his feet up so his crossed ankles straddled the line, then felt the rope sag and sway as he hung upside down and began to slowly work his way, hand over hand, out to the car.

He felt dizzy at first, all the lights flashing in his eyes and the roar of the river growing as he moved out over the dark pit of water. Spooky stuff. The line was bending even more, dipping down so that he dangled only six feet above the surface. "Pace yourself," Lou said over the walkie-talkie, "take your time." It was hard work, gravity tugging at the tools around his waist. He stopped to rest and stared up at the night sky, his arms slack, no bend in the elbows, no sign of cramping in the hands. He counted stars while waiting for his breath to slow and thought, *I'm a damn bat,* then moved on. A wave of icy air rose up from the water to chill his back. The line trembled in his hands. The smell of troutstink was everywhere.

Within ten minutes he was directly above the boulder, its surface wet and shiny. "You're there," the radio squawked, "right on top of it. What can you see?" The battered hood of the car jutted up from the river like a crooked steeple, the front windshield cracked but still intact and revealing a black cavity within. Cruz hung by one arm and unclipped the flashlight, then twisted around to shine the high-powered beam down toward the interior. He was five feet above the car, and foam spray kicked up where the river slammed into the side of the vehicle, creating an arc of water that spouted into the air.

Suddenly Cruz saw a hand pressed against the windshield and he could make out fingers, a palm, then a fist pounding on the glass. "There's somebody in there," he yelled into the walkie-talkie. He swung his legs down from the rope and eased onto the arched pinnacle of the rock below. The surface was slick and mossy and he tested his footing first before unclipping from the rope. He found that his boots held firm, so he popped off the carabiners and crouched low on the boulder.

"Watch your step," Lou said. "This is no place to fall in."

He slid down the face of the rock until his boot wedged against the side door. He expected to hear screaming, someone yelling from within. But the only sound came from the river and the great roar that surrounded him. The car seemed to vibrate and shift when a surge of water rolled into it. He flashed the light through the window and saw a shoulder, the back of a man's neck, his head crushed against the steering wheel, his blond hair matted with blood. Cruz jerked quickly away, stumbled on the wet rock and nearly fell into the river. They must have seen him from shore because the walkie-talkie exploded with Lou's voice. "What's going on? Did you find someone?"

Cruz caught himself, his head spinning. "Yes," he said breathlessly. "There's a body in the front. There could be others in the back seat." He moved to a side window and shined the light in and saw a faint silhouette through the glass. Then the fist appeared again, beating on the window and Cruz bolted upright. "I can see someone," he yelled over the roar, "I'm going in." Lou's voice sounded different, steady, as if coming from a great tower overhead. "Walker's in place," he said.

A web of cracks had already split the glass. When Cruz brought the flat steel head of the hammer down, he was surprised at the kickback. He shielded his eyes, lifted the hammer up again and slammed it into the window. It shattered, raining glass shards on his legs and leaving a space wide enough to crawl through. He peered inside with the light and saw the waterline as the car filled with the river. Then he heard a low moan, deep and guttural, the voice of something hurt and dying. Pivoting the light toward the sound, he saw a young boy clinging to the front seat, blood trickling down his cheek from a forehead gash. His eyes were red and terrified, like some cornered animal waiting to be beaten.

There was a sudden movement, followed by the sound of steel scraping against rock. The car was shifting, and he could feel the swell of the river sucking it under. Cruz went in after the boy, elbows and knees catching on shards of glass. He reached the child within seconds and swept him up in his arms, then felt the sickening motion of the car peeling off the rock, tilting on its side, and flipping.

As they went over, Cruz filled his lungs with air before the water flooded in. He dove for the broken side window where he'd entered, gripped the child to his chest in a bear hug, and rammed through the remaining glass with his helmet. The top of the window raked across his back and shoulder but he pulled free, then pushed off the metal side and kicked for the surface. The life jacket propelled him upward into the glare of the spotlights. Gasping for air, he tried to hold the child with one arm, but felt the weight sucking him downstream. The boy clawed at his neck in a panic, strangling him, and Cruz blindly stroked for shore.

A sudden streak of color flashed to his right, and he saw Walker pivot the cockpit of the yellow kayak in front of them, the back end within reach. A loop of rope dangled from the pointed stern and Cruz grabbed it, then felt the river accelerate, dropping away beneath him. A wave blasted his face and broke over him. The boy had gone limp in his arms and Cruz tried to keep the child's head above the surface, but the water was exploding around them. He could see Walker paddling furiously for shore, dragging them along, his red helmet steady and erect. Suddenly the shore loomed out of the darkness and Cruz lunged for the grey outline of a rock. He clung to it, his arms burning, and for a moment the current tried to rip him loose as his chest heaved against the stone. But he hung on, lifted the boy over his shoulder, and scrambled to safety.

When they were clear of the river, he laid the child on a smooth granite slab and huddled over him. Cruz was shaking and disoriented as he coughed out water, unsure about where the others were or which side of the river they were on. The boy was young, maybe five or six at most, and his dark hair was pasted down over his ears and forehead. Cruz studied the chest, watched for any signs of breathing, then tried to remember what they'd taught about mouth-to-mouth in the first-aid course. But it was all happening so fast, blurring together.

Moving quickly, Cruz propped one hand under the boy's neck and tilted his head back, then forced two quick breaths into the open mouth. The chest puffed up, then lay still. He started again, giving a breath every five seconds *or is it seven* and tried to pace himself *come back to me* because his chest was still on fire from the swim *I need to see your eyes again. Alive.* It went on like this for minutes as Cruz breathed air into the child, rested, then breathed again as if trying to coax a glowing ember into flame.

He fixed an image in his head and focused on it. *A pump,* he thought, *all power and churning air. Electric lungs.* He watched the chest for the slightest fluttering, as if a butterfly might be raising its wings under the boy's shirt. Suddenly Walker was there and kneeling across from Cruz. "We can trade off," he said, then bent to give a breath. Cruz concentrated on where the air was going, and how it might push through to the lungs. At one point he wanted to slap the boy and force him to awaken. *No more dead,* he wanted to scream. *No more dead faces.*

The child suddenly coughed, nearly spit something into Cruz's mouth, then began to choke. Walker turned the boy on his side and they watched as he vomited water onto the rocks. Cruz had never thought that someone so small could hold so much, but the water spilled out as if pouring from a tap. And when the child was finished he leaned back and rested his head against Cruz's shoulder. Walker wrapped a jacket around him. "I'll find the others," he said, then dashed away.

Cruz held the boy close and tried to warm him with his own body. *What should I say?* he thought. The child's eyes were open wide and looked up at him. His thin face and hollow cheeks were shaking from the cold. Cruz wiped away the blood on his forehead. "It's okay," he said to him. "We're safe. You're gonna be fine. Nothing can hurt you now." He stopped and pulled the boy close. The child leaned into him, his head nestled against Cruz's chest like a tiny ship seeking safe harbor, and they waited next to the river for the others to arrive.

When they finally came for the boy and wrapped him in blankets and led him away to a nearby ambulance, Cruz continued to sit by the water. Lou and some of the others came up to shake his hand and congratulate him.

"Damnedest thing I ever saw," Lou said. Cruz felt jumpy as he sat next to Walker, and his hands and legs were trembling.

"Don't sweat it," Walker said, resting a hand on his shoulder. "I used to get the shakes after combat all the time. The adrenaline's gotta go somewhere."

Cruz let Walker drive him home after the boy was taken away. He sat quietly in the station wagon and thought about the dead father, how he'd be zipped up in plastic and driven to the hospital. An autopsy would be done. "The victim was killed instantly from massive trauma to the head and upper extremities." Cruz knew these things. His work had taught him the precise vocabulary of death.

At one point Walker pulled out a bottle of whiskey from under the seat and passed it to him. "I'd say you could use a shot of this," he said. Cruz took a long drink, then gave it back. "Are you all right?" Walker asked. "You're awful quiet."

"No, just tired," Cruz said. "All I need is a little sleep."

"Hell, you deserve a week off."

"Tell that to Lou," Cruz said.

"Damn right," Walker said. "Fucking Houdini couldn't have done any better."

Cruz smiled and said, "I'm glad you were down below in your kayak. I don't think I could've made it otherwise."

"My pleasure. Hell, I figured it was payback time for saving my ass at Don's." Walker took another long swig from the bottle. "We gotta stick together when things get heavy. It's the only way."

Later, after Walker had dropped him off and he'd showered and changed out of the wet clothes, he went into his dark room and sat on the edge of the bed. He thought of the boy again and the look of terror in his eyes when Cruz had first seen him inside the trapped car. Would he remember that moment, how Cruz had come in through the window and carried him away? Or would he hide it someplace in his mind so he wouldn't have to remember. *Just nightmares.* Cruz knew the secret to not remembering. Turn the pain into something else. Something sweet and faceless. Then let go of it as easily as releasing a balloon and watching it sail out of sight.

CHAPTER NINE

Cruz stayed home the next day. He slept in late and woke up sometime in the afternoon. The events from last night kept running through his mind as if he were gazing at one of the mad paintings in Walker's trailer and searching for patterns in the swirling blend of colors and shapes. *Things change so quickly,* he thought. It seemed like only a short while ago he'd been with Rita in her bed as if on some other planet. The next day he'd almost died.

He was resting on the couch when there was a knock at the door. Opening it, he saw Rita standing on the porch with a bag of groceries in her arms. She smiled and said, "Walker called and told me what happened. He said you were okay, but pretty shook up. So I decided to come over."

"I'm glad you did," he said, opening the door. She set the groceries down and they embraced. "It was a long night," Cruz said.

"I canceled my appointments for the afternoon," Rita said. "Laverne was pissed, but who cares."

She hugged him, ran her hand over his face and through his hair. "I'm glad you're safe," she said. She put the groceries in the refrigerator, then came and sat next to him on the couch. He put his arm around her and she rested her head on his chest. The trailer was a mess and Cruz apologized. "I would have cleaned up if I'd known you were coming."

"Don't worry about it," she said. "I almost didn't come over. I thought you might want some time alone."

"I've been alone enough," he said.

"We both have."

Cruz thought about all the nights he'd spent dreaming of being with her and how he knew it would never happen, that something would get in the way. But she was next to him right now.

"Sunday was wonderful," he said. "But I didn't expect it to happen like this."

"What did you expect?" she asked.

"That you were only interested in being friends. I thought it would be all over if I ever made any moves on you."

"Are we still friends?"

He hesitated, looked at the way her hair fell across his shirt. She smelled of lilac.

"I think so," he said. "I don't think anything's changed."

They were quiet then. He closed his eyes and tried to rest, but kept awakening to images of the accident and rescue. He'd escaped drowning in the Kern twice now and knew that he should be afraid, maybe even terrified. But he wasn't. Just the opposite, in fact, as if eluding death had guaranteed him a certain invulnerability that went beyond luck. He'd survived some of the river's most violent rapids and lived to tell about it. And now that he was away from the water, he felt something was missing, a part of him that was confident and wise and self-assured.

"Are you awake?" she asked. He stirred and looked at her. She smiled, brushed her hair aside. "There's something I want you to do for me," she said.

"Name it."

"When you think it's safe and you're ready, I want you to take me on the river."

"Are you sure?"

She nodded her head. "Positive."

"I'd like that," he said. "I know the water's gone down and there are some safe sections to raft now. Give me a few days to get things together."

"Sure," she said. "I'm in no hurry. I just want to see what it's like for you. I still feel like an outsider when you talk about it."

"I could ask Walker to go along with us in the kayak and run a safety boat," Cruz said. "We could go later in the week."

She made dinner for him that evening. Pork chops and scalloped potatoes and salad. He devoured the food and she sat back and smoked a cigarette while watching him. Afterward they washed the dishes together and listened to music on a classical station.

"It's a piano concerto," she said. "Do you like it?"

He closed his eyes. "It's picture music. That's what I used to call it as a kid. I closed my eyes and I could see pictures with the sounds."

"And what do you see now?"

"The two of us," he said, reaching for her. "And there's a waterfall running nearby."

They went down the hallway to the bathroom and turned out the lights and undressed in the dark. He waited for the shower to run warm, then opened the curtain for her and they stepped inside the tub. Within seconds they were wet, skin to skin, and she felt smooth as he stroked her with his hands. Their mouths were playful at first, her lips and tongue slippery and moist, but then he stepped behind her and began to kiss her neck and hair. He used the soap and washed her shoulders and breasts. Gingerly, he slid his hand between her legs and she opened for him, allowed him to wash her there. They cleaned each other with the soap and the water, and when they'd finished, went to his room.

"I want to make love with you," she whispered. "I want you inside me."

He hesitated, pulled her close as they stood next to the bed. "I don't have any protection," he said.

She slid a hand across his chest. "There must be someplace close you could go. I'll wait for you here."

"Are you sure about this?" Cruz asked.

"As sure as I've ever been."

He dressed quickly and walked to a nearby drugstore. He hesitated before going up to the counter, remembering his experience with Teresa and how nervous he'd been, how his hands shook as he tore open the rubber from the truck stop. But he was older now, and there was no need for secrecy or any feelings of shame. He placed the money on the counter without looking at the clerk, then tucked the small box in the back pocket of his jeans and headed back to the trailer.

When he returned, she was in his bed, the sheets pulled up so only her head was showing. Rita pulled the covers back and he went to her and they kissed. She took his hand and placed it between her legs so that he could feel a mossy opening, and he ran his fingers over it. He went slowly, watching her face for signs of pleasure or discomfort. It seemed natural to be with her, his movements guided by a simple rise in her breathing. At one point she led his hand to a place just above the opening and he began to massage a tiny area, kneading it with his fingers until he felt a small bump. She pulled away for a moment and he stopped, but then she brought his hand back, saying, "It's all right."

He kissed her breasts, felt the nipples harden under his tongue, and continued to stroke the spot she'd shown him. Her head was eased back against the pillow, eyes closed, a sigh or sudden gasp the lone sound. Once she'd been able to make him feel like this and he'd trusted her in the same way she was now opening to him, her body tense, her back arched and rigid. He quickened the pace, moving her toward a moment when she might burst and overflow.

Suddenly she pushed his hand to the side and pulled away. She gasped and he could feel her body shudder. For a moment he thought she might be sick, but then he saw her eyes. She was crying. No sobs or other sounds accompanied the tears.

"I don't know what to say," she said. "It's like there's a shadow and I can't get past it."

"Can I help you?" he asked, his hand stroking her back.

She looked over at him and pulled him close, kissing his hair and forehead and neck, her skin warm against his body. "You're doing fine," she said. "I just need to go slow."

"But does it hurt? I don't want to hurt you."

"No," she said, her palm against his cheek. "It's all in my head. You're taking me somewhere I haven't been in a long time. It's scary."

"Then trust me," he said.

"I'll try."

He was cautious at first, easing inside her and waiting for a reaction. He expected something dramatic, that she might cry out or push him away again. But there was nothing, just her hands in his hair as she pulled him down to her. He could see her face. Her eyes were closed and a shy smile played across her lips. He thrust into her, his hands clutching the sheets as he moved, and he felt her thighs locked around his hips as a rhythm began to form. She was moving with him, urging him on, and the smell of her hair and skin was overwhelming, like an exotic spice he could never get enough of. Soon they began to heave and push against one another like children engaged in a tug-of-war. When he finally came and buried his face into her neck, he felt suddenly lost, his head spinning, as if the moment had exploded and they were crashing and he had to hang on or he might fall.

Afterward Rita huddled against him in the darkness and he wrapped his arms around her. She took his hand and held it to her lips and kissed each finger. They didn't talk, nor did they make love again that night. Later, while she slept, Cruz lay awake and listened to the music still coming from the kitchen. He studied every line and curve in her face, then noticed the scar on her chin that was only inches away. Softly, so as not to awaken her, he kissed the small pink crescent. Then he closed his eyes and slept.

* * *

After work the next day he drove to Crawdad's cabin. When he reached the driveway and parked, he realized that the landscape around the house was even more cluttered and uncared for than the last time he'd been there. Empty beer cans and trash were strewn across the brown grass. Thorny weeds had sprung up and were strangling the flower beds and garden. Many of the plants had died, and shriveled buds lay on the ground. The right front tire on Crawdad's truck was flat, and a jack hoisted the bumper up, leaving the tire suspended in midair. A ripped bag of cement had spilled in the driveway and its contents left a grey trail.

"Something's different about you," were the first words out of Crawdad's mouth. The old man was sitting next to the cabin in a folding chair with his broken leg propped on a tree stump. "I can tell by the way you're grinning. You've got a shit-eating look on your face." A pile of crushed beer cans was on the ground at his feet. "Did you get laid or something?" he asked. Cruz ignored the question, then walked over and stood next to the raft, which was still spread out where they'd left it after the patching. The glue had dried into yellowish streaks that zigzagged at odd angles across the rubber surface.

Crawdad looked dirty and unkempt, his clothes ragged and full of holes. Cruz wondered when he'd last bathed. His silver hair grew long and stringy over his collar and it looked as if he hadn't had a haircut in weeks. White stubble coated his cheeks and face with the makings of a beard. As Cruz approached him, a sudden rattling sound erupted from the chair, and he saw that Crawdad held Jasper on his lap, one hand gripping the snake's head while its coils wrapped around his forearm.

"That ain't no house pet," Cruz said, stepping back.

"No, but I take old Jasper out every now and then just to test my reflexes and give him a good stretch." He held the snake toward Cruz and said, "Care to try?"

"No thanks," Cruz said quickly. "I'd rather hold a rabid skunk."

"Suit yourself," Crawdad said, keeping a firm grip on the snake's neck. "I hear you're a hero. I read about it in the newspaper."

"Somebody had to do it. But if Walker hadn't yanked me out, they'd be trying to hook a hero right now."

"Were you scared?" Crawdad asked.

"Out of my mind."

"Good. You need to be scared now and then. Keeps you humble."

Cruz kicked at some of the empty beer cans. "Looks like you've been putting away quite a few."

Crawdad snorted. "Don't tell me," the old man said, "your new girlfriend's a Mormon and you've come on a mission to save my soul from hell?"

"Not quite," Cruz said.

"Be careful with them Mormon girls, Cruz. All they want is a pack of babies. If you don't watch it, she'll turn you into a damn sperm factory."

"She's not Mormon. I was just making an observation about your drinking."

"So you're a damn psychiatrist now? Am I your new patient?"

Cruz just shook his head and stared out at the messy yard.

"Besides, it's good for me," Crawdad said. "Feeds my dreams."

"What kind of dreams are you having now?" Cruz asked.

"Same dreams I told you about before. It's been like a flood ever since the accident. I see things I'm not supposed to be seeing."

"Like what? Are you still seeing the dead people?"

"Sometimes," Crawdad said. "But lately the dreams deal with the living. Things going on around me. Sometimes it's funny stuff. I wake up laughing, tears running down my face. Had a dream about the president of the United States playing *Let's Make a Deal*. 'I'll take door number three,' he told Monty Hall. Won himself a washer and dryer for the White House. The First Lady was thrilled."

Cruz laughed. Crawdad got up and walked over to Jasper's cage. The cast on his leg was dirty and grey. He carefully deposited the snake through a small hatchway in the top, then grabbed a beer and sat back down.

"Had a dream about you," Crawdad said. Cruz looked up. "You were standing in this forest and the trees were covered with birds. All shapes and colors and they were making a racket. Squawks and chirps and whistles. Then

I saw this woman standing in the center of the clearing. She seemed to be waiting for you."

"What did she look like?" Cruz asked.

"I couldn't tell. That's how it is sometimes in these dreams. But there were other things I remember. Mainly her hands and hair. They were shining like gold and sun mixed together. Healing hands."

"Then what happened?" Cruz asked.

"You walked toward her and all the birds stopped their rustling and squawking. They got quiet and seemed to be waiting to see what was gonna happen. You went to kiss her, but stopped to look around at the trees. A big wind was building and everything turned all dark, like a tornado was about to drop out of the sky. The wind swept all those birds off the branches, and they fell to the ground and were dying, their wings all busted up and necks snapping like chicken bones. You never kissed that woman because she started to scream." He paused and gave Cruz a serious look. "She screamed for a long time."

"Then what?" Cruz asked.

"Then I woke up. Had me another dream about being on *The Dating Game* with a bunch of nuns." Crawdad took a long drink of beer and then belched. "Scary shit," he said.

"I drove up to ask you about the raft," Cruz said. "I need to do some training before we go on the upper Kern. It's been weeks since I rowed."

"Well, she's sewed up and patched and glued," said Crawdad. "I think she's ready for the water again."

"I'll check to see if anything leaks."

"Are you gonna take that Mormon girlfriend of yours along?"

"She's not a Mormon," Cruz said. "She's a hairdresser at Laverne's."

"It's good she can cut hair," Crawdad said. "You're gonna need free haircuts for that pack of ten kids you'll end up with. Save you at least fifty dollars a week." Crawdad grinned at him, gestured with the beer can as if offering a toast. "Let's drink to the Mormons," he said. "Holiest and horniest people I know."

"So it's okay if I take the raft?" Cruz asked.

"Yeah. Just don't be showing off and taking her through some hairy stuff. I'm almost out of glue, and that boat is more patched than unpatched."

"Don't worry," he said. "I'll be careful."

Cruz began to roll up the raft. The old man never offered to help. He stayed in his chair, nursing the beer and watching. When Cruz had finally cinched it tight with the bow line, he carried it awkwardly to the jeep and heaved it into the back. Sweating and short of breath, he returned to where Crawdad sat and helped himself to one of the beers.

"So are you scared?" Crawdad asked.

"Scared of what?" Cruz said.

"Of going back on the river. That's what you're gonna do, isn't it? Lou wants you back on the river during the tourist season, don't he?"

"It's only part-time," Cruz said. "Just until he can find somebody new to take over."

"But are you scared after all that's happened? Aren't you worried about accidents and maybe getting yanked under again?"

"I've thought about it," Cruz said. "I know what I'm getting into."

Crawdad laughed. It was more a cackle than a laugh, high-pitched and annoying to Cruz.

"I talked with Walker last week," Cruz said. "I asked him to go with us to the upper Kern and he told me I was crazy." Crawdad sat quietly and listened. "He told me what happened between the two of you," Cruz said. He waited, expecting Crawdad to respond. When the old man remained silent, he went on. "He said that Rose's death was an accident, and that he had nothing to do with it."

Crawdad leaned forward and said, "Of course he'd say that. He believes what he wants to and leaves out all the little details."

"Like what?" Cruz asked.

"Like the fact Rose never went for night walks on high bridges over the Kern. Or that she died only two days after he dumped her for some hot number down in Bakersfield." Crawdad was red-faced now, breathing hard as he spoke. "She didn't mean anything to him."

"He told me it was an accident," Cruz said.

"It was no accident," Crawdad said, his voice firm. "It was a suicide."

"He said he loved her."

"Bullshit. He'll tell you anything you want to hear." The old man stared blankly at the yard. His fingers were moving across the cast, scratching, his nails black with dirt. "What else did he tell you?" Crawdad said.

"That you were close to her."

Crawdad started to speak, then caught himself and stopped. He leaned back in the chair and closed his eyes momentarily.

"I was close to both of them," he said. "Walker even stayed with me at the cabin for a while. He was a good worker, the best rescue man I'd ever seen. No fear of the water at all." Crawdad glanced up and smiled. "He was always a little cocky, but that didn't matter." He looked up at the trees overhead and squinted at the sun. "But Rose was another story. She was beautiful and tough, and if I'd been twenty years younger, I'd have married her. Everybody loved Rose. She was a real looker, but smart on top of it. And she never planned to work in a bar for the rest of her life." Crawdad leaned forward, resting his elbows on his knees and dropping his head. "But Walker handled it all like a fool and she went to pieces."

"I asked him why he ended it," Cruz said.

"And what'd he say?"

"That she loved him too much and it scared him."

"Well, let me ask you this," said Crawdad. "Can a woman love a man too much?" There was no playfulness in Crawdad's voice. His words cut through the air, short and deliberate and sober.

"What do you mean?" Cruz said.

"You figure it," Crawdad said. "Can she love him to the point where she'll do anything for him? It don't matter what it is, she'll do it. Take up with other men to try and make him jealous, or start drinking and doing dangerous things so he'll have to pay attention. Even hurt herself and end up in the hospital so he'd have to come and visit her. Crazy love. Can this happen to a woman?"

Cruz didn't answer at first. "I'm not sure," he said.

"A woman will do all that and then some," Crawdad said. "And so will a man. Trust me."

"Is that what happened, then?" Cruz asked. "Between Rose and Walker?"

Crawdad squeezed the beer can until the metal collapsed and folded in his palm. "I don't remember," he said. "That was a long time ago. Maybe I'm kind of like Walker. I only see what I want to see. And when it comes to remembering the past, I'll only remember certain things and forget about the rest. That's my way."

"Did you try to talk with him back then?"

"I gave him some advice and told him to quit acting like a damn fool, but he didn't hear any of it. We got into a fight and nearly killed each other." Crawdad coughed, then spat into the dust. He reached for another beer. "Two days later she was dead. He didn't even go to the damn funeral. Told me it would be too awkward. Then he went off and joined the army and that ended it." Crawdad slipped off the baseball cap and ran his hands through the sparse hair that remained, allowing Cruz to glimpse the speckled scalp, like the scales of a lizard.

"A lot of hate has built up over the years," Crawdad said, "and it's time to settle things." The old man stood up. "So take the damn raft, but before you leave, you might as well take something else too." He motioned with a little half wave for Cruz to follow. They went around to the side of the house. There was a pile of odds and ends stacked against the back wall. An old lawn mower. A ladder and some buckets of paint. Some water-stained pieces of plywood. There was also a slender box about ten feet long and wrapped in blue plastic with a rope lashed around it.

"Drag that out," Crawdad said, motioning at the box. It was heavy, and as Cruz lifted it, he heard the clink of wood inside. The old man pulled out a knife and cut the rope, then sliced through the plastic and cardboard and began to tear away the exterior.

When he was finished and the lid was ripped off, Cruz saw three wooden oars glistening in the sun. Each was as straight and solid as a tree. He hefted one by the handle to feel the weight, then placed the blade against the ground and leaned on it. There was no flex in the shaft. The wood grain ran smoothly down the length of the oar, undisturbed by any knots or cracks or chips. *Nothing could snap these*, Cruz thought. *Not even Gravedigger.*

Then he turned the oar over and saw the engravings burned onto the blond ash. Each blade had a heron on the surface, its wings outstretched and flowing across the wood, as if the birds might fly into the air and perch on the nearest limb. Cruz ran his hand across the image, letting his fingers trace the carvings.

"I mail-ordered them fifteen years ago," Crawdad said. "Solid Maine ash. Then I hired this woodcarver to do the designs. I just told him I wanted something fancy."

"They're great," Cruz said.

"They're yours to use now," Crawdad said. "Take 'em out and get 'em wet. They're not doing any good just sitting here in the box." So Cruz carried them around to the jeep and lashed them against the roll bar. Before leaving, he turned and saw Crawdad settled in the lawn chair again, a beer in his hand.

"Take care of yourself," Crawdad said, "and take care of them oars. I didn't order them all the way from Maine so they could end up at the toothpick factory."

"I get the message," Cruz said.

"Now get the hell out of here," the old man yelled. "And say hello to Miss Mormon."

"I'll do that," Cruz said.

* * *

On Saturday morning he drove the jeep and river gear to the campground just below the highway bridge. There was a dirt road that led down to a sandy put-in by the river. He met Rita and Walker there at eight o'clock so they could run a shuttle with her Fiat and the station wagon while Cruz unloaded the gear and rigged the raft.

After they left, Cruz was glad to have some time alone by the river. The put-in was shaded with overhanging cottonwood trees, and slabs of granite were scattered along the sand. But the Kern itself had changed. He could see the high-water mark from the early summer, a ring of erosion that extended five feet up the shoreline like a rusty stain in a sink. The green current had slowed to a steady, even flow, and he saw evidence of where spring floods had uprooted and washed away small trees and shrubs.

He was edgy, his eyes tired and sore. He'd stayed at the trailer last night and hadn't slept well after getting the gear packed. Visions of disaster sifted through his mind, and there had been moments when he thought of calling Rita and canceling the trip. But Walker had reassured him that the Kern was safe now and that the rapids were mild in comparison to what he and Crawdad had experienced back in early July. "The river's slowed down a lot," he'd said. "There'll be more rocks, but I'll show you the routes. Don't worry about it. I've kayaked this section a million times."

He'd packed light on purpose, leaving much of the heavier rescue gear behind at Crawdad's so the raft would respond quickly each time he snapped off a turn or made a cut in the whitewater. As he hoisted first the rowing frame, then the oars from the back of the jeep, he felt the familiar weight of metal and wood in his arms and seemed comforted. These were tools he knew how to use. He carried the raft down to the shoreline and unrolled it, then pumped air into each chamber until the tubes were firm.

He moved quickly, a wonderful sense of order building inside him. After cinching down the frame with trucker's hitches, he topped the boat off with more air and watched the frame hug the raft even tighter as the tubes puffed out. Each oar slid smoothly into the groove of the oarlock. He checked the two oar handles and made sure they didn't cross at the center when he pulled them together in an imaginary stroke. Then he eyeballed the load, anticipating the weight to see how it would ride in the waves.

After dragging the raft into the water and watching it glide out over the shallows, Cruz suddenly stopped and realized what was missing. *Crawdad.* The old man wasn't there telling him what to do and how to do it. No cussing him out. No jokes or teasing.

He looked downstream and saw the rippled water catching the sun and sparkling. Everything seemed in its own quiet place this morning, and he dipped his hands into the cold water, brought it to his face, and felt a chill sweep through him. He wanted to share all this with Rita. Tell her stories about when he and Crawdad had trained together and what it had been like. More than anything, he wanted to open up this world to her in the same way she'd revealed the heronry to him.

When Walker and Rita arrived in the Fiat, Cruz helped carry the kayak down to the water. "We left the wagon at a campsite near Remington Springs," he said to Cruz. "We'll get a good seven or eight miles in this morning, and then stop for lunch. I don't feel a need to push it, with Rita being a first-timer and all."

Walker knelt down next to the kayak, took out some plastic flotation bags from the cockpit, and began to inflate them with his mouth. Cruz walked over to the car where Rita was standing.

"How you feeling?" he asked.

"Pretty good," she said. "Walker told me about the river and said the rapids in this section were safe. I'm still a little nervous, but that's okay. I want to do this." She reached out and cupped his neck with her hand and pulled him close, then said, "This is a different kind of dancing, huh?"

"Water dancing," Cruz said, putting his hands over her hips and swaying.

"Knock that shit off," Walker yelled from the kayak. "Don't be getting all romantic around me like a couple of love ducks. That's the last thing I need."

"Sorry," Cruz teased. "I didn't know you were such a sensitive guy."

"About the only thing I've got to keep me warm at night is my dog and my paddle. One has fleas and the other has splinters. Not the best companions."

"I know plenty of women at Laverne's that would like to get you in their barber chair," Rita said.

"I bet they would. I'd probably come out of there looking like Elvis."

Cruz got a life jacket for Rita, then had her sit in the bow. When Walker was ready, he paddled the kayak up alongside the raft. He wore his helmet, and the long ponytail hung down his back.

"Don't you ever worry about flipping over and getting your hair tangled in something?" Cruz asked.

Walker reached under his jacket and flicked out a long, slender knife. "That's what this is for. I brought it back from 'Nam. I'd whack my ponytail off if I ever got snagged. Hell, it's just hair." He tucked the knife back in its sheath, then popped open his spray skirt and pulled out a metal canteen. He took a swig, then held it out for Cruz and Rita. "A little refreshment before we head out?"

"No thanks," Cruz said. "What is it?"

"Whiskey and Coke."

"Is that safe?" Rita asked. "I mean doesn't it affect how you paddle?"

"Relax," Walker said. "I'm not gonna get blitzed. It helps take a little of the edge off." He put the canteen back inside the kayak and sealed the spray skirt around the rim, encircling his waist. Cruz pulled back on the oars and edged the stern out into the pushy current, then quickly pivoted the bow around and pointed into the first wave train rolling downstream.

He ferried back and forth across the current, sweeping the oars with broad strokes. The raft was light in comparison to when he'd rowed with Crawdad. A wave suddenly slapped over the bow and water sprayed into Rita's face. "That's freezing!" she screamed.

"It's snowmelt," Cruz said. "Get used to it. There's more to come."

Suddenly Walker darted in front of them, his kayak paddle slashing propeller-quick through the current. He was shirtless under the life jacket and his bare arms pushed the boat forward at an amazing speed. With a sudden turn, Walker spun the kayak around and pointed the nose upstream into the glassy tongue of a wave, then hung there as if frozen in the center of the water, his paddle blade shifting back and forth for balance. In a flash, the back end of the boat popped into the air and Walker twisted high in a graceful pirouette, then landed smoothly and continued downstream. Like a mischievous dolphin, he cut in and out of the current, sometimes flipping over on purpose, only to roll upright and emerge with a dripping grin on his face.

Rita was loving it, clapping and pointing at Walker's acrobatic leaps above the river. When he paddled close to the raft, she would fill one of the buckets and try to douse him as he passed. Cruz liked her playfulness and tried to see the landscape and river through her eyes. The slanting stripe of limestone plunging hundreds of feet down a cliff only to vanish into the water. The vegetation onshore seared orange and brown from the sun. The green arc of a wave breaking up and over the raft. There were slower places where he tucked the oars under his legs and sat back to rest, letting the current jet smoothly by underneath to pull them along.

They moved through the early rapids carefully. Each one had a colorful name that Walker would call out from his kayak: White Maiden's Walkaway, Dead Man's Curve, Sundown Falls. He'd pause in his boat above each drop, then raise his hand and point either left or right to indicate which side to enter on. As Cruz slid down into the rapid, he discovered that he had plenty of time to maneuver and pull away from the stone obstacles, and that the current didn't suck the tubes under or yank the raft off course the way it had in the early summer.

His runs were clean, and he only brushed against a few boulders and tree branches. Once Walker was through a rapid, he would eddy out below and wait for Cruz to come through. As Rita bailed out any water they'd taken in, Cruz paced himself and tried to relax, flexing his hands and fingers to prevent cramping. He felt strong, using his legs to slide back and forth on the rowing seat when he cranked out a downstream ferry or slammed through a diagonal wave.

When they stopped to rest, Walker would reach into the cockpit and pull out the whiskey for a drink. He always offered some to Cruz and Rita, and when they refused, he'd take another hit and tip the canteen in their direction, saying, "Here's to the river gods." Cruz watched him carefully for any signs of drunkenness, but never detected even the slightest wobble in his paddling or sense of direction. In fact, the farther they moved downriver, the smoother he became. *A magician in a missile,* Cruz thought, studying him as he effortlessly worked the rapid, the kayak weaving in and out of wave troughs and vanishing over small ledges, only to suddenly reappear downstream as if defying gravity with a pop-up, the back end of his boat pointing at the sky.

It was different rowing without Crawdad. No voice chewing him out from over his shoulder. No sense of panic when he scraped up against a rock face or was slapped sideways by a wave. If something went wrong, he'd just correct the angle or straighten out the bow and keep on rowing, making sure to follow Walker's kayak ahead of him. In the slow sections, he let Rita take the oars and tried to teach the basic turns or how to feather the blades. He stood behind her in the stern, his hands on her arms, and guided her through the motions of the portogee and the downstream ferry.

They stopped at a sandy beach to eat lunch on the warm sand. Rita passed out ham sandwiches and bottles of cold beer. Walker kept his canteen close by and continued to sip the whiskey and Coke. At one point Cruz said, "Doesn't that stuff ever make your head buzz?"

"Only a good buzz," Walker said. "You don't see me drinking during the week, do you?"

"No," Cruz said.

"But how much do you put away on the weekend?" Rita asked.

"A lot," Walker said. "And I live to tell about it on Monday."

He walked over to where his kayak rested onshore thirty feet away and sat in the cockpit. His legs dangled off to either side, and he stared out over the river.

Cruz and Rita were quiet for a while, and he leaned his head over until it touched her shoulder. Then he whispered, "I'll be right back," and went over to where Walker sat. Cruz perched on the bow of the kayak and took a sip from his beer, then said, "I talked with Crawdad yesterday."

"Yeah," Walker said.

"We talked about Rose." Cruz waited for a reaction, but Walker's face remained emotionless. "He still blames you for Rose's death," he said.

"Nothing's changed then," said Walker, scowling.

"He said there was a time when things were good between the two of you, and that you lived at his cabin for a while."

Walker stared out over the water and lifted the bottle to his lips again. "Those were the days before Rose," he said.

"He talked about her as well," said Cruz. "She sounded beautiful."

"She was."

"I just wanted to tell you I'm going with him to the upper section of the Kern and it's not because I believe him and don't believe you. I don't know who or what to believe anymore."

Walker sat upright. "Then believe this." His voice was suddenly tense and hostile. "He hasn't changed. When Rose died, he cracked up. And he's never been the same since. He's a crazy sonovabitch, and he'll stab you in the back if you let him. I wouldn't spend ten seconds in a raft with him. He's bad karma, pure and simple."

Then silence. Cruz watched a swallow spin and tumble above the river, blindly plunging toward the surface only to miraculously pull out of its dive and skim along the water.

"It's all pretty clear-cut for you," Walker said. "You just drive up to the cabin, knock on his door, sit down and shoot the breeze. You never really knew him before."

"He's not asking for much," Cruz said. "He just wants to settle things with you. I think you're the real reason he wants to make this trip." Cruz tossed his sandwich crust into the trees for the birds.

"But why should I go?" Walker asked. "There was a time when I'd have gone in a snap. But not anymore. Not after all these years." He suddenly stood up, finished off the canteen, and dropped it inside the kayak with a thunk.

"You drink too much," Cruz said.

"That's your opinion. I believe I drink a little above average," Walker said. Then Cruz watched as he wobbled up the beach to piss in the trees, his feet leaving a jagged pattern in the sand.

After lunch they eased through the remaining rapids uneventfully. Walker was quiet and reserved as he led the way, keeping at least twenty yards between his kayak and the raft. His playfulness and energy had vanished, and he paddled quickly downstream. When they reached the takeout, Cruz and Rita deflated the boat and rolled it while Walker lashed the kayak on top of the vehicle. Then they packed everything in the station wagon and crammed in for the shuttle back to the other cars. Walker was silent throughout the drive and listened to a Grateful Dead tape. When they reached the jeep and transferred the gear, Cruz turned to him and said, "Thanks for showing me the way down today."

"No problem," Walker said. "I could run that section blindfolded."

"I loved watching you kayak," Rita said. "It was magic."

"I definitely like to play in the water." Then he turned to Cruz and said, "I didn't mean to give you a hard time back there at lunch." Cruz looked at him and nodded, but didn't respond. "You do what you have to do," Walker continued. "Follow your own path."

"I'll do that," Cruz said.

Walker's face broke into a smile. "How about coming up to my place for dinner tomorrow night?" he said to both of them. "I haven't had any company in months."

Rita glanced at Cruz, then said, "I don't think we have plans."

"What time?" Cruz asked.

"Six o'clock."

"What can we bring?" Rita asked.

"Just your pretty smile, Rita. We can have that for dessert."

"It's a date," she said.

Walker grinned, then said, "And don't worry. I won't get drunk and sloppy this time. I'll be real civilized."

"I'll believe it when I see it," Rita said, winking at him.

CHAPTER TEN

When Cruz got back to the trailer in Isabella he unloaded the rafting equipment and carried it to a wooden shed where Frank kept his tools and engine parts and auto manuals. Everything was covered with a thick layer of dust, and the smell of iron and oil filled the air. Cobwebs hung like silky veils from the ceiling.

He cleared a space on the floor of the shed, then made three trips back to the jeep until he'd stacked the boat and gear into a small pile. A sudden rustling caused him to whirl around and see his father standing in the doorway. He wore blue jeans, a white T-shirt, and a straw cowboy hat. "Nothing's changed in this old shed," Frank said, clearing away some cobwebs. He stepped inside. "I forgot what a mess this place is."

"When did you get in?" Cruz asked.

"This morning. I took the eight o'clock bus up from Bakersfield."

There was a lull and Cruz felt awkward, sensing that they were both waiting for the other to say something. A mouse scurried in the corner.

"It's good to be home," Frank said.

"Welcome back," Cruz said. "I didn't expect to see you for a while."

"I know. But sometimes things move along quicker than you expect. You know how it is."

"Yeah."

"I talked it over with Father Sam and he agreed that it was probably time for me to leave."

"Great. So things went well?"

"I'm coming off the bottom, if that's what you mean. It's not like I'm back from some Las Vegas vacation." Frank went over to a small table set against the wall. Scraps of wood and metal bolts littered the surface.

"You don't come in here much, do you?" Frank asked.

"No," Cruz said. "Sometimes I might borrow a tool or something. But that's about it."

"Don't think of it as borrowing. These tools need someone using them. Otherwise they're just gonna rust away." He waved his hand at the interior of the shed. "This used to be where I'd go to get away from everything. I was the king and this was my castle." He laughed. "Some castle, huh?"

"You used to spend hours in here," Cruz said. "I guess this was your hideout."

"In a way."

Frank picked up a hammer and swung it through the air. "All of these mean something. I can remember where I bought each one. Like this hammer. It's a Craftsman. I got it at the Sears in Bakersfield. Craftsman's always been the best. Lifetime guarantee. If anything breaks, just take it back and they'll replace it. Remember that."

"I will," Cruz said.

"Maybe I'll start coming out here again and working on something. I need to keep busy. That's what Father Sam told me when I left. Get your mind on other things, or you'll be back on the bottle."

Frank looked down at the pile of river gear and pointed the hammer at it. "Is that all your rafting stuff?"

"Yeah," Cruz said. "I just got back from a training run. I needed to store it someplace for the weekend."

The old man walked around it, staring down at the equipment. "It don't look like much," he said.

"Looks are deceiving."

"You pump up the boat with air and then take off. Is that how it works?"

"Yeah."

"Sounds pretty crazy. You wouldn't get me out on that river for nothing."

They left the shed and Cruz locked the door behind them, then went inside the trailer. Frank's things were in a couple of brown grocery bags and they sat on the coffee table.

"I guess I better unpack," he said.

"We should talk about something first," Cruz said.

"What?"

"A lot has changed since you left."

Frank sat down. He was sweating and the dampness formed a ring around his neck, staining the T-shirt with moisture.

"I've got a girlfriend in Kernville and I spend a lot of time over there now."

"That's good," Frank said. "What's her name?"

"Rita," Cruz said. "She cuts hair at Laverne's House of Beauty and Style."

"A hairdresser, huh?" Frank said. "I'll bet she's a looker." He let out a hoot.

"What I'm saying is that I may not be around much," Cruz said. "When I'm not working, I like to do things with her."

"Fine with me," Frank said. "I don't need a babysitter."

"I'll be around when I can," Cruz continued.

"That's fine. Go spend time with your honey. Hell, that's what you should be doing at your age. That's what I did."

Cruz sat down and looked across the coffee table at his father.

"I'm glad things went well down at the shelter."

"Yeah. Now the hard work starts."

"I want to help," Cruz said. "But I know you've got to do this on your own."

"You said it. That's what Father Sam drummed into my head. I'm responsible for my actions."

"Are you gonna start going to the meetings in Bodfish again."

"Maybe. If things get rough I will."

"If it'd help, I'd go with you."

"Thanks, but right now I'm just taking it one day at a time."

"That sounds like a good plan."

Frank laughed. "The only problem is that the days are awfully damn long and the bars are awfully damn close. He winked at Cruz. "You know what I mean?"

Cruz looked out the screen door and in the distance he could see the flashing sign advertising the Shady Grove. "Yeah," he said. "Real close."

They sat together in the kitchen the rest of the evening and talked about Lake Isabella and the Dodgers and Cruz's work. When it grew late and Cruz rose from his chair to go to bed, Frank said, "Have a good sleep," and Cruz said, "Goodnight." He left Frank sitting under the dim kitchen light. Hours later he got up for a drink of water and found his old man asleep at the kitchen table, his head buried in his arms, his body twitching from some wild dream. Cruz woke Frank up and then led him groggily down the hall to his father's room, where he helped him into bed.

* * *

The next day Rita called and volunteered to drive that evening, saying it was her turn. Afterward, Cruz went to the liquor store to buy a bottle of wine for dinner up at Walker's place. He wasn't sure what brand to get, so he asked the guy behind the register for some help. "This chianti will go with anything," the man said, pulling a bottle of red wine off the shelf, "even beans and weenies. You can serve it warm or cold." He drove home and tucked the wine in its brown bag under the seat of the jeep. He'd pick it up that evening when Rita came by in her Fiat.

That afternoon Cruz listened to the Sunday doubleheader on the radio. He fell asleep on the couch while imagining Rita up at Walker's place as she sipped the chianti, her shoulder casually resting against his, the lights of Lake Isabella sparkling far below like flecks of gold on black sand.

He was awakened in the late afternoon by Frank as he came in from his walk. He'd been going out each day and hiking the strip of road from Lake Isabella to the reservoir. *I need to clean out the rust,* he told Cruz. He was sweating, his T-shirt soaked. He held the bottle of wine in his trembling hand.

"What the hell is this?" Frank asked, pointing the bottle at him. "I drove out to the reservoir today and found this under the seat. Is this a goddamn joke?"

Cruz got up from the couch and said, "It's for the dinner up at Walker's tonight. I didn't want to bring it into the house, so I left it in the jeep. I didn't know you were gonna drive."

Frank licked his lips, examined the label, then wiped a bead of sweat from his cheek. "You know better than this, Roy," he said. "You can't leave this stuff around while I'm on the wagon. I need a clean house to live in right now if I'm gonna make it. You know that."

Cruz walked over and took the bottle from him, then set it on the coffee table. "I know," he said. "It was an accident. It won't happen again."

"It better not."

Frank sat heavily into a chair next to the aquarium. He pulled out a handkerchief and ran it across his face. "You don't have any idea what it's like. I've got to have at least one safe place. And this is it. This is all I've got."

"I'll try to remember that."

"No," Frank said, his voice edgy. "Don't just try. Trying don't cut it."

"Shit," Cruz said. "Everybody makes mistakes."

"Not this time. This time I can't have any mistakes. It's my last chance and it's got to be perfect. Otherwise I'm right back where I started."

They looked across the room at one another. "Okay," Cruz said. "I hear you." He picked up the bottle. "I need to get going. Will you be all right? Can I pick up something for you?"

Frank had taken out a cigarette and was tapping the filter against the aquarium's glass. "No," he said. "I'm fine."

"What are you gonna do tonight?"

He lit the cigarette and took a slow drag as the tip gleamed orange.

"I'll eat dinner and listen to some ball game. I think the Angels are playing the Red Sox in Anaheim."

"Who's pitching?" Cruz asked.

"I don't know," Frank said. He tapped his finger on the aquarium and watched a fish dart away, then laughed. "I don't even know who the damn pitchers are anymore. I have to learn them all over again."

"Maybe we could go to a game sometime. Drive down and spend the night and go to a doubleheader."

"Maybe so," Frank said. "Just like old times."

* * *

When Rita picked Cruz up that evening she was wearing the pearl earrings he'd given her, along with a sleek black skirt and a white blouse that made her skin seem darker than usual.

"Is this a formal occasion?" he asked as he got into the Fiat. "Because I didn't dress for it."

She was running a comb through her hair. "No, but we don't get invited out to dinner very often. I thought it would be a nice change."

"You look great," he said. Then he held up the bottle. "I brought this to add a little class."

Rita looked at the label and smiled. "Very elegant. If I didn't know better, I'd think you were turning cosmopolitan on me."

"Not on your life," he said. "I'm still a noble guy from the country."

"Stay that way," she said.

They drove to Bodfish and he gave her directions on where to turn off the main road. As they started up into the foothills west of town, Rita said, "Pretty isolated, huh?"

"I think Walker likes it that way. He's a real loner."

"Doesn't he have a girlfriend or anything?"

"Used to. I saw her picture when I was over there last time. A nurse at the hospital. Real pretty."

"What happened?" Rita asked.

"He didn't want to settle down and move to Orange County. She had a job offer down there and took it."

"How sad. He's an interesting guy."

"Interesting but angry," Cruz said.

"In what way?"

He leaned forward in the seat and said, "Just pissed off at the world. He and Crawdad are a lot alike in that way."

"Maybe it's their protection."

"Against what?"

"The past. It's like a big force field so nobody can get too close."

"Maybe you're right," Cruz said.

When they reached Walker's place, he climbed out to unlatch the gate. Rita gazed at the statues, which were backlit from the late-day sun.

"What do you think?" Cruz asked. "A little junked up, huh?"

"Those metal sculptures," she said. "Did he make them?"

"Yeah. They're pretty amazing. He made 'em out of chrome bumpers."

They drove in and parked next to the trailer. As they got out of the Fiat, the dog appeared from under the steps and came up to sniff Rita's boots. "His name's Toby," Cruz said. "Walker got him from the pound in Bakersfield."

She bent down to pet him and he rubbed up against her leg. "Hey, boy," she said. Toby rolled over into the dust and she started to scratch his stomach.

The screen door to the trailer opened and Walker stepped out, shirtless and in khaki shorts, a plate with some steaks on it cradled in his left arm.

"Here you are. Welcome to the compound," he said, gesturing at the yard with his right arm. He motioned for them to follow. To the right of the trailer was a large red parasol and under it a picnic table with a cooler perched on top. Smoke rose from a barbecue grill a few yards away. Walker flipped open the cooler lid and said, "Help yourself to some beer."

He forked a steak and placed it on the grill. As Cruz and Rita popped open their cans and sat down, he said, "Don't be shy about dipping into the beer supply. In this heat you can never have enough liquid refreshment."

They sat at the picnic table while he cooked the steaks. The sun was beginning its descent behind the hills, and as they listened to the meat sizzle, the long shadows grew out of the metallic statues around them. Evening light turned the landscape a wheat-gold hue, and Rita pivoted her head around to stare at the sculptures.

"Your statues," she said. "I've never seen anything like them. Have you ever sold one?"

"They're not for sale," Walker said. "I don't make 'em for the money. Who'd want one of those plopped in their yard anyway?"

"I think they're great," she said.

"C'mon," he said, leaving the grill and walking toward the sculptures. "I'll show you around."

They walked behind the trailer and saw what appeared to be an unfinished piece. It wasn't as tall as the others. The chrome seemed darker and more twisted and grotesque, as if seared by a tremendous flame or explosion. "This is a special one I'm working on," he said. "I'm gonna call it *PFC Alonzo Johnson, After the Minefield.* He was a buddy who got blown up in Vietnam when he stepped on a land mine."

Rita put her hand on the tarnished chrome, then walked around it, sliding her fingers along the surface.

"Was he a close friend?" she said, her eyes still fixed on the sculpture.

"He was in my unit," Walker answered. "We looked out for each other."

"You can almost see it, can't you?" she said.

"What's that?" Cruz asked.

"The minefield. The burning and the smell of death."

"Maybe so," Cruz said. "I've never been to war so I'm not sure."

She stopped and surprised Cruz with a smile. "But we've all been through a little bit of combat, haven't we?"

"Yeah," Cruz said, taking her hand in his.

Rita walked over to another statue. "I'd love to learn how to do this," she said. "I'm not sure I could ever weld, but I'd like to try."

"Putting fire to metal and making it stick is no big deal," said Walker. "It's all in how you handle the torch. It takes a lot of time and patience. A steady eye."

"I've never done any welding before," Cruz said. "But I went to a museum once in Bakersfield. It was a field trip for school. I had a teacher who wanted us to see this Chicano art exhibit, all these paintings of Mexicans sitting out on porches or washing their low-riders. I didn't exactly see the point. I mean, why paint all this city stuff when you could be painting animals or birds or mountains."

"He was probably a realist," Rita said. "Their paintings act as a mirror to the rest of the world."

"Then why not just take photographs?" Cruz said. He held up an imaginary camera and clicked it with his finger. "I mean, why not go see it for yourself firsthand. Besides, some people get enough of the real world. They want to dream a little. What's wrong with dreaming?"

"Nothing," Walker said, "but too much dreaming is bad for the soul. Sometimes the only way to get people to really see what's going on is to show them things from a different perspective, then stick it in their faces so they can't look away."

"Exactly," Rita said, looking directly at Walker with a smile. She held his gaze and nodded.

As they went from statue to statue, Walker explained to Rita where the inspiration had come from and how he'd come up with the welding design. Cruz suddenly felt thrust to the outside, a background prop on the set of some movie. He gazed out over the landscape below and felt small against the enormous valley with its web of lights spreading from one end to the other. The reservoir was an inky pool in the center and everything else radiated out from it.

At one point he heard Walker say, "So you're interested in art?"

"I'm trying to get some drawings finished," Rita said. "They're pretty simple compared to something like this. Most of them are charcoal or pencil."

"Her stuff is great," Cruz said. "She just won't admit it."

"It's not that great," Rita said sternly. Her tone surprised him. "I don't need to hear how great it is. I need someone to help me get better."

Cruz didn't say anything back. He could feel his face heating up.

"Well, I'm no art critic," said Walker, "but I did take a few classes at the community college in Bakersfield. I'd be glad to look at some of your drawings and tell you what I think. I've got a pretty fair eye for detail."

"Okay," she said, "if you'll show me how you weld those seams."

"An artistic trade-off," Walker said. "The zen of welding. It's a deal."

When they got back to the picnic table, Walker pulled the steaks off the grill and set them on a platter in the center. Then they went inside the trailer and brought out salad and potatoes and bread. Cruz opened the wine with a corkscrew and poured some into paper cups. Walker carried out a tape deck and speakers and propped them on the steps of the trailer. The first song was Led Zeppelin, heavy on the electric guitar and booming drums, a constant wail in the air. Cruz noticed the songs were loud and scratchy as they came out of the speakers. In between bites of food he tried to catch Rita's eye but she and Walker were talking about the war.

"You're awful curious about what went on over there," Walker said. "Did you lose a relative or something?"

"Not really," she said. "I knew a few people who ended up in Vietnam. Some of my friends' older brothers. I wrote letters to them for a while, and they wrote back."

"Were any of them casualties?" Cruz asked.

"There was one killed in action. His name was Steve. In fact he was the one who wrote me the most."

"And what did he say?" Walker asked.

Rita took a sip of her wine. "Not much. It sounded like a lot of waiting in barracks and tents. They wrote about the heat, but never anything about the war itself. I always got a sense they were holding back."

"It was all a mirage," Walker said. He paused to take a drink of wine.

"What do you mean?" Cruz asked.

"The letters my buddies wrote home made it sound like a trip to the tropics. It's what the officers wanted from us. 'Gotta keep up the morale on the home front,' they'd tell us. 'No need to upset anyone.' So we listened and kept our mouths shut. We were pretty good at that."

"I know it was different from what the TV and news showed," Cruz said. "It wasn't all that GI Joe shit."

"You got that straight."

"We used to watch the news and hope to see somebody we knew in combat or something stupid like that," Rita said.

"They never showed the real war," Walker said, shaking his head in disbelief. "The real war happened in tunnels and jungles so dark you couldn't tell who you were shooting. You just pointed your rifle and fired."

Rita took a bite of salad and finished her wine. "What did you do afterward?" she asked.

Walker pushed his plate away, the steak half finished. "I came back to the States but couldn't stand to see the way vets were treated. I thought the whole country was gonna explode. So I sold some things to get a little traveling money and left."

"Where to?" Cruz asked.

"I bought a kayak in Europe and did some boating over there. 'I'd rather 'yak than go back' was what I used to say. Then some crazy Frenchman told me about this river in the Karakoram Range of the Himalayas with some real kickass water. The Braldu. He said it had never been run and that he'd flown over it in a plane. So I went to India and hung out." He looked at Cruz and slyly smiled, as if the two of them were conspirators in a game. "If you think the Kern is tough, you should've seen the Braldu. A real boat-eater."

"What was it like?" Cruz asked.

Walker took a sip of his wine and leaned forward. "Just getting on the water was tough. After riding a hundred miles in the back of a truck, I found a put-in right next to this village. But the village elders took one look at my kayak and impounded it. They wouldn't let me get near the river and said it was cursed with demons, that it stole their children and swept them away. They even made sacrifices to the Braldu river gods and threw slaughtered calves and sheep into the water."

"What did you do about your boat?" Rita asked.

"I bluffed my way out of it," Walker said with a chuckle. "I told them I was a 'water wizard' and that they'd stolen my powers when they took the kayak. I told them I could slay the demon at the bottom of the river if they'd only let me go into the Chokpo-Chongo Gorge, where the demon had his kingdom. And the elders agreed. Even gave me a prayer flag as a blessing when I got my boat back." He opened another beer, then slipped off his glasses and rubbed his eyes. "It was the craziest thing I'd ever done," he said solemnly. "Sheer walls and cliffs. No way to portage. I had to run everything blind and just hope I picked the right channel. I got pinned a couple of times but was able to crawl out and get my boat unstuck, then keep on going. It was thirty miles of instinct. Rapid after rapid after rapid."

"Was it like the Cataracts?" Cruz asked.

"Yeah," Walker said. "Huge drops and waves and no room for fucking up. When I finally made it out of the gorge I caught a ride back to the village and showed 'em my boat. It was all cracked and poked full of holes. They celebrated with a three-day party and took my kayak to make some kind of a shrine out of it. Hell, one of the elders wanted me to marry his daughter." Walker laughed, drank some more of his wine, and started to pick up the dinner plates.

"You could've stayed and lived like a king," Rita said. "You and your little Himalayan princess."

"Yeah," Walker said, "king of the Karakoram. What a concept."

He cleared the table and began taking the food inside. In the gathering dark, Cruz slid over next to Rita and put his arm around her. He kissed her on the cheek, then expected her to move closer, perhaps rest her head on his shoulder. But she got up from the bench and went over to where Toby lay in the dust and began to pet him. Cruz got another beer from the cooler and opened it.

"Quite a story," Rita said. "He's had a pretty amazing life."

"He's lucky to be alive," Cruz said with a sarcastic edge. "He's done some pretty crazy things. Death wish stuff."

She stood up and said, "I admire him though. He does things his own way and I like that. I mean, look at this place." She pointed at the statues. "Look at that. Were those welded together by a man with a death wish?"

"He's unique all right. I wonder what he'd be like on the river without the booze."

"He seems to be doing okay this evening," she said, staring down at the dog. "How are you doing?"

"I was wondering the same thing about you," Cruz said.

"I'm glad we came. It's nice to get out of Kernville and go someplace different. I like it up here."

Cruz gestured with his beer can at the surrounding yard. "It's different all right."

Just then Walker came out of the trailer with a lantern. He stopped to slide in a new tape and within seconds Cruz heard a whirling blend of accordion, fiddle, and drum rip through the air. "Cajun boogie," Walker said, "New Orleans zydeco." He high-stepped over to the table, the lantern swinging from his hand as pale moths swirled around the light. "This is Queen Ida and her band." Cruz took a long pull from the can. The beer was helping him loosen up. He deserved a little R & R after the accident on the river and his old man showing up.

Cruz set his drink on the table and grabbed Rita's hand. "Let's dance," he said, tugging her up. She seemed surprised and resisted at first, pulling back. But when Walker said, "Shake it, Rita!" she gave in and went with him. Cruz could feel the beer and wine mixing in his head, and his feet were sluggish at first as he tried to catch the rhythm of the music. He seemed a step behind the bass and hurried Rita. It was all an awkward rush, and there was nothing graceful in the way he muscled the turns. The harder he tried to be smooth and relaxed, like the dancers he'd seen at Don's, the further he fell behind the beat. Rita wasn't smiling, her movements stiff and tense. When at one point Cruz stepped on her toe, she pulled away from him with an angry grimace.

"Hold on, Cruz," said Walker, stepping in. "Don't be in such a hurry." He looked at Rita and she gave him a shy smile as he held out his hands to dance. "Just because the music's moving like lightning doesn't mean you have to keep up. Just sit down for a minute. Watch a pro."

Walker slid his hand around Rita's waist, took her other hand in his, and immediately began to high-step across the dirt. "I call this my Louisiana tango," he said to Cruz. He was smooth and efficient, his hands sliding across her back and stomach as he twirled her in a pirouette. Cruz sat down and finished his beer, then opened another. The expression on Rita's face had suddenly changed and she was smiling, spinning with the quick melody as Walker controlled her every move. Cruz tried to study him, but his hand exchanges and quick footwork were dazzlingly fast and Cruz couldn't keep up. Rita was laughing now, her hair fanning out, black and shining in the lantern glow.

He felt awkward and tense, afraid to cut in when she was having such a good time. So he let them go, saw that she seemed happy for the first time all evening and wished he were the one dancing with her. He chugged down his beer and felt the rush to his head moments later. His face was burning and he got another, then pressed the icy can against his face. But before he could open it, the music slowed and Walker was pulling him up and pushing him into Rita's arms. "This one's about your speed, Cruz," he said. But as they tried to dance, he realized that his movements were still slow and wooden. He let her lead him through the dance, avoiding her eyes and staring off into the darkness as his vision became blurred.

When the music accelerated, he stumbled away and let Walker cut in. Quickly, he and Rita were off again, this time moving at a wicked pace. He sat down at the picnic table and watched the moths flutter around the lantern. In the light they seemed golden, and the wild music made him think of gypsies and swirling silk and pirates all dancing on some exotic island.

He wobbled inside the trailer to the bathroom, where he splashed cold water on his face. He sat on the toilet with his head between his knees and cursed at himself. *Stupid ass,* he thought. *Dumbshit.* He should've known better than to drink the beers so quickly. He'd never been much of a drinker, not even in high school, and on the few occasions when he had gotten loaded with his buddies, it usually left him feeling embarrassed and angry. Maybe he was trying to impress Rita with Walker around. *Or maybe just fuck everything up.* After all, he did have a great role model in his old man. The floor tile spun underneath him and his stomach felt bloated and full. When he realized he was going to be sick, he turned and threw up into the toilet, pushing it all out of him.

The music had slowed when he returned and Rita and Walker were still dancing, only now her arms were draped around his bare shoulders and he had both hands on her hips as they swayed to a country-and-western song. He didn't know how long he stood there in the shadows and watched them, his fists clenched at his sides. The moment seemed frozen, timeless, and there was a cruel pleasure to what he witnessed. *It was gonna happen sooner or later,* he said to himself. *Why would she love me anyway?* A great rage swept over him, and he wanted to make a scene and tear them apart.

Then he felt numb and tried to discern if this was all a dream, and whether at any moment he might wake up and find Rita asleep on the pillow next to him. He'd brought her in a gesture of friendship, and Walker was seducing her. Had Walker planned this? Was it just another one of his mind games? Perhaps Walker had known it the first time he laid eyes on her. *St. Rita,* he'd said, looking up at her from the couch as she bandaged his face. *St. Rita of the Crossroads.*

His anger gave way to shame and self-pity. He was drunk. His lover was dancing with a friend in front of him. *Betrayal?* He turned and went to the Fiat, sat on the passenger side and rested his head against the back of the seat. *Why did I drink so fast?* He felt exhausted. The day seemed long, hours that lasted forever and stretched back to a morning that now seemed more like last year. Perhaps he was overreacting. Maybe Rita had recognized Walker's loneliness and was trying to ease him out of it. *Healing hands.* Maybe she just liked to dance. Of course she still loved him. Just a few days ago they'd made love in his bed, rocking back and forth, her head tilted to the ceiling. This was the image he held in his mind as he drifted off to sleep in the car.

He awoke to the engine turning over. Rita was starting the Fiat and easing back out of Walker's driveway. It was dark and the lantern was gone. He didn't see Walker anywhere.

She popped in the clutch and accelerated down the road. They drove in silence for a few minutes, the moon illuminating the desert landscape around them. Cruz looked over and saw Rita's face in the glow from the speedometer.

She glanced at him and said, "What happened back there?"

"I don't really know," Cruz said tersely. He leaned against the door and rested his head on the window frame.

"All of a sudden I looked up and you were gone." She ran a hand through her hair and braked for a curve. "You just vanished."

Cruz didn't respond. His mind was racing and he didn't have any real answers for her.

"I got worried after a while and went looking for you," Rita said. "That's when I found you asleep in the car." Again Cruz was silent as he stared ahead at the road.

"Can you at least talk to me?" she asked, her voice almost pleading.

"It's pretty simple," Cruz said sharply. "I had a little too much to drink and I didn't want to dance."

"Is that all?" Rita said. "Why didn't you tell me? We could've left a little early."

"What am I supposed to say? 'Sorry Walker, I got a little blitzed, so I need the lady to drive me home now.' That would go over real well." He glared at her from the passenger side. "Besides, you looked like you were having a fine time without me."

Rita glanced over again. "Is that what you think?" she said. "Is that what's really going on here?"

"I don't know. I wasn't exactly enjoying myself watching you and him dance."

She shook her head. "What did you want me to do? Sit around and wait for you to show up?"

"No, but I would've danced if you'd been a little more patient with me."

"Believe me," Rita said, "I was plenty patient tonight. It's not my fault that you drank too much. It was your choice."

They drove in silence for a long while. She sounded like a stranger to him, her voice a quick stab each time she spoke.

"When you talk to me like that, I feel like I hardly know you," he said.

"Maybe you don't know me as well as you think," she said, her mouth firm. "Maybe I don't know you."

"How can you say that?"

"It's easy. You don't just make love with someone and suddenly absorb everything there is to know about them. It takes time." She'd raised her voice and was talking above the wind that whistled through the Fiat. Cruz wished she would pull over to the side of the road, but instead she accelerated around a tight bend.

"What else is there to know?" Cruz asked. "I'm curious."

"A lot," she said. "More than you can handle right now."

"Try me. Maybe I'm tougher than you think."

He grabbed the steering wheel and said, "Pull over." She braked and swerved to a halt on the side of the road. "Try me," he said again.

"I don't want to hurt you," she said.

"I want to know what's going on with Walker."

"Nothing," she said. "We danced. You got drunk."

"Nothing happened?"

"No." She looked down at her hands. They were folded in her lap. "When I left he said I should come back and bring my drawings and he'd look at them and we could talk."

"Is that all?"

She looked at him, her face tense and angry. "Would you stop it," she said. "All we did was dance. He's a nice guy, and we danced, understand? Don't start pinning me down like this."

"I'm not trying to pin you down."

"But that's how it feels."

They were quiet then. Off in the distance Cruz could see the lights running along the rim of the great lake and felt overwhelmed by the dark gulf of the valley and its silence. He was angry and embarrassed by how they'd come to this. He tried to backtrack in his mind to earlier in the evening when he'd kissed her cheek and she'd pulled away. Is that where it started?

"I was worried about you tonight," Rita said softly. "Even while I was dancing with Walker." She reached out and touched his arm. He didn't pull away. "Besides, this isn't really about Walker anyway. It's about trust and your being able to talk to me." She paused, her fingers stroking his shoulder. "There has to be some trust. Otherwise we'll never last."

"I know," he said. "I'll try."

"That's all I can hope for." Then she started up the Fiat and headed down into the valley. When they reached the fork in the road at Bodfish, Cruz thought about asking to spend the night with her, but he held off, hoping she might say something. As she turned south toward Lake Isabella he remained silent, figured it was probably for the best. They didn't talk on the drive back. He felt sad, as if he'd torn something delicate that could never be mended or repaired.

When they got to the trailer, Rita said, "Weird night."

"Yeah," he said. "I'm sorry."

"It happens. You'll feel it in the morning."

"I'm sure I'll wake up with a bang."

She smiled as they listened to the hum of the engine.

"Is it okay if we don't spend the night together?" she asked.

"Sure," Cruz said. "We'll sleep better apart."

He didn't look at her, stared straight ahead at a chip in the windshield that sparkled like a diamond. He was trying to be careful about what he said, afraid he might embarrass himself again.

"I'll call you," she said.

"Okay. I should be home evenings."

"Good. Take care."

He waited next to the screen door until she had vanished down the alley in a flicker of streetlights and shadows, then entered the trailer. Frank was awake, sitting on the couch when he walked in. He was smoking a cigarette and had a can of Coke in his other hand. An old movie played on the TV, something in black and white that looked faded and snowy. A man in a tuxedo and a woman in an evening gown were on a beach with the ocean behind them. Cruz could tell the backdrop was fake, that the actors were only standing in front of a screen that showed the breakers and the surf. If it were real, they'd be getting wet from all the spray, but instead they were untouched. *That's Hollywood,* Cruz thought. *Nobody ever gets wet. Not a drop on that tuxedo.*

"You didn't have to wait up," Cruz said.

Frank leaned forward and said, "I know. I was just watching the late show here."

He sat down in a chair next to his old man. On the coffee table in front of them was a stack of old bills that were scattered across the surface.

"What movie is it?" Cruz asked.

"Don't know the name, but it's got Fred Astaire and Ginger Rogers," Frank said. "Did you have a good time?"

"Not bad." Cruz picked up some of the bills and started thumbing through them.

"I found those in the cabinet this evening," Frank said. "They're all overdue."

"I know. I forgot they were in there. I'll take care of it."

"They should've been paid a month ago."

"I know that too," Cruz said, picking up the rest of the bills in his other hand. "Things have been tight, and I haven't had the money."

"You had enough for that fancy bottle of wine," Frank said. "I saw the price tag. Hell, that could've paid off half the phone bill."

"It wasn't that expensive," Cruz said, his voice sharp. "And what if it was? I deserve to buy something for myself after working hard all week."

"Okay. Do what you want. But don't be surprised one day if you come home and find this place all dark because the power's been cut."

Frank took a long draw on the cigarette and exhaled in the direction of the aquarium. Cruz watched the smoke roll off the glass. He waited for the old man to say something else, but he never did, so they sat in silence and watched the movie. Fred Astaire was dancing now, gliding across a marble floor and dropping to his knees before popping up like a cartoon figure. Cruz was tired and wanted to go to bed, but felt he should sit up with Frank for a while.

"Is it good to be home?" he asked.

Frank glanced over, licked his lips, then let the cigarette dangle out of his mouth. The ashtray was full of stubs on the table next to him.

"Not bad," Frank said, "but I didn't exactly get a twenty-one gun salute when I walked through the door."

"You should've called first," Cruz said. "I'd already made plans. If I'd known you were coming earlier, I would've stayed home."

"I just expected you to hang around for a while, that's all."

"I'd made plans," he said again in an exasperated tone. "I had a date."

"Hell, you could've brought her in to meet me."

"Maybe next time," Cruz said.

"Is this the hairdresser you talked about on the phone?"

"Yeah."

"What's her name?"

"Rita."

"Like Rita Hayworth, huh?"

"I guess."

"At least you could've brought her in."

"We were in a hurry," Cruz said. "We were going to a place in the foothills above Bodfish."

"Maybe you're embarrassed and you don't want her to meet me."

"That has nothing to do with it!" Cruz yelled. "What's with you, anyway?" He got up from the couch and went into the kitchen, his ears ringing. "This is great," he shouted into the other room. "We're picking up right where we left off." He poured himself a glass of water from the faucet, then stood in the doorway and looked at Frank, who was still on the couch. "Did you expect a surprise party or something?"

"No," Frank said. "But I didn't expect you to come home stinking like a bar the night I get back."

"What I did tonight was none of your business."

"It is when I'm trying to dry out. It is when you leave a bottle of wine around for me to find."

"It was an accident. I forgot."

"Pretty good timing, though."

"What are you getting at?" Cruz asked.

"What am I getting at? That maybe you're trying to put me back in the shelter. Back where I belong, right?"

"That's a lie," Cruz said, "and you're full of shit."

Frank looked down at the floor, then got up and turned off the TV. He came toward Cruz and stopped a few feet away, his chest heaving under the white T-shirt.

"Don't talk to me like I'm one of your Forest Service buddies," Frank said in a low, menacing voice.

"What do you want from me?" Cruz shouted.

"Not much," Frank said. "A little respect is all."

"You gotta earn respect." As soon as he said it, Frank's hand flashed up and slapped him. Instantly, Cruz lashed out with a wild punch to the old man's face, felt the crack of knuckles on the jawbone, and watched as Frank went down hard on the carpet. At first he didn't stir, and Cruz thought he'd killed him. Then Frank sat upright, his left hand holding his jaw. Blood coated the inside of his mouth and Cruz could see it leaking out onto the white T-shirt.

He helped him into the bathroom. Frank sat on the toilet and Cruz brought him a wet washcloth, then went for a bag of ice. When he returned, his father's jaw was already swollen and Frank held a single tooth in his palm that had been knocked loose.

"Do you think it's broken?" Cruz asked.

The old man shook his head no and held the ice to his jaw.

"Do you want me to take you to the hospital?" Cruz said. The old man didn't respond.

Cruz squatted next to Frank and looked down at his own hands, felt the knuckles on his right fist begin to throb. He hadn't meant to hit him so hard but it had happened fast, all reflex and instinct.

"This won't work," Cruz said. "At least not now."

Frank started to say something but his swollen jaw made the words muffled and unclear. He tried again. "Maybe later. After things have settled." His voice was slurred.

"Yeah," Cruz said. He paused, looked up at Frank. "I'll get a place of my own for a while."

Frank nodded, then winced when he slid the ice bag under his jaw.

"Will you be all right?" Cruz asked. "Are you sure you don't need a doctor?"

"No," he said. "Go on."

As Cruz turned to leave, he felt Frank's hand on his leg.

"Rita," he said. "I'd still like to meet her."

"Sure," Cruz said. "I could bring her by sometime."

Then he went into his room and threw shirts and pants and socks and underwear into an old suitcase, as much as he could cram in. He found a cardboard box in the closet and put in boots and tennis shoes, his old radio, a few books, along with some loose change and paper and pencils. He piled all of this in the front seat of the jeep, then got his old sleeping bag and a plastic ground cloth. Last of all, he hauled the rafting gear out of the shed and packed it in the back, lashing the frame and oars down tight.

He went north along the reservoir and through Kernville. He went to Rita's apartment building and sat in the parking lot, the engine idling, gazing up at her windows. *This is all a mess,* he thought. *How did it come to this?* Slowly, he pulled away and drove up to Crawdad's cabin. He'd never been there at night before, and the place was ghostly and dark. He parked, then pulled out his ground cloth and sleeping bag and found a flat place in the trees to bed down for the night. It was late, nearly two in the morning, and he lay awake for a while, wondering if Rita was thinking about him and their night together and maybe missing him. When he finally shut his eyes, he saw the image of his father's face after hitting the floor, how quiet and still he was, his eyelids closed as if resting.

CHAPTER ELEVEN

In the morning Cruz was awakened by a boot nudging his sleeping bag. He looked up and saw Crawdad standing over him, his grey hair gnarled and unkempt.

"What's this?" Crawdad said. "Did that Mormon girl kick you out of the sack?"

Cruz hoisted himself onto one elbow and felt a throbbing band of pain encircling his forehead. The sun was flashing through the trees, and he raised a hand to shield his eyes from the harsh light.

"No," Cruz said, his voice hoarse. "My old man and I got into it last night. He got back from the shelter yesterday."

"You don't waste much time picking up where you left off."

"He slapped me for something I said and I hit him."

Cruz rose slowly out of the sleeping bag, then stood next to Crawdad.

"I can't go back there right now," Cruz said. "Do you mind if I stay here until I find a place?"

"No problem," Crawdad said. "It's not like anyone's busting down my door. C'mon inside and I'll give you some breakfast."

Cruz followed him through the yard and inside the cabin. The interior was a mess. Garbage bags filled with empty beer cans were piled in the corners, along with stacks of old newspapers. The kitchen table had a cracked leg and the wobbly surface slanted to one side. After sitting down, Cruz rested his arms on the table to make sure it would support his weight. The windows were flung wide open, and the only thing that kept the stench bearable was the forest air that filled the room with its scent.

Crawdad fixed some eggs, then laid out biscuits and hot coffee. Cruz picked at the food, his stomach still woozy from the alcohol. The old man sat calmly on the other side of the table, sipping a cup of coffee as he watched him eat. At one point Cruz glanced down and saw that his knuckles were bruised from where he'd struck Frank. He ate half the food in silence, then pushed the plate off to the side and drank some coffee.

"I'm not real hungry this morning," he said. "My head and stomach aren't feeling so hot."

"Do you need something?" Crawdad asked.

"Maybe some aspirin."

As the old man rose from the table and began rustling through the cabinet next to the sink, Cruz said, "If it's okay with you, I'm gonna leave the rafting gear here at the cabin."

"That'll be fine." The old man returned with a small plastic bottle of aspirin and set it next to Cruz's coffee. "What's your girlfriend's name?" Crawdad asked.

"Rita," Cruz said.

"Why didn't you go stay with her?"

Cruz shook out two aspirin and swallowed them with some coffee. "We had a fight," he said. "Walker invited us up to his place for dinner. He was trying to return a favor. I got drunk, and then things got weird."

Crawdad squinted at him while sipping his coffee. "How weird?" he asked.

Cruz hesitated and massaged his forehead with his fingers. "Walker and Rita were dancing and I thought he was messing around with her."

Crawdad shook his head sternly. "It's not the first time," he said, "and it probably won't be the last."

"What do you mean?" Cruz said, straightening up.

"He's been through a lot of women. That's his style. 'Find 'em, fuck 'em, forget 'em,' is what he used to say." Crawdad came over and took the plate and silverware from Cruz. "He's been with some decent gals, the kind he should've married and settled down with. But that's not his way. He's got that roving eye." Crawdad went over and placed the dishes down into the sink. "If she means anything to you, I'd keep her away from him. Walker's a real hustler."

As Cruz listened, he felt a prickling sensation at the back of his neck. He watched Crawdad clean the dishes in the sink and thought that maybe he'd been naive from the beginning about who Walker really was. There had to be a reason why he stayed to himself on the work crew and the other men treated him with a distant respect that bordered on fear. Cruz remembered how Chico had backed down from him when they were at the river, his eyes like a frightened rabbit after Walker confronted him.

Crawdad finished at the sink and went over to a small desk. A map was spread across the top and he brought it over to the large table.

"It's almost time to head to the upper Kern," he said. "The river level's just about right."

"How can you tell?" Cruz asked.

"I've got some stick gauges down along the shore. I check 'em every day to see what the Kern's running." He looked down at the map and traced the river with his finger. "Are you still up for it?" he said.

"Yeah, but what about your leg?"

"It's healed up real well," he said, reaching down to tap the cast with his hand. "Almost good as new. Don't worry about me. I'll be ready."

"When will we go?" Cruz asked.

"Soon," he said. "Within a few days. I'll let you know." He paused, set the map back on his desk. "Is the raft all ready?"

Cruz nodded. "No leaks. When I took it out the other day, it ran everything dry."

Crawdad sat down with him at the table. "The trip'll be good for you," he said. "Clear out your head."

"Maybe you're right," Cruz said, leaning forward over the table. "But why do you want to go?"

"Old ghosts," Crawdad said. "The kind that need to be reckoned with." He licked his lips and tapped an old finger on the map. "It's time to bury the dead."

* * *

When Cruz left the cabin he had an impulse to call Rita. He was nervous and sat in his jeep outside a pay phone for fifteen minutes, rubbing a quarter back and forth between his thumb and forefinger. Finally he decided against it and kicked the jeep into gear to drive off. They both needed some distance. Besides, it scared him to feel so vulnerable around her, like one of those big targets she would shoot at and then hang in her apartment.

The same thing held true about his father. He'd stay away from the trailer for a few days and maybe look at some apartments in Kernville, where the rent was cheap. *Let him be,* Cruz thought. *Let him get a handle on his life.* He saw the whole thing with Frank like a trial separation where both parties agree to spend time alone. *Until future reconciliation is agreed upon* was what the TV judges always said. But *limbo* was the word repeating itself in his head, a word he'd heard Marta use when talking about her marriage to his father. He didn't know where he stood with Rita, and he wasn't sure if he ever wanted to go back to the trailer with Frank. *Hanging between heaven and hell.*

The next five days were spent clearing tent sites for a new campground in the high country. At the last minute Lou had switched him to Ramirez's detail because they were short a couple of men. They dug out pits for the toilets and chopped away brush and heavy vines with sharp machetes. The work was mindless and tiring and helped him block out all that had happened in the past week. In the evenings he ate his meals at local places, a new spot each night, then drove down to the river for a swim. He slept in Crawdad's yard, often not arriving until long after midnight when all the lights were out in the cabin. Sometimes before sleeping, he'd pull out the oars and hoist one off the ground. In the pitch dark he'd run his fingers over the carvings, probing the intricate designs as if he were a blind man touching braille for the first time and learning a new language.

* * *

On Friday Cruz picked up his paycheck at the warehouse. As he was going past the big sliding doors he saw a shirtless Walker coming in.

"Hey," Walker said, "where the hell you been hiding?"

Cruz folded the check and stuffed it into his pants pocket. "Up at Reed's Meadow. We're putting in a new campground."

"Pretty place to work."

"Yeah," Cruz said.

As they talked, Walker pulled on a yellow T-shirt. "I guess you got a little blitzed Sunday night. I was sorry I didn't get to see you off."

Cruz didn't respond. He looked away, watching the other men as they came into the warehouse to pick up their checks. Laughter and raucous voices surrounded them as the men made plans for the evening.

"I asked Rita how you were doing, and she said she hadn't seen you since Sunday," Walker said.

"When did you talk with her?" Cruz asked.

"Yesterday after work. She drove up so I could show her some of those welding tricks. I taught her how to use the torch, and she was a real quick learner. She brought some of her drawings and we looked at them. You were right, Cruz. The woman's got talent."

"Yeah, she's a helluva lady."

"After dinner she hung out and worked with me on the new sculpture. Some of her tips were real sharp. Rita's got a good eye."

"I bet she does," Cruz said.

"She's driving up again this Saturday," Walker said. "You should come along."

Cruz shook his head. "I've got other things to do. Me and Crawdad are getting ready for the river trip."

"You still going?"

"Yeah. We're waiting on the water level."

Walker stuck his hands in his pockets and rocked back on the heel of one boot. "Like I said before, watch your ass."

"I heard you the last time," Cruz snapped. He tried to look at Walker dead on. "Maybe Crawdad's not the one I should be watching out for."

"What are you saying?"

"I'm talking about Sunday night when you were dancing with Rita."

"All we did was dance," Walker said.

"Then why'd she cool things off with me afterward? I haven't heard from her in five days."

"I don't know. We're just friends. We talk about art and shoot the shit," he said firmly. "That's all."

Cruz suddenly noticed they were standing in the entrance and a few of the men were glancing at them as they argued.

"Let's take this outside," he said to Walker, and they went into the lot and over to his wagon.

"Look, Cruz," Walker said, leaning against the fender of his car. "Maybe you need to go talk to her before running around making accusations."

"I thought I'd talk to you first."

"Why?"

"Because she and I had a good thing going until Sunday night and now things seem different."

Walker crossed his arms. "You can think what you want, but I'm telling you the truth. There's nothing between us."

"I'm not so sure," Cruz said. He felt confused and out of control, a rage swelling inside of him. "Is this one of your mind games too?"

"No," Walker said. "I wouldn't do that. Not to a friend. I don't operate that way."

"Then how do you operate?" Cruz said angrily. "Crawdad told me you find 'em, fuck 'em, and forget 'em. Is that it? The same way you handled things with Rose and all the other women?"

Walker stepped back, pulling keys out of his pocket. "Leave Rose out of this," he said, turning away. Cruz grabbed his arm and tried to swing him back around, but Walker caught his wrist. "That's not smart," Walker said, looking Cruz in the eye. "You could get hurt real bad doing that." His iron grip was firm as he slowly lowered Cruz's arm, then shoved him away. "You need to figure out who the hell to believe. And if you give a damn about Rita, you'll go talk with her." He got into the wagon. Without looking back, he drove off and left Cruz standing alone in the center of the warehouse yard.

* * *

Cruz knew Rita would be working late on Friday. It was the shop's busiest time, since all the local women came in to get ready for their Saturday night dances and Sunday church gatherings. Laverne liked to pack the schedule full on Friday, and Rita used to complain about being on her feet from seven in the morning until seven at night with hardly a break to eat lunch or smoke a cigarette. *Hell Hair Day* was what Rita called it. *Laverne's House of Bondage and Slavery.*

He parked up the street, then walked down and stood off to the side of the building. Her black Fiat was in front and he waited for nearly a half hour before she finally came out, her purse in one hand, a cigarette in the other. She stopped to light up, then dropped the match into the gravel. She saw Cruz coming toward her and leaned against the car door.

"How you doing?" he said, resting his hand on the Fiat's hood.

"Okay," she said. "Laverne asked me to close up. It's been a long day and my feet hurt, but I'm all right."

"You been keeping busy?" Cruz asked.

"I've been running a lot in the evenings," she said. "Work's been crazy all week. The summer season is wild because some of the motels send tourists over."

The paint was chipped on the hood of the Fiat and Cruz could see where the metal had begun to rust. He rubbed his finger against it and watched as it peeled off like flakes of skin. "I'm sorry about what happened at Walker's," Cruz said. "I never should have gotten drunk."

She smoked the cigarette and leaned against the car, her arms crossed. "You're right, you shouldn't have," she said firmly.

He hated the tough, steely tone in her voice, as if she were preparing to deliver bad news without so much as a flinch. If he'd had a hammer he would have smashed the hood of the Fiat and watched the paint fly.

He had his head down low, looking at his boots, and suddenly he felt her hand on his cheek, lifting his face up to where she could see him. Her voice was softer now, and she said, "I'm glad you came by. You've been on my mind a lot." Rita held his gaze for a few seconds.

Cruz hesitated, glanced over at a passing car, then said, "I've missed you. It's been a long five days."

"I know," she said. "It's been hard." She flicked ash off her cigarette. "I've been thinking about how fast everything's moving. I don't know if I'm ready for more. At least not right now."

"I can go slower," Cruz said. "The sex doesn't matter."

"But it does," she said. "That was part of it. You can't just cut that out. You're kidding yourself if you think you can." She came forward and took his hand from the car and squeezed it, then held on. "I love being with you. That's why this is so hard."

"What do you need?" Cruz asked.

"A little time." She said the words quickly, then looked down and dragged a toe through the gravel at her feet. "There's still some things I have to figure out."

"Like what?"

"About what I want to do and where I want to be." She waved her hand at Laverne's pink sign. "I can't stay here forever."

"I'm not stuck here," Cruz said. "My old man's back in town, but I just moved out of the trailer."

"Where are you gonna live?" she asked.

"Crawdad's letting me stay with him for a few days until I can find something." *Move in with me,* he wanted to say. *We could get a place together.* "But I'm not stuck here. I could leave at any time."

She came closer, a painful look on her face. "No, Cruz, that's not what I want."

"What do you want?" Cruz asked.

"I guess that's it. I don't know. And I need some time to figure it out." She took a final puff on her cigarette, then dropped it in the lot and crushed it with the heel of her boot.

Cruz pulled his hand away, then stepped back from the car. The light was starting to fade in the foothills and he could see shadows forming across the street.

"I'm afraid," he said.

"Of what?"

"Of losing you. Of not seeing you again."

"I know," Rita said. "I am too."

She held his hand and led him toward the shop, where they sat down on the front porch. "Just give me a little room," she said.

"But I want us to be close again. Like we were at the heronry."

"I know," she said. "But don't force it. Not right now."

"Okay," he said, "if that's what you need."

She nodded her head. "You have to trust me on this."

She squeezed his hand and he looked at her, saw how the evening light made her eyes beautiful and dark and sad, and he wanted to kiss her. But a different kiss. Perhaps to say goodbye. He leaned forward, pressed his lips to her cheek and neck, then pulled away. He let go of her hand and got up from the step.

"What are your plans?" Rita asked.

"I'm not sure," he said. "Working and hanging out on the river mostly. Crawdad and I are planning a trip to the upper Kern that'll be happening soon."

She ran her hand across his back and said, "Be careful." As he walked away from her, she said, "Where can I reach you?"

"I'll be around," was all he said, and he didn't turn, didn't look back, even when he saw her wave from the corner of his eye. He just bit down hard on his lip and went straight to the jeep. After starting it up, he decided to take the long way back to Crawdad's cabin, the way that paralleled the river. He'd only gone a mile or two when he pulled over and shut off the engine and walked down to the water. He swore at himself and squatted down along the shore, feeling a steady ache in his throat and chest. For a moment he thought he might get sick. When he began to cry, the tears made his eyes burn and he wiped them away with his hand and the dirty front of his shirt. Then he went back to the jeep and continued on to Crawdad's place.

* * *

That night the woods were black as tar when he heard the old man's voice trying to awaken him. At first he thought it was a dream and that Crawdad would just fade away. Cruz hadn't slept well. He'd spent half the night battling the constant drone of mosquitoes outside the shelter of his sleeping bag and his face itched from their tiny bites. Then he heard Crawdad's voice again, followed by a hand on his shoulder.

"It's time, Cruz," the old man said. "Rise and shine."

"What the hell?" Cruz said, pulling his legs out of the sleeping bag. He looked up and saw that Crawdad held a lantern and the slanting light created shadows on his face and upper torso, making him appear tall and ghostly.

"It's time to get on the road for the upper Kern," said Crawdad.

"We're leaving *now?*" Cruz said, letting his head fall back onto the sleeping bag. "It's the middle of the night, for god's sake. Why didn't you tell me yesterday?"

"No need. I figured you had enough on your mind. Besides, I didn't know until last night. The water gauge said it all."

Cruz stood up and stepped back from the bright glare of the lantern. "I'll need to pack my things. They're a little scattered."

"Do it," Crawdad said, "but hustle it up. We're meeting a mule packer at Lloyd's Meadow by seven. We've got some driving to do."

Crawdad walked back to the cabin. Cruz saw the old man's truck in the driveway and noticed that he'd fixed the front tire. Moving quickly, he rolled up his sleeping bag, then went to the jeep and gathered boots and tennis shoes, a sheath knife, a pair of jeans and some T-shirts. He stuffed the majority of his gear into a black watertight bag, then stashed the jeep keys by hiding them under the back bumper.

"Did you pack rain gear?" Cruz asked as he carried his things over to the truck.

"It's all there," Crawdad answered. "Everything we're gonna need."

"What about food?"

"I picked up some canned goods last night. We're set. There's only one thing left to do and I'll need your help."

"What's that?"

"C'mon over here and I'll show you."

Crawdad was sitting in a lawn chair in front of the truck's headlights. He had the cast on his leg immersed in a bucket of water. As Cruz approached, the old man pulled out a large Buck knife from the sheath at his waist. The blade itself was half the length of Cruz's forearm and it glistened silver in the white light. "We've got some late night surgery to perform, Cruz, and you're gonna be my assistant." He took the leg out of the water and braced his foot solidly on the ground, then handed Cruz the knife. "I've been soaking it off and on since last night so you could cut this damn cast off. I'm not dragging it to the upper Kern."

Cruz pulled back and said, "I don't wanna slice your leg open."

"Just take your time. The leg's withered some and you've got a gap to the side." Crawdad took a long stick and jammed it down into the cast, then pushed it out away from his skin. "Start cutting."

Cruz took the knife and balanced it in his hand for a moment, feeling the weight. The blade's edge was like a razor and in the glare of the lights he slipped it inside the cast, then used it as a saw to slice through the softened plaster, always careful to keep the edge away from the leg as he worked. "You should've gone to medical school," Crawdad said. "You could've been some rich sawbones." When Cruz had cut the cast almost to the heel, Crawdad pried away the plaster that remained, then slipped his leg out. The smell of rotting skin filled the air and Cruz said, "It stinks."

"Your leg would stink too if it was stuck inside plaster half the summer." Crawdad chucked the rest of the cast into the yard. "Don't need that anymore," he said. Then he stood up to test it.

"How does it feel?" Cruz asked as Crawdad walked around.

"A little tender, but it's healed up real fine. The doctor told me it wasn't much of a break in the first place."

Then they climbed into the old Chevy truck and Crawdad said, "Put on something warm. We're driving into the high country and it'll be cool this time of night."

Cruz pulled on an old shirt as they drove away from the cabin. He peered into the truck bed behind them and saw the raft and oars and rowing frame.

"You must have been up late to get all this packed," Cruz said. "Did you get any sleep?"

"I sleep less and less," Crawdad mumbled. "Ever since the accident I don't find much comfort in it. I just lie awake and think."

They headed north along the river on a mountain road, driving past a turn-off for the abandoned town of Johnsondale. Crawdad sipped hot coffee from a thermos, the steam floating up into his face and swirling around inside the cab. He was moving fast, the truck hurtling through the night as the old man punched the accelerator, and Cruz could feel the cold mountain air seeping in through the doors and windows. The tires gave off a steady hum from moving over the asphalt, and the truck was sucked into the darkness as if they were being pulled by some enormous magnet. There were no other headlights or passing cars or houses. It was all darkness and woods and mountains and they drove into the very heart of it.

The night was dreamlike, and Cruz's vision was clouded with sleep. He had no idea what day it was or the time or even what road they traveled over. When the pavement changed from asphalt to gravel, a rock bounced up and ricocheted off the windshield. Crawdad cursed, then accelerated to an even faster pace.

"Why are you in such a hurry?" Cruz asked. "We've got time to get there, don't we?"

"We do, but I told my friend Half Pint that we'd meet him early at Lloyd's Meadow. Those mules don't like to wait, and we've got a lot of ground to cover."

They continued climbing up the road's steep incline and passed strange and exotic sights. A waterfall high overhead poured straight out of a stone wall, its surface shining and white in the glare of moon. A blackened section of the forest had been burned away, "a lightning strike," Crawdad told him, leaving it charred and in ruin. An enormous rock dome in the shape of an atomic cloud was surrounded by a jagged parapet of stone towers and spires that loomed overhead like missiles pointed at the heavens.

"It's the Devil's Dome," Crawdad said before Cruz could even ask. "Pretty spectacular in the moonlight." At one point a deer lurched into the headlights, its eyes like two glowing embers, and Crawdad swerved to avoid hitting it. From out the back window and in the brief glow of taillights, Cruz saw the animal fade into the shadows as if it were made of smoke.

"Real living is about getting lost now and then and finding your way back," Crawdad said after they'd driven for a while. "That's what we're doing, getting lost. If something were to happen to us, I'm not sure anyone would come looking. We've covered our tracks pretty well."

Cruz glanced at Crawdad, who was hunched over the wheel. "Does it look the same as when you were up here last?" he asked.

"As much of it as I can see," Crawdad said, "but it's pretty dark." He laughed, then said, "Take it all in now, and look quick before it's gone. I used to come up here to get loose. I could drive for hours and not see a soul. But all that's changing."

The sky turned from grey to a slate blue. Cruz was noticing the first rays of sunlight on the horizon when Crawdad suddenly pulled the truck over onto the shoulder as they came around a sweeping turn. There wasn't much of a pull-off, and he could see they were perched on the edge of a four-hundred-foot drop. Crawdad said, "Let's take a look," then climbed out of the truck. Cruz opened his door and cautiously stepped along the side of the vehicle, a few feet from the precipice. When they were together and looking out over the expanse, the old man pointed his finger down into the canyon and said, "That's where we're headed."

Far below, amid a landscape of scattered rock and lush forest, Cruz saw a section of the Kern. As the sun broke over the canyon, he could see that the water wasn't the typical green of the lower canyons, but instead a solid white.

"That's part of the stretch we'll be running," Crawdad said. "A long time ago I hiked along the shore when the water was lower."

"What will the rapids be like?" Cruz asked.

"A lot of water will be pouring over the big boulders, so there'll be some boat-eating holes. I'll guarantee that the river's steeper and faster than anything you've seen on the lower Kern, except maybe Gravedigger."

Cruz stared at the narrow strip of water. "It looks skinny from here," he said. "Like a creek."

"A kickass creek, then," Crawdad said. "One you'll never forget."

They stood in the silence of the early morning and Cruz looked down at the river twisting its way through the canyon, then at the foothills that led back to Kernville. *Rita.* She'd be waking up soon, maybe going for a run or taking a shower. Cruz knew she had no idea he'd left town and gone off with Crawdad. The idea that Walker might tell her about the dangers involved in the trip gave him a sudden rush of satisfaction. Would she worry about his fate? Would she have tried to persuade him not to go if she'd known?

When they got back into the truck, he felt reckless sitting next to the old man, along with a wonderful sense of being self-sufficient. They had wheels and all their gear and food and a simple purpose of traveling by water through new territory. As the truck climbed higher above the Kern River valley and the distant ridges to the south, Cruz saw himself shedding troubled baggage the same way pioneers had dumped personal belongings from their wagons on the way west, things like pianos and framed paintings and rocking chairs. He felt a sense of lightness and temporary relief, as if he'd left Frank and Rita and Walker somewhere behind him and it had been as simple as throwing stones from the car window and watching them vanish into the canyon below.

They drove for another half hour to where the gradient began to level off, then turned onto a dirt road and followed it for two miles. When they reached the end, Cruz saw a wide expanse of meadow, a combination of mud and grass, and a team of five mules lined up in the parking area. A skinny wrangler was cinching down one of the harnesses when they pulled up alongside him. They got out of the truck and walked toward him and Crawdad said, "When you gonna put some meat on your bones, Half Pint?"

The wrangler turned away from the animal and looked over his shoulder at the two of them, then said, "When you gonna bring me something that's better looking than these here mules." He grinned and Cruz saw gapped, crooked teeth, stained yellow from tobacco. He was in his forties and wore a long-sleeved denim shirt, jeans, and an enormous straw cowboy hat. "You're late," he said. "I've been sitting here for a half hour trying to keep these ladies happy."

Crawdad said, "This is Cruz. He's going along with me on the river."

Half Pint turned away, cursed at the mule, then said to Cruz, "Are you as fucking loco as he is? If you are, then you deserve to be in the same boat if you're going down this part of the Kern."

One of the mules suddenly leaned forward and nipped at the backside of the animal in front. Half Pint exploded, swinging a skinny leg up and kicking the mule in the stomach with his cowboy boot. "Cut that shit out, Bonny, or I'll whip your ass!" The mule took the kick without making a sound, then turned and stared at the three of them with enormous, sleepy eyes.

"Stay the hell away from Bonny," Half Pint said. "This is the meanest, trickiest bitch I've ever seen. Don't even think about walking behind her, 'cause she'll kick you halfway across the meadow." He booted her again, a vicious swipe to the ribs, and the mule sidestepped a little, then held its ground.

"We've got some gear," Crawdad said. "The heaviest thing is the raft."

"Well, pull it out so I can take a look."

They unloaded the equipment while Half Pint tugged the chain of mules over to a tree and tied the lead animal off.

"How long have you known him?" Cruz asked Crawdad as they hoisted the raft out of the truck bed and onto the ground.

"About fifteen years. He used to pack in for me and a few others when we went hunting or fishing in the Golden Trout Wilderness." Crawdad laughed and looked off in the distance at the skinny figure. "He inherited the business from his old man and has spent most of his life up here. We always give each other shit. It's part of the game."

When the gear was laid out on the ground, Half Pint came strutting over and began to peruse the objects individually. He'd bend over and lift up a black bag or the oars or a plastic water jug, then grunt and scowl at Crawdad. Finally, he turned and said, "You pack like a girl, Crawdad. All this stuff just to powder your balls?"

"How much?" Crawdad asked.

Half Pint scratched his jaw and grinned. "A hundred," he said.

Crawdad laughed. "Quit yanking my chain. Seventy-five or I'm hauling the damn gear down on my back."

"Ninety," Half Pint said, "or me and the mules go home."

"Eighty," Crawdad said, "or I'll kick your ass and steal the mules."

"Eighty-five," said Half Pint, "and no lower. That's what I'd pay a whore for a one-nighter."

"Eighty-five it is," said Crawdad, "and that's what you had to pay the whore just to get her to look at your ugly kisser."

"And an extra fifteen to shuttle your truck back to Kernville. Is it a deal?"

"Deal." They shook on it, then Half Pint sent a stream of tobacco juice at Crawdad's boots and began to haul the gear over to the mules. With Crawdad and Cruz lifting the heavy stuff while Half Pint cinched it down, they were finished within a half hour. After locking up the truck, they started down the trail ahead of the mule train.

"Meet you at the junction around eleven," Crawdad yelled to Half Pint.

"Unless I decide to take your money and truck and go to Vegas," he said with a shrill laugh.

As they gradually descended on the dirt path, Cruz could feel the difference in temperature. It was hot, but nothing like down in the valley, and he didn't even break a sweat until they'd gone a half mile. When they stopped to rest, Cruz asked, "How far to the bottom?"

"A few more miles," Crawdad said. "A lot of switchbacks, then a long straightaway that goes right to the river. Watch out for rattlesnakes. Sometimes they like to sun themselves in the middle of the trail, and you wouldn't want to step on one of Jasper's blood relatives."

As soon as they set out again, the trail narrowed and began to drop rapidly toward the canyon floor. The forest was green with stands of ponderosa pine and black oak. As they walked, Crawdad began reciting the names of plants and foliage into the air like a chant or prayer. "Incense cedar," he said, "and deerbrush." He stopped and pointed out the dense, lacy leaves of mountain misery, and the orange petals of the western wallflower. "Bitter cherry and whitesquaw and greenleaf manzanita." They were names Cruz had never heard before but which sounded wild and foreign, as if they came from some tropical country on the other side of the world.

Cruz saw no sign of anyone else's having been there. Isolated and remote, the canyon seemed to swallow them as they descended. Far below he glimpsed enormous sheets of granite that looked as if they'd dripped down the hillside. When the trail began to level off he asked, "Much farther?"

"No," Crawdad said. "We're almost there." The old man was perspiring, his shirt stained in the back and under the armpits. A band of sweat had broken out across his forehead. "We'll get some water when we get to the river," he said.

"Is it all right for drinking?" Cruz asked.

Crawdad grinned. "It's sweet. Glacier on the rocks." His skin was flushed and red, but he was still smiling and pulling the air in with deep breaths.

They stopped to rest in a shady spot at the bottom of a switchback.

"We're up high," Crawdad said. "I can feel it. The air's thinner." He sat on the ground and closed his eyes, then leaned back against the base of a tree.

"I'm gonna walk down ahead of you," Cruz said. "I'll meet you at the bottom. Take your time."

The old man nodded in agreement, then said, "No problem."

When Cruz emerged out of the trees, he saw two streams in the distance, flowing seamlessly together in a mixture of green current: the confluence of the Little Kern and the main Kern. Within minutes he reached the water and sat down on a beach of white rock, the stones sun-bleached and smooth. Crawdad arrived a few minutes later and immediately took his boots off and immersed his feet in the Kern. Cruz soaked his head in a shallow pool and felt dizzy from the icy sting of the mountain water.

"Is this the put-in?" Cruz asked.

Crawdad nodded. "We won't get far today," he said. "By the time Half Pint arrives and we get the boat blown up and rigged, we'll only get a few miles on the river. There's a good place to camp at Freeman Falls."

They waited in silence for the mules to arrive. Crawdad kept his feet in the stream as if unaware of the frigid temperature. At one point he leaned back and stretched out on the rocks and Cruz thought he might have fallen asleep. But then he sat upright and looked out over the river.

"It's been ten years since I was here last," he said, "and nothing's changed. It's exactly the way I remember it."

"Beautiful place," Cruz said.

"This is where I came after Rose died," he said. He leaned forward and dipped a bandanna into the river, then wiped his face off with it. "I threw a few things in a little canvas backpack and drove my truck up into the mountains. I don't even remember why I chose this spot." He shook his head. "I sat here for two days. Didn't put up a tent or nothing. I wrapped a wool blanket around me and stayed by the river and looked out at the water. I guess I was waiting for something to happen or for somebody to come along and tell me why she'd died and why everything was such a mess." He stopped and pulled his feet out of the river. "Sometimes you have to get the hell away and go to where it's quiet if you want some answers." He tied the wet bandanna around his neck, then chuckled, his laugh uneasy. "Do you know what she was wearing when she jumped off that bridge?" He looked at Cruz and his eyes seemed lost, far away. "A red dress I'd bought for her birthday from some fancy store in Bakersfield. Can you believe that?"

Cruz wanted to say *I understand, it's hard,* but he stayed quiet. An image was fixed in his mind: a woman in a flame-colored dress stepping lightly from a rusted bridge girder and dropping away into darkness. Then he remembered Rita standing poised on the bridge railing in Kernville. *C'mon, Cruz,* she'd said to him. *Walk with the devil. I dare you.*

Crawdad turned to him. "I spent two days sitting up here and it was like having a fishhook inside my gut, tearing away at me. Walker cheated her. She might've had a life. But it all ended right there at the bridge."

Cheated. Something he and Crawdad both understood. After all the struggle and time and hoping that Rita could love him, it had all come down to a waiting game. *Don't force it,* she'd said. It was her decision, but it was never that simple. She had other things to figure out. So did Cruz. He'd never settled things with his old man or with Marta, all the family shit. It hung over him like a net waiting to fall.

"It's quiet here," Crawdad said. "Maybe too quiet. Some folks would go crazy. It'd be like they were stranded in the middle of the ocean in a boat and going nuts." He picked up a flat rock and tried to skip it across the current. "But not me," he said. "This is just right."

"I like it up here," Cruz said. "It feels good to get away from Lake Isabella and Kernville."

He looked downstream. The river was a sparkling mint green and gently rippled past them around a distant bend. He wondered how far it was to the big rapids, *the boat-eaters.* The old fear came back. An emptiness in his stomach, along with the need to piss. He got up and relieved himself behind a stand of trees, then walked back to where Crawdad sat.

The old man motioned at the river with his hand. "This isn't like the lower river. You throw a hook into the water down there and you'll pull up all kinds of shit that people have chucked in. Up here it's a different story. You could run a hook through these waters and it would come out clean as a whistle. Nothing under the surface but the purest snowmelt in the Sierras."

Within a few minutes, Half Pint and the mules arrived. They unloaded all the gear on the rocky shore in a green patch of shade. Half Pint was in a foul mood and stomped around, spitting tobacco on the ground and yelling at the mules.

"Bonny damn near jumped off a cliff coming down the trail! She would've dragged the whole team with her!" He cursed at the black mule with the sleepy eyes and continued to unpack the gear, slinging bags and equipment to the ground. They lifted the raft down, and Cruz quickly unrolled it, found the pump, and began to inflate the tubes. Bonny stared at him with her head cocked to the left in a curious way.

When Half Pint was ready to leave, Crawdad pulled out a roll of money from his pocket and handed the wrangler some cash.

"It's all there," Crawdad said. "No need to count it."

"Like hell," Half Pint said, flipping through the money. "I may be a mule packer, but I'm not a jackass."

Satisfied with the counting, he wrestled the mules into a line behind his horse, then climbed into the saddle. He flashed an ugly smile and laughed down at them. "Hope you boys know what you're doing. I'd hate to see you in a body bag strapped across Bonny's back."

"We don't plan on drowning," Crawdad said. "I don't want some donkey carrying my body up that trail."

With a shout, Half Pint yanked at the rope connecting the animals and they scrambled away in a bustle of hooves and curses as he tried to keep them in line. Cruz stopped pumping for a moment to watch the cowboy and his mule train move up the winding, narrow trail. Before he was out of sight Half Pint turned and waved, a big looping gesture with his right arm. Cruz waved in return, then felt a sudden panic hit him as he watched them go, as if his last link to civilization, to Rita, had been severed, and the only path back to her was by going downriver.

CHAPTER TWELVE

There was little talking as they rigged the boat. Cruz finished topping off the tubes with the pump and Crawdad walked around it like an inspector, checking the air pressure by slapping his palms against the bow and stern and feeling the tightness. When he was satisfied, they slid the raft into the water and Cruz lifted the frame, spare oar, and extra gear aboard, then lashed everything down. He was aware of Crawdad watching from shore as he used some nylon line to secure the black bags in the stern. "A tight job," the old man said at one point from the shore. "Bombproof."

They ate cheese and crackers and salami, washing it all down with some canteen lemonade. When they'd finished and Cruz was about to buckle on his life jacket, Crawdad pulled out a green canvas duffel bag that he'd been leaning against. "Hold up a minute," he said. "We need to take some extra precautions this time." He reached into the bag and produced two plastic hockey helmets, then tossed one to Cruz. "Strap this bucket on," he said. "I don't want either of us leaving our brains on some rock downstream."

The helmet was made of shiny yellow plastic and it fit snugly around Cruz's head. Then Crawdad handed him a wet suit, the kind Cruz had seen skin divers wear on TV. It was smooth and black and made him think of sealskin. "It should fit," Crawdad said. "I think you're gonna need it, considering the fact this water's cold as Christmas. I picked up two of 'em at a dive shop in Bakersfield." As they slipped on the sleeveless wet suits, Cruz wondered if this was what soldiers felt as they strapped on military gear before going into combat. He liked how the rubber fit tightly around his body like protective armor. Then he buckled on the sheath knife and life jacket and took his place on the rowing seat.

Crawdad withdrew one more item from the bag, and even before Cruz saw it, he knew what it was by the sound of metal clanking together and the familiar scrape of the barbed edges. Crawdad held the hooks aloft, the yellow line trailing like a snake tail down into the bag.

"What the hell," he said. "You never know when we might need 'em. They do have other uses, you know?"

"Like what?" Cruz said.

"Well, if the boat gets stuck or pinned, we might use 'em to drag the frame out. Or maybe to help portage if we get in a jam." He slipped them back into the bag, then tossed it to Cruz. "Strap 'em in some place extra snug," he said.

There was nothing dramatic said when Cruz pushed off from shore. Crawdad perched silently on the front thwart and waited. As the river streamed around them, Cruz felt as if they were slicing through an emerald green gap in the mountains on a cushion of water. He swung the boat around with a double-oar turn and let the bow drift on the first long straightaway of river. It was shallower than he expected, and from the rowing seat, he could see skeleton white stones on the bottom, vanishing under the raft. The water seemed clearer than the lower river and without any hints of silt or residue from the bottom of Lake Isabella Reservoir. The place had a different feel altogether, surrounded on all sides by steep slopes that stretched as high up the canyon walls as he could see. Cruz thought of jungles in South America, of the river in the Himalayas that Walker had told him about. The sky was electric blue and absolutely cloudless. *Water and air,* Cruz thought, *earth and sky.*

His hands gripped the oars loosely, palms barely touching the wood. The boat responded quickly due to the light packing, and there was no drag or sluggishness when he dipped a wooden blade into the current. Crawdad sat quietly in front of him as they slid around a corner, occasionally craning his neck from side to side and studying the first rapid. It was a boulder garden with numerous granite slabs rising up from the streambed.

"Right looks clean," Crawdad called back, and Cruz pivoted the stern around, then in three quick strokes, ferried to the right shore. It was a swirling channel, not very steep, but an easy place to get hung up or even pin the boat against a rock. Cruz entered slowly, felt the first rush of whitewater slapping over the tubes as they dropped into a chute then rocketed forward. He dug the oars in, slowed, then cranked out two quick strokes to the right. Another tight chute, only this one with a huge boulder splitting the channel at the bottom. Cruz swung the oars in so they wouldn't hit the rocks on either side of him, let the raft accelerate down the drop, then braked again with a backstroke and inched around the boulder, feeling the kiss of rubber and stone as the bow grazed the pebbled granite.

At the bottom, Cruz looked back and saw a foaming staircase where the river was strewn with rocks and small holes. The left side was nasty, as Crawdad had predicted, and would have butchered the raft. "A good warm-up," Crawdad said, "but that's all it is." He bailed water out of the bow, then clipped the bucket to a D-ring with a metal carabiner. "Expect that kind of tight rapid. Only expect it to be coming at you a lot faster." He swung around quickly so he was looking back at Cruz. "Just remember," he said, "keep pulling and don't give up. Even when you think the rapid's about to eat you alive, don't give in to it."

Giant outcroppings of stone jutted from the shoreline. A massive tree, its bayonet-like roots jabbing into the air, had been heaved up on shore and wedged between two boulders. "High water," was all Crawdad said when Cruz pointed at it. They went farther downstream and ran other small rapids which Cruz easily negotiated. Throughout, the old man sat on the front thwart as if he were a casual observer on an amusement park ride.

After a mile and a half they swung around a bend and the channel constricted, the rocky shoreline suddenly tightening into a narrow strait where the streambed dropped away. The current tugged them slowly to the brink of the rapid, and Cruz stood up at the oars to look downriver. It unfolded before him as if he were peering over a ledge, a clean procession of huge diagonal waves that churned through a narrow slot. "Stay off the walls," Crawdad said to him. "The waves are going to try and knock you around, so hold on to your oars and keep it straight."

They plummeted into the rapid and it was quicker than he'd expected, the water heaving him off his mark almost immediately as the breakers came at the raft from all sides and dashed against the tubes. It was enough for Cruz just to hang on to the oars and not get ejected from his seat, much less control the raft. He heard Crawdad hooting from the bow, his words unclear but filled with a violent energy and joy. The old man was standing upright and gripping the front line, his weight pushing the nose of the raft down as the waves exploded over him. He was fearless, as if taunting the Kern to try to flip them. The troughs of the breakers were deep, and each time the boat slid down into the gap, Cruz felt an exhilarating sensation when they rose up the towering spine of the wave, only to be smashed from the left and right by a flurry of water.

When they reached the pool at the bottom, Cruz strained to pull the boat to shore, but it was brimming with water. Crawdad bailed furiously, moving the bucket as if his arms were pistons. Eventually, Cruz was able to muscle the raft into an eddy, then leap onto shore and whip the line around a tree. Then they traded off bailing until the raft's floor was nearly dry.

"It's a tradition," Crawdad said, out of breath, "that we name these rapids. You don't go through something like that and not give it a name."

"What would you call it?" Cruz asked.

"I wasn't doing the rowing. It's yours to name."

Cruz looked back upstream at the narrow rapid and thought for a moment, taking in the billowing rows of waves and how they accelerated through the rock-lined straightaway.

"How about Wave Rider?" Cruz said.

"I like it," Crawdad said. "Wave Rider it is."

They moved on. The rowing felt smooth, and there were only a few moments when Cruz misjudged a stroke and saw the oar flapping loosely in the air where it had missed water. The streambed was steeper than the lower Kern, a sense of sheer gravity pulling them downriver, and their runs were always through tight chutes and boulder-choked rapids. They broached once on a triangular, undercut rock, but Cruz was able to spin off with a double-handed pull on the right oar before the upstream tube could fold and get sucked under. In one spectacular place a formidable wall of stone loomed on the left and overlooked a bubbly, careening rapid that zigzagged past the base of the cliff. As they ran it Cruz paused at one point to stare upward at the dizzying height of the wall. He longed to see a heron leap from the precipice high overhead as a sign of welcome or good passage. But all he saw were twisted vines dangling from the edge, so he set his eyes on the rapid in front of them and rowed on.

He paced himself, tried to rest when they caught eddies and needed to bail. But it was the canyon itself that excited him. No roads or bridges or fishermen in view. It was all wilderness, and he felt an electricity at the thought of taking a raft down this section of river. The wet suit was hot, and sweat poured down his chest and back from where the sticky rubber met his skin.

"I'm cooking in this," he said at one point to Crawdad. "I feel like a lobster in a pot."

"You can thank me later if you go for a swim," the old man said. "Up here, it's like jumping into a pool of ice water. Your arms'll go numb within minutes."

It was late afternoon when they came upon a side stream on the right that poured into the Kern. "This is Freeman Creek," Crawdad said. "We camped here back in the fifties when I was scouting out trails for the Forest Service." They pulled into a small cove and dragged the bow onto a sandy lip of the shoreline. "We'll camp here," Crawdad said, motioning with a sweep of his arm. "We can rest up for tomorrow. The big stuff starts just downstream and once we get into that, there's no letting up."

Cruz undid the ropes that lashed the gear down, then helped Crawdad carry the cooler and black bags up on the shore. In the distance Cruz could hear a steady roar. After setting the bags down he walked into the forest to explore. Through an opening in the veil of pine branches he saw a waterfall cascading nearly fifty feet from an overhang of dark, mossy stone. It was like a ghostly apparition in the afternoon light, a mirage playing tricks in the high mountains. He moved closer. There was a pool at the base of the falls that swelled out and formed a ring of clear water. The air was damp and cool, a true refuge from the heat, as if the pool's green waters and mossy banks had sucked in every ounce of moisture from the region and trapped it in this one tiny place.

"A pretty sight," Crawdad said from behind him. "I found this when I was hiking and never forgot it."

They stripped off the wet suits, then waded into the freezing water. Cruz dove under and then surfaced with a ringing in his ears from the intense cold, his skin tingling with goose pimples. The water was stinging and frigid and he screamed aloud from the shock. He turned and saw Crawdad slowly wading in up to his waist, then dipping his hands into the pool and pouring handfuls of water over himself. Crawdad's withered skin was brown and leathery from too many years of sun and heat, like the brittle texture of leaves in autumn. His chest was still firm, and veins of muscle rippled down his shoulders and forearms.

"You must have Eskimo blood," he told Cruz. "This'll turn your balls into ice cubes."

Cruz laughed, dove under again, and swam to the base of the falls. He stayed underwater as long as he could stand it, then came up directly in front of the waterfall. As he stood in the shallows, a torrent of white spray fell from the heights to pummel his face and chest with its force. He stared upward, wanting to try to step through the sheet of water, but knowing it would only pound him down with its force, like getting hit square in the face with a fire hose. But it was magnificent to look straight up and see a river falling from the heavens and crashing to earth only inches from where he stood.

He swam back to Crawdad, and together they waded to shore. The light was already beginning to fade in the deep canyon, and as they walked back to the raft, Cruz said, "It cools off fast down here."

"Night'll come early," Crawdad said. "The sun don't stay in the canyon very long, and as soon as it's gone, it gets dark quick."

They pitched camp in a sandy clearing surrounded by a natural barricade of thistled bushes. After pulling out dry clothes from the black bags, they draped the wet suits over a thick tree limb for the night. Crawdad produced a small kerosene stove that had been swathed in garbage bags to keep out the water. They heated cans of chili in a small dented pan, then poured it into their bowls and ate it with tortillas. Cruz drank a quart of the lemonade mixed in his canteen and ate ravenously while Crawdad nibbled at his meal.

When he'd sopped up the last of the chili with his tortilla, he asked, "What's the first big rapid like?"

"It's just around the bend down here," Crawdad said, waving at the river. "From what I can remember, there's an upper and a lower section. The bottom part's the toughest. After that all hell breaks loose. Rapid after rapid after rapid, without much letting up."

"Will we have to portage?"

"At this water level, there's always a chance. We'll just have to take them one at a time."

Cruz cleared a pit in the sand and built a fire with driftwood that had washed up onshore from the high water. Then he went down to the raft to make sure that everything was tied securely. If a big wind came up the canyon, it could snatch a life jacket and sweep it into the current, along with anything else that might be loose.

After checking the boat over, he lounged on the rowing seat and let his eyes adjust to the evening light. It wasn't completely dark yet, and he could see the glowing silhouette of the canyon rim to the west as if its crooked edges had been outlined by a golden pencil. Downstream the river swept around a bend, then vanished as it began a steep descent into the first major rapid. Occasionally bats zigzagged through the air above him, and once, upon looking upstream, he saw a sudden flash of scarlet skimming the surface of the water.

He thought of Rita and yearned to be back in Kernville at her apartment. There in the raft, he felt a deep sense of regret as images of her swam through his mind. Rita asleep next to him in her bed. Rita studying the flight of a heron, her own body as lithe and graceful as the birds she adored. Rita kissing his bruised face. *Give her some room or she'll suffocate,* he thought.

When he returned to the camp, Crawdad was still sitting by the fire. Light danced across his face and illuminated the long silver hair and scraggly beard. On the ground was an open ammo can. Cruz recognized the necklaces and rings and bracelets that Crawdad treasured, all heaped inside and wrapped in plastic. In the old man's hand was a string of pearls, and he worked each bead with his fingers as if it were a rosary and he were absorbed in prayer. When Cruz sat down in the sand across from him, Crawdad looked up, then slid the necklace back into the box.

"I didn't know you'd brought those along," Cruz said.

"Yeah," Crawdad said quietly. "I plan to give back to the dead what's been taken away."

"And where will that be?"

"I'm not sure," Crawdad said. "Someplace sacred."

They were silent for a number of seconds as the flames leaped up from the metal fire pan. The ammo can still lay at the old man's feet. Cruz longed to touch the shining contents with his own hands.

"Your father," Crawdad said as he looked across the fire at him, "did you see him before you left?"

"No," Cruz said. "I thought about dropping by. Except there wouldn't have been much to say."

"You decked him, huh?"

"Yeah."

"Did he try to fight back?"

"No. I even helped him into the bathroom so he could clean up. I wanted to make sure he was all right before I left."

"Hit and run," Crawdad said.

"I guess."

"Maybe it was a good thing you hit him."

"How's that?"

"You probably showed him something. That you'd changed."

"But I was the one who flew off the handle," said Cruz. "I'd been drinking that night."

"And maybe he saw a part of himself in you. Probably scared the hell out of him to see his own son half-crocked and ready to punch his lights out."

"Maybe so," Cruz said. "I never looked at it that way."

There was a sudden splash down near the raft, followed by something heavy being dragged across the sand. They waited for a moment as Cruz stood up and peered into the darkness.

Then Walker moved slowly into the firelight, holding his yellow kayak by one of the end loops, his paddle in the other hand. He dropped the boat with a hollow thump as it hit the sand, then set the paddle down next to it. He wore a sleeveless black wet suit, kayak vest, and a red helmet. A large sheath knife with a black belt was strapped around his waist and his enormous arms were wet and shining in the glow from the fire.

"Look who's crashing the party," Crawdad said. "If it isn't Captain Kayak."

Walker didn't respond. His appearance was imposing, almost warrior-like, and for the first time Cruz pictured him in combat fatigues, marching through a jungle in Vietnam, an M-16 cradled in his arms.

"I had to run the last three rapids in the dark," Walker said. "Pretty spooky." He sat down in the sand and took off his helmet.

"How'd you find us?" Cruz asked.

"I went by the cabin and saw that the truck and the gear were gone. So I called Half Pint's pack station up near Lone Pine, and a wrangler said he was taking some rafters down to the Forks." He paused to unzip the front of his wet suit. "After that it was just a matter of dragging my boat down the trail and playing catch-up."

"So what brought you here?" Crawdad asked. "I thought you said to hell with the first invite."

"You're gonna need my help tomorrow."

"Why's that?"

"Because of the big stuff downstream. Things start kicking ass just around the next bend. I've kayaked all of it before at lower flows and know the routes.

If you expect to get that raft through some of the tight spots, you're gonna need my help. Whether you like it or not." He stood up and peeled off his wet suit, then vanished into the dark for a moment. When he returned he wore a faded red T-shirt and some nylon running shorts. "I brought my own food and gear," he said, "so you don't have to worry about that end of it."

"Why'd you change your mind?" said Crawdad.

"Not because of you," Walker said sharply. "This has nothing to do with you. Let's just say I have a personal interest in the situation."

"And what would that be?" Crawdad asked.

He turned and faced Cruz. "I talked with Rita the other night and we both agreed that you might need a little company up here. Somebody you can count on."

The line caught Cruz off guard and made him flinch. "I can count on Crawdad," he said, annoyed. "And I don't need you checking up on me."

"I knew you'd come," Crawdad continued. "Couldn't stay away from it, could you?"

"I'm here because of Cruz," Walker said. "And believe me, that's the only thing that would've got me up here with you."

Cruz imagined Rita with him. Maybe they'd been dancing up at his trailer again and she'd whispered something in his ear. *A favor,* she might've said. *Just this once. Do it for me.*

"You didn't have to come," Cruz said. "We can take care of ourselves."

"Maybe you can," Walker said. "But I know what's downstream and you don't."

"Crawdad and I have been through this stuff before," said Cruz, rising up from his seat. "Whatever's coming, we can handle it."

Crawdad stood and walked over to the fire, where he put on more wood. "Have you eaten anything?" he asked.

"No," Walker said. "I brought my own supplies. I stashed some things in my boat." He went over to the kayak and pulled a bottle of Southern Comfort out of the cockpit. "But right now I'd prefer some liquid refreshment." He uncapped it and took a long drink, then held it out to Crawdad and Cruz. "Peace offering," he said. "Happy hour's the best part of the day."

Crawdad extended his hand and slowly took the bottle as if to drink. For a moment, Cruz saw the honey-colored liquid inside the glass and how it gleamed in the firelight. Then in one swift motion, Crawdad raised the bottle overhead and hurled it toward the darkness of the river.

"What the hell — ?" Walker said as the bottle vanished, a stunned look on his face.

"I don't want a drunk kayaker running safety for me," Crawdad said, his mouth rigid and firm. He sat down solemnly on the other side of the fire. "And if you got any other bottles, get rid of those too. This is a dry run. If you can't handle it, then get the hell out."

Cruz stared at the two men, tried to picture them years ago when they were younger and worked the hooks. He remembered how they'd squared off in the warehouse.

Walker stepped to the other side of the fire. His face was intense and menacing, the same look he'd used to intimidate Chico down by the river. *Mind games,* Walker had said then, *everybody plays them.* At first Cruz thought he was going to strike Crawdad and knock him into the dirt. Instead, he reached down and quickly snatched up the metal ammo can from where it lay at the old man's feet.

"You brought your treasure chest," he said, slanting the box so that the light glinted off the rings and jewelry. "It's gotten bigger over the years." His hand rifled through the items. "Quite a collection. It takes a lot of guts to steal from the dead, doesn't it?"

He made his way back to the other side of the fire and Cruz stepped forward, lunged for the box, but Walker pulled it quickly away. Crawdad didn't budge from where he sat.

"I need those back," Crawdad said. "I need to return them."

"Hell," Walker said, "return them? Let me help." He plunged his hand down into the box and pulled out a fistful of the items, then hurled them into the river. Before Cruz could stop him he'd emptied the remains into his hand and thrown again. Then he whirled around and tossed the empty can at Crawdad's feet. "Now the dead can really party," he said.

The old man stood up, a furious look on his face, and kicked the empty ammo can out of the way. "You forgot about one thing, didn't you?" he said in a cutting tone. He looked directly at Walker, then slipped a gold band off his finger and held it up for him to see. "Do you remember this?" Crawdad said. "It's what Rose was wearing when I dragged her out of the river below

Johnsondale." He waved it in the air and the gold flashed in the firelight. "You'll never have this," he said. "You'll never get her back."

Walker froze when he saw the ring, and Cruz could tell that Crawdad had pinned him down. He glanced over at Cruz, as if hoping for some sign or gesture of support. Then he slowly backed away from the old man. "You bastard," Walker said. He turned and grabbed his kayak and other belongings and silently walked away, fading into the darkness as if there were a black curtain that he'd stepped behind.

"Now it's complete," Crawdad said. "Full circle." The old man unrolled his blanket and wrapped it around himself. "Let's get some rest," he said to Cruz. Then he lay down to sleep in the ring of light cast by the fire.

* * *

Cruz slept fitfully that night, dreaming of rattlesnakes coiled in the scrub brush near his sleeping bag. He looked skyward at the canyon's edges and had the sensation of being trapped in a huge pit where, at any moment, a landslide could thunder down and bury him forever. Images of Walker lurking in the shadows flickered through his mind. Walker with a hunting knife clenched in his hand. Walker the night fighter, the guerrilla warrior, seeking out his enemies. At one point he lay awake and wondered if it was this dangerous quality that women found attractive. Walker was the hardened veteran, the survivor of Vietnam and wild Himalayan rivers, and he'd lived to talk of his adventures.

Cruz, on the other hand, had never been under fire in any situation or known the perils and challenges of war. When he was in high school he'd played with the idea of joining the marines and always pictured himself as a good soldier, the kind of man that others could depend on and trust. Yet he'd never enlisted, never had the opportunity to prove his courage, not even on the athletic field. The possibility of losing his nerve, of folding under pressure and failing, still haunted him.

But he was aware that tomorrow could kill any doubts in his own mind. It would be a day to reclaim a lifetime of missed chances. He looked up and saw the moon hanging in the wedge of sky between the canyon walls. His head ached and he felt incredibly tired, as if his shoulders and arms were filled with sand and he might never lift them again. But he couldn't sleep. He lay awake and saw himself as a sentry, ever steadfast and watchful, longing for the grey-green light of daybreak to seep over the canyon rim and bring with it some hope, some taste of sweet redemption.

* * *

Breakfast was simple the following morning. They rekindled the fire for coffee, then ate cold cereal and dried fruit. Crawdad and Walker didn't talk to one another, but seemed to fidget back and forth, as if about to say something. Walker kept giving Cruz little bits of advice on what the day would be like and how he needed to prepare. Crawdad sat quietly through it all, sipping his coffee and studying the two of them.

"Take my word for it," Walker said, staring over at him. "Before we get into the big stuff, put some heavy-duty safety lines on your oars in case they pop free. And don't be afraid to take on a little water at the top of some of the rapids. You might need the weight to bang through a big hole." He looked away from Cruz, then nudged a glowing ember back into the fire with his foot. "Tie everything down extra tight and rig some of the weight up in the bow next to Crawdad. You want most of your load up front, like a pile driver. When you drop into the steep rapids, take a few strokes at the lip of the drop to slow down so you don't start freight-training out of control."

"Just stay out of our way," Cruz said in response.

"I'll be the least of your problems," Walker said.

"I doubt that," Crawdad said. "Just listening to you gives me one helluva headache."

After packing their gear onshore, Cruz tried to hurry through the rigging. Even though it was early morning, the sun was already heating up the black tubes of the raft. "It's gonna be a real scorcher," Crawdad yelled from shore. Cruz noticed that Walker seemed impatient and edgy, hustling some black bags down to the raft, then quickly suiting up in his kayak gear.

Cruz finished the rigging, then clipped his life jacket on. Walker slid the kayak into the water. Using his paddle as a brace against the shore, he smoothly slipped into the cockpit, his long legs vanishing within the yellow plastic hull. He paddled a few strokes into the eddy and tipped over. Cruz saw the blade of the paddle emerge from underneath and go flat against the surface. Then in a swift, rolling motion, he popped back up, water dripping from his face and beard.

"The morning baptism," he said, shaking the water off. "It's time to get wet." He swung the kayak up next to the raft and grabbed one of the D-rings to steady himself.

"I'll lead today, so follow my route. I'll try to pick channels that I know the raft will fit through. A lot of the rapids are filled with rocks and boulders, and you just go for the cleanest chute. So be ready to do some bouncing. It's a pinball game up here and you just have to keep working."

Cruz stared down at the water and nodded. Crawdad stood onshore with the bowline. He expected the old man to say something, possibly to argue with Walker, but he remained silent.

Walker continued. "If it's a blind drop, I'll point one way or the other to show you the entrance. There's a couple of places where we need to stop and scout and make sure there's no fallen trees blocking the river."

Walker smiled and slapped the raft with his hand. "It's just like going to war," he said. "Only you have to dance in the minefields if you're gonna have any fun."

Cruz let Walker ease ahead of him as Crawdad cast off, then pushed the stern of the raft into the main current. Crawdad stood in the bow, gazing downstream and following Walker's path. Almost immediately the river dropped away and the first rapid began, a big sweeping right turn where all the current piled into a boulder fence on the left. There wasn't time to watch Walker's run, only to see the obstacle and start pulling away toward a narrow chute. Once he'd cleared the rocks, he swung his oars in and let the boat descend over the drop.

"Watch out!" Crawdad yelled and Cruz saw an undercut stone wall waiting at the bottom. He tried to swing his oars back into the water, but there wasn't any room for the wooden blades to grab current. The raft's bow slammed into the wall, rebounded, then the boat slid backward into the pool below, brimming full of water, but upright. Cruz strained for the left shore, where he saw Walker waiting in an eddy, while Crawdad began furiously bailing.

"It's kind of like sex," Crawdad yelled over the sound of the rapid.

"How's that?" Cruz asked, struggling at the oars.

"It doesn't really matter how you do it, just as long as it feels good in the end."

"I'll remember that the next time I get my butt kicked in a rapid."

"I know you will," said Crawdad, grinning.

When they reached the eddy, Walker said, "You're gonna have to do a little better than that. Upper Freeman's just a little test."

Cruz gazed downstream and saw another horizon line where the river dropped away. An enormous tree, its roots splayed and tangled, had fallen from the left shore and extended out into the river.

"That looks nasty," Cruz said.

"It is," Walker said. "Welcome to Freeman Creek Falls."

"Don't worry about us," Crawdad said. "We'll find a way through it. You just take care of your own ass in that plastic boat."

They tied off, then walked down to scout. Cruz could already feel his forearms tightening and he tried to massage them with his fingers as they waded through the high grass to where the tree lay. Walker was crouched on top of the trunk and stared down at the rapid. A black belt of nylon webbing encircled his waist, and Cruz saw an assortment of river hardware dangling from it: a sheath knife, carabiners, small metal pulleys, and a whistle.

The tree blocked at least half the river, leaving a small gap for passage along the right side against a sheer wall. But the streambed leading up to the tree seemed to have caved in, a landslide of rock, and Cruz could hardly make out a passage wide enough for the kayak, let alone the raft. It was a junkyard of a rapid that was steeper, tighter, more complicated than anything he'd seen on the lower sections of the Kern. As if that weren't enough, a violent reversal waited at the bottom, swirling up against the rock wall and plunging down. Crawdad looked at the rapid, spat into the river, then casually pointed to the far side.

"There's your route over there," he said, "hugging that rock wall. You'll have to go slow, but I think you can squeeze it."

"Will we fit?" Cruz asked.

Walker grinned. "Think skinny." Then he shook his head. "At this water level, I was hoping you'd be thinking portage. That run on the right might be possible, but you're gonna hit the hole at the bottom and it'll chew you up."

"No need to portage," Crawdad said. "Just as long as the hole shoots us back out."

"That raft of yours is pretty big to be fitting through all this."

"We'll make it fit," Crawdad said.

The old man walked toward the water and dipped the toe of his tennis shoe in, then turned and said, "I think Cruz'll do just fine. I'm not so sure about you."

"Why's that?" Walker said.

"You don't have your Comfort this morning, do you? You have to think about all the things that can go wrong."

Walker didn't respond. He just licked his lips and studied the water. Then he smiled. "A whole lot can go wrong up here. You gotta keep an eye out for one another."

"Both eyes," Crawdad said sharply. "One in front, and one at your back, if you know what I mean."

They continued to study the rapid. The route was tricky, and Cruz followed the old man's finger as he tried to outline the run, which zigzagged through the center, then quickly cut to the right next to the rock wall. "Stay the hell away from the tree on the left. That's a deathtrap."

They let Walker run it first, and Cruz and Crawdad waited at the bottom with throw bags in case of an accident. From where Cruz positioned himself onshore, the rapid looked even more choked and congested with a multitude of places to pin or wrap, as if a dynamite explosion had littered the stream with shrapnel.

Walker's entrance was flawless and he seemed to toy with the upper part of the rapid. His narrow boat threaded a series of tiny slots on the far left, a route different from the one Crawdad favored. But as Walker descended, Cruz noticed the kayak gaining speed along the way, accelerating in the direction of the downed tree. Suddenly Walker's boat went sideways into a rock, and it was as if some dark arm reached out, seized the kayak, and then flung it upside down.

Cruz gripped the throw line as he tried to keep Walker in sight. He saw a paddle blade rise from under the current and sweep across the surface of the water as Walker swung himself up. His arms moved quickly into motion and propelled the kayak around the tree. He cut back to the right to avoid a barricade of rocks, then swiftly pivoted the boat's nose and dropped into the reversal. Cruz expected it to devour him, but instead, Walker caught the edge and surfed around the deepest part. The reversal caught the rear of the kayak, slammed it down, then catapulted the needle-nose bow into the air in a spectacular pop-up, shooting Walker into the pool below like a rocket. He paddled over, and brought the kayak to a halt next to where Cruz had been stationed.

"Pretty wild ride," Cruz yelled to him.

Walker smiled and shook his head, then used a hand to wipe water from his nose. "Take a different route," he shouted. "And stay away from that tree."

Carrying the throw bag, Cruz and Crawdad hiked back upstream to the raft. Cruz stopped at different places to crouch down and study the run they'd discussed, trying to memorize certain features of the streambed or the specific shape of a rock which could serve as a marker. When he reached the boat, Crawdad was already there, having untied the bowline from a nearby tree. Cruz clambered into the rowing seat and took one more look at the horizon line.

"Got your route picked out?" Crawdad asked.

Cruz nodded. He bent down and cupped some water to splash over his face. The sun was intense and shimmering off the pale stone that lined the canyon. All around him the colors of the plants and shoreline vegetation seemed dusty and brown. He tugged the helmet on and felt it clamp down over his head and ears. *A brain bucket.*

Crawdad pushed off and Cruz didn't waste any time. He cranked out two strokes that took him to the center of the river. The old man was perched in the bow, hunkered down low with his weight forward. Cruz pushed on the oars and drove the boat ahead, slicing between two boulders. Then he stalled the raft momentarily, pulling back to slow down and provide a few seconds to check the entrance. He saw a path that cut crazily through the heart of the rapid and then veered away from the tree.

With a snap of the oars he pitched the boat forward and felt the bow dive into the rocky trough. The upper channel was too tight to have much control, so he shipped the oars in and hung on. The raft took a beating, scraping and sliding over the rocks as it descended. At the bottom, a sneaky wave poured over the bow and buried Crawdad, filling the boat with water.

"Pull!" he heard Crawdad yell as the tree suddenly loomed in front of them. Cruz swung the oars out and felt the bite of the blades in the water, but the raft didn't respond. He crouched down on the rowing seat and used his legs to push upward with the stroke, then felt the boat surge to the right. The water was slower here and in three quick pulls he'd made it around the tree, then found himself perilously sideways as he tried to set up for the bottom reversal.

The raft suddenly rebounded off a boulder, sending the bow spinning in the opposite direction of what he'd wanted. Disoriented, the water and stone a whirling blur around him, he heard Crawdad shout, "Straighten it!" So he ripped off a double-oar turn, hoped for the right angle, then felt the sickening sensation of falling as they dropped backward into the meat of the hole.

The boat's momentum bucked against the current as if trying to pull free, then stalled. The oar handles were ripped from his fingers by the pounding water, and he found himself staring into the thrashing center of the reversal. A surge of water rose up from behind, as if the head of some great beast had surfaced underneath and was trying to tip the raft over.

He heard Crawdad yell, "To the high side!" The old man scrambled past him to the back of the boat as Cruz lunged for the oars, hoping to somehow pull away from the hole. But it was all in vain as the raft's bow was sucked under by the churning lip of the reversal and Cruz felt himself catapulted out of the rowing seat and thrown headfirst over the front thwart. A wall of water smashed him to the floor and he fought to get upright, even though the boat was violently shaking beneath him. *A keeper,* he thought. *A badass muncher.*

Then he heard a voice shouting above the roar, followed by a howl of laughter. "You're doing great, Cruz!" the voice yelled. "Ride it out!" He got to his knees and climbed over the thwart, then looked over at the slanted rock wall they were being slammed against. Perched safely on a narrow ledge a few feet above and leering down at him like some canyon gargoyle was Crawdad, a sly grin on his face. "Don't give up the ship, Cruz!" he yelled.

The raft was pitching about wildly and Cruz clawed his way back to the rowing seat and hung on to the slanted wooden board. He looked over at Crawdad and shouted, "How the hell did you get over there?" The old man made a climbing motion with his hands, then said, "It looked a little drier." There was another shout from the opposite shore and Cruz turned to see Walker hurling a throw bag at him, a spool of white line unfurling behind the airborne nylon pouch. Cruz grabbed the bag and wrapped it quickly around the trembling metal frame, then tied it off. At the other end, Walker was straining to yank the raft free of the hole. Cruz saw his strategy and managed to grab hold of the flailing oars, then regain his position in the rowing seat. He timed his stroke with Walker's pull from shore and after a few tries they were able to pop the raft free. As Cruz felt the surge of current taking them downriver, Crawdad leaped from the wall and landed in the bow, which was overflowing with water.

"Glad you could join me," Cruz grunted as he rowed the heavy boat to shore. "Thanks for all your help."

Crawdad laughed and unclipped a bucket so he could bail. "Once we dropped into that bitch, I knew what was coming and I decided to go someplace high and dry. This old body doesn't need another kicking around."

"True," Cruz said. "A wise choice."

Walker helped tow them into an eddy, then tied the boat off to a pine tree. As they surveyed the dripping gear, Crawdad said, "Helluva tie-down job, Cruz. Didn't even lose an oar." Most of the bags and equipment were intact, although the lines that held them had loosened due to the pounding force of the water. Cruz sat on a rock and took his helmet off, then glanced back upstream at the rapid. "I guess that one took a bite out of me," he said, shaking his head.

"Sit tight and relax," Crawdad said. "I'll retie the load."

Walker came over and began to stuff the loose rope back into the nylon throw bag.

"You did good out there," Walker said. "But this is just a taste of the rapids that are coming. It gets tougher downstream." His voice dropped low. "This river will kick your ass if you don't know what's going on. I know. I've done my share of swimming up here. I know what it's like to get yanked to the bottom of a suck hole."

Cruz tried not to look at him, instead watching Crawdad as he rigged.

"It's okay to be scared," Walker said. "It's also all right to say I'm in way over my head and need to hike out. You'll live a lot longer that way. Don't forget about a certain lady who's waiting for you."

Cruz turned and looked at him, remembered his grinning face as he danced with Rita, the way his hand slid over her hip. He stood up from the boulder and looked down at Walker, his mouth firm as he spoke. "Thanks for pulling me in," he said.

"No problem," answered Walker. "I'm just trying to help." He smiled and nodded.

"As for the other stuff you mentioned," said Cruz, "about being scared and all. I can handle it. Just show me the run and watch out for your own ass. It's that simple." He didn't give him a chance to reply. He walked away with his helmet tucked under his arm and went to help Crawdad finish with the raft.

CHAPTER THIRTEEN

Put it behind you, Cruz thought as he climbed back onto the rowing seat. Even though his words to Walker had been delivered in a confident manner, he felt jittery. The sun was directly above them, heating up the dead air at the bottom of the canyon and quickly evaporating any water on the tubes of the raft. Upstream, the rapid that had trashed him roared on in a seemingly endless cascade. He wondered what a hiker from the shore might think upon seeing the drop. *Such a pretty waterfall. Like something out of a painting.*

He'd smashed his right thumb on the metal frame and the nail was turning purple, so he held it in the river to keep the swelling down. When they were ready, Crawdad stood onshore with the bow line and waited for the signal to push off.

"Not a great way to start," Cruz said to him.

"No, but at least you're breathing," said Crawdad. "Accidents are gonna happen, and the river's going to try and screw you over. Expect it."

"What about downstream?"

"We'll take 'em one rapid at a time," Crawdad said. "Hang in there."

When Walker was ready they pulled out and Cruz tried to pace himself, conserving some of his strength. Walker darted ahead in the kayak, his paddling smooth as he broke through small waves and surfed around holes. Cruz looked for places where they might climb out if an emergency occurred. There were none. No signs of fishermen or hikers or campsites. He struggled to follow Walker's directions above each drop, the whitewater a blur of motion. The main rapids came at them in dark succession, and Walker summoned them by name — Needlerock Falls, Big Bean, Vortex, the Gauntlet — all twisting blind channels where the river suddenly plummeted down into violence.

The day seemed timeless, water billowing around them as the immense canyon walls loomed overhead. The rest places near shore were few and the boat was sluggish to maneuver, overflowing with the river. The Kern whipped by in a racehorse blend of enormous suck holes and razor-sharp rocks. At Coffin Corner the black raft slammed against an undercut boulder, wedging tight. Water began to pour over the upstream tube, threatening to suck the boat under and wrap it around the obstacle. Together Cruz and Crawdad pulled on the lone oar that was loose, straining to pivot the raft around the rock. Suddenly the boat shuddered, then slid free. They scrambled back to their positions, Cruz at the oars and Crawdad bailing. He felt besieged by the fury surrounding him.

After the incident at Coffin Corner there was a half mile lull where they came out of the canyon and into a long straightaway of flat water. It gave Cruz a chance to rest and allow the current to do the work. He relaxed his arms while they ate some bread and salami and cheese. Cruz was starving and he jammed each bite into his mouth, barely taking time to chew before swallowing. At one point Crawdad turned and extended his arms outward in a grand, sweeping gesture. "Look at this place. Can you believe it? Nothing's changed since I was here last. Not a damn thing."

Cruz took his eye off the river and studied the high mantle of trees above the canyon on either side. No sign of fire or beetle plague to scar the landscape. "Is this why you wanted to come back here?" he said to the old man. "To see this again?"

"I've spent half my life dragging people out of the lower Kern," Crawdad said. "I needed to know that some things never die."

Walker floated alongside them, his free hand holding on to the perimeter line. He smiled at Cruz. "You're rowing well," he said.

"Coffin Corner about dumped us, but we got through," Cruz replied.

"Don't let up," said Walker. "It's easy to get lazy in this long calm and think you've made it through the hard stuff."

"What else is there?" Cruz asked.

"Westwall is next," he said. "You'll know it by the huge cliff on the right side of the river. The rapid is nearly a quarter mile long with a big drop at the bottom."

"Are we scouting?"

Walker shook his head. "No time for that. We need to hustle if we're gonna be out of the canyon by nightfall. Just read it as you go and run the last drop dead center."

Cruz took a long drink from his water bottle and nodded. He tried to envision the rapid Walker was describing and form a clear picture in his head.

"As soon as you get through Westwall," Walker said, "start pulling for the left shore. You'll probably be full of water and there's only one eddy to catch. If you miss it, you're in trouble, because the next big rapid, the Horns of the Dragon, is about a half mile downstream. You don't want to run it without scouting."

"What's that one like?"

Before Walker could respond, Crawdad said, "It's the biggie. We'll worry about it when we get there."

Cruz looked at Walker and said, "I won't miss the eddy." He tried to sound convincing and look him in the eye, but it seemed false, and he knew there was a tremor in his voice, as if he were shivering from the cold.

Walker released the perimeter line and drifted slowly next to the raft. "Just in case," he said, "give me a few minutes lead time before you run Westwall. I'll set up safety in the eddy at the bottom. If you come through out of control, I can snag you with a throw line. Just wrap the line around — "

Crawdad cut him off. "He knows what to do with the damn line," he said, snapping at Walker. "Just make sure you're in that eddy."

Walker scowled and pushed away from the raft. "Don't worry, old man. I'll be there."

"Just like you were there for Rose," Crawdad mumbled after Walker was out of earshot.

The kayak accelerated with a few quick strokes of Walker's paddle, then continued moving downriver until it disappeared around the far bend. As they floated, Cruz pulled back on the oars to slow their progress and give Walker a head start. Crawdad turned around in the bow and said, "If he has to throw us a rope, I'll take it. You won't have time to stop rowing and deal with it. Just try to keep your oars free of the line so they don't get tangled up."

As they rounded the corner a gigantic wall of striped granite came into view and hovered in the distance like a mountainous sentry. Cruz pulled back for another minute, listening to the rapid's faint but steady rumble. The river moved straight ahead for a hundred yards before it dropped away. He kept his eyes set on the entrance and continued to study it as they drifted closer. On the right side there was an opening between two granite slabs that looked promising. Everything else to the left and center was a jumbled mess of undercut rocks and half-submerged boulders. "I'm going far right," he said to Crawdad. There was no response from the old man as he crouched down in the bow. Cruz eased the boat into the arrowlike slot and pushed hard toward the right shore.

It was a smooth entrance as the raft split the stone markers. He snapped his oars in at the last second so they wouldn't catch, then scraped over a ledge without taking on a drop of water. *Slick as shit,* he thought. Things felt right, a steady rhythm to his rowing, and he muscled a double-oar turn and spun the boat around to face a series of cresting waves that charged downriver. He accelerated into the first one and was immediately spun sideways, then buried with a curling diagonal that swamped the raft and almost knocked him out of the boat. He recovered, realized that he'd underestimated the size and power of the waves, then saw Crawdad still clinging to the bow and trying to bail. They bombed into the next wave, and the one after that, and each time Cruz managed to pivot the raft so they hit them all dead-on and crashed through.

Then there was a sudden calm, almost a stillness, as if they were in the eye of a storm. Crawdad was bailing at a frenzied pace as the water rolled over Cruz's legs. "Stay right!" the old man yelled. But Cruz had little control over the raft as it collided bow-on with a rock. The whiplash sent Crawdad tumbling backward over the thwart and Cruz helped him to his feet. After returning to the oars Cruz saw the rapid's final descent, a furious channel at midstream that poured over two steep ledges. He stood up at the oars and leaned into his strokes as he tried to coax some speed into the boat. Then they were in it, waves exploding around him as the oars were ripped from his fingers. At the last second he tucked his right leg under the wooden seat and held on through the final savage drop that jolted them once more, then spit the boat out as if it were a cheap rubber toy.

He saw Crawdad still in the bow, water streaming down his face. The old man shouted, "Row for shore!" Cruz grabbed the oars, braced his legs against the frame, and cranked back. Slowly, as if tearing free of some unseen force, the raft budged, then began to inch downstream. Crawdad had the bailing bucket out immediately and was yelling, "Catch the left eddy!" Water sloshed around the interior of the boat while Cruz looked over his shoulder for a glimpse of Walker with the line.

But the eddy was empty. "Where the hell's Walker?" Crawdad said. Cruz wrestled with the oars, tried to pull left, but knew they weren't going to make it. They sped by, gathering momentum as the current propelled them forward. The next little rapid loomed close, another horizon line with only a jagged barricade of rocks visible downstream. If they didn't get over to bail, they'd begin to freight-train and eventually hurtle out of control. Cruz knew it was only a matter of time before his hands and fingers would cramp and become useless claws wrapped around the oar handles. *Jump ship and get the hell out of here.* He wanted to swim for shore and feel the safe, rocky ground beneath his feet. Images of drowning, of going under again, flashed through his mind as he looked ahead.

Then something happened. There was a moment, maybe only a few seconds, when it was clear they'd missed the eddy and were committed to running the next rapid. Crawdad glanced downstream, then quickly back at Cruz. "Switch with me," he said, and climbed over the thwart. "Move, dammit!" he shouted, practically yanking Cruz off the slanted seat. "I'll row and you bail."

Cruz didn't question him. He jumped into the bow and grabbed the plastic bucket. At first Crawdad looked frail at the oars, as if the long wooden shafts would break him. Yet as he rowed, Cruz saw that his strokes were solid and compact. When they dropped into the rapid, the old man didn't fight the raft's momentum or the quick current. He dipped the oar blades into the river, pulled back as they slid over the pinnacle of a wave, then waited to see where the rush of water would take them. "Keep bailing!" he yelled to Cruz.

Each time they were about to collide with a boulder, Crawdad would swing the nose around at the last second, then ram it bow-on. The boat would rebound against the current, slow, then continue. At one point they dropped sideways over a ledge and into a huge reversal and Cruz was terrified they would flip. But the raft bucked through the hole and plowed ahead.

Cruz began to see the old man's strategy. The swamped boat was too heavy to flip or get held by a reversal. He was using the weight like a pile driver, and each time they encountered an obstacle, he tried to face it head-on and use the collision as a sort of brake, a way of slowing down. It was simply a matter of the raft's being able to take the pounding, and hoping a tube wouldn't explode when it slammed into a rock. Crawdad handled the boat as if it were a whirling top, spinning it around with the oars and letting the swift water propel it forward.

Suddenly the river slowed, if only for a short stretch, and Crawdad called out for him to drop the bucket. "Grab an oar," he said. "Maybe the two of us can get it over." Cruz scrambled back to the rowing seat, then grabbed one of the oars and gripped it with both hands. Side by side, they rowed in unison and tried to swing the raft to the left shore. Downstream Cruz could see another horizon line where the next rapid began. "Pull!" Crawdad grunted.

Then they heard a voice from behind shout, "Grab it!", and a nylon throw bag, its line spilling out, came rifling over Crawdad's shoulder. The old man grabbed the rope and quickly wrapped it around the metal frame, then continued to row with Cruz. A few seconds later they hit the shoreline and saw that Walker had tied the rescue line to a large pine tree and they were held firm.

Crawdad dropped the oar and slumped forward, his breath a steady pant. He took the helmet off and lay back on the wooden seat, gasping for air. Cruz saw the kayak beached just upstream from where they'd landed, and he stepped out of the raft and stood facing Walker.

"I'm glad to see you made it," Walker said. "That was a nasty one."

"Nasty is right," Cruz said, out of breath. "My hands started to cramp and Crawdad rowed the last section."

"Where the hell were you?" Crawdad said. "Weren't you supposed to be waiting for us in the eddy? You're the goddamn safety boat."

"I missed it," Walker said. "I tried a cheat chute through the left side and nearly got pinned in an undercut. My head got slammed around on the bottom and I tried to roll, but it took me a couple of tries to finally pop one. By the time I got up, I'd shot past the eddy."

A long silence followed and Cruz looked downstream to where the river narrowed. Three hundred yards away and planted in the center of the current he saw two enormous black rocks, spiked at the top and shaped like tusks. Walker pointed at them. "The Horns of the Dragon," he said. "We have to scout this one."

They made their way carefully along the shoreline, occasionally wading through eddy pools and climbing over boulders, until they drew even with the Horns and Cruz got his first glimpse of what lay beyond. Twenty feet high and spanning the river like a thunderous, steel grey curtain, the waterfall poured into an enormous, recirculating hole that boiled from the undercurrent. *The dragon's lair,* Cruz thought. A picket fence of glistening, pointed rock lay at the base of the falls, unbroken except for a slot in the center directly under the Horns where the water surged through.

They stood on a truck-sized chunk of granite just across from the falls and studied it. "This is the real thing," Walker said. "We've just been practicing until now. The game gets serious here."

"It looks like a portage," Crawdad said.

"It's runnable," Walker said. "I've done it before at lower flows. The waves up above are easy, so you just have to split the Horns dead center, then hang on for all you're worth."

"It looks crazy," Cruz said.

"I'll go first," said Walker, "so you can follow my route. Then I'll set up a couple of safety lines in case something goes wrong."

"Bullshit," Crawdad barked, turning on Walker. "You gonna set up safety like you did below Westwall?"

"I told you already," said Walker. "It was an accident. It won't happen again."

"Like hell it was an accident. I think you missed it on purpose so you could see Cruz and me go for a swim."

Walker stepped forward, his face growing red. "I pull your ass into shore and you throw this shit at me? All that rowing must have drained your brain or something."

"You didn't come up here to watch out for Cruz, did you?" said Crawdad. "You came up here to mess with his head. It's your style."

"How would you know what my style is?"

"I'm telling you," Crawdad continued. "I've watched you pull some weird stuff before. Don't try it up here."

"What stuff?" Walker said, laughing.

"You know. I've seen how you work a crew. All the mind shit."

"That's just playing around."

"Then what about Cruz's girlfriend?"

Walker was silent for a moment. He stepped away from the old man and looked out at the river. Cruz shaded his eyes from the late afternoon sun. He could feel it bearing down on them, warming the granite slab under their feet. The waterfall roared on. He waited for Walker to respond, and when he didn't, Cruz said, "Answer him."

"What about her?" Walker said.

"Are you playing a game with Rita?" Cruz asked.

"There's no game."

"Then what's going on?"

"Everything," Walker said, "and nothing." He turned and glared at Cruz. "What if something was going on? What if I was humping your girl behind your back? What if I was fucking her lights out every night up at my trailer and she happened to like it? Who are you gonna trust then? Are you still gonna love her?" He took a step toward Cruz, fists clenched, and shoved him. "You don't deserve her," Walker said, "and I don't need your paranoid shit."

"Leave him alone," Crawdad said firmly, stepping forward. "It isn't all paranoid and it wouldn't be the first time, would it?"

"How would you know, old timer?" Walker asked.

"I've got a good memory. A few years ago you stole Barreno's girlfriend behind his back, then set him up to get fired."

Walker glanced over at Cruz and smiled, shaking his head in disbelief.

"Your memory's shot," he said to Crawdad. "That's old history and you're forgetting all the juicy details. Like Barreno's girlfriend came on to me, and he was stealing shit from the warehouse."

"It's funny," Crawdad said, glancing down at his wet tennis shoes. He chuckled. "All I remember was that Barreno got his ass fired because he was set up."

"He was stealing tools," Walker said.

Crawdad took a step closer until he was only a few feet away from Walker. *He's crowding him,* Cruz thought. *Turning up the heat.* The old man began to laugh. "Maybe all that Southern Comfort you been putting away is starting to cloud your memory," Crawdad said.

"I doubt it," said Walker.

"And what about right now, the way you're playing with Cruz's head by coming up here. He knows what you're pulling with his girlfriend."

"I wouldn't do that," Walker said. "Not to Rita."

"You wouldn't?" Crawdad said, sarcastically. "But you did it to Rose, didn't you?" Walker's face became sober and he looked straight at Crawdad. "Rosebud," the old man said, repeating her name with relish. "Or don't you remember her, either?"

Walker lashed out at him, a furious swing at his jaw, and the old man's neck snapped back with the impact as he fell, his shoulder striking the surface of the rock. Cruz was stunned by the speed of Walker's hand and how quickly everything had exploded. The old man rose to one elbow, grimacing and massaging his jaw. As Cruz tried to help, Crawdad pushed him away and rose slowly to his feet.

Walker hadn't moved. He stood there, his hands clenched at his side.

"Now we're getting somewhere," Crawdad said.

"You should know better, old man," hissed Walker. "There's a price for saying that kind of shit."

"Nothing's ever free. Not even women."

"You know all about that, don't you?" said Walker. "Sometimes the cost is different than what you expect." Cruz watched them intently, ready to jump in and help if Crawdad needed him. Walker took a step closer to the old man until he was only a foot away and said, "Or did you want Rose all to yourself?" he said harshly. "Maybe that's why she jumped off that bridge. Because of something you did to her."

Crawdad didn't respond at first. He held his ground and waited until Walker had finished. Then he slipped the gold ring from his finger and slowly lifted it in front of Walker's face as if he were performing some ritual and holding a sacred ornament to the sun.

Walker stared at the ring as if he'd seen something ghostly that had suddenly stepped from the river. There was a long moment of silence, and Cruz was aware that the men were breathing hard as they faced one another, that the river was thundering by fifty feet away, and the sun gleamed overhead as bright and intense as the light in a surgeon's operating room, revealing skin and tissue and scar.

Then Crawdad began to speak in a voice that came from some lost place. It was his voice, but he struggled with the words, as if recalling a memory that had slipped through his mind like smoke. It reminded Cruz of the time in Crawdad's cabin when the old man had first shown him the jewelry collected from the drowned.

"When she walked onto that bridge," Crawdad began, "she counted the metal beams, one by one, in this singsong voice just like she'd done when she was a kid. She didn't stop until she counted to fifteen and was out in the center, high above the river. She wore her new red dress and perfume and thought about taking the ring off and chucking it over the side, but she didn't because she liked the way it gleamed on her finger." Crawdad paused, looked at the ring even more intently and Cruz noticed that his hands were trembling. "So she climbed over the metal railing and was real careful not to catch her dress on anything that might snag it. And when she stepped off, she was surprised at how peaceful falling was, just this big quiet before she hit the river. All the way down she saw herself as a little girl again and how she used to go swimming at night down at the Kern and leap out of the trees as she dove into the black water."

He stopped, still holding the ring in front of Walker. "I loved Rose like she was my own. And you abandoned her. Now live with it." Then Crawdad turned away from him.

Walker's face was stricken and drained of color and he raised a hand as if to stop him. "Wait," he said. "I've been living with it for nearly ten years."

Crawdad looked back at him and said, "In what way?"

"You weren't the only one that loved her."

"Then why'd you dump her?" Crawdad said angrily.

Walker lowered his head. "I thought breaking it off was the best thing for both of us."

"It wasn't. Not even close."

"I know that now."

"You might as well have poisoned her."

"I was the one who got poisoned," Walker said.

"You didn't even come to the funeral," Crawdad said.

"I came." He turned away, his face hidden from Cruz. "I was on the hill above the cemetery and watched until it was over. I knew I wasn't welcome."

"You should've been there to help bury her," Crawdad said. "It would have been the right thing to do."

"I know. And I've seen that funeral again and again in my head, maybe a thousand times. I had to stand there and take it all in and there wasn't a damn thing I could do. It's what I've had to live with."

Crawdad was studying Walker intently and took a few steps toward him, then stopped. "You should've said these things a long time ago. I would've listened then."

Walker turned and faced him. "I didn't know what to say. I didn't know the words. But I'm saying them now."

"I'm listening to you," Crawdad said, his voice losing its hard edge. "You're ten years late but I'm listening to every word."

They stood in silence for a long time and stared down at the waterfall. Cruz waited for one of them to speak, but when neither did, he figured it was for the best. Their shadows extended out over the shoreline to the edge of the river, and Cruz looked at the drop and tried to imagine taking the raft over it.

"You're welcome to run it," said Crawdad, gesturing at the falls. "It's your funeral. But I'm walking. We can always line the raft if there's no place to carry."

"What do you say, Cruz?" said Walker. "The ride of your life. You and me. We'll give Crawdad the safety lines and he can wait below for us to come through."

Cruz said nothing. He studied the drop, how the water churned and thrashed at the base of the falls. He wanted to take Walker on, surprise him with something primitive and risky. He wanted Rita to see him take the raft over like some fearless warrior. *Walk with the devil,* she'd said to him. He'd show her he wasn't scared. Then he felt a hand on his shoulder and he turned to see Walker standing close. "Run it with me, Cruz. It's like flying off the edge of the world."

Cruz looked at Crawdad and the old man said, "It's your call. You're the one that's rowing."

He hesitated, looked at Walker and then back at the falls. "I'll do it," he said. "I'll split the Horns with you."

"C'mon then. The dragon's waiting," Walker said.

They walked upstream together, then gave their throw bags to Crawdad. "I need five minutes to get down and set up safety," Crawdad said. The old man paused onshore for a moment and watched as they readied the kayak and the raft. He looked at Cruz and said, "I could tell you all kinds of shit about how dangerous this is, but it wouldn't do a lick of good. So do what you have to. If anything goes wrong, look for my rope."

"Okay," Cruz said.

Then Crawdad went over to Walker, who was seated in his kayak, and crouched down next to him. He held out his hand and Cruz saw the gold ring in his palm. "Take it," Crawdad said. "It's yours now." Walker took the ring from the old man and quietly slipped it onto his own finger. Then Crawdad picked up the throw bags and hobbled off down the shore.

Cruz checked the raft over, making sure that the bow and stern lines were coiled and that the spare oar was fastened down tight. He bailed out any excess water, then took a long drink from the canteen.

Walker glided by in his kayak, watching Cruz as he prepared. He paddled up to the raft and grabbed the perimeter line, then leaned over so that his mouth was only inches from the water's surface. He cupped his hand and drank mouthful after mouthful, as if he'd been parched for hours. When he straightened up and wiped off his mouth and beard, he looked at Cruz and said, "You'll be right behind me when we run it and there'll be nothing fancy. Just remember to swing your oars in early as you cut between the Horns." Cruz nodded and spit into the river. "Think about something nice," Walker continued. "Think about going home to a beautiful woman." Then he paddled away.

Cruz stayed tight in the eddy until Walker hit the short rapid. Then he launched into the current and spun the bow around so he faced downstream. He could see the kayaker ahead of him in the center of the river, rising and falling with each wave, his helmet bobbing like a red beacon. The water was quick, and Cruz was into the rapid above the drop sooner than he'd expected. Panic seized him when a diagonal broke over the side of the raft and threw him to the left. He took his eye off Walker for a moment, frantically slapping at the water with his oars so he could pull back into the main flow. He looked up just in time to see the yellow kayak, dwarfed by the enormous Horns on either side, as it arched up the peak of a wave, then vanished.

Cruz aimed the bow at the spot where Walker disappeared and pushed forward on the oars, hitting each wave square-on and watching as the Horns grew closer, looming ahead like the ruins of some ancient gate. Then he was streaming by the black pillars, plenty of room on either side for him to swing the oars in and lean back. The boat sailed straight up the wave he'd seen Walker climb, the bow pointed skyward, and for a moment Cruz swore he would fly right off the brink and never fall.

He felt the snap of gravity in his neck and back, then the raft plunging into the vertical and dropping, the river yanked out from under like some cheap trick. He saw the churning base of the falls rise up to devour him, a great foaming mouth snapping shut as the raft descended, hit the turbulent water, and tipped on its side. For a split second he hung onto an oar, hoping it would somehow keep him in the boat, then realized that the raft was flipping, a dark cloud descending to cover him. He flung the oar handle aside so he could leap away, but it swung back and glanced off his helmet as his shoulder hit the water.

He was immediately sucked under the surface and slammed into something rock-hard and firm, his head rebounding off the object as water poured into his nostrils. He tried to shut out the river and looked up to see the shadow of the raft as it hung over him. A surge of water pushed him up toward the surface and he went with it, using his legs to kick away from the force that held him. He was somehow under the overturned raft in a black pocket of darkness and air. He filled his lungs, a quick gasp amid the violence, and lunged ahead with his arms to grab onto something solid. But it was no good, his legs suddenly yanked under and down. *It's gonna drown my ass,* he thought as he fought it, holding in the precious air and waiting for another rush of current to push him up.

When it came, he was ready, hands and feet paddling and kicking. He broke the surface again, sucked the air into his lungs and lunged ahead. Only this time it had him by the ankles and nearly tore his tennis shoes off, then jerked him back down again for another cycle. Images of Rita and Frank flashed through his mind as the water flailed at him, his throat and nose burning. *The drowned. The dead.* He stopped fighting, let it take him under, deeper than he'd gone before, until he was pressed into the river bottom, his cheek raking across gravel, the light changing from grey to black.

He was exhausted and battered, the water flooding in, when a sudden, miraculous rush of current carried him away. Tumbling, he scraped along the bottom, then was finally able to push off the streambed and shoot up to the surface. The air was sweet, almost painful as he sucked it in through his nose and mouth. A wave slapped the side of his face, but he managed to get his bearings and start swimming to the left. A gold rope slithered through the water ahead of him and he grabbed for it, took hold, then looked up to see Crawdad at the other end, swinging him to shore in a pendulum motion. The drop-off was steep and Cruz came in chest-up against the rocks. He reached out and grabbed hold of a small granite spire and tried to muscle his way over the top, but he was too weak. So he hung on until Crawdad arrived to seize him by the life jacket collar and drag him from the river.

For a moment he thought he might pass out as he lay panting on the warm stones, but he remained conscious. There was blood in his mouth and he spit it out, then reached up and felt a deep cut on his lip. Crawdad unbuckled Cruz's helmet and eased it off, then slipped a life jacket under his head. "Walker," Cruz said quickly, his voice panting from the swim, "where is he?"

"My god," Crawdad said, "what a sight!"

"Did he make it?"

"Damn right he did. It all happened so fast. First Walker and then you. He made it through the falls, but then got shot into the rocks on the right. I took my eye off him for a moment to watch you come over, and when I looked back, he'd rolled up and was past me." Crawdad laughed. "He's probably sitting in some eddy downstream waiting for your ass to come floating by."

Cruz sat upright and looked back at the falls. Daylight was beginning to wane and shadows fell across the pool, making it appear more ominous than before. "It looks bigger from down below," he said.

"No shit," Crawdad said. "It looked like you were dropping off the damn planet."

"Walker was right. He told me it would be like flying off the edge of the world."

"Hell, flying without a parachute, you mean."

Cruz stood up slowly. One of the wet-suit knees had been ripped open and blood oozed out of the tear. Crawdad kept talking. "When I saw the raft go over, I knew you were in for a bad swim. You must've been under for a minute, and when you finally popped up, it was at least twenty feet downstream."

"What about the boat?" Cruz asked.

"It got kicked out of the falls about the same time you did, so I didn't have a chance to grab it. We should probably go tell Walker you're okay and try to find the raft."

Crawdad coiled up the two safety lines. Then they started out, moving slowly over the slippery terrain because of Cruz's knee. There were odds and ends from the raft strewn along the shore and they picked up what they could. A plastic water bottle. The bailing bucket. One of the black gear bags. Crawdad spotted an oar wedged between two rocks just off the left shore and waded in to retrieve it. Cruz walked ahead.

He came around the first bend and saw the fallen tree, a huge ponderosa pine the length of a semi-truck and blocking the river like a green wall. He knew what it could mean and shouted Crawdad's name, then dropped the items from the raft and began to run, all the while scanning the river for any sign of Walker's kayak. Cruz spotted the raft, its black shape half-submerged under the enormous trunk, then slipped and fell. Pain shot up through his leg and he cursed at the poor footing, but got up and kept moving.

Crawdad was beside him when they both saw the kayak near midstream. The yellow shell was visible from within a tangle of pine and it seemed to tremble as the water piled into it. Cruz swept his eyes across the tree, hoping to see some sign of Walker pulling himself up from the branches to safety or even straddling the trunk as he waved. But there was nothing, only the kayak buried under the mass of green boughs, a flicker of bright yellow in the failing light.

"Hurry," Crawdad said, tugging at his arm and pulling him along. The old man moved swiftly ahead of him over the mossy stones and reached the tree first. They climbed onto the immense trunk, which was nearly as tall as Cruz, and began to work their way out over the water. The pine branches were dense and they had to fight through them, staining their wet suits and life jackets and hands with the vanilla-scented sap. The tree had fallen at the entrance to a rapid and the current was racing underneath them, kicking up an occasional swell of water that licked at their tennis shoes. It was vibrating from the force of the river, and Cruz grabbed fistfuls of pine to steady himself against the shaking trunk.

Within minutes they reached the raft and saw that a few of the black bags had come undone and had washed into the branches around them. "We need the climbing rope and the hooks," Crawdad said, pointing down at the objects. "Find them for me." Then he continued on along the tree, his legs vibrating as if walking an electrified plank.

Cruz was able to stoop down and grab some of the bags. He opened each one and found a variety of dry clothes, some canned food, and eventually, the rope and hooks. He slung the coil of line over his shoulder. Then, lifting the hooks, he started after the old man. When Cruz reached the kayak, he saw that it was upside down and lay at least four feet below them, the pointed stern thrust out from under the tree. Its yellow frame was only partially visible and sandwiched between the trunk and a massive branch that extended from beneath the water like a gnarled tentacle.

"Grab my ankles," Crawdad shouted above the roar as he lay chest-down on the tree. Cruz anchored his feet around a sturdy limb and took hold of the old man's legs, then watched as he slithered headfirst over the side. Unable to see the kayak, he felt the jerk and tug of Crawdad's trying to pry the boat free. Then he heard the old man's voice shouting, "Haul me up!" and he lifted him back onto the trunk.

"Is he in there?" Cruz asked.

Crawdad shook his head. "I don't know. I can't reach that far. I did get my hand on the stern loop and felt the kayak budge a little. If we use the hooks, I think we can pull it up."

They moved quickly into position, Cruz handling the rope and Crawdad working the hooks. No words were exchanged. The old man dangled the steel claws into the water, let them sink and drift under the kayak for a brief moment, then quickly snapped the line taut so the talons could grab the cockpit. When he was sure the hooks had caught, he and Cruz slid to the side for a better pulling angle, keeping an eye on the line as it vanished under the boat. They pulled for half a minute, leaning back with the strain, but nothing moved. The kayak held firm. Cruz didn't have any gloves and the rope tore at his hands. He heard the old man cursing.

"Keep it taut!" Crawdad yelled, and they rested for a moment, then went at it again. Only this time Cruz detected a slight retreat in the rope as if something were giving way. They pulled on and the kayak began to withdraw, foot by foot, the dark river swirling around it. He cursed the dusk, wished for a flashlight or lantern that would allow him to see under the surface. When they had the boat nearly free and there was still no sign of the body, Cruz eased up for a few seconds and took a long, slow breath. Then the kayak tilted as they swung it up against the tree, and he saw the flash of red under the surface, the shadowy outline of Walker's limp upper body still inside the boat, his left hand floating in the water as if reaching for help.

"Sweet Jesus," Crawdad said. "Pull him up!" Cruz tried to haul in the line, but the kayak was full of water and he could barely keep it from getting sucked back under the tree. Crawdad quickly rigged a sling with the rescue rope and, as Cruz held the boat tight, he slid it under the hull. With both of them pulling, they were able to hoist the boat up onto the trunk as Walker's body hung lifeless out of the cockpit. His helmet had cracked and there was a large scrape across his face from where a rock must have struck him. The front hull had caved in and was folded around his legs, pinning him inside.

There was no pulse. They leaned Walker onto the back deck and tried CPR to revive him. At first Crawdad worked feverishly on him alone, then traded off with Cruz when he began to get winded. As Cruz placed his mouth over Walker's to breathe, he remembered the young boy they'd brought back to life, the two of them working together in the darkness. They labored over Walker for five minutes, then fifteen, then thirty, hoping for some sign of recovery. But there was no response. Nothing. Eventually Crawdad eased away from the body. Cruz knelt by the side of the kayak.

"We should've gotten here sooner," Cruz said, gasping. "I had no idea — "

Crawdad cut him short. "It's no use second-guessing yourself. None of us knew there was a tree down here. I should've been there to pull him in after the falls."

"But you said he looked okay."

"He did look okay!" Crawdad snapped. "He just missed the eddy. Hell, he was probably looking upstream and checking for you when he went into the strainer."

For a long moment they said nothing as they knelt atop the tree next to Walker's body. Cruz closed his eyes, knowing what he needed to do. A routine he'd started after the first one, the girl they'd pulled from the lower Kern. Mental morphine. *Never look at the face. Focus on some piece of clothing or jewelry and keep your eyes trained on it. Block out any questions that might creep in. Avoid the personal. See it as an object. Something no longer alive. Something to be moved.*

He tried to do this with Walker, tried to keep some distance from what he felt and the task he needed to do. But it was no good. A life had been taken, and he felt the need to respect that, to look at Walker's hand and see the ring and think of a time when Rose was alive and in his arms. He thought of Rita and how he might tell her of Walker's death. *He looked peaceful. He died doing what he loved best.* But it sounded like bullshit to him. Cruz untied the bandanna from around his neck and wiped the blood from Walker's face.

"He saved my life once," Cruz said, staring down at the body, then up at Crawdad. "He pulled me in. I should've been there for him." He reached over and touched Walker's hand and felt the cold skin against his palm.

He looked at Crawdad and saw that the old man's head was bowed and that he held the hooks in his hands. "Goddamn," Crawdad said, his voice cracking. "He was almost home." He rattled the steel as he got up from his knees. "I never would've expected it. Not him. Not like this." He looked over at Cruz. "And the goddamn hooks finally dragged him out." Then he turned and flung the steel into the black river and Cruz watched them vanish under the swift current.

It took them nearly ten minutes to get Walker out of the kayak. He was jammed in tight and they had to cut the thigh straps, then grab under his arms and work the legs out. They left the boat perched on top of the tree and carried him to shore. Cruz stayed with the body while Crawdad went back out to the raft. In the gathering darkness he kept his hand on Walker's chest as if trying to reassure or soothe him in some way. The haunting image of Walker plunging over Cataract Falls replayed itself again and again in his mind. At one point Cruz felt his throat tighten and he fought back tears as his hand gripped Walker's T-shirt.

When Crawdad returned he had some rope and the big canvas tarp. "We ain't leaving him," the old man said firmly. "We're hiking out and he's going with us."

Cruz nodded in agreement. "We'll carry him home," he said.

"Damn right," Crawdad said. "This is one trip he's gonna finish."

After retrieving the upstream oar, they spread the tarp out on the shore and placed Walker in the center, then carefully folded the canvas around him. They set the oar on the ground and lashed the bundle to the pole so they could carry it on their shoulders. Then they peeled off their wet suits and stuffed them into a black bag that they left near the tree.

"Leave everything else," the old man said, pointing at the remaining gear. "It's not going anywhere. If we want it later, we can come back for it."

Crawdad was in front as they set out, the body dangling like some hunting trophy between them. It was awkward at first, the swinging weight throwing them off balance, but then Cruz began to match his steps with Crawdad's. It was slow going in the darkness and occasionally they stumbled when one slipped and threw the other off balance. After a while, Cruz's shoulder began to ache from the heavy burden, and he tried shifting the weight from one side to the other, but it didn't really help.

Every now and then Cruz could hear Crawdad talking under his breath. He'd say things like, "Not far now," or "Almost there, son, almost there." His voice was low and gentle, as if he were calming a sick child. Cruz couldn't tell if he was talking to Walker or to him. Cruz just listened and took some comfort in the old man's words. "Doing fine," Crawdad said. "Doing real fine."

They found a trail that arched away from the river, and Crawdad took it. Cruz had lost track of time, and as they marched up the steep grade, he imagined they were wading through some inky jungle. He expected Rita to somehow emerge from the darkness, her arms open wide. But how would she react? Would she embrace him first, or go to Walker's body to grieve? A cluster of bats danced above their heads for an instant, then flew away.

The trail was overgrown with bushes and thorny plants that tore at their legs, and Cruz was constantly alert for the sudden resonant chatter of a rattler underfoot. A partial moon had risen over the canyon mouth, and a pale light slanted down to illuminate the hillside. At resting places they eased their burden to the ground and Cruz stood below it, bracing the body with his feet so it couldn't roll down the slope. Crawdad slumped to one side, his breath wheezing out in short rapid bursts. Cruz looked up and saw a shadow glide across the trees, then cut down toward the river. An owl? A heron? He couldn't be sure.

When they reached the top of a ridge and the trail leveled off, he felt a second wind kick in. The slow, steady ache remained in his arms and shoulders, but he'd eased into a quiet place in his head, as if he were sitting in the blackest part of a cave and listening to the rhythmic pulse of his own heart. He saw himself as a soldier in the jungle, hauling a casualty home through enemy territory.

During one rest stop, Crawdad looked down at Walker's body and said, "He was a lot like you when he first started on the hooks."

Cruz nodded his head. "In what way?"

"After we pulled out a couple of bodies, he saw what it could do to a man. It scared the hell out of him."

"I never saw him as being scared of anything," Cruz said.

"He wouldn't show it," Crawdad said, "but it was there." Crawdad wiped his face with a bandanna. "He was different after he came back from the war. Pretty fearless. He didn't have any respect for the river or himself. He started going down into the Cataracts. Crazy shit like that." Crawdad paused and crouched down next to the body. "There's nothing wrong with being a little afraid. Sometimes it's what keeps you alive."

Cruz looked away from the body and the old man. Far below he could see the surface of the Kern, the whitewater sections flashing silver in the moonlight. At that moment he realized the river had always carried a double meaning for him of both fascination and fear. As a small boy he'd been seduced by the lustrous surface and the musical rush of water. But he'd always been terrified of diving into the depths to where the luster faded and there was total stillness. No air to breathe. No light to guide your way. It was this thought that always sent him fleeing upward, a child clawing for sound and light and air.

The trail eventually slanted downhill and they had to move carefully over the loose scree and dirt. Cruz moved to the front and set a slow, steady pace. They'd gone another mile or so when he saw the bridge in the distance. It seemed to rise out of the darkness, an immense iron structure that loomed above them as if it were the high parapet of a castle. "Look," he said to Crawdad, "we're almost out."

Then, for a brief moment, he imagined a woman standing on the edge of the bridge, her hand resting on a steel girder as she stared down at the river. She might hesitate, dangling one shoe out into space, maybe even kicking it off and watching it plummet into the abyss, fascinated by its slow descent. Then she would step into the void and fall.

They trudged ahead through tangles of chamise and manzanita, then climbed up to the road, swearing and grunting with each step. When they reached the flat, solid surface of the pavement, they set the body down. There were no cars or headlights in sight, and the white light from the moon illuminated the cracks and potholes of the road. Crawdad eased down on the bridge, his back against one of the beams. "Thanks for taking the lead back there. You were shouldering most of the load on that hill."

"You'd have done the same for me," Cruz said. "I'm gonna try to find somebody with a car. There's gotta be a few campers around here."

Crawdad looked up at him. "You do that. Find someone with a big soft backseat, maybe a Cadillac or something. I could use that right now."

As Cruz headed down the road, he waited for the exhaustion to hit and settle over him like a blanket. But just the opposite was happening, as if some electrical thread were tapped into his brain, making his senses Technicolor sharp. The darkened trees and shoreline next to the road seemed almost hallucinatory to him in an array of color and sound. A wind swept through the canyon, lifting tree branches upward, and he thought of the dancers at Don's Crossroads and how they raised their arms with the music to twirl a partner. He kept walking, putting one foot down and following it with another, keeping his eyes trained ahead like radar in search of car lights.

He'd gone maybe a half mile when something glistened off to the right and he saw a truck parked down near the river. There were people sitting in the back and he could see the glowing tips of their cigarettes as they talked and laughed. He drew closer and saw they were probably high-school age or older. They'd been drinking beer and their discards littered the ground around the truck. He stopped in front of them and they grew suddenly quiet and stared at him as if he were a ghost.

"Who the hell are you," he heard one of them finally say, "some kind of night owl?" The boy started to hoot and the others joined in.

"I need some help," was all Cruz said. "A friend of mine has drowned. Another friend is up the road with the body. I need you to drive us to the hospital." He didn't give them a chance to question him or even think about whether he was telling the truth. "Let's get moving," he said. "Now."

One of the young men, who wore a Jack Daniels baseball cap, swung down from the truck bed and into the cab, where he started the engine. Cruz pulled himself up into the back and kicked some beer cans out of the way so he could sit down. The truck lurched into reverse and backed up, then charged forward over a slight rise to the main road.

He pounded on the window when he saw the bridge ahead and the driver slowed, then pulled over. Two of the others hopped out of the cab and went to Crawdad to help him with the body.

"What the hell you two been doing?" said the kid behind the wheel as they lifted Walker's body into the truck bed.

Crawdad held a finger to his head and made a shooting sound. "River roulette," he said coldly. He hoisted himself into the back of the truck and sat down on the spare tire. Then he looked around at the others, who were staring at him as if he were some crazed hermit who'd just returned from thirty years in the wilderness. "Isn't anybody gonna offer me a beer?" he said.

When they handed him one, he opened it and took a long drink. He stared at Walker's body, which lay at his feet. As the others looked on, he held the beer up to the moon as if delivering a silent toast to some phantom only he could see. "For Rose," he said, "and for Walker." Then he gulped the rest down in one clean motion, tossed the can in a corner of the truck, and they headed back to town.

CHAPTER FOURTEEN

Cruz called Lou from the hospital. When he told him about Walker and the accident, Lou said, "You're bullshitting me." His voice was rough and disbelieving. "Walker's dead?"

"He got pinned by a strainer," Cruz said.

"Goddamn trees. We oughta just cut 'em all down." Lou spit the words out angrily. "Every fucking one."

"Can you come down?" Cruz asked.

"Give me about twenty minutes."

"No rush," Cruz said. "We got all night."

When Lou arrived they took Walker's body to a room in the hospital basement. They knew the usual procedures for a drowning victim: the paperwork and autopsy and some kind of report to the local paper. At one point Cruz lay down on the cold tile floor and slept for at least an hour. When he awoke, Lou was gone and Crawdad sat in the chair under the fluorescent ceiling lights that buzzed and flickered.

"Lou's gonna take you back to the cabin," Crawdad said. "He went to pull his truck around front."

"But I'd like to stay," Cruz said.

"There's no need for us both to hang around. Go on back to the cabin. I'll take care of things here."

Cruz nodded in agreement. "It's been a long day."

"The longest day of your life, I'll bet," Crawdad said. "Get some rest."

Cruz walked over to the body. He rested a hand on Walker's chest and thought about the last time he'd seen him alive. It seemed only minutes ago that they'd been in the eddy above the Horns of the Dragon. *Think about going home to a beautiful woman*, he'd said. *But was it Rita or Rose?* Cruz wondered. It didn't really matter anymore.

"It's a cheat," Cruz said, looking down at Walker's face.

"I know," Crawdad said from his chair.

"After all the crazy things he did," Cruz said, "he dies like this. Pinned under a tree."

"It doesn't seem right, does it?"

"No way." The body felt cold under his hand. He expected some movement, a breath perhaps, to ripple the still surface of the chest. There was nothing. "There were times I didn't trust him," Cruz said. "I wanted to, but couldn't." He paused, took his hand away from the body. "He never really gave anyone a chance to trust him, did he?"

"No," the old man said. "He never did." Crawdad stood up and placed a hand on Cruz's shoulder. "Go on now. Get some sleep." So Cruz left the room without looking back and climbed to the first floor, his bootsteps echoing in the quiet of the stairwell.

Lou drove him to Crawdad's cabin in the grey light just before dawn. When they arrived Cruz saw that his jeep was still parked there.

"I'm sorry about Walker," Lou said, the engine idling. "He was my number one man when it came to rescues. A lot of people are alive because of him." Cruz nodded in agreement and Lou added, "He'll be missed around here."

Cruz swung open the truck door and went to get out, but hesitated. He swerved around in the seat and looked back at Lou. "I'll be quitting soon," he said. "I'll stay on another week until you can find someone to take my place. I thought you should know."

Lou's face was illuminated by the green glow of the dashboard and he said, "I figured you might. Especially after all this. It's not exactly a job with a future." Lou reached across the seat and extended his hand. Cruz shook it. "Best of luck to you, son. I appreciate all your hard work."

"No problem."

"I guess I'll be looking for someone new to work the hooks," Lou said. "Any recommendations?"

Cruz smiled. "Give Chico a try. I think he's cut out for the job."

Lou laughed and said, "I might just do that. Gotta keep Chico busy or he gets into trouble."

Then he drove away and Cruz watched the orange taillights fade as the truck went back down the road. He turned and looked around at the cabin and yard, and for a brief moment he thought of driving into Kernville to see Rita. Instead he went inside and sat down at the kitchen table. He was beyond exhaustion, but felt wired for anything but sleep. He cleaned up the big room, taking all the newspaper and old cans and bagging them in some green trash bags he found in a cabinet. *It's the least I can do,* he thought.

He opened a can of beans and took it outside and ate it cold while gazing down at the river. When he was finished he went over to the tin shower stall by the side of the cabin and stripped off his clothes and cleaned himself with warm water and soap.

Afterward he lay down on an old cot in the corner of the living room and slept for eight hours. He dreamt about Rita, that they were leaping from a bridge and falling into a bottomless gorge. When he awoke in the early afternoon and saw Crawdad was still not back, he changed clothes and drove into Kernville.

He went to Laverne's and scanned the lot for Rita's Fiat but didn't see it. After parking he went inside, and upon opening the door, felt a rush of cool air sweep over him as refreshing as anything he'd ever felt. He walked to the main desk where Laverne sat behind the cash register. She looked him over and said, "I haven't seen you in a while, honey. Where you been hiding yourself?"

He ignored her question and said, "I'm looking for Rita. Is she working today?"

Laverne laughed, a shrill cackle that hurt his ears. "Not today or any other," she said, her voice suddenly angry. "Saturday morning she ripped in here late and threw a fit when I docked her pay. Ain't nobody going to call me a bitch and still be employed when the smoke's cleared." Laverne took out a cigarette and tapped it on the glass counter, then stuck it in her mouth. "I've never been so upset," she said. "Insulted me right in front of my own customers. Can you believe it?"

Cruz tried to picture the scene in his mind as Rita raged through the shop. He smiled, then asked, "Did she say anything about what she was gonna do or where she was going?"

"Hell if I know," she said. "Probably back to L.A. where she belongs. Back with all those other crazies." Laverne shrugged, the unlit cigarette still dangling from her ruby red mouth. "You know," she said, "I'd be careful if I were you. I wouldn't be surprised if that girl was on drugs or something. Either that or she might be one of them hair spies."

"A hair spy?" Cruz said.

"You know," Laverne said, "sent up here by one of those big L.A. shops to steal some of my beauty secrets. I wouldn't put it past them. I do have a state-wide reputation, you know."

Cruz smiled as he turned and headed for the door. "I doubt if Rita is that type," he said. "I'm sure your secrets are safe."

"A professional can't be too careful in this day and age," Laverne said.

"You're absolutely right," Cruz smirked. "These are dangerous times."

He left the shop and drove over to Rita's apartment. He knocked on the door and waited, but no one answered. He tried to look into the front window, but the blinds were drawn and he couldn't see a thing. Then a flashing thought came to him, more a reaction than anything else, and he went back to the jeep. He turned left out of the parking lot and drove north along the Kern.

* * *

Cruz found her camped near the heronry. She'd pitched a tent in the meadow at almost the exact place where they'd once eaten a picnic lunch. He hesitated when he came down the switchbacked trail and saw her things. Maybe he shouldn't disturb her in this place. Just let her be and give her some room to think. But he knew she'd want to know about Walker. He stopped for a moment and closed his eyes, just like she'd told him to do the very first time. He listened for the river, strained to hear the steady rush of water over the rocks. After a few seconds he began to pick it up as if tuning in to some far-off radio signal.

Then he heard a voice, *her* voice, say, "You're back," and he looked up and she stood outside her tent in jeans and a T-shirt. She was barefoot. "You're the only one who'd look for me here," she said.

He smiled. "I went to Laverne's. She told me you'd taken off to L.A. with all her beauty secrets."

"Why didn't I think of that?" Rita said, laughing. "I could've made millions."

He walked over to the small canvas tent and placed his hand on one of the wobbly poles. She stood off to the side of the campsite and brushed the hair from her eyes.

"When did you get back?" she asked.

"Last night."

"And how was the trip?"

Cruz hesitated, took his hand away from the tent and stepped toward her.

"Walker drowned." At first he wasn't sure what else to say, but then continued on. "He got pinned under a tree. By the time we got to him and tried CPR it was too late." He didn't look at her. Instead he kept his eyes on the ground and watched the dappled sunlight flicker across pine needles and frayed twigs.

"Drowned?" she said. Her voice was hushed, almost a whisper.

"Yes," Cruz said, looking up at her. "We took the body to the hospital. Crawdad's taking care of all the arrangements."

She turned her back to him and walked a few steps in the direction of the river, then stopped. "I had no idea it would turn out like this," she said.

"None of us did. It was an accident." He could see that she was crying and she brought her hand up to wipe away the tears. Cruz came up from behind and put a hand on her shoulder. He wanted to pull her close and comfort her.

"Oh God," Rita said. "This is all so fucked."

"I know," he said. "It's hard."

"You don't know," she said, turning around so he could see her bottom lip quivering. He wanted to kiss it. "You don't have any idea." Then she staggered away from him and leaned against a nearby tree. Her head was bowed and she crossed her arms. For a moment Cruz thought she might be sick or suffering from a cramp. Then she straightened up and faced him.

"There's something we have to talk about," Rita said, her voice shaking. "Something you need to know about Walker." Then it hit Cruz and he seemed to know what was coming. All the dark possibilities come true. The betrayal. *I slept with him,* would be her next words. *Things got out of control.*

He felt suddenly dizzy, the forest spinning in the background. *All to dust,* he thought. *A family curse.* His first instinct was to slap her, knock the words right out of her mouth before she could speak them. He'd seen Frank strike his mother and he knew how it silenced her, and he wanted to silence Rita. He stepped back and turned away from her, his head reeling. *I'll kick the lies out of you* was what Frank always said.

"I asked him to come over the night before you left," Rita said. "I was in a bad place after we'd talked at Laverne's. I was angry at everything." She came toward him, her hand reaching out to touch his arm. "He brought some beer and we started drinking." Cruz pulled away. He could see them together in her apartment, his hand confidently stroking her hip as she slid her arms around his neck. He wanted to hurt her, humiliate her, say something nasty and penetrating and then turn and run up the hill. *Leave the whore with her herons.*

He felt her hands encircle his waist. He'd let her in for just a moment, let her think she was getting through to him and then slam the whole thing back in her face. He wanted to tighten the screws until she felt betrayed the way he did. A slow burn. No healing salve. No ice. He wanted scars that would last. So he waited for the kisses on his neck, in his hair. Delilah kisses.

But they never came. She was behind him, her breath on his neck, her hands resting across his stomach. There was a time when he would've given anything for her to hold him like this, and he remembered when she rose out of the river, water streaming down her thighs and breasts in the moonlight. He'd loved her even when she was the ghost of someone else.

"At one point he talked about you," she said to him. "He said you reminded him of who he was before the war." She paused, her voice dropping. "I've never seen anyone in such pain. It's no wonder he drank so much."

Cruz took a long breath of air, held it, then exhaled. He put his hands over hers. *There has to be some trust,* she'd said to him. *Otherwise we'll never last.* The hot anger was still pulsing through him and he tried to let go of it, let it seep away like water trickling into the ground and vanishing.

"When he left that night, I asked him to go up with his kayak and make sure you were safe. He laughed at me and said, 'I owe you one. I'll take care of him.' That was the last time I saw him alive." Her mouth was next to his ear and she whispered, "I can't believe he's gone."

"I know," Cruz said.

Then Rita took his hand and led him across the meadow and down to the trail along the river. They went silently to the rookery, the ripple of the Kern's swift waters accompanying them. Once again he saw the birds looming in the distant trees and smelled the sharp odor that wafted out of the place.

"I started drawing again after talking with Walker," she said, pointing up at the herons. "He told me to go somewhere and learn about light and shadow. So I came back here." She went to the center of the glade and Cruz followed her. "I think he would've liked this place."

He studied Rita from the back, the sleek neck and gentle curve of shoulder and hip that he knew so well. Overhead the sun was slicing down through the trees, and he could feel the warmth on his face and neck. He reached out and touched her shoulder, then brought her toward him. She was trembling and he kissed her forehead.

"I need to get away," Cruz said, stroking her cheek, "and I want you to come with me."

"Where?" Rita asked.

"I don't know yet," Cruz said. "Maybe south into Mexico. Just about anywhere will do, as long as it's away from the river and Lake Isabella. I need to tie up some loose ends."

She looked at him and smiled. "I'd love that," she said, "but right now I have to be here." She looked up and made a sweeping gesture at the herons with her arm. "I need to draw them. And who knows?" she said, smiling. "They could be gone tomorrow and I'd never get the chance again." She placed a finger on his lips. "But if you need to find me when you get back, don't bother looking in town. I'll be right here."

"I know," he said.

"I'll miss you."

He answered by kissing her. The heron sounds, the squawks and shrill chirps, rained down on them, and he felt drunk with the moment. They stood silently in the clearing for a long while, holding on to each other, and it was as if the previous anger had cooled under her touch. When they finally separated, he looked at her and said, "Walker didn't deserve to die the way he did."

"He was in a lot of pain before. Maybe he's at peace now."

"I hope so," Cruz said. "Maybe that's what death is all about. To end the suffering and find a little peace."

"Like what we've found right here," Rita said.

Absolutely, Cruz thought.

* * *

After saying goodbye at the jeep, he went back to Crawdad's cabin and picked up the rest of his belongings. Then he drove into Lake Isabella and rented a cheap motel room. It had an old black-and-white TV and a cracked mirror and a dented metal shower. He cranked the air conditioner up to full power, then collapsed on the small bed.

For the next three days he worked on the trail crew. He ignored the other men and kept to himself, his eyes low to the ground, working at a furious pace with a pickax and rock bar. There were times when he overheard the men talking about him and Walker behind his back, but they said nothing directly to his face and never mentioned Walker's death. They left him alone. Even Chico kept his distance, eyeing him warily when they passed each other on the trail.

After work he would drive down to the Cataracts and park along the shore. He liked to sit alone and watch the violent water as it thrashed downstream like some white serpent. There was something primitive about the Kern that would always frighten him, no matter how many times he floated its waters. It was as if something uncontrollable lurked below the surface, a force that could never be tamed, only feared. He would think of Walker and remember his stories about the accidents on the Kern and Vietnam and the river in the Himalayas where villagers threw slaughtered animals into the rapids to satisfy the demon. *There'll always be sacrifices,* Cruz thought. *Offerings of blood and water.*

Then he would head back to the motel when it was near dark. He'd spread out a map of California and Mexico on the floor of the room and work on a travel route close to the Pacific. Afterward he'd lie awake and listen to the hum of the air conditioner and think of white sands and blue surf and running on the beach with Rita. Always with Rita. He'd fall asleep and dream of places with exotic names like Baja and La Paz and Mazatlán.

* * *

His last day of work at the Forest Service was Friday. He picked up his paycheck from Lou and said goodbye to a few of the men. Even Chico shook his hand and with a sly grin said, "Good luck with the ladies." Then Cruz drove over to the trailer in Lake Isabella. It was late afternoon, *siesta hour,* as Frank used to say, and he knew his father would be at the Shady Grove. He needed to pick up some things, and he didn't feel like talking to Frank right now, so he went to the trailer and searched for the key that was usually hidden under the cement-block steps. All he found were a few cobwebs and some scrap wood laden with spiders. He cursed, kicked at the trailer door, then went across the alley to the entrance of the bar.

When he stepped over the threshold it took his eyes a moment to adjust to the dim light. It was like an air-conditioned cave, the only window being at the front near the entrance. He found his old man at the shuffleboard table along the side wall. As he approached, he saw Frank poised above the narrow wooden alley, his right hand deftly touching the small puck. His father hesitated for a split second, then slid the rubber disc the length of the sawdust-covered table until it collided with the other pucks, then hung balanced at the lip of the drop.

"Helluva shot!" bellowed Frank's playing partner, an old fat man with pudgy fingers. Frank looked up at Cruz, his chin cocked with an arrogant tilt, then placed a hand on his hip.

"You picked a good time to show up," he said. "Whadya think of that shot?" Cruz detected an exaggerated slur in his words, typical of when he'd been drinking.

"I need the key to the trailer," he said. "There's a few things I have to get."

"You checked under the step?" his old man asked.

"Yeah. Nothing there but a bunch of spiders."

His father walked over to the bar and reached for a glass of beer, hesitated, then turned around and faced Cruz while he scratched his head. "Damn," he said. "I locked myself out the other day, but I swore I put the key back."

"Well, it isn't there," Cruz said, "and I'm in a hurry."

"Where you headed? You got a date with your little sweettart?"

Cruz pushed away from the bar. "Does it really matter? All I want is the key. I'm not here to visit."

Frank threw a dollar on the bar top, then turned to his shuffleboard partner and said, "Keep it hot, Fingers. I'll be back."

When they stepped out into the daylight, Frank squinted and brought up a hand to shield his eyes.

"It's hot," he grunted. "A real scorcher."

"Yeah," Cruz said, walking a few paces in front and hurrying him along.

"You been working lately?" Frank asked.

"I was," Cruz said. "The Forest Service job is over for me, so I'll be looking for something new. I'm taking some time off to go south. Maybe I'll visit a few friends in Los Angeles, then go to San Diego and see Marta. I don't think I'd recognize Donna even if I saw her."

"It's been a while, ain't it?" said Frank.

"Yeah."

"Well, give 'em my best."

"I'll do that."

"If I'd known you were going, I'd have gotten something for little Donna."

"She's not so little anymore," Cruz said. "She's almost a teenager."

"Is that right?" Frank said. "What the hell do you buy a teenager anyway?"

"I don't know. Jewelry. Maybe some skin lotion."

"Oh well," Frank said. "I guess it don't really matter."

When they reached the steps of the trailer, Frank fumbled around in his pockets until he found the key, accidentally dropping some change and an old pocketknife in the dirt. Cruz helped him gather up his things, then Frank unlocked the door and stepped inside and said, "Are you clearing out?"

Cruz ignored the question and went straight to his room. He still had a few belongings he wanted to get out of the trailer. A floor lamp with an adjustable stand that Marta had given him for Christmas. His blue three-piece suit and black dress shoes. Some books and photo albums that he kept on the top shelf in the closet. His fishing rod and reel and tackle box. He hurried through the room as quickly as possible and left behind anything he was uncertain about. He wanted to get out of there before his old man could stall him by starting up a conversation, then maybe try to hit him up for some money. Cruz had a large green garbage bag and he emptied his drawers into it. The last few things he grabbed were his old baseball glove, a nylon windbreaker, and his heavy winter coat. *Keep it light,* he thought. *Don't take anything that'll drag you down.*

It took him two trips to cart all the stuff to the jeep. Frank sat on the trailer steps. He didn't say a word and never once asked if he could help carry anything. On his last pass through the trailer Cruz took a quick look around and was surprised at how neat the place was. The carpet in the living room looked as if it had just been cleaned and vacuumed. A new reclining chair was next to the sofa. The kitchen was immaculate, with new dish towels folded in half and draped over the front of the empty sink and snow-white linoleum that had recently been washed. The fist-sized hole in the cheap paneling had been repaired.

Cruz went outside and stowed the last of his things in the jeep. Frank said, "You got room for everything in that little tin can? You can always leave something here if you need to."

"It'll fit," Cruz said. He turned around and looked at the trailer. "The place looks great inside. It hasn't looked that good in years."

"Yeah," Frank said. "I've been doing some cleaning up. I got that reclining chair on sale at Sears and had it special delivered. I wanted the place to look nice if you ever came back." The last sentence hung in the air and Cruz could see the longing in his father's eyes and imagined him in the kitchen fixing the damaged paneling.

"I'm not coming back," Cruz said. "I'm leaving for good. I may be in town again in a month or so, but I'll just be passing through on my way to Kernville."

His old man got up from the steps and shuffled out into the yard. He kicked at an automobile part lying in the dust and Cruz heard the twang of his boot striking the metal.

"I know," Frank said. "I know you need to move on. This ain't really a home anymore." He looked over at Cruz and smiled. "It's just a detour."

"I'll be sure to tell Marta and Donna how you're doing," Cruz said.

"You mean that I'm still drinking," Frank said. "I'd rather you didn't say nothing about me. Let 'em use their imagination." He spit into the dirt. "Except for Donna. Tell her to send me a postcard of San Diego. One that has the ocean in it."

"I'll do that."

Frank walked over to the jeep, his head tilted down as if he were studying the tire treads. "You got any more room in there?" he asked.

"I got a little space in the front," Cruz said.

"Then hold on a minute." Frank turned and shuffled over to the metal shed. He vanished inside for a few moments and Cruz could hear him rustling around. Then he reappeared carrying a cardboard box in both hands. He set it down in the dust and Cruz came around the jeep to see the contents.

It was his father's silver toolbox, the one Cruz had called the treasure chest as a kid. The polished metallic surface caught the sun and reflected like a mirror. Frank unfastened the latches and opened it, and Cruz saw the tools inside, shiny clean and neatly arranged like a snug puzzle. There were wrenches and screwdrivers and ratchets and pliers. A tape measure. A socket set that fit into the lid.

"It's all Craftsman," Frank said, picking up a hammer, its handle burnished gold from wear. "The best you can buy. Lifetime warranty. If anything goes wrong, just take 'em back for a replacement."

"Hold on," Cruz said, glancing down at the toolbox. It looked beautiful to him as it gleamed in the afternoon light. "You'll need these more than me. You've still got that old car to put together."

Frank shook his head and coughed. He waved his hand across the yard at all the junk parts and said, "That Chevy's moving about as fast as it's ever gonna move."

Then Cruz understood. "Thanks," he said. "I'll try to put them to good use."

"It ain't much of an inheritance," Frank said, "but it's the best I can do right now."

Cruz stared down into the box and imagined them in his own hands. The tools had limitless possibilities.

"I've always loved good tools," Frank said. "Hell, it's the one thing you'll probably remember about me. I could always handle tools."

"Yeah," Cruz said, "you sure could."

Cruz picked up the toolbox and placed it in the front seat of the jeep. When he turned around, his old man had moved to the door of the trailer and stood on the steps with his hand on the screen.

"Go on," Frank said. "You've got a lot of driving ahead of you." There was twenty feet of yard separating them, and Cruz walked half of it and stopped to look up at his father.

"You won't stop drinking, will you?" Cruz said.

Frank shook his head. "Not likely. I'd say the chances are slim to none. It's all I've got left."

Cruz nodded. Frank came over from the door until he stood a few feet away. "I understand why you're leaving," he said. "It's time for you to move on. There's no need to feel bad. You did all you could."

Frank reached out and took his hand and shook it. "We had some good times together, like when we were out fishing or playing baseball. That's what I'll remember. Those times."

His father's grip lingered for a second, then released, and Cruz walked back to the jeep. He heard Frank's voice behind him and he swung around. "Your hands have changed, Roy. I could tell when we shook just then. You've got working hands now."

Cruz held up his palms and smiled. "It's from all the shoveling and rowing," he said.

"Whatever," Frank said. "Still, it's a good thing."

Then his father was gone, slipping inside the screen door and letting it slam behind him. Cruz started the jeep and eased down the alley without looking back. As he drove off, he placed his free hand on the shiny toolbox lid and let it rest there, feeling the warmth of the metal through his callused fingers.

He had one more stop before leaving town and he pushed the jeep hard, accelerating around the reservoir as he drove toward Kernville. He'd decided to leave that night and drive straight through to Los Angeles, stopping for coffee when necessary, or sleeping at a rest area if he got tired. He didn't want to hang around for anything else. He'd waited long enough.

He arrived at Crawdad's cabin in the early evening. The old man was standing by the truck when he pulled up, and it looked as if he were loading a box into the passenger side.

Crawdad glanced over at him as he got out of the jeep. "I figured you'd come around sooner or later," he said. "Where you been hiding?"

"I stayed at a motel for a few days while I finished up with the Forest Service. I needed some time to myself."

"When did you quit?"

"Today," Cruz said.

Crawdad turned away from his truck and silently nodded. Then he walked over to the jeep and looked at the boxes and bags that had been packed in the rear. "Heading out, huh?" he asked.

"Yeah," Cruz said. "Just for a while. I'm gonna drive south. Maybe go to Mexico."

"Sounds like a smart thing to do. I bet you could use a little vacation after all that's happened." They stood in silence next to the jeep and Crawdad tapped his knuckles on the lid of the metal toolbox.

"I took care of Walker," Crawdad said. "I thought you might like to know. I arranged to have him toasted in the morning."

"Toasted?" Cruz said, a puzzled expression on his face.

"Cremated," Crawdad said. "I'm gonna take the ashes back upstream to the Forks and put him to rest there. I think he'd like that. It's a real peaceful place."

"Thanks for doing that."

"Don't mention it."

Cruz studied the old man's withered features. He looked exhausted and worn out.

"Have you gotten some rest?" Cruz asked the old man.

"A little," he said. "I'll sleep well tonight." He leaned on the hood of the jeep and rapped his knuckles against the surface. "So," Crawdad said, "have you seen Miss Mormon lately?"

"Yeah. We talked on Monday. We had to straighten a few things out."

"I figured out that much on my own," Crawdad said. "And did they get straightened?"

"For the most part."

"Then why isn't she going south with you?"

Cruz looked over at the old man. "When did you get so nosy?" he said. "This is a private matter."

"Simple curiosity," Crawdad said.

Cruz tapped the toe of his boot against the jeep tire. "She needs to be here right now. We'll get together when I get back and make some plans for the fall."

Crawdad grinned. "Enough said. Just promise me that you'll bring her by."

"I'll do that," Cruz said.

Then Crawdad walked over to the truck and opened the door on the driver's side. "Which way are you heading out?" he asked.

"Through the canyon and over to the interstate outside Bakersfield," Cruz said.

"Well, I'm going as far as the canyon mouth. I've got a little job to take care of down there."

"What's that?"

"Just follow me," Crawdad said. "I can always use a little help."

The canyon was dark by the time they got to it, and Cruz drove carefully past the Cataracts and around the sharp, winding curves. At the bottom, just before the flats leading to Bakersfield, Crawdad pulled over onto a narrow strip of gravel next to the warning sign at the entrance to the canyon. They got out and Crawdad carried a box that had paint and brushes and rags inside.

"This used to be Walker's job, you know," Crawdad said. "He called it 'the changing of the sign' and he took it pretty seriously. Whenever there was a drowning, he was always down here the next day to update the count."

They stood in front of the wooden sign. It read: WARNING: 55 PEOPLE HAVE DROWNED IN THE KERN RIVER SINCE 1930. PLEASE BE CAREFUL!

Cruz watched as the old man bent down and pried off the lid of the can of white paint with a screwdriver and proceeded to whitewash the 55. Then he picked up a smaller brush and some black paint and slowly daubed a crude 56 in its place. Cars rushed by as headlights flashed across their faces.

"I'm no artist," the old man said, "but I guess that'll do."

"It doesn't have to be pretty," Cruz said. "Just accurate."

They gathered up the paint and brushes and walked back to the truck, where Crawdad placed the box on the floor of the passenger side. Then he turned and looked at Cruz.

"Next time you see me, I could be floating real pretty on that pink houseboat out in the middle of the reservoir," he said.

"You should get together with Laverne and start a floating hair salon," Cruz said. "Customers can fish while getting their hair cut. You could call it 'Trout 'n Trim' or something."

Crawdad chuckled. "You cast while we cut," he said.

"Exactly."

Cruz rested his elbows on the hood of the truck. "When do you plan to scatter Walker's ashes?" he asked.

"I'm not in any hurry," Crawdad said. "It's not like I have to do it tomorrow or anything. I'll wait a few days and rest up, then probably hike over to where we left the river gear and bring down what I can. I'll take the ashes up to the Forks soon afterward." The old man put his hands on his hips and walked around the front of the truck to the canyon edge. Cruz joined him and gazed at the black opening, unable to see the river at the bottom because of the darkness.

"I love being next to the Kern at night," Crawdad said. "It's my favorite time."

"Why's that?"

The old man closed his eyes. "Because you can't see it real clear and you have to pay attention to what it sounds like. You have to shut your eyes and wait. And when you finally hear it, you want to stay up all night and just listen. It makes the prettiest music on the planet."

"I know what you mean," Cruz said.

"That's good," Crawdad said. "I've known too many men who went down to the city and got used to all the traffic and construction noise and forgot what a river sounded like. It's like they got amnesia or something and just wandered around lost." He was looking at Cruz now and his hand came up and gripped Cruz's arm. "That's what happened to Walker. He went away to the war and forgot what the river sounded like. It took him years to remember."

"But he heard it again," Cruz said. "He was listening."

"Yeah," Crawdad said. "He finally remembered."

The old man took his hand away and walked over to the truck and got in. Cruz followed him and stood next to the open window.

"I could never forget," Cruz said. "Not after all that's happened."

Crawdad started up the engine and turned on the headlights. "I know," he said. "I know you couldn't." Then he did a creaking U-turn in the center of the road and as he passed Cruz, he yelled, "Take care," and waved from the open window. Cruz stood for a long while and watched the sputtering truck as it began its slow labor back up the canyon. Then he got into the jeep and drove south toward the distant lights of Bakersfield.